Nottingham Harbor

DEDICATION

"To my deceased parents, Ed and Helen, for all their help and encouragement for all my endeavors during my lifetime. To my brother, Edward, and sister-in-law, Marilyn, and the rest of my family for their encouragement."

A SPECIAL DEDICATION

"A special dedication in loving memory of seven year old Josephine Grace: May our family cherish and celebrate her and remember her in our minds, in our hearts, and in our prayers forever. May we pray for her parents and siblings."

Jack Lorenz

authorHOUSE®

AuthorHouse™
1663 Liberty Drive
Bloomington, IN 47403
www.authorhouse.com
Phone: 1-800-839-8640

This is a work of fiction. All of the characters, names, incidents, organizations, and dialogue in this novel are either the products of the author's imagination or are used fictitiously.

Published by AuthorHouse   05/05/2016

ISBN: 978-1-4969-4946-2 (sc)
ISBN: 978-1-4969-4944-8 (hc)
ISBN: 978-1-4969-4945-5 (e)

Library of Congress Control Number: 2014919120

Print information available on the last page.

This book is printed on acid-free paper.

Contents

The school teacher works part time at Gilley's Pub at the right side of the cover picture. The rape takes place at the golf course on the left. The chief of police is at the police station. His deputy also covers the fire house. The mayor is at the city hall. They all to the diner. The Simpson family's farm is 25 miles in land from the Harbor. Sergeant Bill Simpson is the primary character for our story. Enjoy the story and embrace the logic.

CHAPTER 0

FICTIONAL STORY NOTE

This is a fictional story about a state police task force identifying and capturing a number of criminals in three New England states. Except for the names of the small cities in New England all of the names of towns where the crimes take place are fictional. All of the names of the persons in the story are fictional. Any similarity to the names of real persons is purely coincidental. Any similarity to actual crimes is purely coincidental.

AN INTRODUCTION

Several TV documentaries and news stories have summarized the rape problem across the United State. There are literally thousands of random street rapes each year. Very few jurisdictions run DNA on the rape kits. Some in law enforcement and other researchers believe that there are many unreported rapes. It is a sad state of affairs for the women of our country. The fact that a different rapist commits each of the rapes can be questioned. Statistically and practically it is more likely that most of the rapes are committed by serial rapists. The fictional story is based on these premises.

AUTHOR'S COMMENTS ON THE STORY

Over the last few years I have read and seen on TV that many jurisdiction in the US apparently do not run DNA analysis on the rape kit evidence. There appears to be two reasons for not running the analyses. The first is financial. Each test cost between $600 and $800. There are various reasons for not spending the money on the DNA analyses, but I believe in the real world that politicians cannot claim to be tough on crime and then not process the best identification available. The second fact is that the results do not match DNA in the national databases. This second fact may be because rape is a unique kind of crime. This is the real world. In our fictional story the politicians and police are tough and thorough in their efforts to stop crime. Like my main character Sergeant Bill Simpson and his lady friend Mattie Greene, I personally believe most random street rapes are committed by serial rapists. They move from town to town and state to state. This is the basis for the fictional story Nottingham Harbor. Enjoy the story.

CHAPTER 1

THE BACKGROUND FOR THE STORY

The Simpson farm is located 25 miles inland from the coast of Maine and the town of Nottingham Harbor. William Simpson the father of Bill, John and Evelyn and his wife, Marcia, took over the operation of the farm from Bill's grandfather, Thomas, sixty-six years ago. The dairy farm has been in the Simpson family for five generations. They also raise chickens and turkeys. The farm is large enough to feed lot cattle and breed some cattle. John is now operating the farm. He has taken over the operations more and more as his father grew older, but has basically worked the farm with his father since John was Twenty-two. He and his wife Clara have two teenage children William and Hannah. Evelyn lives in Bangor with her husband Charles, Charlie, and two teenage children, Charles Jr. and Linda. Bill, the oldest son, is in law enforcement since he left the Coast Guard. Bill lives in New Hampshire. He married his high school sweetheart, Marge, at age twenty, while still in the Coast Guard. Bill is a Sergeant with the New Hampshire State Police. He works at the Attorney General's Office and concentrates on major crimes and violent crimes. He and his wife, Marge, had three children. Marge died of cancer about five years before our story begins.

When Bill and John and Evelyn were growing up on the farm they would make regular trips to Nottingham Harbor. They would play at the small beach or go to a movie. It was typical small town farm life. Their friends lived the same way. Twelve years ago Nottingham Harbor added a golf course on the west end of town. There has been a small marina on the east end of town. It is on an inlet or cove along the coast.

The town has a part time mayor and a chief and couple of police. The biggest crimes over the years were parking violations, speeders, and an occasional fight at Gilley's Pub. Once in a while, someone tries to leave town without paying the bill at one of the two local Motels or one of the two gas stations. This all changed in November of this past year. A young woman, a schoolteacher and part time waitress, was raped on the golf course as she walked home. She worked as a waitress at Gilley's Pub on Saturday evenings for some extra money. The last crime this serious was a murder about forty years ago. The state police have been and are investigating the rape with little success. They ran a DNA analysis, but the DNA matches nothing on the national databases. Identifying the rapist was at a dead end. The physical description of the rapist is one that could fit many guys, but in another way it fits no one from the area.

The young woman is from a prominent family in New Hampshire. The New Hampshire Attorney General thru his assistant Linda Symth is contacting the Maine ADA, the Mayor and the chief of police about progress in the case. There has been little progress. It is early March and a snowstorm is coming. George Bernard, the mayor, wants to talk to the Chief, Carl Kramer, about the progress in the rape case. He also wants to discuss the other enforcement issues in the town. Carl has been chief for ten years and was a policemen for twenty years before becoming Chief. He had spent a few years on the Boston force where he got his training.

The Sun has not risen. Looking across the Ocean there is just a thin line of light on the horizon. Mornings in Nottingham Harbor are very uneventful Carl usually drags himself into the office by 9 AM sometimes 10 AM. Tim is retired, but he trains search and hunting dogs. He also drives the fire truck. He is a hunter and goes to back woods in Maine to hunt deer and other game. Some people say he got his nickname "Sure Shot" because he is an excellent marksman. Some people say he got the nickname because he photographed wild life at night. Neither Carl nor any of his deputies have experience with major crimes.

Spot jumps on the bed, which wakes Carl. Spot wants to go out into yard. Carl named Spot for the large brown spot on his side. Carl's house has neighbors, but their houses are not too close. There is a small stream valley on the east side of the property. Carl reluctantly gets out of bed and goes to the back door. On opening the door, Spot darts into the yard. Carl returns to bed. He dozes before the alarm awakens him. Carl slides out of the bed. He walks to the bathroom. After splashing some water on his face and disturbing his brain, he convinces himself to head into the kitchen for coffee. He had set the coffee maker for 6AM and now the time is 6:35 AM. He pours a cup and adds a spoon of sweetener. He looks into the refrigerator and fortunately checks the half & half. It is sour. He dumps it in the drain. He finds the powered creamer and adds it to the coffee. He checks the answering machine and sees there are no messages. He thanks God under his breathe. It does not bother him that a crime happened over night, but no crime is always better. He goes to the bathroom with the coffee to get ready for work. A half hour passes and he has finished in the bathroom and dresses for the office. He lets Spot back into the house and places his food on the floor. Carl scratches Spot's back as the dog starts to eat the food. Carl changes the water in Spot's water bowl. Carl walks to the window and looks out at the weather. It is getting cloudy and snow was predicted by evening on the weather show last night. Snow always increases the problems in Nottingham Harbor. It is the beginning of March and snow is common. Broken down vehicles, cars in ditches, power outages and a few usually simple problems, but the snow makes them more critical. Carl has told his two deputies to try to take it easy on the day prior to a snowstorm.

Carl pulls up to the office and parks his SUV behind the building. When on duty he drives the chief's car unless he is working undercover. Undercover is a misnomer in Nottingham Harbor because everybody knows him and the Deputies. He has on occasional rented a car or SUV to fool the local troublemakers. The biggest trouble is usually a fight at Gilly's tavern on the waterfront. Gilly is really a good guy and supports the town activities, but on Saturday night some of the locals get drinking and arguing. There is always the need to watch for drunk driving late on Saturday.

Carl enters the office, "Good Morning."

Lillian and Tim reply almost simultaneously, "Good morning, Chief."

Carl asks, "Anything happening."

Tim says, "The snowstorm is coming, I assume you already heard the weather."

Carl replies, "Yes. Try to take it a little easy today, because we will need to cover tonight."

Lillian replies, "I was thinking of taking the afternoon off and coming back in at 8PM. I have some paperwork to complete."

Carl replies, "What paperwork?"

Lillian answers, "Several tickets from the last two days."

Carl says, "When you finish the paperwork. Go home and come back tonight at 8PM."

Lillian answers, "Thank you."

Carl continues, "Tim try and plan to leave about 4PM and come back about midnight." One of the problems with a small department is regular shift work is impossible to schedule. Everybody has to do three shifts a day. Tim and Lillian nod their approval of Carl's comments. Carl goes to his office and starts to review some of the paperwork on other rapes and assaults, which have happened in several other towns in Maine. He has talked with Sergeant Bill Simpson of the New Hampshire State Police about some rapes Bill is investigating in New Hampshire and Vermont. Carl is going to New Hampshire to meet with Bill Simpson next week.

The mayor comes in about 10AM. He says, "Where is Carl?" Tim answers, "In his office." The Mayor walks in without knocking. "Carl, how come Lillian is not writing parking tickets? There are several cars parked along Main Street at expired parking meters."

Carl answers, "The parking meter tickets are important, but I sent Lillian home because of the predicted snow storm tonight. She is going to work the second shift because of the storm and Tim is covering third shift. Remember we are a 'four person' department and the snowstorm is going to hit around midnight. The parking is really a secondary problem to the overnight response to the storm. If we are not on duty overnight the town population will be writing you and the newspaper letters and complaining to the Radio Station about our lack of response. I am just covering your butt for the storm. We will clear Main Street and several other streets for the storm when Lillian and Barney come in at 4:00PM."

The Mayor continues, "Have you made any progress on the rape and assault?"

Carl replies, "I have a meeting with Sergeant Bill Simpson of the New Hampshire State Police next week. He has discovered several rapes with similar MO and physical characteristics to our suspect. Carol James with the New Hampshire State Police collects the statistics on crimes also has a number of possible suspects. I know Bill Simpson casually. He has a good reputation for solving crimes. He told me he has an idea of how to identify the suspects using DNA and something he referred to as Geographic profiling. So we are meeting at his Barracks near Concord. All three of us believe this rapist and several others are traveling across all three states committing these crimes."

The Mayor continues, "The Town Council is wondering why you are trying to solve crimes in other places. So am I. And why we are supporting the solution of crimes in other places besides Nottingham Harbor. You are not being paid to solve the crimes all over the state. And now you tell me possibly three states."

Carl replies, "I am trying to solve the crime here. I will explain to you and the Council after I meet with Sergeant Simpson why the other towns need to be included in our investigation. He did explain to me that practically we are solving the crime in any one location by narrowing the number of unknown suspects. Looking for the rapist in a town like Nottingham Harbor is useless. Some mathematical analysis is being used by some of the larger city departments to effectively find criminals. The real problem is that many of the smaller towns and county district attorneys are unwilling to run DNA on the evidence. Apparently most places do not even bother to run DNA."

The Mayor asks, "I saw in some big city there are thousand of rape cases for which no DNA analysis has been done. What can I do?"

Carl answers, "First your support and understanding is critical to our success. You can generate letters to several of the other mayors and encourage them to have the DNA testing done. Encourage them to support our efforts and be patient with the progress. We need all of us to practice secrecy until we have identified and arrested the rapist."

The Mayor starts to leave, "I will be awaiting your explanation."

Carl replies, "I will have an excellent explanation after the meeting in Concord next week."

Carl heads home at about 3 PM. Carl knows he is going to return at midnight because of the storm. He calls his lady friend, Paula from the SUV before starting to drive. The phone rings four times and Paula answers. She says, "Paula Peters, fourth floor nurse. How can I help you?"

Carl says, "Paula it is Carl. We need to do a short supper tonight. Because of the storm I must cover overnight. See you about six. Can you bring a pizza?"

Paula replies, "I can. See you about six."

They both hang up.

It is five minutes before six when Paula rings Carl's doorbell. Carl checks to be sure it is Paula. He opens the door. Paula says, "Pizza delivery. How are you?"

Carl replies, "I am fine. How are you?"

Paula answers, "I am fine. What's happening?"

Carl continues, "As you know there is a storm coming around midnight. My deputies and I have to be prepared. So I have to be in the office by midnight. After we finish eating I am going to take a nap until 11 PM. I have to suspend other work until the storm response is over."

Paula replies, "I understand. I am going to leave when we finish dinner. Did you accomplish anything today except signing parking tickets?"

Before Paula arrived, Carl had set the table with plates and glasses and dinnerware from the kitchen. Carl put a slice of pizza on their plates. Paula pours herself a small glass of wine. She takes Carl's glass and fills it with ice. She returns with the bottle of Cola and the glass. They sit down and start to eat.

Carl pauses to finish the part of a piece of pizza and responds, "I and my deputy Lillian have found several other rapes in Maine with similar MO and the rapist had similar physical characteristics. I drafted a letter to the other towns. I ask them if they had DNA analysis done on the rape kit. I ask them if they can provide the physical characteristics and any sketch of the rapist. George came over and questioned why Lillian had not ticketed several parked cars. I explained we had to cover the snowstorm tonight and I was sending the deputies home so they could work this evening and overnight. I explain that the rape investigation was on hold until the snowstorm was over. I am meeting with Sergeant Simpson next week about the rapes. Sergeant Simpson of the New Hampshire State Police is originally from this area. He heard about the rape and wants to look at the facts. He believes our rapist could be the same guy as one several rapists he is investigating."

Paula interjects, "Does he believe we are dealing with a serial rapist?"

Carl replies, "He believes it is possible. In fact, he says it is highly probable."

Paula comments, "That is interesting."

Between bites on the pizza Carl continues, "I do not have the training or experience to pursue this investigation without help. Sergeant Simpson is an expert at serious crimes. I casually know Bill Simpson. He does not put policemen like me down for lack of training or experience. He is always teaching his techniques to the rest of us. I am looking forward to working closely with Bill Simpson."

Paula says, "That is very good. It should please George that this person is doing the investigation."

Carl continues, "I believe George is pleased. He and the council want to know what is going to happen. We need to solve this rape for the good of the town and the protection of the women of Nottingham Harbor and our visitors."

Carl and Paula finish the pizza and the drinks. Carl says, "I hate to throw you out when we finish, but the snow storm is the first priority tonight. Lillian, the other deputies, and I are going to be busy with the snow storm and will not be working our normal schedules."

Paula replies, "I understand. I want to get home before the snow starts. I will talk to you tomorrow and come over to the office the next day after my shift at the hospital. Love you." Paula gets up.

Carl responds, "Love you." Carl gets up with Paula. He walks her to the door. They kiss. He continues, "Thanks for the pizza. Spot will thank you. I am going to give him the last piece."

Paula opens the door and says; "I will see you in two days. Hope Spot enjoys the pizza. Be careful in the storm." Spot is sitting in the rocking chair watching them. His ears perk up every time they mention his name.

Carl says, "See you after the storm." Carl goes out on to the porch with her.

Paula says, "Don't come to the car." Carl waits until she starts the car and drives away. He waves as she leaves. Paula see Carl wave and honks the horn.

Carl returns inside and picks up Spot's bowl. He cuts the pizza. Spot comes over. Carl sits the bowl on the floor and picks up the water dish. He fills it and puts it back down. Spot is obviously enjoying the piece of pizza."

The snowstorm was over before morning. Carl and the deputies spent the night rescuing a few stranded motorists, investigating a few minor accidents, and clearing some parked cars. Carl and Sure Shot acted as crossing guards at the elementary school because one of the normal guards was out sick. Everything was more or less normal by 4 PM. Carl dismissed the deputies at 4 PM. Carl went home and Lillian locked the office at 4:30 PM.

The next day was normal for Nottingham Harbor. Lillian arrived at 9 AM. Sure Shot dropped in about 9:30 on the way to the firehouse. Carl arrived at 10 PM. The mayor did not call about parking tickets or any other problem. This was a little different. Paula arrives after her shift at the hospital is over for the day. As she enters the outer office she greets Lillian, "Hello, how are you today?"

Lillian answers, "I am OK, Paula. How was the hospital today?"

Paula's replies, "It was about usual. Is Carl in?"

Lillian replies, "Yes, he is waiting for you."

Carl says, "Hi, how are you today."

Paula answers, "I am fine. How are you?"

Carl replies, "I am fine. How about dinner Saturday at about 7 o'clock?

Paula answers, "Fine. Are you making any more progress? Several of the nurses were talking about the rape, today."

Carl replies, "I did talk to chiefs in two towns upstate and they had DNA analysis run on their respective rape kits. The DNA did not match any DNA in the criminal databases. They were somewhat discouraged by the results. I explained to them about the meeting next week. Once we set up a proper protocol for collecting and processing the data, I will ask them to send the results of the DNA and the other data to Sergeant Simpson. I explained that Sergeant Simpson has a program to identify these guys. He will need all of our data to help identify the rapist."

Paula continues, "Do you think Sergeant Simpson is on the right track?"

Carl answers, "I hope so. But he has a good arrest record and a good reputation for identifying and catching violent criminals."

Paula continues, "I hope you and he are correct. The nurses are worried since the victim in Nottingham Harbor was on the way home at night. Several of the nurses work second jobs like the victim. They are genuinely worried."

Carl says, "Bill and I do not think this rapist is from the area around Nottingham Harbor. It is more likely he will strike again in some other area. This conclusion is not 100% absolute, but Bill is of the mind that these guys move around so as not to be caught or identified. Bill has a lady friend who is math teacher and is helping him and the New Hampshire Attorney General Office with a technique to take advantage of the very fact that these guys move from place to place. I am not sure of the details. This is why we are meeting on next Tuesday. There is going to be a Maine State Policeman, Ed Woodworth, at the meeting. I know Ed. He has a good reputation also. There is going to be several people from Vermont also. Bill is interested in our case, because he is from this area. His family owns one or more farms about 25 miles inland from here. He told me that he and his brother and sister would come to Nottingham Harbor when they were kids and teenagers. He has a real connection to Nottingham Harbor."

Paula continues, "Sound like progress. George should be pleased. I will see you about 7 PM tomorrow night. Bye for now." Paula gets up to leave. She whispers, "Love you."

Carl says, "See you tomorrow night at 7." He blows her a kiss and winks.

As Paula goes through the outer office she says, "Lillian, you have a good weekend."

Lillian responds, "You have a good weekend, Paula."

THE NEXT WEEK

Monday is normal day in Nottingham Harbor. Carl contacts Ed Woodworth and they agree to meet at the AG's office in Augusta at about 7 AM and drive to Concord New Hampshire together. Ed says he can drive a state police car to the meeting. Lillian tells Carl the two towns upstate send their DNA results to her on Friday. She put the data along with the DNA from here on a thumb drive for him to take to the meeting. Carl gathers some of the papers on the rape from here to take to the meeting.

Carl checks and signs a few parking tickets. He reads a brief report by Barney on a disturbance at Gilley's Saturday. Barney did not arrest anybody, but he sent two of the participants' home. They were town residents, so Barney tried to calm the disturbance without arresting the participants. Carl leaves for home at 4:00 PM. Paula calls at 6:30 PM and wishes him a good trip.

Tuesday morning comes early. Carl is in the SUV by 6AM. He drives to the state police barracks near Augusta. Ed lives upstate but he stayed in the barrack overnight. He is ready to leave when Carl arrives. Carl tells the desk Sergeant which car is his. The desk Sergeant writes the info down so they know he is on official business with Ed. They head for Concord New Hampshire. The meeting is at 10AM. During the drive they discuss their families and some work, but ignore the rape cases.

In the next chapter we skip backwards to a few weeks before Christmas and a month or so after the rape in Nottingham harbor. While the preceding events were occurring in The Harbor a series of events were taking place in New Hampshire. Sergeant Bill Simpson of the New Hampshire State Police was beginning to chase information on rapes in New Hampshire and Vermont.

CHAPTER 2

NEW HAMPSHIRE

Bill Simpson had several open rape cases, but no identifiable suspects. He has read or seen on TV news stories about how many unsolved rape cases there were in just the East Coast cities. He was aware that very few DNA analyses have been run on the rape kits. Many of the politicians talked about being tough on crime, but when it came to spending $600 to $800 per analysis they simply forgot about being tough. He believed that most of the rapist did not perform a single rape and then quit. Most of the cases were tied together by a number of serial rapists. How he could prove these beliefs or use them to identify suspects was not clear.

Bill heard about the rape in Nottingham Harbor shortly after it happened. Bill as we know is from the area. He knew the chief of police Carl Kramer casually from visiting the Harbor with the family. He contacted Carl about the details.

Bill called Carl the phone rang several times. Carl answered, "Carl Kramer chief of police Nottingham Harbor."

Bill says, "This is Sergeant Bill Simpson of the New Hampshire State Police. I heard about the rape in Nottingham Harbor. Can we discuss the details?"

Carl replies, "I would like to discuss the details. I believe you have more experience than me with this type of crime."

Bill answers, "More experience in general maybe, but more success at identifying rapists is questionable.

Carl continues, "My experience and success is zero."

Bill continues, "Did you have a DNA analysis performed on the rape kit?

Carl answers, "Yes. However the results did not match any DNA in the various criminal data bases."

Bill continues, "The few DNA results that I have do not match any in the data bases either. My theory is that rape is a unique type of crime. Most criminals do not rape so DNA of criminals who commit other types of crimes are very rarely going to match rapist DNA.'

Carl replies, "Your theory may be correct. However it does not help us catch rapists."

Bill continues, "Please send me the description and DNA results for the Nottingham Harbor rape. My family is from the area near The Harbor. I will check and compare your data with several cases in New Hampshire."

Carl answers, "I will FAX all the information to you. Just give me your Fax number"

Bill answers, "Here is my FAX number." Bill gives Carl the number and verifies it.

Carl replies, "Thank You and Good bye."

Bill says, "Have a good day, Carl."

They both hang up.

Bill gets a cup of coffee. He pulls the files on several recent rapes. He looks thru them to refresh the details. Sandra his assistant walks into his office. She says, "Bill, a FAX from Carl Kramer just arrived. Here it is. What is the connection to our cases?"

Bill replies, "As you know my family is from the area near Nottingham Harbor. When I heard about a rape there I decided to call the local Chief to see if the rapist description matches any of the rapist from the recent crimes here. I need to look at the data. I have no idea if the data and DNA from their case will match the data from our cases."

Sandra asks, "This goes along with your theory that most of the rapists are serial rapist or at least repeat offenders."

Bill replies, "Yes."

Sandra leaves. Bill picks up the FAX from Nottingham Harbor. The DNA is in an electronic file. Carl notes he sent Bill an E-mail with the DNA file attached. Bill studies the FAX for several minutes. He then slowly studies the eight files from rapes committed near Concord. These are not the only rapes he is tracking but they are a start. The rape in Gilbert gets his attention. The rapist has similar physical characteristics and MO to the rapist in Nottingham Harbor. Unfortunately there is no DNA. Bill lays the file from Gilbert on top of the FAX from Nottingham Harbor. He looks at the clock and sees it is 4:50 PM. He decides to start in the morning. He will try to have the DNA analysis run by the lab the state police utilize. He may have to get the analysis paid for by the AG's Office. It will be better to start calling in the morning. He gets up to leave. As he goes out of the office Sandra says, "Have a good evening, Sarge."

Bill replies, "Sandra, you have a good evening. By the way one of the cases I have been following from Gilbert matches the physical characteristics of the case from Nottingham Harbor. I am going to pursue getting the DNA analysis run on the Gilbert case. It's too late today to start. I will start in the morning."

Sandra replies, "Can I help?"

Bill answers, "You certainly can. We will discuss it tomorrow."

Bill drives home.

It is the second week in December. Bill looks at the calendar and realizes that there is Christmas Bazaar on Friday at the local church. He decided a couple of weeks ago to attend the Bazaar and maybe fine some gifts for the kids and friends. He sits down looks at a couple of bills. He gets up and goes to the kitchen. He decides on a simple sandwich for dinner. He takes the food and a soda into the living room and places them on the desk. He sits down turns on the TV with the remote. He begins watching the news and the weather. The game show comes on following the news. He has finished the one and half sandwiches. He takes the checkbook from the desk and makes out three checks to pay the bills. He casually is answering the questions related to the game show. Two hours pass. He turns off the TV. He turns on the radio to a music station. Before he goes to the easy chair from the desk, he lets the dog in. He cleans up the sandwich stuff and feeds the dog. It is about 9:30 and he sits down in the easy chair. He drifts off to sleep. He wakes up at 10:50 and decides to turn on the news before going to bed. A traffic accident on the main road, a fire near the ocean, and the weather prediction about a snowstorm on Sunday are the main stories. He turns the TV off and goes to bed. He thinks as he is dozing off another exciting day in New Hampshire.

The alarm goes off at 7:00 AM. Bill takes a shower and shaves. He stops on the way to the office and gets a coffee and donut. He arrives at about 9:00 AM. Being on the serious crime task force his hours are more like office hours. As he enters the office area he greets Sandra, "Good morning, Sandra."

Sandra responds, "Good morning, Serge."

Bill says, "I am going to call the AG's office about the DNA for the one rape case. Then we can talk. Is there anything happening that is more urgent."

Sandra answers, "Nothing."

Bill goes to his office. He looks up Linda Smyth's number. She is the ADA he deals with at the AG's office. He dials the number.

The phone rings four times and Linda answers, "Linda Symth, ADA in the attorney General's office. How can I help you?"

Bill replies to her question, "This is Sergeant Bill Simpson of the state police."

Linda responds, "Hi, Bill. What's up?"

Bill jokingly replies, "Apparently the cost of DNA analysis."

Linda continues, "Do you need help with a DNA analysis?"

Bill continues, "Short answer yes. Did you hear about the rape a few weeks ago in Nottingham Harbor?"

Linda says, "Yes on the news. Are we now solving crimes in Maine?"

Bill responds, "Yes and no.'

Linda interjects, "This is going to be a good explanation."

Bill continues, "For a lawyer you are sometimes funny. I probably told you in the past, that I grew up near Nottingham Harbor. I casually know the chief there. I talked to him about the case. He sent me the particulars of the Unsub. The Unsub physically matches an Unsub on one of my cases from New Hampshire. It is the rape in Gilbert. There is no DNA on the

Gilbert rape. Carl Kramer had the Maine state police run the DNA on the case from Nottingham Harbor. What I need is the DNA run on the Gilbert rape. The state police have not run the DNA analysis. Can you get them the funding etc. to have the DNA analysis done?"

Linda says, "I believe I can, based on what you have told me. If there is a match then we know the rapist is repeat offender."

Bill says, "It would also confirm my belief that these rapists do not commit one rape and quit."

Linda says, "Is the rape kit in Gilbert?"

Bill replies, "I believe so."

Linda says, "I will call you tomorrow after I talk to the Gilbert chief and instruct him to have the kit taken to the lab."

Bill says, "Thank you."

Linda continues, "You know it will be next week before we have results."

Bill says, "That is fine. I will talk to you next week. Have a good day."

Linda says, "You have a good day also."

They hang up.

Bill walks out to the bullpen area. Sandra asks, "How did it go with Linda?"

Bill says, "She says she should be able to get the analysis run by next week."

Sandra says, "Sounds like good news."

Bill replies, "Yes." He gets another coffee and goes back to the office. He decides to look at some of the older cases and compare the physical characteristics of the rapist in those cases.

Lunchtime goes by. After Bill returns from lunch, he continues the search. He fines another case that matches the Gilbert case. It appears that two other cases match, but not to the Gilbert case.

He calls Linda again.

The phone rings five times. Linda answers, "Hi, Bill. Do you have more information?"

Bill replies, "I have been going through some more cases. A rape in Wilbert has a very similar physical description of the rapist as in the Gilbert case and the Nottingham Harbor case."

Linda responds, "Send me a FAX with the details. I should be able to get a second DNA run."

Bill replies, "Right away. Have a good day."

Linda says, "Ok."

They hang up.

Bill takes the file to Sandra. "Can you send a FAX to Linda Smyth?"

Sandra answers, "Yes, immediately."

Bill says, "Thank you."

Bill goes back to his office and thinks to himself. This is real police work, but it is boring and slow.

He leaves at about 5:30 PM. He goes home and the evening goes about the same as yesterday.

Friday he comes in at 9:00 AM. He reviews a couple of E-mails and looks at a serious robbery case. He looks at a few more of the rape case files. He thinks the robbers are serial criminals also.

Five o'clock comes around. He decides to leave and head over to church and the bazaar. He changes clothes and picks up his personal car before going to the church. The bazaar started at 5:30 PM. There is light food and none alcoholic beverages. He knows the lady working the table selling knickknacks is Mattie. He does not know much about her. He decides to talk to her and find out her story. Mattie knows his name is Bill, but not much else. He says, "I am Bill Simpson. I am a sergeant with the state police. I am not here to arrest you. What do you do?"

Mattie says, "I have seen you in church. That didn't answer your question. I am a high school math teacher. I am glad you are not here to arrest me."

Bill says, "I was obviously kidding. Do you have a family?"

Mattie replies, "Yes I have two children. My husband died in the service several years ago. Do you have a family?"

Bill answers, "Yes. I have three grown children. My wife died of cancer five years ago. I am sorry about your husband. Did he die in combat?"

Mattie replies, "Yes, ten years ago. He loved the service. He loved me and the kids"

Bill asks, "Do you every go out."

Mattie replies, "do you mean on a date?"

Bill says, "Yes, I suppose I do."

Mattie continues, "Ok."

Bill looks at her for a minute and then says, "How about Dinner tomorrow night?"

Mattie thinks, "Ok."

Bill says, "Can you tell me where you live and your phone number?"

Mattie looks around for a pen and piece of paper. She writes her name and phone number on the paper and her address. She explains how to find her house.

Bill takes his card from his pocket and borrows the pen and writes his personal cell phone number on the back. Bill says, "I will pick you up about 6:30PM tomorrow night. You understand as a police Sergeant I could get called to work. Normally that does not happen because my job is looking at cases that have been investigated by other policemen. I do want to go out with you. So if I would have to cancel it would be because of an emergency.

Mattie says, "I understand. Math teachers do not have those types of emergencies."

Bill continues, "I am going to walk around and look at some of the other tables. I might fine a few Christmas presents."

Bill stops back at Mattie's table. She is engaged in a conversation with a customer. Bill waits on the side until she finishes the conversation. Then he says, "I am leaving. Good Bye. I will see you tomorrow night."

Mattie replies, "Good Bye. I will see you tomorrow night."

Bill leaves. As he walks out of the church hall he thinks I am as nervous as a teenager.

Bill goes shopping in Concord for some Christmas gifts for his kids and his sister's kids.

He gets home at about 3 PM. He had set the alarm for 4 PM. He takes a short nap. He gets up and takes a shower. At 5:15 he gets dressed. He leaves for Mattie's house at 5:50. He arrives in front of her house at

6:25 PM. He parks in the driveway. He walks to the front door and rings the bell.

Mattie answers the door. As she opens the door she says, "Hello Bill. Come in and have a seat. I am almost ready. I need just a few minutes."

Bill replies, "Hello to you. Ok. I will sit here. Take your time." He sits down in the one chair.

Mattie goes upstairs. About five minutes later she comes down. She says, "I am ready now."

Bill gets up and walks over to Mattie. She reaches in the cupboard for her coat. Bill takes the coat and holds it while Mattie slips it on. She slips on a pair of gloves. She checks the door to see that the lock is set. Bill opens the storm door and Mattie closes the inside door and checks the handle to see that it is locked. Bill offers her his arm and walks her to the passenger side of the car. He opens the door. Mattie slides into the front seat. He goes around to the driver's side and get in. He starts the car.

Bill says, "I made reservations for 7:15 at a restaurant near Concord. I hope you will like it."

Mattie replies, "I am sure I will."

Bill begins the conversation. "You said you have children."

Mattie replies, "Yes. I have two children. "Brenda is in the last year of high school. Her grades are excellent. Her SAT scores were excellent. She applied to Johns Hopkins and Georgetown. Sam is finishing up the first year at Princeton. He likes the math, but some of the electives not so much. He still is getting good grades. My husband was killed in combat and the children are covered by the military benefits. How about your children?"

Bill answers, "Sam is following in his mother's footsteps. My wife died of cancer five years ago and our three children are grown and only Linda is still in college. Linda is in prelaw at the University of Chicago. William is in Baltimore building Electronics. It is defense work. He kids me that if he tells me what he is doing he will have to kill me. I always remind him I have a gun. Jane is at NASA near Washington and is doing computer science. She says unlike William she could tell me what she is doing, but I probably would not understand it. She is right. You may understand it.

Linda has been accepted to Michigan State in Lansing for her law degree. She will start there next year." They are paying off some college loans and I help some with Linda's bills.

Mattie continues, "I found out something interesting about Johns Hopkins. Did you know where the name of Johns Hopkins originated?"

Bill replies, "I don't know. Was it named after John Hopkins?"

Mattie answers, "no and yes. But I would have thought the same thing. When Brenda visited Hopkins they told her about the name. Johns was or is Hopkins' mother's maiden name and of course Hopkins was or is his father's last name. The full name of the university and the hospital is "The Johns Hopkins University" not just Johns Hopkins."

Bill says, "That is interesting. Sounds like a good trivia question."

They ride quietly for a few minutes.

Bill says, "There is a Diana Krall CD in the drive. Would you like me to turn it on?"

Mattie replies, "I like Diana. Please play it."

Bill pushes the buttons to turn on the CD and it starts playing a Diana Krall jazz recording.

Mattie starts to hum along.

They reach the restaurant in about fifteen minutes.

Bill parks the car. He walks around to the passenger side and opens the door for Mattie. She gets out and thanks him. They walk into the restaurant.

The receptionist at the front desk asks, "How can I help you?"

Bill replies, "I have a reservation for two. My name is Bill Simpson."

The restaurant is in a large old house. The receptionist directs them to the second floor and leads the way to their table. After they are seated Mattie starts the conversation. "Bill, you said when we met at the bazaar that you deal with serious crimes."

Bill replies, "When serious crimes like murder, rape or major robberies occur. The local state police respond along with local town police. What happens next is myself or other detectives take over the cases and do the investigations. It is interesting work. Once in a while I do end up in some chase to catch a criminal. It is not quite like the TV shows, but they are not too exaggerated."

Mattie continues, "Did you hear about the rape in Nottingham Harbor Maine a few months ago?"

Bill answers, "Yes. I did. How did you hear about it?"

Mattie continues, "The young lady that was the victim went to high school where I teach."

Bill says, "I cannot talk about individual cases. I have theory. I believe that many of the rapists are serial rapist. It is hard to believe different rapists have done each of the rapes. I believe many of the rapists are serial rapists, but they move around enough that it is not obvious they are committing multiple rapes over a period of time.

Mattie replies, "That is an interesting theory."

Bill continues, "I only have DNA on a few of the rapes. But I did match a rape in Vermont with one here in New Hampshire. I am trying to have more DNA analyses run and compare them. But even if I can match up DNA from a number of rapes, how do I connect a name to the DNA?"

Mattie says, "Maybe we can apply some mathematical analysis."

Bill says, "Enough work. We can talk about any ideas you have. Christmas is a week away. Are you doing anything for the holidays?"

Mattie answers, "Yes. I am going to Maryland to visit my Brother, Ted. He works at NASA. He has a wife and three kids. I will be down there three days. I am going down on Amtrak."

Bill says, "My kids are coming up here. We will go to my brother's farm. Actually it is the Simpson family farm. The farm has been in the family for five generations. My sister will come for New Year's Day. The farm is twenty miles inland from Nottingham Harbor. We would go to the Harbor to fish and play on the beach as kids and teenagers. The chief of police at the Harbor is older. He believes he still does not have the experience to solve a major crime."

Mattie continues, "I would think you do not have any jurisdiction in Maine."

Bill answers, "I don't technically. Ed Woodward, a state trooper in Maine, does similar investigations and does have jurisdiction. He is a friend. If crimes occur in both states we can cooperate on the investigations. I got off the track for a minute."

The food arrives with wine. Bill and Mattie start to eat. The conversation slows. They do talk about the pending snowstorm. They talk about the families some more. An hour passes. Bill and Mattie are ready to leave. Bill drives Mattie home. When they arrive at the house Bill walks Mattie to the front door.

Mattie says, "Bill would you like to come in for few minutes."

Bill answers, "Yes."

So they go inside. Mattie says, "Have a seat. Can I get you a soda? I don't have any thing stronger?"

Bill says, "I will take a glass of soda."

Mattie gets two glass of soda. She returns to the living room and sit down on the sofa.

Bill says, "I enjoyed the date tonight."

Mattie replies, "So did I?"

Bill says, "Next week is Christmas. Are you going to be here for New Year's?"

Mattie answers, "Yes. Why?"

Bill continues, "There is a New Year's Eve Party at the country club at the golf course in Nottingham Harbor. Some members of my family are going and my friend Ed Woodward and his wife are going. I would like you to go."

Mattie thinks for a minute. Then she says, "Yes."

Bill says, "The party starts at 8PM and goes to 2AM. I will have to pick you up at about 7PM."

Mattie replies, "That will be OK. We are talking about New Year's Eve?"

Bill answers, "Yes. 7PM on New Year's Eve."

Bill finishes the soda. He says, "I guess I should get going. But I am looking forward to another date for New Year's Eve."

They walk to the front door. As Mattie opens the door she looks at Bill. He put a hand on her back. They kiss like a couple of teenagers not sure whether they should kiss. Bill steps out the door and says, "Good Night."

Mattie answers, "Good Night."

Bill walks to car. Mattie watches. Bill turns at the car and waves good bye. Mattie turns and goes inside. Bill drives off.

Sunday Morning Bill goes to church. As he walks in he looks around and sees Mattie sitting in a full pew. He takes a seat several pews back. As the service is finished he walks to the back of the church. Mattie comes out with a couple of friends. Mattie sees Bill and walks over with two friends. Bill is not sure what to say. Mattie says to her two friends, "This is Bill."

Bill says, "Hello."

Mattie says, "This is Linda and Clara. This is Bill Simpson. He is state police detective. I met him at the bazaar last week."

Linda says, "This is the guy who asked you to go out New Year's Eve?"

Mattie replies, "Yes."

Linda says, "Go for it."

Bill just smiles.

Mattie says, "I guess the cat is out of the bag. I will see you, New Year's Eve."

Bill replies, "I will see you at 7:00 PM. Until then have a good Christmas holidays with your family." He turns and walks to the car.

Mattie's friend Linda comments. "Is he a keeper?"

Mattie replies, "It not that serious, but he is a widower with three adult children and a good job. He is working on some rape cases that may be connected to the teacher that was raped in Nottingham Harbor. He is working with a friend from the Maine police and believes there may be a connection. Bill is from the area near Nottingham Harbor. His family Farm is still near the Harbor."

Linda says, "The case is the young teacher that went to high school where you teach."

Mattie answers, "Yes. He came to the church Bazaar. We went to dinner yesterday. Then he asked me out for New Year's Eve. I had not been on a date in ten years. I was sort of nervous about it. We talked about our kids and family. I am looking forward to New Year's."

Linda continues, "I can tell you are enthused about dating again. I will see you on New Year's Day and I will want a full report."

Mattie responds, "Merry Christmas to you and your family."

Linda says, "Same to you and yours."

They both walk to their cars and head for home.

CHAPTER 3

NEW YEAR'S EVE

Bill leaves for Mattie's house at about 6:15 PM. He is early at her street. He sits on the side of the road. He waits until 6:50. He drives up and parks in the driveway. He rings the bell and waits.

Mattie comes to the door. She looks through the peephole and sees it is Bill. She opens the door and says, "Good Evening, Bill."

Bill says, "Good Evening." As he walks inside he continues, "That is a beautiful dress."

Mattie replies, "Thank you. It is not new. I got it for a friend's wedding about eight years ago. I have not had any chance since then to wear it."

Bill continues, "You are going to be the Belle of the Ball."

Mattie answers, "Maybe. I imagine there is going to be other beautiful outfits at a country club party."

Bill says, "Well, you will be my Belle." He helps Mattie with her coat."

Mattie picks up her purse and checks for her door key. Bill ushers her to the passenger side of the car and opens the door. Mattie gets in and Bill shuts the door and goes to the driver side and gets in. They drive to the country club. They turn on a Diana Krall CD for the trip. As they enter the club he sees his family. Bill says, "My family is over there. They got a table for the evening." Bill and Mattie walk over to the table.

Bill walks up to the table with Mattie on his arm. He says, "Family this Mattie Greene my date for the evening."

Mattie says, "Hello."

Bill goes around the table and introduces the family. This is my brother John and his wife, Clara. Next to my sister-in-law are my sister Evelyn and her husband Charles or Charlie. Next are my Father William and his wife, my mother, Marcia. John and Evelyn both have two children. The next two people are Ed Woodworth and his wife, Melissa. Ed is a Maine State Policeman.

Bill and Mattie sit down next to his Brother, John, and Bill's sister-in-law, Clara.

Clara asks Mattie, "What do you do for a living."

Mattie answers, "I teach mathematics in high school."

Clara asks, "How did you two meet?"

Mattie answers, "We met at the church Bazaar three weeks ago. Bill asked me to dinner. And then to come tonight."

Clara asks, "Do you have a family?"

Mattie answers, "Yes. I have two kids that are in their late teens. My husband was killed in action. I am an army widow. It was about ten years ago. We were happily married for twelve years when he was killed. He liked the army. He had just made Captain. The first couple of years were tough. The kids were young and I was not ready to be a young widow. I buried myself in my teaching. Now I remember the good times. The kids are my life."

Clara says, "Losing a loved one is tough anytime."

Mattie replies, "Yes it is. Bill told me that he lost his wife to cancer."

Meantime Bill is talking to his brother about Mattie.

John asks Bill and Mattie what he can bring them to drink. The band starts to play. On the second song Bill asks Mattie if she would like to dance. She agrees. They excuse themselves and get up to dance. Bill's sister and brother-in-law get up and go to the buffet. Bills brother comments to his wife, "Bill and Mattie look like a couple out there dancing." His wife nods yes.

The evening goes by quickly. There is a celebration at midnight for the New Year's. At about 1:00 AM Bill's brother says they are ready leave. He is taking Mom and Dad home. Bill says, "Have a safe trip little brother."

His brother says, "You all have a safe trip home. I was nice meeting you, Mattie." The other people nod a wish their mom and dad to have a good year."

Bill and Mattie get up for one more dance. Bill says, "I guess we should get going also. It is over an hour drive back to your house.

Mattie replies, "I agree."

When the music stops Bill and Mattie walk back to the table. Another couple is sitting at the table with Bill's sister. His sister introduces them to Bill and Mattie. Bill says, "We are going to go sis. It is over and hour back home. I will see you in a few weeks at the farm one weekend."

His sister and brother-in-law both say have a safe drive and we will see you at the farm one weekend and definitely bring Mattie. Mattie waves good-bye.

Bill and Mattie pick up their coats and walk to the car. They head home.

On the way home Bill tells Mattie he spoke to the chief of police from Nottingham Harbor about a meeting he is setting up about the rapes. He says, "You had some ideas about using Mathematics to connect these guys together and identify them. I think you should be at the meeting. But it may be during the week not on the weekend."

Mattie says, "I can take off a day from school, if it will help."

Bill replies, "I would like you to explain the mathematical techniques we can use to identify the criminals. I am inviting an ADA's from Maine, Vermont and New Hampshire. My friend from the Maine state police, the chief from Nottingham Harbor, and a state policeman from Vermont will also be at the meeting. Maybe I can arrange the meeting on Martin Luther King Day. You do have off from school for MLK Day? I have to verify all of the participant can make it that day.

They drive to Mattie's as they listen to a Diana Krall CD. They exchange little stories about the children and the families. When they arrive at her house, Bill walks her to the door. Mattie says, "Would you like to come in for a few minutes."

Bill replies, "Yes, I would. I cannot stay too long. I have to get up tomorrow. I volunteered to work New Year's Day. Being Single I can relieve one of the married guys on the holiday. Otherwise I would invite you to do something tomorrow."

Mattie replies, "I am going to visit some friends tomorrow. What time do you get off?"

Bill replies, "At 4:00 o'clock. Why?"

Mattie answers, "Well you could join us. My friends always tell me to bring a guess. It is only twenty miles from here. My daughter is coming. The party doesn't start until about 4:00 PM."

Bill thinks a moment and then answers, "I could pick you up, but it would be about 5:00 PM. Obviously, there is room in the car for your daughter."

Mattie replies, "I am going to drive with my daughter. I am going to help with the preparations. Can you just come to the party when you get off from work?"

Bill says, "Yes, I can do that. Give me the directions."

Mattie writes the direction on a piece of paper.

Mattie says, "It sounds like a date. I will see you at 5:00 PM."

Bill gets up and says, "OK."

He goes toward the door. Mattie follows. He turns at the door and gently pulls Mattie toward him and kisses her and then kisses her again and says, "I think I am falling in love. Hope that is OK with you?"

Mattie replies, "Very much."

Bill leaves. Mattie stands by the door and watches until Bill drives away."

Bill drives home. Mattie locks the door and gets ready for bed.

CHAPTER 4

ROBBERY AT LOVETT

The morning comes early. The alarm rings at 6:00 AM. He takes a quick shower and gets ready to go to work. He puts on his uniform. He is covering the highway today. By about 7:45 AM he is at the Barracks. There is short roll call. Captain James at the end says, "Bill need to see you in my office. Need you to change your assignment."

Bill walks to the captain's office. He instinctively wraps on the doorframe. Henry James says, "Come on in, Bill."

Henry says, "I know that you volunteered to replace a patrol officer. I know you do it so one of the guys can be with his family on the Holiday. Normally I would tell you to go on the patrol. But last night someone was shot in Lovett in a convenience store during a robbery. He is going to eventually be OK. But I need you to do your regular job. Go to the Hospital and interview the victim and then talk with the responding local police. I think there are three other related robberies. I want to put an end to these robberies before they become an epidemic. You can continue tomorrow on the case or cases as part of your regular assignment. You have some ideas on the rape cases. How are they coming?"

Bill replies, "I could use some help getting DNA run on the rape cases. I will go over to Lovett and start the investigation. A lady math teacher I met at church knew the latest rape victim from Nottingham Harbor. She has an idea of using mathematics and the DNA results to identify criminals. I am going to ask the Attorney General to hire her as a voluntary consultant so she can be officially on the cases. I am working with the Vermont and Maine AG offices to consolidate our efforts."

Henry continues, "Ok. Keep at it."

Bill gives Henry a casual salute and Henry returns it. Bill leaves for Lovett. The victim is in the Hospital about seventy-five miles from the Barracks near Concord. Bill drives to the hospital. He arrives at 10 AM. He identifies himself to receptionist in the lobby. He asks to see the victim's nurse or doctor. The receptionist directs Bill to the second floor nurse's station. As he walks up to the station he identifies himself even though he has a uniform on. The nurse, Jane Worthwood, asks, "How can I help you?"

Bill answers, "John Lipsome, is victim of a shooting last night. I am here to investigate what happened. Can you show me, which is his room? Can you ask his doctor to come to the room also?"

Jane answers, "Sure can. The local chief of police requested he be placed in a private room for several days. His wife is there. The room is 216."

Bill walks down the hall. As he enters the room he says, "Hello, I am Sergeant Bill Simpson of the state police."

John's wife says, "Please come in."

Bill comes in and says, "How are you this morning, John."

John answers, "I am as OK as can be expected after being shot."

Bill continues, "I am Sergeant Bill Simpson of the state police. I work serious and violent crimes. There have been several armed robberies and couple of other shootings. Every law enforcement agency has problems with identifying the criminals. Did you have a chance to give a sketch artist a drawing?"

John answers, "No I haven't."

Bill continues, "It is New Year's Day and I have a call into my headquarters to get a sketch artist up here today. I know the artist and he has three kids and a wife and other family. But he should be here by noon. He knows it is important to make the sketches while the information is still fresh. The only question is are you up to the effort? I asked your doctor to come here."

John answers, "I feel good enough to help."

A doctor walks in. He says, "Good Morning. I am Dr. Jack Smyth. Mr. Lipsome's Surgeon has left, but I have been briefed on his condition. So how can I help?"

Bill says, "I am Sergeant Bill Simpson of the state police. I am investigating the shooting and the crime in general. I ask John if he felt up to providing a sketch of the robber. I just wanted your opinion on whether you believe it is OK for him to spend a half to one hour working with an artist to make the sketch. Basically he can lie in bed, and his wife can be here, etc. The artist will ask him questions and show him the sketch as they work on it."

Dr. Jack answers, "It should be OK. If he feels he needs a break I assume the artist will comply."

Bill says, "Our artist works with patients all the time. We try to do sketches as soon as possible. We try to get the sketch while the information is fresh in the victim's mind. The artist should be here about noon. His name is Jeff Woods. He has a wife and three kids. John, do you have children? You obviously have a wife."

John answers, "Yes, we have two kids."

Bill continues, "Thank You Doctor."

Dr. Jack says, "You are welcome. I will stop by in a little while to just check on John. There will be nurses coming in from time to time."

Bill continues, "Thank you again, Doctor. John, can you please explain what happened during the robbery? I know you have told the other officers, but as a detective I like to hear the story myself."

John begins, "It was about 11:30PM. I was preparing to close the store at midnight. It was New Year's Eve and traffic was slow. A car pulled up with two people inside. I could not see the second person well, but I could see there was a second person. He went over to the aisle where the chips and crackers are displayed. I thought he was a regular customer. I was standing at the counter waiting for him to come up and pay. When he came around the aisle and up to the counter he was holding several bags of pretzels. He dropped them on the counter. I started to ring up the pretzels. I asked him if he needed anything else. He answered yes give me your money. He had pulled a revolver from his right coat pocket and pointed at me. I said OK. I push the button on the cash register and the drawer open. He grabbed the money from several of the slots in the drawer. He picked up the two bags of pretzels. He started out of the store. Suddenly he turned and fired the revolver at me. I was behind the cash register and ducked but the bullet struck me in the side."

Bill interrupts, "Was he wearing gloves?"

John answers, "No. Is that important?"

Bill says, "Yes. Our forensic team is testing for fingerprints. But there are a dozen prints on the counter. We may get lucky."

John says, "I just remembered something. He brought three bags to the counter and he only took two with him. When he stuck the gun in my face, I dropped the one bag on the floor behind the counter. He had handled the bag. I have four employees and one of them put the pretzel bags on display. If you can find the bag, we may get lucky."

Bill says, "You may be correct. Let me make a call to the forensic team."

Bill gets up and walks out of the room. He calls the officer in charge of the team."

The team leader is Bill Parsons. The phone rings seven times and Bill answers, "Good Morning."

Bill Simpson says, "Bill I have some very important information on the robbery and shooting last night. I hate to make you go back to the scene on New Year's Day, but the information may be the break we need. The victim remembers he was holding a package of pretzels when the robber stuck the gun in his face. He dropped the pretzels under the counter somewhere. Did you guys find something like the bag of pretzels? It may have the robber's finger prints on the bag."

Bill Parsons answers, "Don't remember finding a bag. I will get someone back to the scene, immediately."

Bill continues, "Thank you, Bill. Have a Happy New Year. I am at the hospital with the victim."

Bill Parsons answers, "You have a Happy New Year also. I will call you as soon as I have some information. Good Bye for now."

Bill replies, "Good Bye.'

They hang up.

Bill returns to the room and says, "John that information on the bag may be important. I just call the head of the forensic team. He is sending someone to check on the pretzel bag. This could be the break we need to solve your robber and several other robbers."

John says, "Some of my employees could have handled the bag also."

Bill replies, "That is OK. We will eliminate employees as soon as we have the prints. Can you think of anything else?"

John says, "The car was black or very dark blue. I am pretty sure it was black."

Bill continues, "My artist has a book with photographs of most modern cars. He can show you the pictures. You may be able to identify the model."

John says, "I hope this helps. Has the robber hit other places?"

Bill replies, "We believe he has hit four places in New Hampshire and several in Vermont. The bag of pretzel may be the break we need."

Bill says, "If you think of anything else please call me. Here is my card. You can tell the artist something else also. I hope you completely recover. Mrs. Lipsome you have a good New Year's. Hope your children are OK.'

She says, "My name is Helen. Sergeant, do you have children and a wife?"

Bill answers, "I have three grown children. My wife died of cancer a few years ago. I took the duty today to relieve another officer with children."

Helen says, "That is generous of you."

Bill says, "I have just met a lady at church a few weeks back. She invited me to join her later today. She is widow. Her husband died in combat."

Helen says, "I am sorry for your losses, but I hope you have a good day."

Bill says, "Thank you. I am glad John is going to recover. You both have good day. I will be in touch with any progress."

Bill gets up and leaves just as a nurse enters the room.

The nurse says, "Happy New Year."

Bill replies, "Same to you and the staff."

The nurse, "Thank you."

Bill walks down the corridor and the steps. He goes to his car. He starts the car. He picks up the radio mike and calls station. The Desk sergeant answers the radio call, "Sergeant James Woody here."

Bill replies, "This is Bill Simpson. I am going to the store that was robbed last night. I asked Bill Parsons to send a forensic team member to the store."

James answers, "Bill sent Linda Gabriel to the store. She is our best finger print person. She has about an hour drive."

Bill replies, "I am going to the store and wait for her. This pretzel bag could be important. I am going to stop for a coffee on the way, but I should still get there first. Can you tell the Captain I will explain the details when I return? We may or may not have the robber's finger prints."

James answers, "I will tell the captain. I hope we are lucky."

Bill replies, "I hope so also. I will see you when I get back to the station, James."

James says, "Signing off."

Bill starts to drive toward the store in Lovett. He knows that a local service station will be open even on New Year's Day. He stops. He instinctively locks the car. He goes inside.

The guy at the counter says, "How can I help you officer?"

Bill says, "I just want to get a coffee. Is it fresh?"

The guy answers, "Yes officer."

Bill fixes a medium size coffee and returns to the counter. He pulls out his wallet.

The counter guy says, "The coffee is free to police."

Bill says, "Thank you." He continues, "I am headed to Lovett."

The counter guy says, "Are you investigating the robbery at the store? I heard the owner was shot."

Bill replies, "I obviously cannot talk about the investigation. I can tell you the owner is going to be OK. Do you know the owner?"

The counter guy continues, "I casually know him. I am glad he is going be OK. I know he has a family."

Bill says, "I do have to go. You have good day."

The counter guy says, "You have a Happy New Year's officer."

Bill replies, "Thank you."

Bill leaves and unlocks the car. He gets in and places the coffee in a holder. He looks around and sees it is clear to back out. He heads for Lovett. He arrives early. He thinks it may fifteen to twenty minutes before Linda arrives. He parks in front of the store. He puts the seat back down and lays back. There is nothing to do until Linda arrives. A little rest will go a long way later at the party. About twenty-two minutes pass. He dozes off. Linda arrives and parks near Bill's car. He wakes up.

Linda gets out of the car and walks over to Bill's car. Linda knows Bill. He opens the window. Linda says, "I have the key. Do want to get started?"

Bill says, "Yes."

Linda goes to the door and unlocks it. She moves the crime scene tape. Bill follows her to the door and then inside.

Linda says, "I was told to look for a bag of pretzels near the counter or under the counter."

Bill replies, "The victim told me the robber brought three bags of pretzels to the counter and in his haste only took two with him. The victim, John, said he was holding the one bag to ring it up. The robber grabbed the money and started to leave then he turned and fired his gun. John said he ducked and dropped the pretzels on the floor. Ducking saved him from a shot to the body."

Linda goes behind the counter. She bends down and looks under the counter. There is a bag of pretzels on the floor. She says, "How did the forensic team miss the pretzels?"

Bill says, "I don't care why they were missed. Let's process them."

Linda says, "Please hand me an evidence bag and the forceps from my kit."

Bill opens the top of the kit and sees the forceps and a bag. He hands them to Linda.

She says, "Thank You."

She kneels down and reaches under the counter and picks up the pretzel bag with forceps. She gets up and says, "Can you hold the bag open."

Bill holds the bag. Linda places the bag of pretzels in the evidence bag.

Linda says, "The bag is wrinkled. I am going to take it back to the lab. I can process it more carefully in the lab. I know you want the finger prints as quickly as possible."

Bill replies, "Yes. But I am reminded that as quickly as possible could mean never. You know the results are more important than speed at this juncture."

Linda says, "I believe the team did finger print the counter and did not find any shell cases. I was told the robber was using a revolver.'

Bill says, "Yes, he was. A fingerprint could be the break thru we have been looking for. This guy has robbed here and in Vermont."

Linda says "I should have results tomorrow late."

Bill says, "Let's lock the store and head for home."

Linda says, "Have a Happy New Year as she locks the door and straightens the tape."

She says, "I think we can release the crime scene tomorrow. I am glad the victim was not seriously hurt and is recovering."

Bill replies, "Yes that is the best piece of good news this pretzel bag is the second best piece of news. Have a good New Year's Day. Are you getting together with family for the holiday?"

Linda answers, "Yes. We are all meeting at my brother's place. So I am not cooking today."

They leave. Bill heads for the Barracks. Linda heads for the forensics lab.

Bill gets to the barrack in about an hour. He stopped for a sandwich and a soda on the way. He thinks I don't want to eat too much. Mattie and her family are going to have dinner at about five. When he gets to the barracks he sits down at his desk and starts eating the sandwich. Captain James comes in. He says, "Finish your lunch then come to my office."

Bill says, "We can talk while I eat."

Captain James sits down. He says, "OK."

Bill begins once in while interrupting to take a bite from his sandwich. "I first went to the hospital. The victim, John Lipsome, and his wife were there. His doctor said that John should recover completely. That is good news. He told me the same story he told the first two police on the scene. However he remembered a detail he had not told them. The robber had brought three bags of pretzels to the counter. When he pulled the gun two of them were on the counter, John was holding the third one to check the guy out. He grabbed the cash from the register drawer and started to leave. John was still holding the third bag. Two cars came into the parking lot. The guy turned and shot at him. The cash register blocked a direct body shot. John said he drop the one bag and kicked it under the counter. The two cars panicked the guy enough to leave without firing again or firing at the cars. There is a possibility he left his fingerprints behind. Linda and I met at the store. We found the bag under the counter. She is going to process it tomorrow. She said one of the other guys in lab has a technique that has worked to reconstruct partial prints. He will be in tomorrow."

Henry interrupts, "I can ask him to come in today. I know it is tough to work on a holiday. But it sounds like this is important enough to process the bag in a timely fashion."

Bill says, "I agree. Except he is in Maryland with his family and he would not be here until midnight. I think we need to be sensible and wait till the morning."

Henry continues, "Ok. We will wait till tomorrow."

Bill continues, "Also we need to fingerprint the young clerks who possibly handled the bag when stacking the display. They are not involved in the robbery. Two of them are under eighteen and the parents will need to be there while they are finger printed. They are not involved in the robbery. I think ADA, Linda Smyth, will need to be there to talk with the parents. The young clerks may not be home either. We need to proceed as fast as possible, but with caution. We do not want to screw up the evidence."

Captain James replies, "Ok. You are correct. Proceed and be sure we are crossing all T's and dotting all the I's. Ok I will let you finish your lunch. Are you going on patrol or are you going home?"

Bill says, "I am going to look up some information on the other robberies before I leave. Considering the time it makes more sense than setting up on patrol."

Captain James says, "Do that. I'll see you tomorrow. You can take over the case. It belongs in your department,"

Bill says, "Ok. I will see you tomorrow. Have a good holiday or at least what is left of the day."

Captain James replies, "You too, Bill."

Bill spends about an hour on the details of several other robbery cases. It does appear they have a serial robber on their hands. He will need to check with Maine and Vermont tomorrow. When he leaves he heads for home to change.

CHAPTER 5

NEW YEARS DAY PARTY

Then he heads to meet Mattie at the New Year's Day Party. He arrives at about ten minutes past five.

Bill rings the doorbell. He can hear the party. Mattie answers the door. She says, "Hi. Come in. The party is just getting a glow on."

Bill says, "I have been all over lower New Hampshire today. I will be glad to sit and relax for a little while."

Mattie says, "Over here I saved us a pair of seats. I will introduce you at dinner. Linda is in the back with Marlene and my daughter finishing up dinner. We are going to eat at about 6:30. Linda's son and daughter-in-law and their baby are not here yet. You know how it is with a baby. Why were you running around so much on New Year's Day? I thought you were going to be on highway patrol."

Bill responds, "I was supposed to be on highway patrol. When I arrived this morning, Captain Henry Jackson called me into his office. He explained that the patrol was important, but there was a robbery overnight in Lovett and the owner had been shot. He wanted me to investigate the crime. Fortunately the victim is going to make a full recovery according to the doctor. It was not the way he and his wife intended to spend New Years."

Mattie says, "We should say a prayer for the victim."

Bill continues, "I went to the hospital near Lovett and spoke to the victim and his doctor. The doctor believes he will make a full recovery. So I talked to him and asked him to tell me the story of what happened. It always sounds like we are pestering the victim and not communicating with the first responders. In this case he remember something that he had missed earlier. When the guy shot at him the owner drop a bag of pretzels the robber had brought to the counter. Linda Gabriel a forensic specialist met me at the store in Lovett. We searched and found a bag of pretzels under counter. She is going to try and construct the fingerprints. It is a tricky technique to construct a fingerprint from an irregular surface like the bag. She said they have done it before. Anyway I was running around until almost 3:00 PM. The fingerprint could be a big break. We believe the same guy has committed robberies here and in Vermont. So how was your afternoon?"

Mattie replies, "Uneventful. I got here at about three and helped Linda finish vacuuming. The guests have been arriving since about four."

Bill says, "As I said I can use the time till dinner to relax."

Mattie says, "Here is Brenda, my youngest."

Brenda walks up and says, "This must be Bill the guy you been talking about."

Bill stands and reaches out to shake Brenda's hand. Brenda kisses him on the cheek instead.

Bill says, "I hope the talk was all good."

Brenda replies, "It was."

Mattie says, "Bill is a little tried right now."

Brenda says, "I will talk to both of you at dinner or after dinner. I am helping Linda."

Mattie says, "OK. Bill I think the guys have a game on the TV in the family room. If you want to join them it is OK with me."

Bill says, "Maybe later. I am content with sitting here with you. Should you go to the kitchen to help the other ladies?"

Mattie says, "I set the table earlier and there are at least three women in the kitchen. Too many cooks spoil the stew. We are not having stew for dinner. Dinner is Turkey and Ham with all the trimmings and Pie and Ice Cream for dessert. Linda is a good cook."

Bill sits back in the chair. He says, "I am dozing off, not a very attentive date."

Mattie says, "I am going to look at the paper. Relax. I will wake you for dinner." The stereo is playing Christmas music. Every now and then there is a cheer or groan from the Family Room. Several of the kids are playing with the Christmas Garden. Several of the teenagers are playing a board game. It is a typical New Years Day party. Granddad is dozing also. Grandma is holding the two year old and reading a story.

Bill does doze off. Mattie finishes reading an article. She gets up and goes to the kitchen. Grandma motions to her. She says, "It appears your man is tried."

Mattie replies, "He is a state policeman and had to work today. He had to investigate a robbery and shooting in the town of Lovett. He did a lot of driving, today. I am going to join the women in the kitchen. I will be back at dinner." Mattie continues to the kitchen.

As she comes in Linda asks, "Is Bill a keeper?"

Mattie replies, "This is only our third date. We do have a lot of things in common. His kids are a little older than mine. He has three and I have the two. The dates have been good. He had a rough day. He had to investigate a robbery and shooting up near the town of Lovett. He says the victim should recover, but it is still hard on the victim's family. I am going to wait until dinner to introduce everybody. How is dinner progressing?"

Linda replies, "About an hour."

The women continue to prepare dinner and chit chat about a number things and their families.

An hour has passed. Bill wakes up and needs the bathroom. He walks to the kitchen and sees Mattie. He motion to her. She comes over. He asks, "Where is the bathroom?"

She replies, "There is one down the stairs in the family room and the other is about two doors down the hall at the top of stairs."

Bill says, "Thank you. I will be down in a few minutes."

Mattie says, "Take your time. Dinner is about ten minute away

Bill goes up the stairs. Mattie returns to the kitchen.

Bill washes his hands and then washes his face before returning to the living room.

Mattie comes in and says, "Dinner is ready. Linda serves it buffet style. Let me get the little table." She places the table between the rocker that

Bill is sitting in and a chair for herself. She goes to the top of the basement stairs. She says in a slightly raised voice, "Dinner is ready. Better come up now or go hungry."

Mattie comes back to her chair. She looks at Bill and smiles. He smiles back. Several minutes pass. Linda walks in and says, "Dinner is ready. Let us gather in the dining room for Grace."

Most of the guys are up from the basement. Linda walks to the top of the stairs and calls down, "Dinner is served. Let us get up here in the dining room for Grace." The remaining two guys come up and join everyone in the dining room.

Linda gathers around the table. She says, "I know you all know each other. We have a new guest this year. You can introduce yourselves during dinner. This Bill Simpson, he is Mattie's friend and date. So say hello Bill."

The guests say, "Hello Bill."

Linda continues, "Bill is a state policeman. He is slightly tired tonight. He had to investigate a robbery and shooting in Lovett. Mattie said it has been a long day. Fortunately, the victim, John is going to survive. So let us all hold hands and say an Our Father for John before Grace. They bow their heads and say the Lord's Prayer."

Bill says as they finish, "I am sure John and his wife and kids appreciate the prayers. I will be seeing them again and tell them what you all did. Thank You. Christians do believe the prayers help."

Linda continues, "Let us keep holding hands and say Grace for this good food and the company of good friends."

They say Grace. Linda continues, "There are plenty of plates and dinnerware, but they don't all match. When you finish please place the plastic ware in the kitchen dishpan. I wash everything. We will have dessert a little later. The drinks are in the kitchen. You can take the food to the living room or the Sun porch next to the kitchen or to the basement. There are card tables and small tables around. I know you have all been here before so let us make ourselves at home. Enjoy."

The guests begin to take the food and go to various tables. The guys returned to the basement. Most of the guests introduced themselves to

Bill. Mattie stands next to Bill. They know Mattie from previous parties. Finally everyone has food and has found a seat. Grandma says to Mattie, "So how did you two meet?"

Mattie replies, "At church just before Christmas. Bill came to a Church Christmas bazaar and asked me to dinner. Then he asked me to a New Year's Eve Party with his friends and family. So I asked him to join me today. Linda always says I should bring a date, so this year I took her up on the offer."

Grandma continues, "You two sound like me and this guy I met 62 years ago. We were younger than you two."

Mattie answers, "Bill and I were both married before. His wife died of cancer. My husband died in combat. Between us there are five children. But I understand what you mean."

Grandma continues, "Well we met at church. We have five children and twelve grandchildren. I remember from last year. You are a school teacher."

Mattie replies, "Yes. I teach mathematics. Bill is a sergeant and a detective for the state police."

Grandma continues to eat.

Bill and Mattie smile at each other and continue to eat dinner. Bill finally says, "The food is good. I like the turkey seasoning."

Mattie replies, "Linda is a good cook."

Linda walks through and says, "We are going to wait a little while before putting the dessert out."

Bill says, "Linda the turkey is delicious. I like the seasoning."

Linda replies, "Thank you. Mattie knows the recipe."

Bill looks at Mattie. She winks. Bill just smiles and keeps eating the turkey.

Twenty minutes pass. Bill has gotten a little more food. Mattie is finished. She waits until Bill has finished the second helping. She says, "Are you finished?"

Bill replies, "Yes."

Mattie says, "Let me take the dishes. Several of us ladies are going to clean up a little before dessert. Do you want to join the guys downstairs? It is OK with me."

Bill says, "If you are going to help the other ladies with clean up I guess I could. As a guest it would be polite to join the guys for a little while until dessert s served."

Mattie says, "Go ahead. They are going to ask questions. We have been having this party for fifteen years. My Husband was still alive for the first few. Do not let them intimidate you with their questions."

Bill answers, "As a detective I am rarely intimidated. But thank you for the advice."

Mattie says, "I know you can handle the questions."

Bill says, "Have fun with the dirty dishes.'

Mattie answers, "I will. You have fun with the questions."

Bill gets up and goes to the basement. Mattie goes to the kitchen. As he gets to the basement, he sees the basement is really fixed up as a family room. Several of the younger kids are playing games in the one corner. There is a Christmas Garden with trains being run by several of the older kids. The men are gathered around a big screen TV that is playing a football game. Two or three teenagers are working on computer games. One of the guys says, "Bill, please join us." He gets up opens a folding chair. It is Linda's husband."

They sit there for a couple of minutes. Finally the intensity of the game slows. Carl asks, "Linda told us that you and Mattie just met."

Bill says, "Well I started going to the church in the fall where Mattie was going. I just decided to change from my former church. It was closer and I heard the church was active in the community. Someone told me Mattie was a widow around Thanksgiving. As a widower I decided to talk to her. So about four weeks ago there was a Christmas Bazaar. I went to the bazaar to buy some gifts for my grown kids and a couple of friends. Mattie was working one of the tables. I took the opportunity to introduce myself. I felt like a teenager. She told me a little about herself. So I asked her out to dinner. We have gone to two parties. That is about all that has happened."

Carl says, "We have known Mattie since her husband was alive. You are the first guy she has shown any interest in."

Bill replies, "It is very casual at the moment. We will see. My wife died five years ago of cancer. So I may or may not be ready for a relationship. Now you guys can tell your wives all about the interview."

Carl says, "you are a Detective with the state police?'

Bill answers, "Yes. I generally handle serious crime. I have volunteered to do highway patrol, but there was a shooting during a robbery and I had to investigate what happened. I was running around all day. I guess I was tried when I arrived here. I dozed off before dinner. Mattie let me sleep."

George says, "The game is getting intense."

Bill says, "Who are the teams?"

Carl answers, "University of New Hampshire and the University of Vermont. It is the fourth quarter and U of V is ahead. George is suffering because he is a grad of U of NH. I am U of V. The other guys are from other universities."

Bill says, "I am a graduate of the police academy. We only had a shooting team no football."

Carl replies, "Do you have competitions?"

Bill says, "NO. I am kidding. Once in a while a couple of the Barracks will have a friendly competition."

The guys start concentrating on the game and there is quiet. Linda's husband, Sam asks, Bill would you like a beer."

Bill answers, "Yes, I am off duty and with friends. So I will have a beer."

Sam holds up three bottles of beer. He says, "Which one?"

Bill says, "I'll take the Bud."

Sam grabs a glass off the table and hands the beer and the glass to Bill.

Bill says, "Thank you."

Vermont wins the game is over. George says, "Ok I owe you and Susan dinner." I can't do it next weekend, but Helen and I will do it in two or three weeks. I will tell Helen to call Susan and set it up."

Carl replies, "That's ok."

Sam says, "They have this dinner bet every year."

Bill says, "Sounds like they are good friends."

Sam continues, "Yes it is one of those friendly rivalries. Actually the wives are the winners. They get to go to an excellent restaurant. Maybe you and Mattie can join Linda and I for dinner in a few weeks after the holidays slow down."

Bill answers, "I have to talk to Mattie, but if she wants to do dinner it will be Ok with me. Linda and Mattie should arrange it."

Sam says, "I will tell Linda to talk to Mattie. Are you into sports?"

Bill replies, "I ski a little. I played amateur softball. I think my wife was a better skier than myself. I grew up near Nottingham Harbor. My Brother still operates the family farm about twenty miles inland from the Harbor. We fished near the Harbor when I was younger. The funny thing I was never a hunter as a cop that probably sounds silly. We have shooting competitions between the Barracks. I compete but just for the fun and association with the other guys. Much of the time I am isolated from most of the other guys and girls because as a detective I am in the office and not out on patrol."

Sam continues, "So you investigate serious crimes."

Bill replies, "Yes. Crimes like murder, armed robbery, rape, assault. It keeps me busy."

Sam continues, "I think I better check on the coolers and the beer. I will be back in a while."

Bill says, "Ok. Talk to you later."

Sam gets up and goes to the cooler and checks on the beer and soda supply.

Bill picks up a National Geographic lying of the table and thumbs through the pages. A couple of the guys are playing chess. Two of the guys are entertaining the smaller kids. Sam walks back down the stairs and says, "Dessert is going to be ready in about fifteen minutes. Pie, ice cream, fruit, cookies and some other snacks are the desserts." He goes back upstairs to help.

Bill reads one of the articles. One of the chess players calls "Check mate." Several more minutes pass. Mattie comes down stairs. Bill does not see her at first. She walks over to the chair. She says, "Hi."

Bill says, "Hi yourself. Are you finished cleaning up?"

Mattie replies, "Basically the dishes from dinner are cleaned. There are few pots that are going to need more time to soak. Dessert is ready. Sam should come down any second to tell us to come up. Do you want to sit here or upstairs for dessert?"

Bill replies, "Here is OK with me."

Sam walks down and says, "Dessert is ready. Come on up and get some."

Mattie and Bill get up and go upstairs. Ten minutes later they come back down carrying dessert. One of the guys moves a more comfortable chair from the chess table for Mattie. Bill says, "Thank you."

Carl replies, "You are welcome."

Mattie sits down next to Bill has moved a small table over in front of them to hold the desserts. They smile at each other as they work on the desserts.

Bill finally says, "I need you to explain the general idea for the math. I am going to talk to the Attorney Generals from here and in Maine and in Vermont. I need them to bring you on the team as a consultant. I am not sure what the whole procedure is, but the AG from here has already indicated that a consulting position is the way we need to go. I already told you we are planning a meeting. We can discuss the math next weekend."

Mattie says, "Let's discuss some of it now. The party is getting a glow on. Are you ready to leave?"

Bill replies, "No. After my little nap I am refreshed. Do you want to leave?"

Mattie answers, "Not now. Do you want to discuss my ideas?'

Bill answers, "Yes. Explain the general concepts. I am going to see the ADA this week. I can better explain what we are proposing to try and identify these guys."

Mattie begins, "I assume there is a physical description of each suspect for each rape. My first effort would be to list the physical characteristic from each case in a spreadsheet format. This would allow us the ability to sort the cases based on the physical characteristic. If we can determine the DNA for each case then we will be able to show we are dealing with serial rapists not individual rapists. This will allow us to look at the descriptions provided by the victims and attempt to develop a composite sketch of each rapist. Rapists like other human beings need to eat, sleep, stay warm, etc. I believe we can take advantage of those needs. We need to look at the hotels and motels and other residences at the time of each rape and determine if there are common names amongst the residents. If they are working at jobs across the area and their permanent residents are not close then we should have a better chance of determining their identities. The mathematics and the sorting is not that complicated, but gathering the information is going to be time consuming. Do you understand and can you explain it to the ADA's?"

Bill replies, "I can explain the technique enough to peak their interest. Then when we have a follow up meeting you can go into more detail and answer their questions."

Mattie says, "OK."

Bill says, "We should enjoy the rest of the party."

Linda comes over in a few minutes. She says, "How are you two doing tonight?"

Mattie replies, "We are enjoying ourselves. Bill is a little tired. He worked till 4:00PM this afternoon. He had volunteered to take the place of one of the younger guys so he could have off with his family."

Linda says, "That is nice of you, Bill."

Bill replies, "The Jewish officers volunteer for Christmas. We pay them back by volunteering for Jewish holidays. We are all in this together."

Linda says, "You are from Nottingham Harbor?"

Bill answers, "My family owns a farm North of Nottingham Harbor. We have been going to the Harbor for years. I know the Chief of Police of the Harbor."

Linda continues, "There was a rape a few months ago at Nottingham Harbor. Mattie said you are looking at the case."

Bill says, "I am New Hampshire State Police. The Harbor is in Maine. But one of my longtime friends is Ed Woodward a Maine State Police. Ed and I believe these rapes are connected with some in Vermont also. Mattie has volunteered to use some math ideas to try and connect the data. I don't want people to know about Mattie in general because criminals are dangerous. She knew the victim in the Harbor."

Linda continues, "I know the victim also from school."

Bill says, "We are in the beginning stages of the search."

Linda says, "I am glad someone is going after these criminals."

How many rapes are there each year in New England?"

Bill answers, "In the three states we are going to look at, there are about 400 a year total."

Linda says, "How many of the criminals have the police caught? Four hundred is rather high."

Bill says, "Only few have actually been caught. Four hundred is low compared to some other areas of the country. Every woman should be armed and prepared to defend herself all over the country. It is discussing."

Linda stands there contemplating Bill's comments. She says, "I guess I should circulate a little. You two enjoy the rest of the evening."

Mattie says, "People are really surprised by the statistics. I was when we first talked about the problem."

Bill replies, "Yes. Do you want something else to drink?"

Mattie says, "Yes. A cup of tea would be excellent."

Bill says, "Ok. I think I am ready for a soda."

Bill gets up and heads for the kitchen. Mattie relaxes.

Bill returns with a can of soda and a cut of hot tea. He says, "I think the tea needs to steep a little more. Here are a couple packs of sugar and a little cream."

Mattie sits everything on the table and says, "Thank You." They smile at each other and sit quietly for fifteen minutes. They talk to each other for the next hour.

Bill finally says, "It has been pleasant this evening, but do you think we should go in a little while."

Mattie replies, "In maybe ten minutes. I am going to check on the ladies room."

Bill says, "Ok."

Mattie returns to the chair in about ten minutes. She says, "Give me a few minutes. Are you going to drive me home?"

Bill replies, "I can. What about your car?"

Mattie answers, "Brenda can drive it home. She probably wants to stay longer with her friends. It is ok with me. Let me find her and give her the keys."

Bill replies, "Ok, when you are ready."

Mattie goes upstairs. Brenda is sitting with several of the teenagers. She says, "Bill and I are getting ready to leave. Here are the keys to the car. I want you to start home at midnight. I can trust you to drive carefully. No cellphone or texting. Remember after midnight there are more and more drunk drivers on the road. Drivers are also tired late at night. I want you to be alive in the morning."

Brenda answers, "Mom you can trust me. I will start home near midnight. Thank you for letting me stay here a little longer. I want you and Bill to behave yourselves."

Mattie giggles and replies, "Very Funny."

Brenda says, "I like Bill. He seems good for you."

Mattie replies, "I like him. I need more time before we get serious."

Brenda says, "I will see you when I get home. Thank you again for trusting me."

Mattie goes back down to the basement and walks to Bill. She says, "I gave her the mom lecture. She obeys me in general and does understand the hazards of driving."

Bill says, "From what you have told me Brenda seems very responsible."

Mattie says, "Yes in general she is but I reminded her the hazard of driving after midnight because of drunk drivers and being tired.

Bill gets up and says, "We are ready. We need to get our coats."

They walk upstairs and get their coats. Bill sees Brenda and says, "You enjoy your friends. But as a policeman I see bad accidents. Please be careful driving home."

Brenda answers, "I will. You guys be careful also."

Mattie comes out of the bedroom with her coat and Bill's coat."

Bill says, "Thank you." He helps Mattie on with her coat."

Brenda says, "Ok, mom I will see you later."

They walk to the car. On the way to Mattie's place they talk some about the math and their kids.

Bill walks Mattie to her door. Mattie unlocks the door and says, "Come on in for a few minutes before driving the rest of the way home."

Bill says, "Ok, I do have to go tonight. The robbery case is going to be hot in the morning."

Mattie says, "I understand. They sit down for a few minutes."

Bill says, "I had good time even though I was tired. Hope you had a good time?"

Mattie replies, "I did. It is enjoyable to do things with friends and a date."

Bill smiles at her. He says, "Should I call you about another date? I do have to call you about the math work."

Mattie replies, "Yes, call me for both reasons."

Bill says, "Should we go to dinner next weekend? On the math I will call you as soon as I know something." He gets up and says, "I better go tonight because tomorrow is going to come early."

They walk to the door. Bill turns and faces Mattie. She steps close and Bill kisses her. She kisses him a second time. He says, "Until next weekend." He turns and opens the door and exits. Mattie watches through the storm door until he drives away. Mattie thinks to herself, 'I haven't felt like this in a long time. I think I am falling in love with Bill.'

Chapter 6

THE NEXT DAY JANUARY 2

Bill arrives at the office at about 8:00 AM. He picked up a sausage sandwich at the local grocery. He sits down with a coffee and starts through the paper work from the robbery. Captain James sticks his head in after roll call. He says, "don't get up, Bill. What are your plans for the robbery?"

Bill replies, "I am going to call Linda about the finger prints on the bag. She may need the morning to process the bag. It is a little tricky to process prints from a wrinkled surface. I will give her a few minutes to settle in this morning."

The captain continues, "How is the investigation of the rape cases progressing?"

Bill replies, "My math teacher friend, Mattie, believes we can use information from motels and hotels to identify the rapists. If the DNA matches from multiple rapes then the identities can be matched from the motels and hotels in each area. I like the idea. I am going to talk to the ADA's from here and Vermont and Maine about a cooperative effort."

Captain James replies, "I am not sure I understand, but if the math teacher thinks the technique will work then go for it. I know you want the rapists from here and the one from Nottingham Harbor."

Bill says, "I am going for it. I want this robber also. I am going to get him. I don't like robbers, but one that shoots the victim after he has the money is really bad."

Captain James says, "I will leave you to your problems. Just keep me up to date, please."

Bill replies, "You bet, Captain."

Bill picks up the phone. He dials Linda's number. Well he really punches in the digits.

The phone rings in the forensic lab. Linda gets up from her stool at the lab bench. She answers the phone, "Linda Wood, forensic specialist. How can I help you?"

Bill replies, "This is Bill Simpson, I am not bugging you, but I wanted to check on the progress on the finger prints."

Linda says, "There appears to be six prints on the bag. Two of them are small and probably a woman's prints. Two are along the top border and are probably the owner's prints from their location. You said he was holding the bag when he was shot. The other two are on the main part of the bag and are probably the robber's. We have dusted the bag. The prints on the main part of the bag are discontinuous, but we are going to photograph them and using some computer techniques we should have a thumb and finger print. We may be able to use them to identify the robber, but the reconstruction gets questioned in court. You can understand the questions that can be raised about this kind of technique. Give us till after lunch to finish the reconstruction. I am with you on this, Bill."

Bill answers, "Ok. I will talk to you later. Good luck with the reconstruction."

Linda replies, "Good bye, till later."

They hang up.

Bill calls Linda Symth at the AG's office in Concord. The phone rings four times and Linda answers, "Linda Symth, assistant district attorney. How can I help you?"

Bill replies, "This is Bill Simpson. I have some details on the technique we plan to use to identify these rapists. Do you want the details?'

Linda replies, "Yes I do."

Bill describes the technique. Then he says, "Basically the technique assume that the rapist have to eat, sleep and live like normal people. It assumes that they are living near the site of the rapes, but essentially not next-door. We need to supply Mattie my math teacher friend with the physical characteristics of the rapist and other information on each rape.

We definitely will need DNA on every rape. Getting test run is going to fall on you for the money."

Linda replies, "I believe I can bring Mattie on board as a consultant for at least 6 months. I will have more details by the meeting with the Vermont and Maine ADA's."

Bill says, "It sounds good. Things are coming together."

Linda answers, "Yes. I will talk to you over the next several weeks. I have to go to court this afternoon. Good bye until next week."

Bill says, "Goodbye, Linda."

They hang up.

Bill calls Ed Woodworth in Maine. The phone rings five times and Ed answers, "Sergeant Ed Woodworth Maine State Police. How can I help you?"

Bill replies, "This is Bill Simpson. How are you Ed?"

Ed answers, "I am fine. How are you?"

Bill continues, "I am fine also. I called to tell you several things about the rape cases. Do you have time to talk?"

Ed responds, "Shoot."

Bill continues, "I am not at the range. So I guess you mean shoot the words."

Ed says, "Funny."

Bill continues, "I have talked to the New Hampshire ADA, Linda Symth. She is going to bring my friend Mattie on board as a consultant. Linda says she can actually pay her a small stipend. We are going to meet on Martin Luther King Holiday because Mattie has off from school. Linda said most of us have to work the holiday. Linda is going to call the other two ADA's. I am calling you and will call the sergeant from Vermont. Can you contact Chief Carl from Nottingham Harbor? Right now I was planning to meet at about 11AM at Linda's office in Concord. 11AM should give time for everyone to get to Concord without starting at a ridiculous hour."

Ed replies, "I will call Carl and the ADA. We can probably car pool to the meeting. Till then have good day."

Bill says, "Good day Ed."

They both hang up.

Bill calls Sergeant Charlie Wilson at the Vermont State Police. The phone rings four times and Charlie answers, "Sergeant Charlie Wilson Vermont State Police. How can I help you?"

Bill replies, "This is Bill Simpson. How are you today?"

Charlie replies, "I am fine, Bill. What can I do for you?"

Bill answers, "I am going to help you. I am arranging a meeting for Martin Luther King's Holiday. Several people from here and from Maine are coming. Can you bring at least the ADA from Vermont and yourself to the meeting? The meeting is about the combined effort to solve some of these rape cases. My friend Mattie the math teacher is going to explain her ideas for using math to identify the rapist. We are going to talk about DNA analysis and the general logistics of the effort. Your ideas are obviously welcome. Linda Symth will be contacting the Vermont ADA for their cases."

Charlie answers, "We will be there. What time and where?"

Bill responds, "At 11AM at Linda Smyth's office in Concord. I made it 11AM to give everyone time to travel. I think we should be finished by 2PM."

Charlie replies, "Sounds good to me. See you then."

They hang up.

Bill picks up the paperwork on the robbery. It is almost lunch. He gets up and walks to the outer office. He says to Sandra, "I am going to the diner and get some lunch.'

Sandra replies, "Can you bring me back a sandwich?"

Bill replies, "What do want?

Sandra says, "Corned Beef on rye with mustard and horseradish. Bring me a Diet Cola."

Bill leaves for the diner.

He returns with Sandra's lunch and his own.

As he comes through the office Sandra says, "How much do I owe you, Bill?"

Bill replies, "You owe five fifty two. Here is the receipt."

Sandra opens her purse and finds five fifty. She says, "thank you. I don't have two pennies."

Bill replies, "You are welcome. Forget the two pennies. When you finish come in. We need to discuss setting up files to track the rapist."

Bill goes to his office. Sandra walks in. She says, "Let's talk while we eat."

Bill says, "Ok."

Sandra says, "It is your idea that these rapists are actually serial rapists."

Bill replies, "Yes. What we need to do is get a file started on each rape and then using the DNA results and other information sort the files on the individual rapes into a combined file for a single rapist. My friends from the Maine and the Vermont State Police believe these guys have raped in all three states in some cases. Linda Symth is going to work with the ADA's from Maine and Vermont to developed combined files. My lady friend Mattie is going to analyze the data from all three states. We are having a meeting in a week about all of this. All three Attorney Generals are going to fund Mattie to help identify the actual rapist. We are all going to share the information. Once we identify a suspect then one of us will lead a search for the suspect and arrest him. You will be sharing all the collected information with someone in the other two states as we proceed with the investigations."

Sandra says, "I can round up the rape cases from the last three years from around the three states. I will assembly a list."

Bill says, "That will be a good start. It will be several hundred cases for the last three years."

Sandra replies, "Yes. As a woman I follow the rape cases a little, but we have caught very few of the rapists over the years."

Bill says, "Well that is what this effort is all about. We will probably concentrate on a hundred or so cases. If we have success with the selected cases then we can try to solve more of them."

They finish lunch. Sandra returns to her desk. She makes some notes and uses the computer to look up some information about the rapes in New

Hampshire. She looks at the criminal statistics for Maine and Vermont. She is surprised by the number of rapes each year in all three states.

Bill's phone rings. He answers, "Sergeant Bill Simpson, New Hampshire State Police. How can I help you?"

Linda replies, "This Linda Gabriel at the forensic lab. I have some good news."

Bill says, "Let me have it."

Linda continues, "We were able to construct a thumb and a fore finger print from the pretzel bag. I have run them in the Aphis Database. We have a match to a known robber, Harvey White."

Bill says, "You are sure?"

Linda replies, "I and my assistant are sure. We do not know where he is living, but we are sure he is your guy. I am going to FAX the data to your office. Sandra your assistant should have it in a few minutes.'

Bill continues, "Thank You. I will take it from here. I want this guy. He shot the storeowner for no reason. I am going to get him off the street for a long time. Thanks again. Linda Symth will want the evidence also. Have a good day.'

Linda replies, "I will send it to Linda also. You have a good day.'

They hang up.

Bill calls to Sandra. "Sandra there is a FAX coming from Linda Gabriel about the robber that shot the store owner. See what you can find out about the guy who Linda identified as the shooter. I want this guy."

Sandra replies, "I will get the FAX. I will check the databases for the information on the robber."

Bill sits quietly for a few minutes. Sandra walks in and says, "I made a copy of the FAX for myself. Here is your copy."

Bill says, "Thank You." He takes the FAX and begins to review the information. Bill remembers the name. He goes to his file cabinet and looks for the name on a case file. He arrested this guy ten years ago for a home invasion in Lovett. He was less violent, but just as stupid."

He calls to Sandra, "I arrested this guy ten years ago. I guess he served his time."

Sandra replies, "His record show he was released from prison about six months ago. I am going to check with his parole officer for an address. Let me get the information on his parole officer."

Bill says, "Get the information, but I will call his patrol officer."

Sandra comes in to Bill's office in a few minutes and says, "His parole officer is William Strong. Here is his number." Sandra hands Bill a piece of paper with the number on it.

Bill says, "Thanks. I'll take it from here. As I said I want this guy."

Bill calls William. The phone rings five times and William answers, "William Strong Parole Officer. How can I help you?"

Bill replies, "This is Sergeant Bill Simpson with the State Police. I am trying to locate Harvey White. He is one of your Parolees."

William responds, "So am I. He has not checked in for two weeks. I have started the paperwork to issue a warrant for his arrest."

Bill says, "We have identified him as a suspect in an armed robbery. He shot the owner of the store. I want the low life."

William says, "Is the owner going to be OK."

Bill replies, "He is going to recover. The guy shot the owner after he got the money. It was Christmas Eve. John was in the hospital for Christmas. Call Linda Symth at the AG's office. She will expedite your warrant and add mine to the warrant."

William replies, "Right away."

Bill says, "Can you FAX me all the information you have on the guy?"

William replies, "I will get the info together. You should get the info in about fifteen minutes."

Bill says, "Here is my assistant's FAX number and our phone numbers. Fifteen minutes is fine."

William says, "I just need time organize the papers and FAX them. You have a good day. As soon as I send the paper I will call Linda at the AG's office. Do you have her number?'

Bill responds, "Let me put Sandra, my assistant, on the line. She has all the numbers. She keeps our files up to date. Have a good day. I will be in touch. We will get this guy."

Bill calls to Sandra. "Sandra can you pick up the line and help William with the contact information."

Sandra answers. "OK, Bill.'

Sandra picks up the line. She says, "Hello. This is Sandra Davenport."

Bill says, "Have a good day William. Sandra this is William Strong the parole officer."

William replies, "I am going to FAX you information on Harvey White. I need Linda Smyth's phone number and contact information.

Sandra replies, "Just give me your E-mail address and I will send you an E-mail while you are FAXING the information to us."

William says, "Good idea." He reads his E-mail address to Sandra and verifies it. He says, "Have a nice day Sandra."

Sandra says, "You too."

They hang up.

Sandra composes an E-mail on the computer. William on the other end organizes the paperwork and FAXES the information to Sandra and Bill.

Fifteen or so minutes pass.

Bill looks over the FAX.

Bill sees that this guy lives near Farmville. Lovett is twenty miles away. He thinks to himself I got this guy. He calls to Sandra, "Do you want to go on a little trip to Farmville tomorrow?"

Sandra responds, "Get out of the office for the day is fine with me. Why are we going to Farmville?"

Bill answers, "Harvey White lives there. I am going to ask Frank Black to go with us for extra back up. I could send someone else, but I want this guy."

Sandra says, "I am game."

Bill picks up the phone and calls Captain Williams at Frank's Barracks.

The phone rings four times. Ed Williams answers, "Captain Ed Williams, how can I help you?"

Bill replies, "This is Bill Simpson. I want to borrow Frank Black tomorrow for trip to Farmville to help arrest a robber?"

Ed answers, "I have no objection, but Frank is on night shift this week."

Bill continues, "I am going to Farmville to arrest the guy that committed the robbery in Lovett and shot the store owner. The guy is a parolee and is armed, so besides my assistant Sandra, I want a second back up. This guy is bad, but I am worse."

Ed says, "Let me call Frank and tell him to skip tonight. I can cover his shift. I understand why you want this guy. Sometimes it just feels right to do it yourself."

Bill says, "Thank You. Tell Frank I will pick him up about ten tomorrow morning at your Barracks. Remind him to wear a vest."

Ed responds, "See you at ten. Have a good day."

Bill replies, "OK. See you at ten. You have a good day."

They hang up.

Bill calls to Sandra, "We will leave here about 7:30AM. Don't forget your vest. You can wait to put it on until we meet Frank. This guy is violent. So be prepared."

Bill calls Linda Symth. The phone rings four times and Linda answers, "Linda Smyth, Attorney General Office. How can I help you, Bill?"

Bill replies, "Do you have the arrest warrants for Harvey White?"

Linda replies, "Yes. I am getting ready to send them by courier. You know he is wanted for a parole violation, also."

Bill answers, "Yes, I know."

Linda asks, "Are you going to execute the arrest"

Bill replies, "Yes, I am taking Sandra and Frank Black to assist."

Linda says, "Be careful. This guy is bad."

Bill says, "That is why I am doing this myself. I am bad, also. Plan for an arraignment but not for tomorrow but the next day. Or plan a funeral."

Linda says, "OK. See you in two days."

They hang up.

The courier arrives at about quarter to five.

The desk Sergeant calls Bill. "Bill there is courier with a package for you. Can you come down?"

Bill replies, "Yes, I will be down momentarily."

Bill walks down to the front desk.

The courier asks, "Are you Bill Simpson?"

Bill answers, "Yes, as he points to the nametag under his badge."

The courier says, "I have a package from Linda Symth. Can you please sign here that you received it?"

Bill replies as he signs the tablet, "Yes."

The courier hands the package to Bill and says, "Thank You."

Bill goes to his desk and opens the package. There are three warrants and subpoena in the envelope. One warrant is for the robbery of the store in Lovett. The second is for violating his parole by not reporting as scheduled. The third is a search warrant for Harvey's residence. The fourth is a subpoena for a DNA test. Bill walks out to Sandra's desk. He says, "Sandra, here are the two arrest warrants and a search warrant. There is also a subpoena for a DNA test. They appear to be in order. Can you read them to be sure? I am about ready to leave. I will see you about 7:30 AM. OK."

Sandra replies, "I will read them before I leave. I will see you in the morning. I will call you after I read them. I will just leave the message if they are OK."

Bill says, "Have a good evening."

Sandra's message is that the warrants are in order.

THE NEXT DAY

Bill arrives at about 7:25 AM. Sandra comes in a few minutes later. Bill calls Frank. The phone rings five times. Frank answers, "Frank Black. How can I help you?"

Bill says, "It is Bill Simpson here. Are you going to be ready at about 9:00?"

Frank answers, "Yes, I am up. I am going to have a little breakfast with the family. Otherwise I am ready."

Bill says, "See you about 9.

Frank also says, "See you at 9."

They hang up.

Bill and Sandra head for the SUV.

After they have started toward Farmville, Sandra says, "Before we execute the search warrant, we better check the address. In the small towns and farm land some properties include more than one address."

Bill replies, "I agree. Thanks for reminding me. The arrest warrants are not tied to an address."

They drive for a while. The SUV is an unmarked state police vehicle. It does have a commercial radio. Sandra turns it on to local station.

After an hour and half of drive they arrive at the barracks where Frank is stationed. Sandra says, "I'll go in and get Frank."

Bill says, "OK."

Frank and Sandra return in a couple of minutes. Frank walks up to Bill's side of the SUV. He says, "Marked or unmarked car?"

Bill replies, "Take a marked car. Sandra and I can approach the house and you can hang back till we get the lay of the land. Got your vest?"

Frank answers, "Yes on the vest. I will follow you till we get there."

Bill says, "That's good. Let's go."

Bill pulls toward the parking lot exit and waits for Frank to follow."

They head for Farmville.

It is about eleven when they arrive at the address of the farm where Harvey is living. Bill pulls up the driveway near the front of the house. Frank stops down the road. Bill says, "I am going to walk up to the door. This guy may be living in one of the smaller houses."

Sandra gets out and walks toward the side of the porch. Bill rings the doorbell. An older lady opens the inside door. She says, "How can I help you?"

Bill continues, "I am looking for Harvey White. Is this where he lives?"

The lady says, "He lives over there in the third cottage. He rents the space."

Bill continues, "I am with the state police." He shows her his badge.

He continues, "Please stay inside. We are here to arrest Mr. White."

Sandra can hear the conversation. She has called Frank on the radio. Frank is turning into the drive as Bill comes off the porch. Bill says, "Frank and I will take the front. Sandra, can you cover the rear?"

Sandra replies, "I can, Serge." She is trotting toward the cottage.

Frank joins Bill and they head for the front door. Bill says, "That's his car so Harvey should be home."

Harvey is home. He is watching television. Sandra calls Bill on the radio, "Serge I am in place near the back door. Go for it."

Bill raps on the door standing to one side. Frank is on the other side. Bill yells, "HARVEY WHITE, STATE POLICE. OPEN THE DOOR, NOW. WE HAVE A WARRANT FOR YOUR ARREST."

Bill waits about 20 seconds. There is no response from inside. He yells again, "MR.WHITE OPEN THE DOOR. THIS IS THE STATE POLICE."

Harvey has crawled to the hallway that leads to the back door. Reaching the back door he looks out. He sees no one. He is holding the same gun he used in the robbery. Sandra is standing to the side against the wall. She is holding a broom and has unfastened her holster. Sandra can hear him unlock the door. He opens the door and steps out. Sandra sticks the broom between his legs. Harvey trips and falls and drops the gun. Sandra has drawn her gun and says, "Police, stay where you are." She presses the mike button and says, "I got him guys. Come on around back."

Bill says, "Frank stay here. I will go around back." Bill runs around back. He stops next to Sandra. He kneels and pulls Harvey's arms behind his back and handcuffs them together.

Bill says, "Sandra, you got the prisoner. Let me go through the house and let Frank into the house."

Bill draws his gun and enters the house cautiously. He gets to the front door and opens it to let Frank in. He says, "Need to check the bathroom."

Frank says, "I'll get it." He looks into the bathroom and says, "Clear."

Bill calls to Sandra, "Bring Harvey inside."

Sandra brings Harvey inside. Bill says, "You are being arrested for violating your parole. You are also being arrested for robbing a store in

Lovett and shooting the owner. I am going to read you your rights. Then I will be taking you to Concord for arraignment tomorrow or the next day."

Bill reads Harvey his rights. Sandra and Frank serve as witnesses. Harvey immediately requests a lawyer. Bill says to Sandra, "Please get the leg irons from the SUV for Harvey."

Sandra gets the leg irons and comes back in. She puts them on Harvey.

Bill says, "OK. Mr. White, do you need to use the bathroom before we leave?"

Harvey says, "Yes I need the bathroom."

Bill says, "Frank can you and Sandra check the bathroom?"

They both answer, "Yes." They find a knife and a straight razor.

Bill helps Harvey stand. Bill says, "I am going to remove the handcuffs. Leave the door open. Frank and I are going to be right by the door."

Harvey hobbles in with the leg irons on. He uses the toilet and washes his hands. He hobbles out. Bill puts the handcuffs back on.

Sandra takes Harvey to the SUV.

Bill says, "Frank, we have a search warrant for the property. Before you execute the warrant check with the lady at the main house to be sure the address is correct. We do not want a mistake for the search. You understand. Call Linda Symth, if there are questions about the warrant. Can you handle the search?

Get a couple of officers from the local barracks. I think you only need to search this cottage. Check with Linda about the address of the cottage compared with the main house."

Frank answers Bill, "Have a good trip to Concord. I know you want this guy. I will talk to you tomorrow about the search."

Bill says, "Yes. This guy shot the owner of the store for no reason. He is just a mean SOB. Thanks for the help. I will talk to you tomorrow. We should not need any evidence you find for the arraignment. The parole violation will keep him in jail. No judge is going to release a suspect that has violated parole."

Bill and Sandra arrive in Concord at 3:30PM. They go to the county jail. They take Harvey inside. The jailer on the desk inquires as why they are bringing the prisoner there. Bill explains the prisoner is wanted for a parole violation and a robbery and shooting. He explains the prisoner has been read his rights in front of witnesses and has requested an attorney. He tells the jailer to please call Linda Symth for further instructions. Jim, the jailer, says Linda has already notified them about Harvey. He calls one of the jail officers to come and get Harvey. He checks the paper work and identity of Mr. White. The other officer takes Harvey to be finger printed and locked up. He explains to Harvey that an attorney will be here in the morning.

Bill and Sandra return to the Barracks. They leave for home. Bill says, "See you in the morning."

Sandra responds, "See you tomorrow. This was a good day's work."

Bill says "Yes, a very good day's work."

THE NEXT DAY

The phone rings at Bill's desk at about 8:15 AM. It is Linda. She says, "Hi, Bill."

Bill says, "Hi yourself. How can I help you?"

Linda continues, "First the arraignment is at 2:00PM. Can you and Sandra be here?

Bill answers, "Sure."

Linda continues, "I don't need the evidence, which Frank uncovered at the cottage."

Bill says, "The gun we found when the guy tried to run has not been tested yet."

Linda says, "I just need you testify Harvey tried to run when you went to arrest him."

Bill says, "OK."

Linda continues, "For the rapes cases I have arranged a meeting for Martin Luther King Day to accommodate Mattie. There will be someone at the meeting from the AG's offices in Vermont and Maine. There will be a state police representative from all three states. I have received approval to hire Mattie as a consultant. I already told Mattie, yesterday.

Bill says, "It sounds like the team is coming together."

Linda replies, "Yes. Good bye till later today."

Bill says, "Good bye."

They both hang up.

The arraignment goes as expected the judge remands Harvey to jail until the trial. Linda tells Bill that the meeting on MLK Day will be at 11 AM.

CHAPTER 7

MONDAY MARTIN LUTHER KING DAY MEETING

Bill picks Mattie up at her house at 8AM. After they get in the car Bill starts a conversation. "Mattie I am worried about your involvement in one way. Some of these guys can be violent and could decide to attack any of us. I know the ADA's and other state police are aware of the possibility of revenge."

Mattie responds, "I am going to be isolated from actually chasing any of the guys."

Bill replies, "Yes, and we want to keep it that way. I want you to route all the data through Sandra. You should have very little direct contact. Your name should be like a ghost."

Mattie says, "That is OK with me."

They stop at the Barracks and meet Sandra for the ride along to Concord.

They are listening to the local radio station. The News comes on. The announcer reports that there was a rape on Saturday evening in Greensburg Vermont.

Bill says, "In one way I hate to say it, but this rape will give the Vermont ADA a real incentive to participate in this combined effort to catch some of these rapist."

After several minutes Bill says, "The weather is fairly nice today for January."

Mattie replies, "Yes. How about changing from the radio to the CD?"

Bill replies, "OK with me."

Mattie fusses with the CD and finally puts a Patsy Kline CD in the player. She says, "This is about my era of music. I do like country music."

Bill answers, "I do too."

They ride along listening to the CD and Mattie hums along with a couple of the songs."

About ten o'clock they stop at small diner and get some breakfast. They arrive at Linda's office at about ten minutes before eleven. Linda motions for them to go to the conference room. A couple of the other people are already in the room. Bill casually knows a couple of the people. He introduces Mattie. They make themselves a coffee. Mattie makes a tea. The ADA from Vermont arrives. The conversation turns to the rape on Saturday in Greensburg. Linda comes in followed by the ADA from Maine. The last of the state troopers and the chief of police of Nottingham Harbor arrive.

Linda stands and introduces herself. "I think all of you know me. As just a formality I am Linda Symth the ADA from New Hampshire. Some of you already know each other. But I am going to ask you to go around the table and introduce yourselves. I am going to sit down. This is an informal meeting with a very serious topic.

Bill is sitting to Linda's right. Bill starts, "I am Bill Simpson a sergeant with the New Hampshire State Police. I investigate serious and violent crimes all over New Hampshire."

Mattie is next. "I am Mattie Greene. I am a High School Math teacher. Bill got me involved in the chasing the criminals when I pointed out how some math and profiling could be used to identify criminals like the rapists. I will explain more in a few minutes.

I am Sandra Davenport State Police Officer from New Hampshire and Bill's assistant. You will get to know me because I will be clearing the information to Mattie and between the various offices. Just call me Sandra.

Carol James is the crime statistics lady. My job is to collect a list of the crimes in New Hampshire. I keep a comprehensive file of the crimes and the victims and criminals. Statistics do not solve the crimes, but Mattie's ideas can make use of the statistics to combine the crimes committed by the same criminal.

Vivian Bush, I am the ADA from Vermont. Obviously after the crime in Greensburg over the weekend I am more interested in Mattie's and Bill's ideas on how to identify the rapist. I was already interested because I believe some of the rapists have committed crimes in all of the New England States.

Carl Kramer I am the chief of police from Nottingham Harbor. There was a rape in the harbor last fall. I have been the chief for ten years and an officer for twenty years before becoming chief. The biggest crimes were parking and speeding and once in a while a drunken brawl on Saturday night. I have no experience with violent crimes like rape.

Frank Butler, I am a state police sergeant in Vermont. Like Bill I have dealt with serious crimes, but have not been very successful at catching rapists. I am very interested in a technique that works to identify rapists and leads to their capture.

Charlie Wilson, I am a state police sergeant in Vermont. Like Bill I have dealt with serious crimes, but have not been very successful at catching rapists. So like Frank, I am very interested in a technique that works.

Jane Cordova, I am the ADA from Maine. The crime in the fall of last year in Nottingham Harbor is my problem. I like the rest of you have had little success in identifying rapists. I am getting some pressure about the Nottingham Harbor rape. The young lady is from a prominent family in New Hampshire and they do have political connections. I try to treat all crimes equally, but I do understand political pressure.

Ed Woodworth, I am a state police sergeant in Maine. I have known Bill for more then twenty years. I do about the same thing as Bill, Frank, and Charlie. Mattie explained to me her ideas when Bill and she had dinner with my wife and myself. Sounds like a good idea.

Linda says, "I am going to let Mattie explain her idea. Then we can have a general discussion. Mattie the floor is yours."

Mattie explains, "Several large city police departments have used various mathematical techniques to identify criminals or to track them. Sometimes it has worked and sometimes it has not worked. In the

Washington DC suburbs several years ago the police tried some math techniques to catch the two guys targeting random citizens. I have read that the math premises used for the shooting case did not fit the case. The shootings were not totally random. All this means that sometimes math logic works and sometimes it doesn't. So what is our logic and premises?

First the mathematics: Actually the math I propose is simply utilizing spreadsheet logic to sort the information and organize it. The second part of the logic is to realize that even rapist need to eat, sleep, and live somewhere on a day-to-day basis. They do not travel hundred of miles to commit a crime and then travel back to their own neighborhood. Many criminals do not commit crimes directly in the neighborhood where they live. Combining these ideas mathematically gives us the ability to search for the criminals. The other part of the equation is the DNA analysis and comparison from a number of cases. Many of the crimes we are dealing with occur in more rural areas where the possibility for residing locally is limited. There are a total of several hundred rapes over the last three years. Bill says he doubts that we are dealing with that many individual rapists, the more likely scenario is that we are dealing with a few serial rapists.

If we look at rapes from the last few years to start and sort the data based on the physical characteristics of the rapist, we can group the crimes. Bill pointed out to me there is nothing illegal about comparing the evidence and physical description and the DNA from multiple crimes to identify a serial criminal. Since it likely that the criminal will move from place to place living in essentially temporary residences like a motel or rooming house while working in an area or visiting the area. We should be able to check records at the time of the crimes and compare guest's names. I think we may need to search outward twenty to forty miles from the location of each crime. In the rural areas there should not be too many residences to search. However this is where your police effort will be needed. If we connect a series of the crimes with DNA and physical characteristics then we can sort the names from those areas to look for a common name. Just as little bit of encouragement, Sandra and I had DNA on four crimes two in New Hampshire and two in Maine. I compared the DNA and found one crime in New Hampshire and one in Maine had the same DNA. The physical characteristics matched. The two crimes are far enough apart that the criminal was probably residing at a two different temporary residences for each of the crimes. It is a start. Sandra is going to collect the information from all three states for the other individual crimes. I will start collecting and processing the data as soon as the three AG's approve the participation in the program. Are there any questions?

Jane Cordova, the ADA from Maine, says, "My AG has already agreed to our participation and we will be paying you a consulting fee. He asked you to sign a confidentiality agreement. You have agreed to do this. The agreement allows you to share the information with the other states in the program. For your protection I will route all our information to Sandra."

Mattie says, "I will sign the papers when we are finished this meeting."

Vivian Bush, the ADA from Maine, says, "My AG has agreed to the same thing."

Mattie says, "I have agreed to your papers also. I have already signed the New Hampshire paperwork."

Sandra says, "Do I need to sign agreements also?"

Linda answers, "No. You are a State Policewomen and you are under oath to protect all criminal data. You can supply Mattie with all the data necessary for her processing. You can ask me about the data, but I do believe any of the data from the three states on these crimes can be shared as necessary."

The other two ADA's answer, "Yes. Any of the data with regard to this program can be shared freely."

This is going to involve other police and law enforcement. They should maintain confidentiality and only process data to the ADA's or Sandra. No one in law enforcement is going to release information. Chief you need to inform the Mayor of Nottingham Harbor he must maintain strictest confidence.

The meeting comes to a close. Mattie gathers with ADA's and signs the consulting agreements. Sandra makes sure all the participants have her information card. Bill talks with the other state police about collecting the information and eventually making the arrests.

Linda finally says, "I think we are finished for today. Several of us are going down to Mom's Café for lunch. It is a block and a half from here. Mom's Café should have a table that can accommodate us. So you are welcome to join us before starting back. Everybody agrees. They walk to Mom's for lunch. After lunch they exchange pleasantries and start for there respective offices.

Bill, Sandra, and Mattie start back to Bill's Barracks. They discuss the few cases for which there is DNA. Carol already told them that she would put together a list of rapes from the last few years. Carol told them she would talk to her cohorts in crime statistics from Vermont and Maine. Sandra asks, "Mattie, you did look at four cases where you had DNA analysis?"

Mattie replies, "Yes I did. Two of the cases matched. One is from New Hampshire and one is from Vermont."

Sandra comments, "The match sort of confirms Bill idea that these rapes involve serial rapists, not lone wolves."

Mattie replies, "More or less it does confirm his idea. However two is not good statistical sample."

They ride several more miles without comment.

Bill finally says, "I am going to stop at the Barracks for a few minutes. Mattie you can come in. I will introduce you to Captain James. Then I will take you home."

Mattie says, "OK. I should meet him."

When they come to the Barrack, the three of them go inside.

Captain James walks up to them and asks, "How was the meeting?"

Sandra replies, "Good."

Bill says, "It was good. We are set to start the pursuit. Mattie is on board. The people from Vermont and Maine are on board. The information should start flowing tomorrow."

Bill replies, "It is good, but now the real work needs to be done."

TUESDAY AFTERNOON

The State Police Lady, Carol James, catalogues the crime statistics and keeps the reports for the serious and violent crimes in New Hampshire. Carol calls Mattie directly after school has ended for the day. Carol provides Mattie with access to the database as the ADA's consultant. She also tells Sandra how to access the database. Carol explains to Mattie how to access the criminal database and provides her with a password and ID. Mattie verifies that she can access the database. While talking to Carol, Mattie agrees she has access. Carol ends the conversation with, "have fun."

Mattie replies, "I am sure I will."

They hang up.

In the evening Mattie does run several searches on the database, but the database is made to store the information not to select information. Mattie has decided for the initial search to limit the crimes to the last three years. The one good thing about the data is that the suspect's description is at the beginning of the entire description of each crime. Mattie restricts her selections to suspects with brown hair, between 5 foot 8 inches and 6 foot in height and identified as white. When she finds a suspect meeting these general characteristics she records the crime and the file number assigned by the state police. She records the town and county where the rape occurred and was reported. Mattie knows that she and Bill will need more information, but the objective is to select at least 50 crimes meeting the general description of the suspect in Nottingham Harbor. Mattie recognizes that mathematically she must identify suspects with the same general physical characteristics. The main problem is that most of the other jurisdictions have not run the DNA analysis on their respective rape kits. Mattie's quick look at the data confirms this is true about the DNA. The next two evenings after finishing her school preparation, she spends some time on the database.

Diane Phillips calls Mattie on Thursday. When Mattie answers her phone Diane says, "This is Diane Phillips. I am the statistician for the criminal database for Maine. Carol James gave me your number. I was told by my boss to provide you with access to our database. Carol explained to me, approximately what you need. I keep a similar database to what Carol keeps for New Hampshire."

Mattie says, "Yes. Basically I need an ID and password to bring the database to my computer.

Diane continues, "Let me give you your ID and password." You should change the password after you access the database the first time. I provided you with a private folder to store or transfer the data to your computer."

Mattie says, "Thank You. It will be next week before I can search your data. I have to grade papers this weekend for my Math Classes."

Diane continues, "I understand. You teach high school?'

Mattie answers, "Yes. I told the ADA that the class work preparation must come first."

Diane continues, "We understand, but I was told setting up the access would be quick,"

Mattie replies, "I want the access as soon as possible. Have a good day."

Diane says, "Same to you."

They hang up.

A few minutes later the phone rings again. Mattie answers, "Mattie Greene, how can I help you?"

Bill Foster says, "This is William (Bill) Foster. I am the statistician in Vermont. I do a similar job to Carol James in New Hampshire. She gave me your number. You need an ID and password for our criminal database.

Mattie replies, "Yes, I will need it. I want the access as soon as possible, but I must take care of my students and the class work. I will start using the database next week."

Bill replies, "You need to work it on your schedule."

Mattie answers, "Thank you."

Bill replies, "You are welcome. Have a good day."

Mattie replies, "Same to you Bill."

They hang up.

CHAPTER 8

THE LETTER

The rape in Greenberg Vermont and Mattie's success with matching the DNA from two of the four rapes has given a boost to the process. Mattie has searched the databases from all three states. She has approximately one hundred cases with similar physical characteristics. No DNA from any of the cases is listed in the three databases. With Sandra help, she listed the physical characteristics for the rapist in each case in a spreadsheet. There are similar characteristics, but no definite matches. The towns are from all the three states with NO real pattern. Bill reviews the list and suggests he will meet on Saturday with Ed Woodworth and Charlie Wilson of the Vermont State Police and possibly Carl Kramer.

Bill generates a letter to be sent to the towns, which Mattie selected, where the rapes with similar physical characteristics occurred. Bill finishes the letter early afternoon on Thursday. He asks Sandra to proof read it. She read the letter and suggests a few corrections or changes.

THE LETTER

New Hampshire State Police Barracks
Concord, New Hampshire

Ladies and Gentlemen:

I am going to address each of you with this letter simultaneously. I know this is different, but there are more than 100 towns and small cities involved in this problem and the eventual solution. A consultant for New

Hampshire State Police Department and the Attorney General's Office is compiling the information on the rape at each of your towns. The towns are in Maine, Vermont, and New Hampshire. The state police in Maine and Vermont are working with me in New Hampshire on solving the rapes in the three states. The consultant has the mathematical expertise to develop and process the information that this letter requests from your chief of police or the head of your respective police departments.

As some of you have probably seen in the newspaper or heard on the news, about a rape in Nottingham Harbor about four months ago. There was a rape in Greenberg, Vermont three weeks ago. The rape in Nottingham Harbor was of a young woman who is an elementary school teacher. Physically she has recovered from most of her injures. But her emotional injures will require much more time. The rape in Vermont was very similar. We have searched the records in Maine, New Hampshire, and Vermont about other rapes with similar modis operandi. We have searched for suspects with similar human characteristics. This letter is asking you as the chief of police to provide more information about the rape in your town.

The attached form provides a list of the information we need to make progress in finding the unknown suspects for these rapes. The math program has been generated to sort and classify the data you are being asked to provide. Using what is called geographic profiling our consultant will match the names you provide to the names that the other towns provide. By doing this we believe and our consultant specifically believes the unknown suspect list will be self-narrowing over a number of rapes. We are working with the District Attorneys from the three states to gather this information from all over the three states. This hopefully will simultaneously solve a number of rapes in the various towns. The offices of the three District Attorneys involved in the task force do have some money available for having DNA analysis run on the rape kits.

The consultant and I believe that each of the rapes is one of a number of rapes performed by a serial rapist. The computer program is used to match DNA from all the rapes that are on our list. This will not identify a suspect, but will connect the different rapes to a suspect. We believe the rapist must temporarily reside in the vicinity of the town where a specific rape occurred. Even rapist must stay in motels, hotels, or rooming houses. Rapist must eat and do other things normal individuals do every day. The geographic profiling depends on these needs of every human. Rapist work and earn a living like other individuals. We are asking you to provide lists of names from the records of the motels, hotels and rooming houses for a twenty to thirty mile radius around your town for the five days before and after the rape occurred in your town. We are asking you to provide the names of out-of-town contractors that were working in your town during the same time frame. Any other transient workers in town during the time frame surrounding the date of the rape will be useful. We recognize some of this information is relatively easy to gather while some is going to be more difficult. The more diligent your search, the better the chance of solving the rape in your town and helping us solve some of the other rapes. Information about the victims will be kept confidential in the computer information files. We are assigning numbers to each rape not the name of the victim.

Please provide us a point of contact in your police department with a phone number and E-mail address. Our numbers and E-mail addresses are listed on the attached form. My deputy Sandra is the collection point. I need to keep my consultant confidential for now.

Thank You

Bill Simpson, Sergeant Violent Crimes Davison
New Hampshire State Police
Concord, New Hampshire

Bill calls Mattie and verifies she can make a 10AM meeting on Saturday. Bill calls Ed, Charlie, and Carl to invite them to the 10 AM meeting on Saturday. All respond that they can make the meeting. With the letter complete and Mattie's search method available, the meeting should lead to some very good progress.

Bill calls to Sandra and says, "Can you please review this letter and make any corrections?"

Sandra walks into Bill's office. She brings her flash drive. Bill loads the letter onto the drive. Sandra loads the letter on her computer. She reads the letter and makes a couple of minor corrections. She prints a couple of copies. She returns to Bill's office. She says, "Looks good Serge. I printed a couple of copies. You need to sign one of the copies."

Bill takes the copies and says, "OK." He takes a pen from his desk and signs the one copy.

Sandra says, "I should make a hundred copies."

Bill responds, "Yes. One hundred copies should be enough. I will get the list of towns from Mattie on Saturday."

Friday went as usual. Bill continues to review the rape cases. He consults with several of the people involved with the task force.

THE MEETING ON SATURDAY AT BILL'S OFFICE

Bill arrives with Mattie at 9:50 AM. After he gets a cup of coffee and Mattie gets her usual tea he shows Mattie a copy of the letter. She sits quietly and reads the letter. Sandra arrives a few minutes before ten. Ed and Charlie arrive at 5 minutes pass ten. They both greet the desk sergeant. They walk back to Bill's office. Bill sees them and calls, "Get a cup of coffee and join us."

They both say hello to Sandra. She says, "Hello."

Carl arrives at 10:10. He walks to the outer office. He goes to the coffee mess and says, "Good Morning Sandra."

She responds, "Good Morning Carl."

Carl walks into Bill's office. He says, "Good Morning."

Sandra walks into Bill's office.

Bill says, "Well we are all here. Let's get started. I have a letter to send to the various towns. Here is a copy for each of you." Bill passes out the signed copies. He continues, "After you finish reading we can discuss the letter." Bill waits a couple of minutes before continuing. He says, "Carl, if you received the letter, how would you respond?"

Carl responds, "I would respond in a positive way. I would want to help. I understand what you are asking us to provide. I might call you with some questions, but it is a good start."

Bill says, "Thank you. I want everyone to route the information through Sandra. Sandra will send it to Mattie. Mattie is obviously not directly law enforcement. So we need to protect her identity."

Charlie says, "Mattie, can you explain a little more about how you are going to use the information?"

Mattie responds, "I plan to enter the data from each rape in to a spreadsheet. By being consistent with the data entry I can sort the data by each physical characteristic. So as not to bias the data I will give the cases numbers. Once I have DNA data for the cases I can sort the cases to compare the DNA data. The DNA data takes precedence over the other physical data when determining which cases match. We have few cases with DNA. I have matched the DNA on two of the cases. This result reinforces the idea that we are dealing with serial rapists. If we find that the same person was living near several of the towns where the DNA matches then the probability is that the person is the rapist. Thus we are asking for the names of guys staying near the town where each of rapes took place. I have a list of approximately 120 cases in the three states. The physical characteristics are similar to the Nottingham Harbor case, but not exactly the same. By coincidence the Greenberg case in Vermont the rapist has similar physical characteristics."

Ed says, "The letter looks good. You are going to send a copy to the ADA's in each state. As soon as I have the list I can work on getting DNA run on the rape kits."

Charlie says, "I agree, the letter looks good. I can do the DNA also as soon as I have the list of cases we are going to concentrate on solving."

Bill says, "We have looked at a few cases. There is the possibility that one or two of these cases will match the Nottingham Harbor case. We will be concentrating on all the cases as time goes by. Sandra will be keeping files on all the cases. I need you to send us copies of your records from Vermont and Maine so we can have a unified file on each case. The ADA's made a task force agreement to share all the information on the cases we decide to pursue. All the information will be kept confidential between the team members. Sandra will pass information to Mattie. As a consultant I really want to isolate Mattie from the task. She is not a policewoman and I worry one of the criminals would come after her."

Ed says, "We will protect her."

Charlie says, "I talked to Vivian our ADA and she told me Linda and Jane have agree to vigorously pursue subpoenas and warrant concerning these cases."

Bill says, "They told me the same thing. Mattie and I talked last Saturday about a number of cases for which we some information. This all started from the Nottingham Harbor rape. None of the other cases are more or less important than the Nottingham Harbor case or the Greensberg case. We should not be influenced by outside pressure for any case. We go where the information and evidence takes us."

Ed says, "I agree. Bill, you casually know Jake Burns. I want to bring him on board. He has a good background in violent criminal cases."

Bill says, "Just tell Jane and have her add his name to the task force. Charlie you should do the same thing for someone from Vermont. Carl, Check with Jane to see your name is on the task force also. Sandra is already on the list of the task force members. Mattie is a consultant in all three states. The fact the task force exists is confidential for now. When we get around to catching these guys, we should record all incidences of reading their rights and any information during interrogations. For now we can relax for a week or so until we have the list ready and some other information organized. In the next week or so we will ask you to take an oath to up hold the laws of all three states when working on the task force."

Ed says, "I have no problem with supporting the task force."

As they are talking Captain James walks in. Bill says, "This is my Captain. Captain James obviously knows about the task force. If for some reason you cannot reach Sandra or me, you can ask for Captain James."

Captain James says, "Please have your commanding officer contact me so if I need any of you I have his or her contact information. Good luck."

Ed and Charlie both nod yes. Carl says, "My next in command is the mayor. I will have him contact Sandra with the information."

Captain James responds, "That is fine, Carl. I authorized Bill to take you all to lunch at the café down the street. The food is good and plenty of it. We are picking up the tab. So enjoy."

They all nod thanks. Captain James leaves.

Bill says, "Does anyone need the facilities before we walk down the street?"

Mattie says, "The Empress does."

Ed says, "Mattie is the Empress on this project."

Mattie gets up and heads for the ladies room. Sandra follows."

Ed says, "What is the empress joke."

Bill says, "There is a slang German expression for going to the men's or ladies' room. It is the room where the Emperor or Empress go by themselves. We were at dinner and I used it when leaving for the men's room."

Charlie interjects, "I have to remember that."

Ed and Charlie also go to the men's room.

Bill and the rest of the guys sit quietly and wait for the others to return. After a few minutes they all walk to the Diner. After lunch they walk back to the barracks. After the usual pleasantries they leave for their homes.

Bill and Mattie stop at the grocery store on the way to Mattie house. Bill drops her off at home. They agree to go to Dinner at 7 PM. Bill heads home.

CHAPTER 9

THE LETTERS RETURN

The next week Mattie gives Sandra the list of towns and Sandra mails the letters. Bill examines a couple of robbery cases and a homicide. Another week passes before there are any responses to the letters.

Monday and Tuesday go like most days at Bill's Barracks.

The mailman arrives at the barracks at 10:15 AM on Wednesday. He comes inside and walks to the desk sergeant's desk and says, "Amongst the general mail I have three letters that appear to be official. They are from three different towns."

The desk sergeant replies, "We have been expecting them. I cannot tell you what they are about. You should not talk about them. They are official and important."

Bill hears the conversation and comes out of his office. He says, "They are official and important, but they are nobody's business."

Silas, the mailman, says, "I do not tell people what mail I deliver to what address."

The sergeant hands Sandra the letters. Bill responds, "Don't think you do, Silas. There are going to be some more and I know anyone would be curious seeing the return addresses. It is important official state business."

The first letter is from Bluebank New Hampshire. The rape was the first major crime in Sixty years. The state police actually handled the crime investigation. The one policeman is a part time employee of the county. His primary duties are traffic control and emergency response to fires and medical emergencies. The policeman is Phil

Orlando. Bill reads the letter to himself. "Dear Bill: The state police did the DNA and have that evidence. I will contact them and ask them to forward the results to your assistant Sandra. I talked with them about the crime a couple of weeks ago. There has been little progress in two years. The enclosed sketch by a local artist of the only suspect was done a couple of days after the rape took place. It is as accurate as one may expect. There are not any real places to live in this town if you are a transient. I will go to the nearby towns and get a list of persons, obviously men, who resided there at the time of the rape. The victim could only partially describe the suspect. He was 5 feet 10 or 11 inches with brown hair and had rough hands like he was a manual laborer. Hope this helps. I will be looking forward to hearing if you are successful. It is signed, Respectfully, Officer Phil Orlando."

The second letter is from Grindal half way across the state of Maine. Again the rape was the first major crime in thirty years. Again the state police handled the major portion of the crime investigation. There are two policemen on the Grindal force. The more senior officer is Samuel (Sam) Foster. The younger officer is Larry (Tex) Mandal. The nickname Tex is because he is originally from a small town in Texas. Grindal reminds him of his home in many ways. Both men had retired from larger police forces. Bill reads this letter also. "Dear Bill: The state police did the DNA and I will have them forward the data to your assistant Sandra. The DNA did not match anyone in the criminal databases. A state police artist made the enclosed sketch. There is a rooming house here in town. It has been in business since the 1950's. There is a small motel about two miles from town. There are three or four places in a couple of towns about twenty-five miles from Grindal. I will get a list of names and registration information over the next week and forward that information to you and Sandra. The victim estimated the rapist was between 5 foot 9 inches and 5 foot 11 inches and had brown hair. He wore a partial mask. He was not very heavy. He was strong enough to hold her down in a wooded area at the west end of town. He did have a knife, but did not cut the victim. Hope this information helps you. It is signed, Respectfully Yours, Officer Tex Mandal."

The third letter is from Kingwood. The two-officer department is small and primarily deals with problems created by the ski area visitors. One problem is created by a few speeding skiers on their way thru town. Once in a while someone does not pay their bill at one of the two of the local rooming houses or the motel. The pub will have an unruly guest, usually from out of town. The girl that was raped 3 years ago was from Portland and a visitor, but with local relatives. The local relatives have some political connections and have put some pressure on the state police to solve the crime. Jack Smith is the older of the two officers. Miles Waterford is the second officer. Both worked for the Augusta police department until they retired. Both are locals. Bill reads the letter to himself. "Dear Bill: I hope you are successfully with this effort. My department and the state police are receiving a little heat about the crime. The young lady is the niece of a prominent family in this area. You can imagine they are not happy with the lack of progress in the case. The state police have made no progress either. The suspect was about 5 foot 9 to 6 feet tall with brown hair. DNA analysis was performed, but the DNA did not match anyone in several criminal databases. I will have the DNA information forwarded to your assistant Sandra. I have enclosed a sketch, but the suspect wore a mask over his lower face. Over the next week or so I will check guests at the local rooming houses and motels. The ski area housing was closed by the late May time frame of the rape. There are some transient employees working cleanup in the ski area housing. I will try to get a list of those names also. I am sure the ski area will cooperate. They obviously do not like the publicity from a rape in the area. It is signed, Respectfully Yours, Officer Miles Waterford."

The search has started. Bill realizes the search will become more intense over the next several months. Bill calls to Sandra, "Sandra, we are going to need to set up an orderly filing system as these letters arrive."

As Sandra comes to the office door she replies, "How much space are we going to need?"

Bill answers, "Probably about a half drawer of space. Mattie sent a total of 120 letters to other departments. We will need a folder for each case. I am sort of guessing. I think we will file them by some assigned number. I think Mattie has an idea for the numbering system."

Sandra takes the letters, "OK. I will take care of it."

Bill sits back and thinks about the crimes and the work ahead. Lunch comes and goes. The afternoon is uneventful.

Around 4:30 PM Mattie shows up. As she enters the office she says, "Good afternoon Sandra. How are you today?"

Sandra replies, "Very good. And how are you today?'

Mattie answers, "OK. Busy with school work."

Sandra continued, "We received three letters today. Bill read them and I filed them. The information is starting to flow. You are going to provide a numbering system for the cases according to Bill."

Mattie walks toward Bill's office and answers, "Yes. I will send you a list."

Mattie enters Bill's office and says, "Bill you got three letters today?"

Bill answers, "Yes. I read them. Sandra is going to receive the DNA data. She will forward it to you. I will have Sandra make copies of the letters. None of the letters listed any names. The local police indicated they were going to check the local motels and so forth and send us a list of the names and related data."

Mattie says, "I will look at my E-mail for the DNA data from Sandra. I have to grade a test for two of my classes and check homework. It will be Friday evening before I can get to the data and the letters."

Bill replies, "You have to put the kids and your full time job first."

Mattie continues, "I know. It only slows the process a little, if at all. We have to wait for the data from the towns."

Bill continues, "If we get more letters by Friday, I will call you. Sandra or I can run the copies over to you. You will have the letters for Friday evening. I will see you Saturday. We can talk about dinner on Saturday or Sunday."

Silas, the mailman arrives at the police station at 10:30 AM on Friday. He comes inside and walks to Sandra's desk and says, "I have three more letters that appear to be official from three different towns."

Sandra replies, "As I told you the other day they are official and important."

Sandra hands Bill the letters.

Bill says, "Sandra, after I read them you can make the copies and file them."

Sandra replies, "I will."

The first letter is from Fishingtown Maine. The rape was the first major crime in Twenty-two years. The state police actually handled the crime investigation. There are two policemen on the Fishingtown force. The one policeman is a part time employee of the county. The more senior policeman is a full time employee of the town. He is Harry Johnson. The part time officer also the drives the fire truck like Sure Shot in Nottingham Harbor. His primary duties are traffic control and emergency response to fires and medical emergencies. The younger policeman is Tim Johnson. He is Harry's younger Cousin. Bill reads the letter to himself. "Dear Bill: The state police did the DNA and have that evidence. I will contact them and ask them to forward the results to your associate Sandra. I talked with them about the crime a couple of weeks ago. There has been little progress in the two years since the rape occurred. The enclosed sketch by a local artist of the suspect was done a couple of days after the rape took place. It is as accurate as one may expect. There are only two places to live in this town if you are a transient. One is a rooming house and the other is a small motel. There are a number of motels and boarding houses within twenty miles. I will check here and then go to the nearby towns and get a list of persons, obviously men, who resided at each place at the time of the rape. The victim could only partially describe the suspect. He was 5 foot 10 or 11 inches with brown hair. Hope this helps. I will be looking forward to hearing if you are successful. It is signed, Respectfully Yours, Officer Harry Johnson."

The second letter is from Turnerville, New Hampshire half way up the state toward the Canadian border. Again the rape was the first major crime in about Fifteen years. Again the state police handled the major portion of the crime investigation. There are four policemen on the Turnerville force. The chief is Edmund Cassidy. His friends call him Hop-a-Long for the movie cowboy of the nineteen forties and fifties. Of the other three officers the more senior one is Timothy (Tim) Linden. He retired from the Hartford Connecticut force twelve years ago.

The youngest is Carroll Filbert. He spent three years on the Boston force. His father owns several farms around Turnerville. His father has had some medical problem and Carroll and his brother James have come back to the area to help with the farms. James is a cross-country truck driver, but is home enough to ease the burden on his father. The third officer is Phillip Simpson he is a third cousin of Bill on his father side of the family. Phillip trained as a State Police officer. He moved back to Turnerville two years ago with his wife and their two children. The wife's mother lives with them and has various medical problems. His wife is an accountant and works for a local bank. Bill reads this letter also. "Dear Bill: The state police did the DNA and I will have them forward the data to your assistant Sandra. The DNA did not match anyone in the criminal databases. A state police artist made the enclosed sketch. There are several rooming houses here in town. There are several motels about two miles from town near I-91. There are three or four places each in a couple of towns about twenty miles from Turnerville. I will get a list of names and the registration information over the next couple of weeks and forward that information to you and your assistant Sandra. The victim estimated the rapist was between 5 foot 9 inches and 5 foot 11 inches and he had brown hair. He wore a partial mask. He was not very heavy. He was strong enough to hold her down in a wooded area at the north end of town. He did have a knife, but did not cut the victim. Hope the information helps you. Hope we find the rapist. It is signed, Respectfully Yours, Chief Edmund Cassidy."

The third letter is from Pleasantville, Maine. The three-officer department is small and primarily deals with problems created by the ski area visitors. One problem is by created speeding skiers on their way thru town. Once in a while someone does not pay their bill at the local rooming houses or the one motel in town. One of the bigger problems is ski thief but the state police usually are involved with that problem. Sometimes the pub will have an unruly guest, usually from out of town. The girl that was raped 3 years ago was from Boston and a visitor, but with local relatives. The local relatives have some political connections and have put some pressure on the state police and the Pleasantville Department to solve the problem. The Pleasantville Department has the same problem as Nottingham Harbor. A non-local criminal with no ties to Pleasantville was probably the perpetrator of the rape. Chief Jack Francis is the older of the officers. Mike Breakstone is the second officer. Youngest officer is Vince French. Jack and Mike both worked for the Augusta police department until they retired. Vince was with Augusta for five years until he moved back home with his wife and kids. All three were from the area around Pleasantville originally. Bill reads the letter to himself. "Dear Bill: I hope you are successfully with this effort. My department and the state police are receiving a little heat about the crime. The young lady is a cousin in a prominent family in this area. My Youngest officer Vince French attended the local to high school with the young lady. You can imagine her parents and relatives and Vince are not happy with the lack of progress in the case. The state police have made no progress either. The suspect was about 5 foot 9 to 6 feet tall with brown hair. DNA analysis was performed, but the DNA did not match anyone in several criminal databases. I will have the DNA information forwarded to your assistant Sandra. I have enclosed a sketch, but the suspect wore a mask over his lower face. Over the next week or so I will check guests at the local rooming houses and motels. The ski area housing was closed by the late May time frame of the rape. There are always some transient employees working cleanup in the ski area housing. I will try to get a list of those names also. I am sure the ski area will cooperate. They obviously do not like the publicity from a rape in the area. It is signed, Respectfully Yours, Chief Jack Francis"

Sandra comes in as Bill is finishing the reading of the letters. Bill says, "Sandra, please make me copies for Mattie. I will run them over to her after work."

Sandra replies, "I will file them and get copies for Mattie."

Bill calls Mattie at 4:45 PM. She answers after two rings, "Mattie here. What can I do for you Bill?"

Bill replies, "We have three more letters. I am going to bring them over to your house. Is that Ok?"

Mattie says, "Fine. Make it about six. I am still at school."

Bill continues, "Want me to pick up a pizza or some chicken?"

Mattie answers Bill's question, "Get the chicken. I can warm up some vegetables. I have some nice rolls. I know you generally like bread with your meals. I still have a half a bottle of wine. I also have some regular and diet soda."

Bill arrives at about 6:30 PM. He knocks on the front door. Mattie answers in a few seconds. Come on in. I am warming the vegetables and have the table set. You might as well just go directly to the dining room table."

Bill answers, "Ok." He takes a seat on the long side of the table. Mattie has a plate on the other side of the table. She brings in the vegetables and the wine bottle. Then she brings in the soda and glasses of ice on a tray. Bill watches her but says nothing. She finally comes in and sits down.

Mattie says, "Should we say grace."

Bill replies, "Yes."

Mattie starts and Bill joins in.

They start to eat. They engage in some small talk during dinner. They do not talk about the crimes during dinner. After dinner Mattie gets some hot tea and Bill take his soda into the living room. They sit the drinks on the coffee table in front of the sofa. Mattie brings in some napkins and coasters for the drinks. She brings in a tray of cookies. They are sitting next to each other on the sofa.

Bill says, "I guess we should get the serious business out of the way first."

Mattie says, "I agree."

Bill takes the copies of the letters out of his little case. He hands them to Mattie. She reads them.

Mattie comments, "The DNA has been run in all three of these towns."

Bill answers the implied question, "Yes. You should have E-mails with the data."

Mattie says, "I looked at my mail with the service 'Mail2web.com', but did not download them to my computer. I will when we finish talking."

Bill says, "That is Ok. I just wanted you to have the letters. The similarity of the information in these first six letters is interesting. The description of the suspect, the DNA, and the sketches are useful information. The combined information has not provided the solution to the crimes."

Mattie responds, "Well if we catch the rapist the information can be used in court."

Bill asks, "Do you want to go to Dinner tomorrow evening?"

Mattie answers, "Yes. I do, maybe about 7:30. Do you want to watch some TV now? I can relax for an hour before I continue working."

They watch a couple of game shows. They talk a little about nothing special. When the second show is over Bill says, "I guess I better go so you can finish your school work and the DNA research."

Mattie says, "Yes. I will see you at the office tomorrow. Until then be safe." They both get up. They walk to the front door. They kiss. Bill opens the door and goes out. Mattie watches as Bill goes to his car. As he drives away she closes the door and makes sure it is locked.

SATURDAY AT THE OFFICE

Mattie drops into the office at noon. Bill normally works part of the day on Saturday. Mattie has come over today to discuss the results of the DNA analysis and the six letters. Sandra is sitting at her desk working on some minor paper work. Mattie speaks, "Hi, Bill and you too Sandra".

Sandra replies, "Hi, Mattie. I am going to get us some lunch in a few minutes. Do you want something?"

Mattie inquires, "Bill, are we going to work here?"

Bill replies, "Yes, this is as good a place as anywhere. Get me a hamburger, fries, and a diet coke, also a piece of the apple pie. What do you want Mattie?"

Mattie answers Bill and Sandra; "Tuna on toast with lettuce and mayo, bag of regular chips and a diet iced tea. Thank you, Sandra."

Sandra is writing the order on a piece of paper. She speaks, "I'll be back in a few minutes." She gets up and leaves.

Bill speaks as she is heading to the door. "I'll cover the tab, Sandra."

Sandra does not reply. She closes the door behind herself.

Mattie starts the discussion. "The FBI provided the program to do the DNA comparisons on Thursday. I was able to run the DNA from our case and the other six cases. The good news is we have a DNA match to the crime in Fishingtown. The suspect in Turnerville did not match." She pauses.

Bill speaks, "This is very good news in one way, but bad news in that we could have a serial rapist or several serial rapists working in Northern New England. As you know I believe these crimes are the result of serial rapists rather than individual criminals."

Mattie continues, "Yes, on both counts. But now we have a reason to get the AG's here and in Maine and Vermont to use their offices to have the DNA in the other cases tested. It is going to very difficult to argue against testing the DNA in at least the eight cases that match the general description of the Nottingham Harbor suspect."

Bill sits quietly contemplating the results. Mattie sits quietly also. Bill finally speaks. "I will contact the AG's office on Monday with these finding. We will also contact the AG's offices in Maine and Vermont. The AG may want to talk to you about the accuracy of the results and the program. I will find out. I think at this stage we can handle the discussions over the phone."

Mattie nods in concurrence.

Sandra returns with lunch.

Bill clears the a few things off the table. Sandra puts Mattie's lunch and Bill's lunch on the table and starts to take her order to her desk. Bill speaks, "Join us Sandra. We are discussing the rape case. I think you will be interested in what Mattie has discovered. You're a deputy so you can hear the details."

Bill continues, "The DNA match is not from the first three towns for which we received letters."

Mattie says, "The DNA from those three towns did not match the DNA from Nottingham Harbor. However, the DNA from Grindal matches the DNA from Turnerville. The DNA from Bluebank and Kingwood do not match any of the other rapes."

Bill says, "There is the case in New Hampshire in the town of Gilbert. Do we have a match on the DNA?"

Mattie says, "Not sure. I sort of forgot about that case. You mentioned that the physical characteristics were similar to the Nottingham Harbor case."

Bill questions, "The evidence points to at least four rapists."

Mattie's reply, "From the DNA evidence it is true there are four different rapists."

Sandra injects a comment; "You are saying there are four rapists in Northern New England. That is hard to believe."

Bill replies, "The number of random rapes in the country is very large and the prosecution of these crimes is very poor. In most cases the DNA is not determined from the rape kits."

Mattie says, "Only a few of the cases we are investigating have had the DNA evidence done. We are going to ask the AG's office to have the DNA analysis run for the cases we are investigating. This is between 80 to 100 cases."

CHAPTER 10

THE DATE AT SEABROOK

MATTIE AND BILL MEET FOR DINNER
ON SATURDAY EVENING

Bill arrives at Mattie's at about 7:00PM. Mattie answers the door, "Hi. I will be ready in a few minutes."

Bill answers, "Hi, I will just sit here."

Mattie goes back to her room. She is fixing her face and straightening her dress.

A few minutes she returns to the living room. "I am ready. Are you?"

Bill answers as he stands, "Let's go. I am ready and hungry, also."

Bill and Mattie walk to the porch. Mattie turns and checks the front door. She turns back and walks to Bill's car. Bill opens the passenger side door. Mattie slides into the front seat. Bill makes sure Mattie is clear of the door and closes it. Bill walks around the front of the car and opens his door and slides into the driver's side seat. "Let's go."

Bill backs out of the driveway and turns toward the main street of town. Mattie sits quietly. Bill pushes the button on the CD player and it starts playing a Diana Krall jazz recording. Mattie likes Diana's music. She starts to hum along. The drive is about 45 minutes to Seabrook.

Bill says, "How are your kids?"

Mattie says, "The kids are fine. My kids like you. As you know they have not had a father figure for ten years. Sam particularly wants to do some guy things with you."

Bill continues, "My kids like you. Linda said one day that they both approve of you."

Mattie said, "Maybe when Sam comes home you could go to a car race or sailing. He would like that. He also likes Baseball. Maybe you two could go to a Red Sox game in Boston. He likes Ice Hockey also. Maybe if William is visiting here you guys could do something together."

Bill replies, "Sounds like a good idea.'

They both talk about National Politics. They speculate on George's political ambitions. They talk about the food and clothing drive being run by four churches in the area around Nottingham Harbor. Mattie changes the Diane Krall CD to a different one.

Mattie and Bill show up a few minutes after eight at the Restaurant in Seabrook.

Bill asks, "Do you want something to drink?"

Bill motioned to Brenda the waitress as Mattie answers, "I want a glass of wine. I may need a strong cocktail to deal with this problem and the details."

Brenda asks, "What kind of wine?"

Mattie thinks for a moment and answers, "Merlot." Brenda turns and leaves.

Mattie is carrying a large folder, which she lays on the table and begins to open. She addresses Bill, "I generated a list of the rape cases from Maine, Vermont, and New Hampshire. I did not realize how many rapes occur every year. It is discussing and frightening."

Bill kind of answers, "that is why we are here. At least, if we can stop this one, there will be one less rapist on the street. So what do we have?"

Mattie pulls a couple of sheets of paper from the file folder. "This is a list of twenty two rapes. The MO of each of the cases sort of matches the rape case in Nottingham Harbor. Only two of the cases have had the DNA determined. The towns in the other cases have limited funds for the tests.

Mattie lays a couple copies of the spreadsheet on the table for her and Bill.

Mattie says, "I listed the two cases where DNA is available at the top of the list. I believe one of them is a better candidate than the other because of the MO. The Unsub used a knife as a weapon and was 5'-10" to 5'-11" tall just like the Nottingham Harbor rapist. He also has brown hair, and wore a mask." She continues, "In the second case the Unsub was shorter only about 5-7 and had black hair."

Bill interjects, "Carl Kramer has the DNA results for the Nottingham Harbor rape suspect. You know how to match any two DNA files?"

Mattie resumes, "The method we need to use to identify the suspects is a modified Geographic Profiling Program. Unfortunately beside the DNA for the Nottingham Harbor suspect there are only two other DNA results available. It appears that at best our suspect will only match one of the other two suspects. We need a few more suspects with matching DNA to use the geometric profiling method.

Bill stops Mattie with a question. "You indicated there are several other likely cases with similar MO's?"

Mattie stops for a moment as Brenda, the waitress, approaches the table with Bill's iced tea and her wine. Brenda comments, "Iced tea, Bill. Wine, Mattie."

He replies, "Yes it is killing me, but the doctor gave me medicine for the viral cold and told me not to drink alcohol with the medicine. I have only two more days on the wagon."

Brenda interjects, "Are you ready to order?"

Bill motioned to Mattie, who says, "I will take a Caesar Salad and the Chicken Breast entree."

Brenda scribbles the order on her pad and asked, "What vegetables Mattie?"

Mattie answers, "Green Beans and Apple Sauce, Brenda."

"What about you, Bill?" Brenda asks.

Bill answers, "I will take the House Salad with French Dressing. And can I have extra dressing on the side? For the entree I will take the Pork Chops and the same vegetables as Mattie."

Brenda scribble the info on the pad and says, "OK, I will be back shortly with the Salads." She turns and walks away.

Mattie continues with an answer to Bill's question. "There are six to eight other cases with MO's and suspects that basically match the profile of our Unsub. You notice I picked up the Unsub term (unknown subject) from a couple of TV shows. I listed them as the next eight cases on the spreadsheet. The last twelve cases listed are less likely to be a match for the Nottingham Harbor suspect."

Bill replies, "I got the reference." He picks up the list in front of him and studies the next eight listing. Mattie studies her couple of Unsub's for a couple of minutes there is silence at the table.

Brenda returns with the salads and breaks the silence. "Mattie, here is your Caesar salad and, Bill, the house salad with extra dressing." Brenda obviously knows the two people having dinner. They have both been to the restaurant before with some of their friends. They were there together in January.

She asks, "Are you two working on Police work tonight?"

Bill answers, "Yes, but we cannot discuss the cases or the information."

Brenda replies, "I don't want to know, just asking to be polite."

Bill replies, "We understand."

Brenda leaves.

Bill says, "I like cases 1, 2, 3, 4, 6, and 8."

Mattie answers, "I agree but 5 and 7 each have some sketchy input from the victim. So I believe we should keep them in the list of most likely candidates."

Bill continues, "That is fine with me."

Mattie speaks, "the first 5 of the 8 in the list are from Maine. If we have a match from the first two with our suspect, we should have more influence with the Maine Attorney General's Office in Augusta. There is some political pressure on the AG to solve the Nottingham Harbor case."

Bill interjects, "He is bringing some pressure to bear on the State Police Department in Maine. I hope he can bring pressure to find funding for the DNA analysis."

The conversation has slowed as Bill and Mattie enjoy their respective salads. A few minutes of silence passes. Mattie speaks, "How is Hazard?"

Bill thinks and then answers, "He is fine. He chased a couple of cats yesterday, then jumped into the inlet and got pretty wet. Just typical dog tricks or just dog fun. Why do you ask?"

Mattie replies, "You usually have some comment about Hazard a few minutes into our conversation start."

Bill comments, "How are your Brother's children and grandchildren?"

Mattie replies, "They are fine. I guess you comment on Hazard and I comment on my Brother and Sister-in-law's kids by this point in our conversation anytime we are together. I think our conversation is much more serious tonight."

Bill replies, "Well it needs to be more serious, but we need to relax and be casual also to solve the problem. It is a very serious situation, but we have a life outside of our work. We are beginning to develop a life with each other. Don't you agree?"

Mattie answers Bill, "I do agree.

Brenda comes over to the table carrying the entrée's. Bill and Mattie move the papers and Brenda place dinner in front of each of them. She says, "Enjoy."

Bill and Mattie reply simultaneously, "Thank You and we will."

Brenda asks, "Do you need any more tea or wine?"

Mattie replies, "I will take another glass of Merlot, and I think Bill could use a refill on the Iced Tea." Bill nods in agreement.

They both fuss with the food and pass the salt and pepper in silence. Bill takes a roll from the basket, breaks, and butters it. Mattie tastes the beans and the applesauce. Bill takes a cut from the corner of the pork chop. He tastes it. Mattie speaks, "Chops Ok?"

Bill answers, "Yes, how is the Chicken?"

Mattie answers, "Good."

Bill and Mattie make some more small talk about the dog and Mattie's Nieces and Nephews. The subject material is much more pleasant than the work discussion.

Mattie turns the subject back to the cases. "I have a file of 35 to 40 more cases. The suspects in each case are similar to the suspect in the earlier cases. Can Sandra try to find the phone numbers for the various police departments for each of these cases? The phone number would help us to contact them about the case files."

The conversation turns back to the family and friends for the remainder of the dinner.

After several minutes Brenda comes over to the table and asks, "Do you want any dessert? Bill, I will bring you some more iced tea. Mattie do you want another wine?"

Bill replies, "Thank you for the iced tea. Could we see the dessert menu?"

Mattie replies, "I will take a cup of hot tea with the dessert."

Brenda answers, "Yes." She leaves to get the menus and the iced tea refill and the hot tea.

Brenda returns with the menus and the drinks. "I will give you a few minutes to select a dessert. OK?"

Bill answers, "that's fine."

Bill addresses Mattie, "I am going to have the apple pie a la mode. What are you going to have?"

Mattie answers, "The chocolate Mousse, no question."

A few minutes pass and Brenda returns, "made a decision?"

Bill answers, "Mattie wants the chocolate Mousse and I will have the apple pie a la mode with Vanilla Ice cream."

Brenda replies, "Good choices. I will be back in a few minutes."

Mattie says, "I have a couple of students that are having real trouble with the algebra. I think I will need to tutor them for the next couple of weeks. It is going to impact my time."

Bill replies, "Your job comes first. We have time on the rape cases."

Mattie continues, "I think some of the students just do not study enough."

Bill replies, "did you study enough when you were their age?'

Mattie pauses before replying, "when I was their age I was a complete nerd.'

Brenda returns with the desserts and says, "Enjoy."

Mattie smiles and Bill says, "Thank You."

Brenda walks away.

They stopped talking and eat the desserts and drink the tea.

Brenda passes the table and says, "Do want the check now?"

Bill answer, "Yes, please."

Mattie says, "I think I will use the ladies room before we leave."

Bill replies, "OK. I will use the other room when you return."

Mattie returns and Bill goes to the men's room. "The money includes the tip and I do not need change if Brenda comes back while I am gone."

Brenda comes over and picks up the tray and book with the check. "Do you need change?"

Mattie answers her, "No, the tip is yours?"

Mattie says to Bill when he returns, "One of the teachers went to Germany on vacation. The Germans have a slang expression for telling someone they are going to the men's room. They say 'It is the room where the Emperor of China goes by himself.' For the woman's room it changes to the Empress."

Bill says, "Ok, Empress Mattie, are you ready to leave?"

Mattie laughs as she answers, "Yes, Emperor Bill."

Mattie gets up, picks up her purse and small coat. Bill and her walk toward the front door. Brenda is standing with the Maître-D at the desk. Bill speaks, "Have a good evening Brenda."

Brenda replies, "You two have a good evening also."

Bill says as they walk to the car, "Nice evening for the late March."

Mattie answers, "Very nice for this time of year."

They get into the car and head back to Mattie's house.

CHAPTER 11

THE SECOND TO THE FOURTH WEEKS OF MARCH

After the first few weeks the letters from the other towns come to Bill at three or four a day. The information is generally not complete. Most of the cases have not had the DNA analysis done on the rape kits. Most have some kind of sketch and list of the suspect's general characteristics like height, weight, hair color, eye color and description of the clothing worn by the suspect. From the general characteristics Mattie has sorted the list of suspects into ten groups. Some of the groups overlap. Of the sixty-five cases represented by these additional letters only twelve have DNA. There are now twenty-five cases with DNA. Three of the ten groups determined by the general characteristics match three sets of DNA. There are now three cases with the same DNA as the Nottingham Harbor case. The data provided only has some names from local temporary residences such as motels, rooming houses or campgrounds. Mattie designated the one set of data as the second suspect. The same name is listed as a resident of three motels in three different towns.

It is Saturday Morning in the second week of March and Mattie comes to Bill's office. As she enter Sandra says, "Hello Mattie. How are you today? How is the search coming?

Mattie replies, "I am fine. The search is only fair. I have several matches but not enough to start searching for an actual suspect. The best match so far does not involve the Nottingham harbor rape case. Is Bill in today?'

Sandra replies, "Bill is in. He went to the Diner to get a Danish. He should be back momentarily."

Mattie continues, "After I get some tea, I will wait for him in his office."

Sandra answers her, "OK."

Several minutes pass. Bill returns.

As he enters the office Sandra speaks, "Mattie is in your office."

Bill replies, "I brought several Danishes. I put them next to the coffee mess." He enters the office and continues, "Good morning Mattie. How are you today?"

Mattie replies, "I am OK. How are you?"

Bill answers her question, "I am fine. So what is the prognosis from the data?"

Mattie answers the questions. "The general data sorts into ten different groups for seventy some cases. Three of the groups have three to five DNA matches. There are three cases with matching DNA data to the Nottingham Harbor case. A second set of cases has several matches from three towns. There is nothing definitive beyond these minor matches. I need more names and DNA to definitely provide a match for any of the suspects. The data does indicate there are several serial rapists involved in the cases as you suspected. I have generated a spreadsheet showing the data we have and the data that is missing. There are nine of the fifteen cases with DNA that do match other cases. The DNA on two other cases matches but the general characteristics do not come close. That is the summary so far. I need the Attorney General to fund more DNA tests. We, more probably you, need to contact the various towns and look for more residences and more names. This search is going to fall more on you than I at this time."

Bill replies, "That is OK with me. Let me look at your spreadsheet over and make sure I understand the entries." He examines the list for a few minutes and then continues. "I see the ten groups of cases. You have listed the characteristics and town where the rape occurred. You show the number of names provided for each case. You entered yes or no for the DNA. What is the last column the number of names again?"

Mattie answers Bill's question, "The data in that column is the number of names from the town where the particular rape occurred that match any names from the other cases in the particular group. This is where the data at present has the most significant weakness."

Bill thinks and then replies, "OK. I will start contacting the towns and attempt to find more names for each case. I may have to actually visit some of the towns. Hopefully I can convince the AG to fund the travel."

Mattie continues, "Yes, you will need to talk to the officers in many of the towns. I am going to talk to Linda Symth, the assistant to the AG, on Monday about the DNA. She said some time ago the AG would help with the DNA funding. I think the two groups with some DNA matches will convince the AG to help gather the DNA data. I need to talk to Jane and Vivian the ADA's in Vermont and Maine also."

Bill replies, "It is little more we can do till Monday. See you about 7 for dinner."

Mattie replies, "OK. I agree Monday is the earliest we can do much more. See you about 7 for Dinner."

The third and fourth weeks of March have brought more letters but only a few cases have DNA and only a few have some names. Bill, Mattie, and Linda have talked about the need for financial help with the DNA and the travel for Bill. Jane and Vivian are attempting to obtain additional funding. Success on any one of the cases would help.

THE FOURTH MONDAY IN MARCH

Mattie calls Linda Symth. The phone rings five times before Linda answers. "Linda Symth Assistant to the AG, how can I help you?"

Mattie answers, "This is Mattie. I have the lists of the rapes and need to forward it to you. I also need to call Vivian and Jane."

Linda replies, "OK."

Mattie continues, "It is on an Excel spreadsheet. I will attach it as a file to the E-mail. Can you read a 2007 version of Excel?"

Linda replies, "That is OK."

Mattie continues, "Only fifteen of the seventy or more cases have had DNA processed. We need more of the cases processed. The good news is that there are three cases in which the DNA matches the Nottingham Harbor case. There are three matches for two of the other cases. We do not have a match for many of the names at present." There are some name matches, but these are too few to be conclusive. Bill is going to contact the towns and try to obtain more names. We probably need to widen the search around each town. This is the other area where we can use some help. Bill is going to need to travel to some towns to help with the name search."

Linda replies, "I believe we can help with both items, but I will talk to the AG about how much help we can provide."

Mattie continues, "The data indicates that the rapes are being committed by only a few men. Bill believes that most of the rapes were and are committed by a few serial rapists. We definitely need the DNA to prove that this is the case. Maybe the AG could provide a letter that we could forward to the local law enforcement indicating the AG supports our search for more names. Maybe asking the local law enforcement to widen their searches around their respective towns will help. A letter from the AG would give a little more credibility to the searches."

Linda replies, "I can do a letter. I can generate a letter and ask the AG sign it. It may take a week or so. I am going to ask the AG to send a letter to the state police requesting they arrange for more DNA tests."

Mattie says, "Obviously the list I sent you can be forwarded to the state police to help with their selection of cases for the DNA testing. Bill is going to call the towns about the name search information. It is obviously somewhat of a nuisance to gather the name information, but Bill and I believe the name information will identify a specific suspect for each series of cases."

Linda replies, "OK. Let me get with the AG and start the letter that you need."

Mattie answers, "Thank you. I will be in touch next week."

Linda replies, "We want to catch these criminals. I am sure the AG agrees. If nothing else it is good reelection help. Have a good day and goodbye."

Mattie answers, "I am calling Vivian and Jane after we hang up. Goodbye."

Both ladies hang up the phones.

CHAPTER 12

GRINDAL SET OF CASES.

Mattie must spend the time with preparing her classes for the mid-semester exams. Bill calls almost all the towns. Two and one half weeks pass very fast. It is Saturday and she stops by the Diner for lunch with Bill. She starts the conversation, "Hi, Nice day."

Bill answers her, "Yes, it is a nice day. I was waiting to order until you arrived. Mary brought me an iced tea while I was waiting." He nods to Mary, the waitress.

Mary walks to the table, "Hi, Bill. What can I get for you and the lady?"

Bill responds, "This is Mattie. She is a high school Math teacher."

Mary replies, "Yuk, It is a good thing our cash register can add. So Mattie what would you like?"

Mattie answers, "How about a tuna salad sandwich on white toast with lettuce and tomato? I will take a hot tea to drink and a glass of ice water."

Mary scribbles the order on the pad and turns to Bill, "What can I get for the Serge?"

Bill answers, "How about some brain food, a hamburger with onion, relish, lettuce and tomato? I will take some more ice tea also."

Mattie starts the serious conversation about progress on the case. "I have charted the names for all five groups. We need more information for the Nottingham Harbor group. The Grindal group has the most towns covered. Of the fifteen towns in the Grindal group we have matching names from twelve towns. Two of the rapes occurred in suburbs of Portland and Concord the geographic profiling does not necessarily work well around a large city. I got three name matches from at least eleven of the towns in the Grindal group. Linda Symth from the AG's office was able to pull the driver license pictures for the three names that showed up in most of the thirteen towns. A couple of the names occurred twice, but I ignored them from the overall list as being too few occurrences. Of the three names one occurred in eleven of the towns. He is a salesman for a food distributor in Boston. He obviously travels all over Maine. He is 55 with graying hair. Linda and I both think he is an unlikely candidate for the suspect.

The second name was found in ten of the thirteen towns. He is an African American truck driver. He works for a trucking company that makes deliveries from all over New England to and from Maine. Linda was able to verify he is very dark skinned and only 5 foot 6 inches. We know the rapist was white and about 5 foot 10 inches tall. We ruled the driver out.

The third candidate meets the general description of the rapist. He is 5 foot 11 inches tall, white and 35 years old with brown hair. Linda and I both think he is the best suspect of the three names. I have the details on his statistics in this folder. Mary is coming over. I am going to hold."

Mary brings the food, "Mattie, here is the tuna sandwich and Bill your burger. I will be back with your drinks." She turns toward the counter.

Bill speaks, "thank you, Mary."

Mary returns, "Your tea and ice tea."

Mattie speaks, "Thank you."

Mary says, "Have a good lunch."

Mattie continues the case discussion, "His name is Richard Robinson. He is apparently a construction worker that works light construction like houses and small buildings. Linda is trying to find where he is working at present. His name and location is only associated with twelve of the fifteen rape cases. However two of the rapes were near Portland and Concord. We may not have looked in the right area for the third missing location. Linda would like you to review this file and the information. You should tell her Monday if you agree with our conclusions. She will obtain a subpoena to search bank records and employment records to locate where the alleged suspect is working now."

Bill answers Mattie, "Ok. Let me have the files. I will review them today and tomorrow. I will call Linda on Monday." Bill takes the file folder from Mattie.

Bill and Mattie finish their lunch sandwiches. Bill asks Mattie, "Do you want to go to Seabrook for dinner."

Mattie answers, "Yes, about 7."

Bill replies, "OK. Pick you about 7."

Mary comes over to the table, "Any desert folks?"

Mattie thinks for a few moments and replies, "How about a dish of chocolate ice cream?"

Bill replies, "How about a piece of Mom's apple pie."

Mary says, "Ok." She turns and goes toward the counter.

Mattie continues, "Linda says she can meet with us at the end of the day on Tuesday. If you agree that Richard Robinson is a good candidate for the suspect in these cases, Linda will proceed with acquiring a subpoena for his income and employment records. She believes we can locate his present whereabouts from his records."

Bill replies, "Good idea. I'll read this information and call her Monday with my conclusions. So until Tuesday we can hold on this case. I know that Carl is going to ask me about the Nottingham Harbor case and our progress. I know what you said the other day." Bill sees Mary coming with the deserts. He says, "Here comes Mary with the desert."

Mattie waits with her reply. Bill says nothing.

Mary brings the deserts. "Here is the Apple pie for you, Bill, and the Chocolate ice cream for Mattie."

Bill replies, "Thank You, Mary."

Mattie begins her discussion of the progress on the Nottingham Harbor case. "As I told you I found sixteen cases from the last three years with the same DNA. A couple of the cases are around Portland and Concord. I did not expect good results for those two cases. A couple of the cases that are three years old I did not expect good geographic information because many businesses destroy records after three or four years. There are three groups of towns. One group is around Nottingham harbor the other group is upstate 50 or more miles north of Bangor. The third group is over here in New Hampshire."

Bill stops her, "What is the significance of the three groups? I thought it is the same DNA for all the locations."

Mattie replies and continues, "I believe the suspect was living and probably working in each area. He may have traveled between the three areas regularly. The three groups are not grouped in time. The time of the rapes in one area and in the second or third areas overlap. This indicates he travels to the three areas in a random pattern. Nottingham Harbor was the last case. I am trying to identify a common denominator for the cases. This could be a particular business or a family connection. No luck as of now. In six of the towns there are several common suspects, that is, names. In five other towns there are several common names. There is NO cross over between the two groups of names. The cases in New Hampshire Do not connect. I think we do not have enough names from either area. How do we proceed is the question?"

Bill thinks quietly for a few minutes eating his pie. Mattie sits quietly eating her ice cream. "What about the names from Nottingham Harbor?"

Mattie answers, "The names from Nottingham Harbor match several names in the group of five. The names from Nottingham harbor do NOT match any of the names in the group of six or the New Hampshire names. The names from five of the towns match none of the other towns."

Bill thinks for a few moments as he finishes his pie. He comments, "I will call the police chiefs of the six towns on the other list. I will call the towns with no matches. I would imagine that the police in those six towns with no matches simply did not include enough area in their searches of the motels or the rooming houses. Could the suspect be camping in reasonably nice weather instead of staying at a motel?"

Mattie replies, "Never considered that way of living. But it could be an answer also. I am going to check the time of year of each case and search the weather history for the dates around each case. It could provide a method to identify the suspect. As far as I know camp grounds keep the same records as motels or rooming houses."

Bill continues, "Obviously Mayor Bernard is looking for results for the Nottingham Harbor case. I understand why, but we just have to work the math and search and worry about getting the right answer. For the Nottingham Harbor cases, the question is whether the list of inns for each town is comprehensive.

Mattie answers, "From your list of inns around each town the local police have not checked more than 50% of the inns in any single town and in most of the towns on the list, only 30% or so of the inns have been checked."

Bill comments, "I will have to call them again. Linda, Jane, and Vivian may need to call them also. What about the name information for the other three groups of cases?"

Mattie answers, "For each of the other three groups the lists of names are sketchier."

Bill continues, "I think we need to concentrate on the Grindal group. If we can arrest the suspect for the Grindal group of rapes then the arrest should motivate the other towns to do more work on the names."

Mattie replies, "So far the rapes in the smaller towns like Nottingham Harbor have been isolated incidents, but not around the cities and several larger towns. The rapes in those areas appear to be committed by several different rapists. It could obviously happen anywhere. The rapes appear to be random crimes of opportunity."

Mattie stops talking.

Mary comes toward the table, "Do you need anything else?"

Bill answers, "Mattie do you want something else?"

Mattie answers, "No. You can bring the check."

Mary turns and walks toward the counter. She punches some keys on the register and the totals the bill. The bill is still hand written and the cash register is from the 1970's. She writes the total on the bill and returns to the table. She hands the bill to Bill. "I will be back in a few minutes."

Bill picks up the check. He looks it over. He mentally calculates 20% and takes the money from his wallet. He lays the money on top the bill. Mary returns to the table. Bill speaks, "Mary, I need a receipt."

She answers, "OK. I will be right back."

Mattie says, "I am going to make a quick trip to the ladies room."

Bill says, "OK. I will go to the other room when you come back. I don't want to leave the paper work alone on the table."

Mattie gets up and walks toward the ladies room.

Mary returns with the receipt. "Several of my friends were discussing the rape that happened in Nottingham Harbor. Is there any progress?"

Bill thinks and then replies, "I cannot discuss the case. But several people are pursuing various leads. I cannot say anything else."

Mary says, "OK. Have a good day, Bill."

Several minutes pass and Mattie returns. As she approaches the table Bill gets up and head toward the Men's room. Mattie takes a seat and begins to gather the paperwork into a carry bag. In a few minute Bill returns. He speaks, "Ready."

Mattie gets up and replies, "Yes, let's go. Are we going back to your office?"

Bill replies to her question, "Yes. I do not know if there is more to discuss."

They leave the Diner and walk back to the office.

Several people nod to him. Bill usually wears street cloths rather than a uniform, but he always wears his state police cap when he is on duty. Betty, one of Mattie's students is coming the other way on the walk. "Miss Greene, how are you?"

Mattie answers, "I am fine, Betty. Do you know Sergeant Simpson?"

Betty replies, "Sort of."

Mattie thinks that the students report everything to their friends and then she replies, "The sergeant and I are studying some mathematics about criminal activity. You probably have seen on the TV or on the Internet that math can be used to track and catch criminals. The sergeant has an idea we can apply a similar technique to some criminal activities here in New Hampshire. Remember math can be applied to many of life's problems. What are you doing in Concord today?"

Betty answers her, "My mother is antique shopping. I just came along for the ride. I will see you in math class on Monday."

Mattie replies, "I will see you in class." She pauses a moment until the student walks away. "They observe everything. If you were holding my hand by Monday the class would be speculating on the date for the marriage."

Bill giggles and says, "That's funny."

They walk to the office. Bill opens the door and lets Mattie go in first."

Mattie walks in and sees Barney, "What are you doing here on Saturday?"

Barney answers, "Just hanging out. I am going to the firing range later. Nothing is happening today."

Bill is walking behind Mattie and speaks, "Hi, Barney."

Bill and Mattie walk into his office. Bill takes a seat behind the desk and Mattie sits down on the sofa. Bill asks, "Want to go to Dinner about 7?"

Mattie answers, "Yes. I'll print a list of the towns, which need to be contacted. I have phone numbers and names on the computer. Monday you can contact the police official in each town. I am going to head home. I have some preparations for next week. I will see you about 7." She gets up to leave.

Bill says, "See you at 7. Good bye for now."

Mattie leaves. She says, "Don't shoot yourself at the range. Have a good day Barney."

Barney answers, "I am always careful. Mattie, you and Bill have a good weekend."

Mattie answers, "We will."

Bill and Mattie have Dinner in Seabrook on Saturday evening. They do not discuss any of the cases. They just enjoy each other's company and talk about the families.

MONDAY MORNING IS APRIL FOOL'S DAY

Sandra arrived at 9:00 AM. She fixes some coffee and hot water for tea. Bill arrives at 9:30 AM. As Bill enters Sandra says, "Coffee is ready Serge."

Bill says, "Good Morning, Sandra. Thanks for the coffee. I need to make several calls about the one rape suspect. Mattie and Linda have identified an alleged suspect by name for Grindal group of rapes."

Sandra answers, "That is good for Grindal, but how about the other cases?"

Bill replies, "Not yet."

Bill goes to his office. Before starting to make the phone calls, Bill takes the file on the Grindal cases and begins to review the information. He carefully looks at each location where each rape occurred and matches the date and location to the place the suspect was residing. Twelve of the dates and locations match. In each case the suspect was staying about twenty to twenty five miles from the rape location. The three cases where there is no location appear to be just missing a definitive residence. There is no reason to reject the other twelve matches. He picks up the phone and calls Linda.

Linda answers the phone, "Attorney General's office, Linda Symth."

Bill replies, "This Bill Simpson. How are you today, Linda?"

Linda answers, "I am fine. Good to hear from you. What do you think about the data on this suspect?"

Bill replies again, "I believe the suspect is a good match. He was within twenty-five miles of twelve of the locations on the dates of the rapes. Two of the rapes were near Portland and Concord. The math technique is hard to apply near a larger city. For the one location there appears to be insufficient names. The location matches gives him the opportunity to commit the crimes. The DNA matches on all the rapes. Can you get a warrant to search his employment records?"

Linda answers, "I believe I can get a warrant to search his employment records and verify his employer at each location. The subpoena should allow us to locate his present employment and location. I am going to ask to search his bank records."

Bill comment is, "Go for it. I'll talk to you once we have the employment information."

Linda answers him, "Have a good day. I'll talk to you in a couple of days. I will send Mattie the information on the employment as soon as I have data. My technician already has his driver license data and his physical characteristics match."

Bill replies, "You have a good day, also."

They both hang up.

Bill places the file on the corner of his desk. He picks up the folder for the Nottingham Harbor cases. Mattie listed the motels and rooming houses that were checked at each location. The local police only checked two or three temporary residences for several of the towns. No campgrounds were checked. Five of the dates were between June and the beginning of September. The campgrounds or camper parks could be valid for these dates.

The list from Mattie points out that the names from Nottingham Harbor match several names in the group of five. The names from Nottingham harbor do NOT match any of the names in the group of six.

Bill ponders these results. The DNA from all eleven towns matches the Nottingham Harbor DNA. He thinks to himself, that we just do not have enough information. To visit each town is going to take two weeks of travel. He realizes that the case in Fishingtown was the first DNA match to the Nottingham Harbor case. He decides to start by calling Fishingtown. Fishingtown is in the group of six and none of the names match any of the names in Nottingham Harbor. He decides to call Harry Johnson the senior member of Fishingtown police department.

Bill calls the Fishingtown police department. The phone rings several times and Tim Johnson answers, "Fishingtown Police Department, Officer Tim Johnson. How can I help you?"

Bill replies, "This is Bill Simpson of the New Hampshire State Police. Can I speak to Harry Johnson?"

Tim answers, "Harry is not here at present. Can I take a message? You are the state policeman that has asked us to supply information on the rape here."

Bill responds, "Yes, Asked Harry to call me. I need the strictest confidence about what I am going to tell you. Please only tell Harry. Do you understand?"

Tim replies, "Yes. Tell no one, but Harry."

Bill continues, "The rapist from Fishingtown is the same guy that raped in Nottingham Harbor and ten other towns. We need you and the police in the other towns to collect more names from local motels, inns, rooming houses, and campgrounds. We do not have enough names to narrow the suspect list. Ask Harry to call me about detailed information on the name lists, please."

Tim responds, "I will tell him when he gets here this afternoon. I will keep the information confidential."

Bill says, "thank you."

Tim says, "No problem. Good bye."

Bill says, "Good bye."

They both hang up.

The town of Gilbert in New Hampshire is one where the DNA matches Nottingham Harbor. Bill thinks I was looking at Gilbert several months ago. I was checking the physical characteristics of the rapist against several of the other cases, but I didn't have the DNA to compare.

Bill spends Monday afternoon and Tuesday morning calling the other towns including Gilbert from the Nottingham Harbor list. Bill explains how the technique used on the Grindal cases lead to the identification of an alleged suspect. He urges all the police departments to widen and increase their search of local motels, rooming house, and campgrounds for names. He points out the attorney general is supporting this effort along with the DNA testing.

Bill arrives on Wednesday at about 8:30 AM. Sandra is not in yet. Bill makes some coffee and puts water on the hot plate for tea. He looks over the paper work on two robberies and a murder near the Canadian border. Sandra arrives at 8:50. As she enters Sandra says, "Hi Bill."

Bill replies, "Do you have any news about the additional names?"

Sandra answers, "I received two letters in the mail with list of names from several temporary residences around each town. One list is hand written and the other is typed. I am typing them on to computer lists for Mattie. As soon as I am finished I will E-mail them to Mattie. I also received two E-mails, which were also sent to Mattie directly. She probably hasn't seen any of these yet because they just arrived today. I also had two phone calls from two other towns. They needed to obtain her and our E-mail addresses to send the additional names. They all are from towns with the same rapist as Nottingham Harbor.

Bill replies, "This sounds like good news for a solution to the Nottingham Harbor cases. I will talk to Mattie later today or tomorrow about any additional name matches. I will be talking to Mattie later today and probably tomorrow again." He goes into his office and sits down. The afternoon passes without incident. At four fifteen he calls Mattie on her cell.

He remembers Mattie is home. The phone rings several time and Mattie answers, "Hi, Bill. I am just up the street from my driveway. Can you hold till I park the car? Don't want you to arrest me for driving while talking on the cell." She lays the cell of the passenger's side seat.

Bill replies, "Very funny. I will hold." Bill waits.

Mattie parks the car and picks up the cell phone, "OK, I am now legal.

Bill continues, "We have more names. You should find four lists in your E-mail. Two came directly from different towns. Two lists were mailed here as hand written or typed paper list. Sandra typed those into Excel spreadsheet files and sent them a little while ago to your E-mail. These are related to the Nottingham Harbor case. Also two other towns have contacted us to verify yours and our E-mail addresses. You should get two more lists from those two towns in the next couple of days. I am going to need to concentrate on the Grindal list and suspect for a couple of weeks."

Mattie responds, "I will be ready to discuss these new names on Saturday."

Bill responds, "I will see you on Saturday. Meantime have fun. Goodbye."

Bill continues, "There is more. Linda has subpoenas to allow her tech to search Richard Robinson's employment and tax records. She is pursuing him on paper. She wants me to go down to locality where he now residing and work with the locals to verify the DNA and finally arrest him. She knows the AG will cover the trip. Linda also verified he was working near Portland and Concord when those two rapes occurred."

SATURDAY MORNING

Several officers not working on the rape cases are in the outer office. About ten o'clock Bill arrives. He is expecting Mattie around ten thirty.

The desk sergeant walks into Bill's office and says, "Mattie called. She said she is running late. She should be here by quarter to eleven. Said she has some good news on the rape cases. A Linda Smyth from the AG's office called. She said you can call her back until noon. She is working this morning. Is this about the rape cases?"

Bill answers, "I assume it is about the cases. You do understand that the information on the rape cases is confidential." Bill makes himself a cup of coffee.

The desk sergeant replies, "I understand it is police business. It is confidential to the department."

Bill enters into his office.

Mattie enters the outer office, "Hi, Serge. How are you today?"

He answers, "Fine Mrs. Greene, how are you today."

She replies, "I am fine, also. Serge you can call me, Mattie. You are not one of my students."

He continues, "OK, Mattie, Bill is in and waiting for you."

Mattie continues, "Thank you. I am going to get myself a tea and then join him."

She addresses Bill, "Bill I am getting a tea. I will be there in a few minutes."

Bill calls back, "OK."

A few minute pass and Mattie enters Bill's office. She says, "Good Morning." She winks at Bill.

Bill winks back and says, "Better close the door because we need to keep the information about the rape cases confidential at this time. We never know who is in the outer office. From the number of people that walk through here, you would think this was the Mall."

Mattie begins, "Linda is pursuing the Richard Robinson case. I am sure she is going to have locations and information about his whereabouts soon. The main good news is about the Nottingham Harbor case. The names we got over the last two weeks have changed the suspect list positively. Linda provided an interesting piece of data also. Let me tell you Linda's information. As you know we had a match in six towns for one name. The person operates vending machines around the state. He services the machines and supplies product to several other people for the machines. He happens to supply the vending machines at the AG's office in Concord. Linda casual knows him. He is in his early fifties and has Graying hair. He does not meet the physical characteristics of the rapist. I think we can eliminate him as a suspect. It is good news because the information reduces the suspect list and lets us concentrate on the other suspects. It is slightly bad news because it eliminates a suspect with the highest number of matches for a single suspect. However, the rest of the news offsets the bad news.

"The suspect that matched in five towns now matches in nine. The new names did increase a couple of matches. Two names that occurred in two towns each now show up in three towns each. The one name that matched in four towns now matches in five. The Nottingham Harbor suspects DNA was found in sixteen towns. There are still five towns without a name match to more than three other towns. The towns in New Hampshire are hanging free, except for Gilbert."

Bill interrupts, "I thought there were fifteen towns."

Mattie replies, "There were."

Bill questions, "What changed?"

Mattie answers, "The small town of Gilville sort of fell into a crack. The state police had investigated the crime and had good rape kit. They forgot to send it to the lab for testing and DNA determination. Some people realized the kit was in the evidence locker and sent it to the lab. The DNA did match Nottingham Harbor. Gilville has a one-man police force and so the name list is just being generated. The one man is a young officer and wants to solve his case. We will see what we get from Gilville. Linda is going to ping the other towns. You need to do the same thing. So that is the good news. There is no bad news about the Nottingham Harbor case. There is simply more information needed."

Bill continues, "On Monday, I will start calling the towns where we need more names. Several of the towns on the original list are near enough for me drive there during the day. I will see you around 7."

Mattie gets up to leave and replies, "Bye. See you at 7."

The weekend passes to quickly. On Monday Bill comes to the office at about nine. He has a list from Mattie of the towns where they need more names. Mattie has listed the phone number for the chiefs of police in each town. He thinks Mattie is very thorough. It is good Mattie is thorough because Bill can't find his list this morning. By about 2:00 PM he has called and talked to all of the various chiefs. He explains that there is a match to single name in nine towns. Please widen their search area and find twenty to thirty new names. All agree to work on additional names over the next week. They all want the rape in their town solved. They all know a solution to the rapes is one common suspect.

Chapter 13

THE RICHARD ROBINSON CHASE

Wednesday morning Linda Smyth calls. Bill answers, "Sergeant Bill Simpson speaking."

Linda replies, "Bill, this is Linda Smyth. How are you today?"

Bill replies, "I am fine, Linda. How are you?

Linda replies, "I am fine also. I have some good news. My staff has located Richard Robinson. Since leaving Maine he has lived in a town in South Carolina for about five months and then moved to a small city on the Tennessee-Kentucky border. It is all in the E-mail I just sent to your office. You could make some phone calls to towns near where he lived in South Carolina and Tennessee about any rapes in those areas. Mattie's statistics showed that the rapes in Maine and New Hampshire were in towns 25 to 40 miles from where he stayed and worked. If we locate one town in each location where a rape occurred with the same DNA as Grindal, the odds of Richard Robinson being the rapist would be almost 100%. I can get the DNA results if you believe one of the rapes down south is connected to our case."

Bill responds, "OK. I will make some calls after I study the maps of both areas. I know about Mattie's statistics. She is good with the math. I was never that good with math."

Linda continues, "The AG has authorized me to proceed with subpoenas, search warrants and arrest warrants for this guy. He is convinced we have the right guy, so am I. A rape by the same person, that is the same DNA, would seal the deal."

Bill continues, "It is Wednesday. Give me tomorrow and Friday to make some calls. I will talk to you on Monday If I make any progress."

Linda continues, "I have a personal day on Monday. So you have till Tuesday. I have confirmed he does housing construction. He was up in Maine and New Hampshire building houses for several different companies. The companies he worked for in New England had operations around each town where he was residing. According to my tech here at the AG's office all of the information ties together. I have given you and Mattie the information to review. How is Mattie?"

Bill continues, "Mattie is fine, but busy with her school work. She is scheduled to teach summer school. Do you have time to discuss the Nottingham Harbor case?"

Linda replies, "Yes."

Bill continues, "I think you know we got more names and have tied four more rapes to the Nottingham Harbor rape. But I received a letter from a tenth town Gilville and one of names on the list is the same name as on the nine towns. I called seven other towns for more names. Gilville was missed on the original information because the state police had the evidence locked up properly, but it was at an upstate barracks and apparently no one looked at it. However they did now. Gene, the Gilville policeman, sent us several names and the DNA data. I don't believe the evidence chain is broken, but you should verify the chain before using it in court. There is no question the DNA matches and the suspect is the same as Nottingham Harbor just being thorough about the evidence chain."

Linda answers, "That is good news. I will have my research assistant and the state police verify the chain of evidence. We are doing that with all the evidence before going to court for subpoenas and the other paper work. I have an associate checking the evidence on each case in all sixteen towns. So far we have not seen any legal problems. I will add Gilville to the list. We have all been very careful assembling the information."

Bill says, "Good. I want all five of these guys. Of course the one from Nottingham Harbor I want the most. Nottingham Harbor is my hometown. Goodbye, until next Tuesday. Have a nice weekend and personal day."

Linda says, "Say hello to Mattie and you two have a nice weekend."

Linda and Bill hang up.

Sandra comes in and says, "We have got several letters and E-mails for the other three cases. I have been typing the names and information in the letters on the computer and sending them to Mattie. I also forwarded the E-mails to Mattie. I think it is a total of fifteen towns which have responded to your inquiries in the past two weeks."

Bill responses, "Just keep sending the information to Mattie and filing it here. We have the one guy identified. Linda the assistant AG is closing toward an arrest warrant. There are now ten towns where the same name is listed in the Nottingham Harbor case. Gilville was the tenth. I am going to talk to Linda next Tuesday about the two cases and any additional names in the Nottingham Harbor case. The guy on the Grindal case is living down South at present. I am going to check for rapes in the area where he lived and is living. One case with the same DNA in each area would make it almost impossible for the court to refuse various subpoenas and arrest warrants."

Sandra says, "Carl and the Mayor are going to be surprised."

Bill replies, "Yes, but do not say anything to Erin. Let me tell the mayor next week. I should have even more information by next Wednesday when I have a meeting with Carl and the Mayor."

Sandra replies, "Mums the word Serge. I want you to give him the good news. I know anything I tell Erin will go right to the mayor. You know Erin has a crush on you."

Bill replies, "Yes. Can't you and Mattie and few of the other women find her a nice interesting man? Erin is a nice looking and good woman, but I am not interested. I am interested in Mattie, but I haven't told Mattie how much."

Sandra replies, "We have been working on it. So far nobody seems to interest her."

Sandra returns to her office. Bill gets a coffee. He says to Sandra, "Can you print out that latest E-mail and documents from Linda about the locations and whereabouts of Richard Robinson. I need to start calling the towns. You can forward it to Mattie for her information.

He goes back to his office and sips the coffee. Several minutes goes by. He hears Sandra curse at the printer. He gets up and walks to the outer office. Bill says, "What is the matter?"

Sandra replies, "The DAMM printer jammed. I'll fix it. Just when you are trying get something done the machine fails to cooperate."

Bill says, "Seem that way. I will let you alone. I know you can fix it."

Bill goes back to his office.

Sandra fusses with the printer and clears the jam. She prints the document and E-mail from Linda. She takes the printed material to Bill. She enters and says, "Bill here is what Linda sent you."

Bill replies, "Thank you. Is everything OK with the printer?"

Sandra answers, "Yes. It is just a normal day at the office."

Bill says, "Thank you again. Why don't you walk over to the diner and have an afternoon snack. It will relax you."

Sandra thinks and replies, "Maybe I will." She leaves and Bill hears the front door open and close."

He hears the desk sergeant and her exchange pleasantries.

Bill thinks to himself Sandra is a good deputy but I guess she just gets frustrate with things. He begins to read about the area in South Carolina and Tennessee where their alleged suspect is now residing. He turns on the computer and waits for it come up. He goes to the Internet and calls up MapQuest. He sees the town where the guy was working is maybe 12 blocks by 10 blocks. He types in Lindon South Carolina police department. A few second pass and the address and the phone number come up on the screen. He writes the information down on the paperwork from Linda. He picks up the department cell and calls the number.

The phone rings several times and then someone speaks, "Deputy Steve Maynard, Lindon police department, how can I help you all?"

Bill responds, "This is Bill Simpson. I am a state police sergeant in New Hampshire. I need some information about an alleged suspect from up here."

Steve replies, "Never been to New Hampshire or Maine. So I don't know how much I can help."

Bill continues, "Come visit. The information I need is about the same suspect living in the area near Lindon, South Carolina about a year to year and half ago."

Steve continues, "Well that I may be able to help you with."

Bill continues, "Our suspect has committed a number of rapes in New Hampshire and Maine. We know he was living in your town a year ago. I am trying to determine and to slightly investigate if any rapes that have occurred in your area from twelve to eighteen months ago."

Steve replies, "There has not been a rape here in the last five years."

Bill continues, "This guy does not rape where he is living. He usually rapes in a town or city 25 to 40 miles away. This is his MO. So do you know of any rapes in towns around Lindon that would fit those distances during the time frame he was living in Lindon."

Steve says, "Let me think." He pauses and there is silence on the phone. He continues, "I believe I have heard of three. One was in Mudville about 35 miles from here. It was about fifteen months ago. You will need to contact Mudville for more details. One was in Forestville about twelve months ago. One was in Clintonville probably almost eighteen months ago. I have phone numbers for all three police departments. Do you have a piece of paper?'

Bill replies, "Yes right in front of me."

Steve continues, "Let me give you the names and phone numbers of the local police. The chief in Mudville is a second cousin of mine, Gaylord Maynard. The other two policemen I do not know personally." Steve reads off the names and numbers and repeats them with the proper spelling to Bill. Bill repeats the information back. "Hope the information helps you 'all' to catch the rapist."

Bill replies, "You are very helpful. You will be hearing from me, or the Attorney Generals of New Hampshire and Maine, when we catch this guy. Thanks again. Good day for now."

Steve responds, "Good day to you 'all'."

They both hang up.

Bill goes out and gets another coffee. Sandra comes in. Sandra says, "The milkshake did the trick. But it doesn't help my waistline."

Bill says, "Ok. Good to see you have calmed down. I have some interesting news. There were at least three rapes down in South Carolina near the town where Richard Robinson was living a year ago. I am going to call each of the towns where each of the rapes occurred. Linda will be excited about this news."

Bill calls the Mudville police department. The phone ring a few times and is answered, "Mudville police department, Chief Gaylord Maynard speaking. How can I help you?"

Bill replies to the request, "This is Bill Simpson. I am a state police sergeant in New Hampshire. You are exactly whom I was told to talk to about the information I need."

Gaylord replies, "Well how can I help my Yankee brother?"

Bill continues, "Sometimes a Dam Yankee. According to your cousin in Lindon there was a rape about fifteen months ago in your town."

Gaylord answers, "Yes there was. If I catch him I might forget I am a policeman."

Bill continues, "Can you tell me his physical characteristics like height, weight, skin color, and so forth."

Gaylord replies, "He was white, brown hair, in his thirties, about 5-9, about 180 pounds. He raped the woman on the way home from the second shift at the local clinic. If I catch him, he is toast."

Bill says, "I understand, but I need to know another piece of information. Was the DNA run on the rape kit?"

Gaylord answers Bill's question, "Yes it was. The state police had the DNA run and should have the results. The detective is Justine Jones. Let me give you his number. Do you want the DNA results?"

Gaylord gives Bill the number. Bill continues, "Yes, we want the DNA results. The Attorney General of Maine will formally request the results. If this is the same rapist as here in New Hampshire and Maine, I am sure that our AG will ask for the first chance to prosecute the guy. We have him for fifteen alleged rapes."

Gaylord continues, "I see why you want the first chance to prosecute the guy. Your cousin gave me two more towns where rapes occurred. They are Clintonville and Forestville. Do you know anything about those rapes? I am getting ready to call the police at each town. Just thought I would ask.

Gaylord replies, "If you are looking for a white guy, forget Clintonville the rapist was a black guy. If I remember the rapist in Forestville was only about twenty. I do not think either of them has been caught."

Bill continues, "Thank you for your help, Gaylord. Good bye."

Gaylord replies, "Good talking to you and good hunting. Goodbye."

They both hang up.

Bill calls Clintonville. The phone rings a number of times. Just as Bill is ready to hang up and try later. There is an answer, "Deputy Conrad Foresight, Clintonville police department. How can I help you?"

Bill answers, "Bill Simpson, I am a state police sergeant in New Hampshire. I need some information about a rape that I was told occurred about eighteen months ago in your town. We have a suspect and DNA results from fifteen rapes in New Hampshire and Maine. He is white about thirty. Does your suspect fit these physical characteristics?'

Conrad answers, "No, Sergeant Bill. Our suspect is a dark skinned African-American. Not quite sure of his age. He was 5-6 and fairly heavy."

Bill continues, "He is definitely not a match for our suspect. We believe our suspect was living in Lindon at the time of at least one rape in South Carolina. His MO is to commit rapes 25 to 40 miles from where he is living.'

Conrad answers, "Good hunting. Sorry I can't help. Have a good day."

Bill continues, "Thank you anyway. You have a good day. I may call you about the math we are using to track suspects. It could help with your case. But I need to call some more towns today. Goodbye Conrad."

They both hang up.

Bill turns to the computer. He starts a new word document. He is not the greatest typist, but he needs to record what he has found. He can get Sandra to clean up the document with additional dictation. He soon gets frustrated with the typing but continues to outline the information."

He stops typing and picks up the cell. He calls Forestville. The phone rings several times and Linda Longstreet answers, "Forestville police, Deputy Linda Longstreet speaking. How can I help you?"

Bill speaks, "This Bill Simpson, I am a state police sergeant in New Hampshire. I am calling about a rape in your town. Can you help me?"

Linda continues, "Yes, it was about twelve months ago. It has not been solved."

Bill continues, "The police in Mudville told me the suspect was young maybe only twenty. We have an alleged suspect in fifteen rapes in Maine and New Hampshire. We know he was living in Linton between twelve and eighteen months ago. This is why we are interested in rapes around Forestville. His MO is to go 25 to 40 miles from where he is residing at the time. If your suspect is about twenty, then he does not fit the physical characteristics of our suspect. I would still like to get any DNA result you have on your suspect."

Linda replies, "The state police did run DNA on the suspect. There were no matches in any existing databases. I will give you the name of the state police detective that handled the case."

Bill says, "OK."

Linda continues, "The detective's name is Justine Jones. I can give you his phone number.

Bill says, "I have his contact information. He handled the case in Mudville also."

Linda continues, "How do you find these animals?"

Bill says, "We have a mathematician using some sophisticated programs to track the suspects. It uses geographic profiling and good old fashion police data gathering to identify suspects. I will have her contact you and explain more. You cannot reveal her name for security reasons. It is her security we are worried about."

Linda says, "Ok. Think she can help us with our case?"

Bill replies, "Not right away. She is busy on five groups of cases in New England. Maybe in a few months she and I can help. Good bye for now."

Linda replies, "Good bye."

Bill calls Sandra in to his office, "Can you help with this document? I am frustrated with my typing."

Sandra sits down in front of the computer and Bill gets a cup of coffee before dictating some information. Sandra cannot type as fast as Bill can talk. He does one sentence at a time."

He takes sips of the coffee. Let us start with Lindon South Carolina. He says, "That is Lindon, L-I-N-D-O-N." he continues slowly. It takes about a half an hour to finish the dictation.

Sandra says, "Let me read this over and correct spelling and grammar mistakes. Then I will read it back to you to make any additions and fill in some information.'

Bill agrees, "Ok." He goes to the men's room and gets another coffee. He comes back to his office and sits in the chair across from his desk. Sandra is still fooling with the document."

It is about 4 PM when Sandra says, "Let me read this back to you once. Then we can read it again paragraph by paragraph"

Bill responds, "Shoot. That's not very good to say to a woman with a gun."

Sandra reads the document. Bill nods a couple of times. Sandra then starts through the document slowly. He asks her to make a couple of corrections and additions. Bill finally says, "I think we got it. Thanks Sandra. You can send it to Linda and Mattie."

Sandra answers, "I have to get my flash drive from my desk and transfer the document to my computer. I will file a printed copy, also."

Bill replies, "Good." He stays sitting while Sandra goes to outer office and returns to copy the file. Sandra finally takes the electronic file to her computer and completes the task. Bill continues to finish his coffee. Nothing else is happening. At about 4:30 PM he decides to call Mattie.

He calls on his personal cell. Mattie's cell rings several times before she answers, "Hi, Bill. What's up?"

Bill replies, "Business as usual. How was your day?"

She replies, "Business as usual, also."

Bill continues, "I have one interesting bit of news. I called several towns in South Carolina. There was a rape fifteen months ago in Mudville. The physical characteristics of the rapist match our suspect, Richard Robinson. The state police should be able to provide DNA. Linda is going to request the DNA info. You should have an E-mail with a document I sent Linda about the research on three rapes near where our suspect was living. You can read all the details. I am sure Linda will request a full set of details."

Mattie asks, "What about the other two rapes?"

Bill replies, "One suspect was very young and the other was African American. But we only need a DNA match from one suspect. If the DNA matches it will confirm with a high probability as you pointed out that we have the right person. I am going to call the Tennessee towns tomorrow."

Mattie replies, "It sounds like success. I talked to Linda and she told me her office is proceeding with subpoenas and other documents to charge the guy with the rapes in New Hampshire and Maine."

Bill continues, "Yes. I know. We are still waiting for more letters on the Nottingham Harbor case. There has been some letters and E-mails on the other cases. Sandra has been typing the letters into electronic files and sending them to you. I have not talked too much about the other three cases."

Mattie continues, "There are seven towns in one of the cases and five or six in the other two with matching names. Most of the other matches are only two names maybe three in the one case. We definitely need more names for the other three groups of cases. It is my opinion, that once the arrest in the first case is announced names for the other cases will flow like water."

Bill comments, "That is a good analogy."

Mattie continues, "Have fun calling Tennessee tomorrow. I am going to have fun grading papers tonight. Tell Sandra to send the E-mails. I should have time on the weekend. See you Saturday evening."

Bill continues, "OK. See you Saturday about 7 PM."

They both hang up.

Bill shows up at the office around 10 on Friday. He is carrying his Danish and gets a coffee. Sandra is in the restroom. She comes out and says, "Hi, boss. Are you ready for the day?"

Bill answers without turning around, "Hi. Yes."

He goes to his office without further comment. The Portland paper is lying on his desk. He picks up the paper while he finishes his Danish. There is story about a shooting. The shooting is probably drug dealer related. Bill worries about drug violence coming to Concord. His favorite Hockey team won last night. There is a cartoon about a small town chief of police hunting gofers on the local golf course. Bill thinks Carl probably feels like the chief in the cartoon. He lays the paper down. He gets up to get a second coffee.

He comes back in a few minutes. Sits down and picks up the E-mail from Linda. The first town in Tennessee is Riverton. The chief is Donald Harrison. Bill calls Riverton. The phone rings five times and Susan Brown answers the phone, "Riverton police department, Officer Susan Brown speaking. How can I help you?"

Bill answers, "Susan, this is Bill Simpson. I am a sergeant with the New Hampshire State Police. I would like to talk to Chief Donald Harrison. I am calling with regard to an investigation of several rapes. Our principle suspect is living in Riverton to the best of our knowledge."

Susan answers Bill, "Let me check if Don is available. I must put you on hold."

Bill continues, "I will hold."

Susan switches to the other line. She busses the chief. The chief says, "Yes, Susan."

Susan answers him. "I have a State Policeman, Bill Simpson, from New Hampshire on the line. He wants to talk to you about a rapist living here. Do you have time to talk?"

Don says, "Yes. If he knows a criminal is living here. I definitely want to talk to him. Put him on my line."

Susan punches the button on the phone. She says, "Are you there, Sergeant?"

Bill replies, "I am here."

Susan continues, "The chief wants to talk to you. I am sorry for the hold, but he has some meetings today and I needed to know if he had enough time for a conversation."

Bill says, "I understand. He was not expecting me to call."

Susan connects Bill to Don's phone. Don picks up the line. "This is Chief Don Harrison. How can I help you?"

Bill speaks, "We have been putting together a case against an alleged suspect in at least fifteen rapes. We have identified the suspect. To best of our knowledge he is living in Riverton. What I am interested in is if there have been any rapes 25 to 40 miles from Riverton in the last year."

Don says, "I know there have been six to eight rapes around Riverton in the last year. But I have to defer the details to my detective John Griffin. He tracks sexual attacks here and in the area. I hope we can help."

Bill continues, "I understand chief. How many police are in your department?"

Don answers Bill, "We have thirty at present."

Bill says, "I understand why you need to depend on other members of the force. I hope we can help your department. The math program we are using to identify suspects can be used by other departments to identify suspects."

Don says, "Sound interesting. Susan will connect you to John Griffin. I have a meeting in about ten minutes. Hope we can help. Have a good day. Stay on the line, while Susan transfers the call."

Bill replies, "You have a good day."

Don busses Susan. He says, "Susan transfer Bill to John Griffin and gives him John's phone number."

Susan punches the phone and connects to Bill. She says, "Bill let me give you John Griffin's number." She gives Bill the number. She transfers Bill to John's phone.

The phone rings. John answers, "This is John Griffin, detective. How can I help you?"

Bill speaks, "I am Bill Simpson. I am a sergeant with the New Hampshire State Police. I have identified a rapist that the Attorney General here in New Hampshire believes that he is living in Riverton. I need various help from your department."

John replies, "Do you need us to find and arrest him."

Bill continues, "We probably will, but first I need some information on rapes near Riverton in the last year. The AG here has definitely found that the suspect has lived in Riverton for the last year. This has been done with the utmost legal care."

John interjects, "What do you need from me? I am always ready to help identify and catch sexual predators."

Bill continues, "Bear with me while I explain the details and ask for specific help. There are at least fifteen rapes in New Hampshire and Maine with matching DNA. That is the same suspect. A person with the same name was residing within 25 to 40 miles of each rape at the time of the rapes. Using a math program and good police work we have identified the suspect. The AG traced the suspect to South Carolina about eighteen months ago and then to Riverton about twelve months ago. Yesterday the police in Mudville, South Carolina, verified that a rape that was committed by a suspect matching the physical characteristic of our suspect. We are going to verify if the DNA matches. While the suspect was residing in New Hampshire and Maine he committed fifteen rapes. If the DNA in South Carolina rape matches the DNA in the rapes in New Hampshire and Maine mathematical probability rules out other suspects. If the same suspect committed a rape near Riverton then the probability we have the correct suspect increases somewhat more. The AG believes we have enough evidence to request an arrest warrant, but we are just adding a little more evidence to the case."

John responses, "There were several rapes in the last twelve months. Let me get the files. But several of the rapes are not in my jurisdiction. What are the physical characteristics of your suspect?"

Bill thinks and feels it is OK to provide the characteristics. He speaks, "The guy is white, with brown hair and is about thirty five. Do you have any suspect that fit that profile?"

John answers, "There was a rape about five months ago in Coalton and rapist had those characteristic. The police department is a small department. They called us about the rape and the evidence including DNA. The state police ran DNA as far as I know. Here is the phone number of the state policeman that handled the case. John tells Bill the number of the state police detective that handled the case. Call them and they should provide the DNA. I will check the other cases here, but I cannot remember any cases in the last twelve months with those physical characteristics."

Bill says, "Thank you, John. I will be in touch. Have a good day."

John says, "You have a good day, also."

They hang up.

Bill calls Linda. The phone ring four times and Linda answers, "Hi, Bill. Is there any news?"

Bill replies, "Yes. In Tennessee at the town of Coalton there was a rape. The rapist generally fits the physical characteristics of our rapist. Need you to call the state police and get the DNA for their suspect."

Linda replies, "I will call as soon as we hang up. If we have a match after Mattie checks the DNA she can call us later today."

Bill says, "Good. Have a good day Linda. I am sure Mattie will call me if the DNA is a match."

Linda replies, "You have a good day, Bill."

Saturday morning Bill does some shopping at the local grocery store and meat market. He takes the groceries home and then goes to the office. He arrives at about 11 AM. The desk sergeant looks up as Bill enters and says, "Mattie called. She said there is good news about the rape in Coalton. Where is Coalton? I have never heard of it."

Bill is getting coffee and replies, "Coalton is in Tennessee. Our suspect in the one case is living near there now."

The desk sergeant responses, "We are solving cases for Tennessee now?"

Bill answers, "The AG traced our suspect to Tennessee. We thought that during the last year he might have continued his criminal activates in Tennessee. Apparently he has. There is another case in South Carolina. What the information confirms is that there is a very high probability we have the right guy. That is why it is good news."

The sergeant continues, "Your friend, Mattie is really good."

Bill continues, "Linda at the AG's office tracked the guy to South Carolina and Tennessee. Mattie and Linda are confirming we have the right guy. I am surrounded by smart women."

The sergeant continues, "Oh, Mattie said she would be over at about Noon."

Bill starts towards his office and says, "OK."

Bill sits down with the coffee and picks up the Portland paper from yesterday. He reads a couple more articles until Mattie arrives. He hears Mattie come in. Looks at his watch and sees it is 12:05.

Mattie speaks to the sergeant, "Hi, how are you today?

He replies, "I am fine Mattie. I told Bill the good news. He explained to me why it is good news. He is in his office. How are you?"

Mattie answers, "I am fine. I am going to get some tea and join Bill."

The desk sergeant says, "OK. It is funny how we guys like coffee. My wife is like you, she likes tea."

Mattie walks in to Bill's office and says, "How are things?"

Bill replies, "They are fine. I got some groceries this morning. Then I came here. How are you?"

Mattie continues, "I am fine. The sergeant told me that he gave you the good news. Linda thinks it is very good news for us. The commission of a rape is not good news, but the DNA matching is good for our case and the identification of our suspect."

Bill replies, "I obviously understand. Crime is not good news, but catching the right suspect is."

Mattie continues, "A few more names for the other three cases arrived this week. I, or should I say Sandra compiled them in the spreadsheets, but did nothing else about those cases. There were no new names related to the Nottingham Harbor cases."

Bill continues, "Linda may want me to go to Tennessee with the arrest warrant. I do not have any jurisdiction in Tennessee, but being there will influence the local team to do it right. Once there is an extradition hearing and a ruling, I will have two state police transport the guy back here."

Mattie says, "That's OK. As long as I don't have to get involved"

Bill says, "There is NO need for your involvement."

Mattie continues, "See you about 7. Have a good day."

Bill says, "OK. See you about 7."

Mattie leaves. She waves to the sergeant on the way out.

Bill fusses around the office a little and then goes home. Mattie and Bill go to dinner in Concord.

Linda calls about 10 AM on Tuesday morning. Bill answers, "Sergeant Bill Simpson here. How can I help you?

Linda replies, "Bill this is Linda. How are you?"

Bill answers, "Fine. How are you, Linda?"

Linda answers, "I am fine. Have some news. I am going to get an arrest warrant for Richard Robinson. The AG is going to pay your way and reimburse your time to make a trip to Tennessee. Make arrangements to go on Wednesday and return next Monday. You are just there to observe, but if you get a public DNA sample it won't hurt. I will give you all the information about where he is working and living. I will send down warrants on Friday. Can you do this?"

Bill says, "Yes. I did a similar thing a number of times in the past."

Linda continues, "I will have the travel people here make arrangements for you to fly from Augusta Maine to Knoxville, Tennessee. They will make arrangement for a rental car. They will call you in a little while for your personal information. Have a good trip and definitely call back with any and all relevant information."

Bill replies, "I will. Good bye."

Linda answers, "Good bye Bill."

The travel agent calls and Bill provides the necessary information.

Bill calls Carl Kramer in Nottingham Harbor. When Carl answers Bill says, "Carl, this is Bill Simpson. I have some good news and some less popular news. It is not necessarily bad news. I am making a trip to Tennessee to arrest the suspect in the Grindal series of cases. It is good news from two points of view. First the math technique has worked. Second good news is these rapists are definitely serial rapists. The less popular news is we will need to postpone our meeting with the Mayor. You cannot tell the Mayor or Erin the details."

Carl responds, "Mums the word. Thank you for the heads up. I will tell the Mayor you need to go out of town. It is a minor emergency.'

Bill says, "Thank you."

Carl responds, "Have a safe trip."

Bill replies, "Thank you. See you in about a week."

Carl says, "OK."

They hang up.

Bill walks back to his office. At about 4:30 he calls Mattie.

The phone rings four times and Mattie answers, "Good Afternoon, Bill. How are you today?"

Bill replies, "I am fine, Mattie. How are you?"

Mattie continues, "I am fine, also. What is up?"

Bill continues, "The AG and Linda are sending me to Tennessee tomorrow, Wednesday, and I will be returning on Monday. I am only an observer and will be working with the local police to arrest the suspect, Richard Robinson. I am going to try on Wednesday, Thursday, and Friday to obtain a public DNA sample. Linda says she will be forwarding the arrest warrants and subpoena for a DNA sample by Friday. We will probably do the arrest on Monday morning. Linda is coordinating with the local authorities. Linda says the local court should hold this guy until the DNA is tested. Anyway it will be interesting as usual."

Mattie says, "How dangerous is it?"

Bill answers, "For me not very since I am an observer. I won't be breaking down doors or anything like that."

Mattie Says, "I will say a prayer that you and the locals will be safe. I always worry."

Bill replies, "Yes, I know you do. We will have to skip doing anything this weekend, but I will call you from Tennessee. I postponed a meeting with the Mayor of Nottingham Harbor and Carl Kramer until I return."

Mattie replies, "I did get a couple of E-mails this morning, but have not had time to include them into the spreadsheets. I will talk to you tomorrow. Good bye."

Bill continues, "Good Bye, Mattie. Love you."

They hang up. Bill sits for several minutes and then gets ready to leave. As he goes out he says, "Sandra, have a good evening. Hold the fort down."

Sandra replies, "Serge you have a good evening."

Bill leaves and heads for home. After eating some dinner he packs for the trip.

On Wednesday Bill arrives at about six. Barney comes in a few minutes after six. Barney says, "Serge, are you ready to go to Augusta."

Bill answers, "Yes, the flight is 10:15AM."

They leave for Augusta.

Bill and Barney chit-chats as they drive to Augusta. As they approach the Airport Barney asks, "Which Airline?"

Bill answers, "Southwest."

Barney pulls up in front of the Southwest sign. He says, "Have a good trip, serge."

Bill answers, "I hope so. You have a safe trip back to Concord. See you next week. I will call the office when I know which day I will be back. Can you come and get me?"

Barney replies, "Sure serge. See you then."

CHAPTER 14

THE TRIP TO TENNESSEE.

Bill gets out and walks into the airport building. He stops at the ticket counter and checks his bag. He takes a book from the bag before checking it. He walks to security. And then to the gate."

The flight to Knoxville is uneventful. Bill arrives at Knoxville. He picks up his bag at the carousel along with the other passengers. Bill walks to the rental car counter and picks up the car. He drives to Riverton. He first goes to the motel and checks-in. He checks the information from Linda about where the suspect is living and working. The suspect is not living or working too far from the motel. He drives to the place where the suspect is living and then to the place where he is working. It is a housing development with several dozen houses. He observes there is a small café or coffee shop on the main road near the work site. When he was in Boston he managed to observe a suspect going to a similar café for breakfast. He was able to pick up a cigarette butt from the can outside the door and thus had a public DNA sample. It gave them a temporary positive identification on that suspect. Maybe he can do a similar thing here.

He drives to the Riverton Police headquarters. At the desk Bill introduces himself and asks to see John Griffin. The desk Sergeant calls John. When John answers he says, "I have Sergeant Bill Simpson from New Hampshire here to see you."

John replies, "Please send him in."

Bill goes in. John is standing at his desk and motioned to Bill. John and Bill have never met before face to face. Bill goes over to the man standing. When he gets closer Bill can see John's nametag. Bill says, "Good Afternoon, John. How are you?'

John replies, "I am fine. How are you and how was the flight from New Hampshire?"

Bill continues, "I am fine and the flight was uneventful. I am here to observe. I recognize I have no jurisdiction here. I do know what the guy looks like from his driver's license."

John asks, "Do you know where he is living and working?"

Bill replies, "Yes. Linda Smyth the assistant to the AG in New Hampshire has located the suspect from employment and tax records. Here are the addresses. Linda is sending the arrest Warrant on Friday and a subpoena for a DNA sample. I assume the District Attorney here will want to check the paper work before authorizing the arrest. The suspect has no idea we know who he is. We can move slower and be sure we are doing it by the book."

John continues, "If we get the paper work on Friday, then we should be able to arrest the suspect on Monday at the latest."

Bill continues, "OK. I would appreciate a call when you are going to arrest Richard Robinson. I will let you do all the work. I will just observe for the AG of New Hampshire. We want this guy. We need to be sure the arrest and subsequent arraignment are done legally. Everything should go fine. This is why the AG's in New Hampshire and Maine have confidence in my ability to check on things concerning this arrest."

John continues, "See you when we make the arrest."

Bill responds, "See you then." Bill leaves the police department building and returns to his room at the motel. After a little cleanup Bill stops by the office and asks the desk clerk about a restaurant. The clerk says, "About two blocks over on the main drag is Kathy's. Kathy's is a good family style restaurant. About six blocks further is a Sam's Pub. The beer is OK, but the food is marginal. About three miles further are three very good restaurants, but they are expensive."

Bill replies, "Kathy's sound OK for tonight." Bill gets into his car and drives to the restaurant. At about 8 PM he returns to the motel and prepares for bed. He sets the alarm for 5:30 AM. He wants to be at the café near Richard's worksite by 7 AM.

The next morning Bill gets up and leaves the motel at about 6:30 AM. He parks on the street where he can see the parking lot of the café and waits. Several cars arrive and park. None of the drivers are Richard. A pickup arrives. It could be Richard. Bill gets out and starts toward the café. He tries to time his approach to arrive at the door when Richard reaches the door. Richard snuffs out a cigarette in the ash can next to the door. He holds the door for Bill. Bill drops his car keys next to the ash can. He says, "I dropped my keys." Bill holds on to one edge of the ash can. Richard goes into the café. Bill picks up the cigarette with the glove on his left hand. As he pulls the glove over the cigarette he puts it into his coat pocket. He goes into the café. He sits at the counter away from the suspect Richard. He orders breakfast. Richard is eating breakfast. Bill does not look over to where Richard is sitting. He does not want to tip his concern. Richard gets up and leaves. Bill stays so as not to attract any attention. Final Bill leaves after paying the bill. He goes to his car. He checks where the local post office is located. He drives to the post office. He puts the glove and cigarette into a small bag before going into the post office. He picks up a small flat rate box and puts it together. He puts the bag into box and seals it. He looks in the small address book he has in his pocket. He addresses the box to Linda. He pays the postage. He goes back to the motel. He waits until 9:30 before calling Linda. He relaxes the remainder of the day.

On Friday Linda has a rush place on the package with the cigarette from Bill to obtain a DNA analysis. The Lab comes through by Friday afternoon. The preliminary DNA from the cigarette butt is a match for the rapist DNA. Linda calls Bill and tells him the result. This DNA is not going to be used in evidence, but it gives the Attorney General and Linda confidence to seek a warrant for Richard Robinson's arrest. Linda gets the Judge in Concord to issue the warrant and a subpoena for a DNA sample after Richard is arrested. Linda talks to the local district attorney in Tennessee and the Chief in Riverton about the delivery of the subpoena and warrant.

Linda calls Bill, "Linda this is Bill. What's up?"

Linda responds, "The cigarette had the Grindal rapist DNA on the butt. The judge has issued a subpoena for an official DNA test and an arrest Warrant."

Bill says, "That is very good news."

Linda continues, "After the local DA checks the paper work you should be ready to execute the arrest."

Bill continues, "We should proceed with the arrest on Monday."

Linda continues, "Ok. I will talk to you on Monday."

Bill responds, "Fine. I will call once the arrest has occurred. Good bye until Monday."

Linda comments, "Be careful Bill. Good bye till Monday."

Bill calls Mattie on Saturday.

Mattie answers the phone, "Hi, Bill."

Bill says, "Did Linda tell you, I got a public DNA sample. Robertson is our guy."

Mattie says, "That's good news."

Bill continues, "Linda is sending an arrest warrant and a subpoena for DNA. The arrest should happen on Monday."

Mattie says, "Great. You should be home by Tuesday. I have missed you."

Bill says, "Same here. Love you. So until Tuesday."

Mattie says, "I love you, too. Be careful, I want you back in one piece. Good bye."

Bill replies, "I will be careful. See you on Tuesday. Good bye."

They hang up.

Monday morning at 7:30 Bill arrives at the Riverton police Station. John Griffin is already there. John says, "Hi, Bill. We are ready to go. We are going to the housing development to perform the arrest. The DA has reviewed the documents from Linda Smyth. They are in order. I am taking two other officers with us. You know you are just an observer on this operation."

Bill replies, "Yes, I am aware I have no jurisdiction here."

John says, "You can ride with me. Fred and Kelly will be in the second car."

They go outside. Fred and Kelly are sitting in front of the station. John motions to them to follow. They do. It is only a few minutes to the housing development. John stops at the construction trailer. He goes in. Sally the woman at the desk says, "How can I help you?"

John says, "We are looking for Richard Robinson."

Sally gets up and walks outside. She says, "Please follow me." There is a time clock and a file cardholder on the wall. The shed is only partially covered. She looks at one of the cards. She says, "Mr. Robinson has not checked in yet. He should be here by 8:00 AM. He has to come by here to check in."

John says, "Thank you. Please do not say we are looking for him."

Sally replies, "I usually do not see the guys. They check in and go to the work site for the day."

John says, "We are going to wait behind the trailer."

He goes back to the cars. He says, "Fred, park behind the trailer." He gets in the car and pulls it behind the trailer. He says to Bill, "Richard is not here yet."

Bill says, "Since I am not in uniform, can I just stand near the side of the trailer and signal when I see him arrive."

John says, "I am going into the trailer. I would worry some body may consider you spotting for us as involvement."

John gets out and slowly walks around the trailer. He goes over to the cardholder and removes Richard's card and takes it into the trailer. He says to Sally, "If there is no card in the holder will Richard come in here."

Sally answers, "He should."

John flips the radio open and says, "Fred come on in and have Kelly get out and stay behind the trailer."

Fred answers, "Coming in." Fred and Kelly get out of the car. Bill gets out and stays with Kelly. Fred checks around the side of the trailer no one is there. He quickly goes into the trailer."

Sally is looking out the window next to her desk. She can see the front gate to the construction site. John says, "We are here to arrest Richard Robinson. Please stay seated."

Sally replies, "Ok."

A few minutes go by. Several employees arrive and check in. Sally says, "I think the car that just came through the gate is Richard's."

The car stops and the driver gets out. John says, "I think you are correct." He flips the radio open and says to Kelly, "He just arrived."

When Richard gets out of the car and walks to the shed, he does not see his card. He turns and walks into the trailer. Fred is standing behind the door as he enters. John is standing in front of the door. Richard says as he enters, "Where is my time card Sally?"

John says, "Are you Richard Robinson?"

Richard answers, "Yes."

John says, "Mr. Robinson you are under arrest. Turn around and place your hands behind your back."

Richard realizes that Fred has slammed the door close behind him. He complies with John's command. John hand cuffs him and says, "We have a Warrant for your arrest from New Hampshire. We also have one from Tennessee."

John flips the radio open and says, "Kelly you and Bill can come in. It is over."

Richard says, "Why am I being arrested? Please go outside and I will explain the charges."

They go outside. John says to Richard, "The arrest warrant is for a number of rapes you alleged committed in New Hampshire and Maine. Bill here a represents the Attorney Generals of New Hampshire and Maine. We have an arrest warrant for a rape in Tennessee. We are going to read you your rights. When we return to the police station you can read the warrant with the list of charges. You have the right to remain silent. The Tennessee District attorney will meet us at the police station and get you an attorney if you want one."

Richard says, "I definitely want one."

John says, "I have to ask one question that does not directly have anything to do with your arrest. Is that your vehicle with the engine running?"

Richard answers, "Yes."

John says, "I am going to have my fellow officer drive it back to the police station."

Richard says, "That is OK."

They all leave. Kelly drives Richard's car to the police station.

When they arrive back at the police station the Assistant District Attorney, Tara Willson, is waiting. John takes Richard into an interregration room. Tara enters. John says, "Tara, Mr. Richard Robinson was placed under arrests about fifteen minutes ago. He was read his rights before Fred, Kelly, Bill Simpson, and I. Bill is the consultant from the AG's office in New Hampshire and Maine. He witnessed the process, but did not participate. Also Mr. Robinson has requested an attorney in front of the four of us. Tara says, "Thank you, John."

Tara speaks, "I will call an attorney here in Riverton to represent you in any interrogation. The arrest warrant alleges you committed a number of rapes in New Hampshire and Maine. There is also an arrest warrant for a rape you allegedly committed here in Tennessee. That is why we arrested you. I am not going to ask you any questions about the charges. John is going to lock you in a cell. When the attorney arrives you will be brought back here for questioning. You will be given time to talk with the attorney in private. Do you understand this?"

Richard says, "I understand what you have told me."

Tara says, "Good. Are you on any medication that we need to be aware of.

Richard says, "No"

John takes Richard to a cell. He lets Richard get a drink of water.

Tara goes to the front desk and calls the attorney.

Bill goes out to the front desk with John. Bill says, "Thank You."

John says to Bill, "Call the AG in New Hampshire and tell her we arrested him and she should contact Tara. He turns to Tara and says, "Better give Bill your contact information."

Tara replies, "Ok. I have already talked to Linda and gave her my contact information. I will give it to Bill also."

The next few days are in the hands of the attorneys. At the advice of his attorney Richard waves an extradition hearing. The New Hampshire state police pick him up on Friday and return him to New Hampshire.

CHAPTER 15

THE NEXT PHASE

Richard Robinson the alleged rapist in the fifteen or more rapes has been extradited to New Hampshire and Maine for trial. The story has been on the news all over New England. Bill is trying to keep from identifying Mattie by name. He is worried that one of the other suspects could target her. Suddenly the towns where the other rapes occurred are more interested in providing names and locations for their particular case. The police all over New Hampshire, Vermont, and Maine realize the method that Bill and his consultant and the assistant to the AG are utilizing is producing positive results. In the first week Mattie has received 800 new names from the various towns. Mayor Bernard asks Erin to call Bill and invite him to meeting on Tuesday. He wants Carl, Ed, and Charlie in the meeting also.

Bill arrives at the mayor's office at 1:30. As he enters he says, "Good afternoon Erin. How are you today?"

She replies, "I am fine, Bill. How are you?"

Bill answers, "I am fine, also. Is the Mayor in?'

She buzzes the Mayor, "Bill is here."

George answers, "send him in."

Erin says to Bill, "Go right in."

Bill walks into the Mayor's office and says, "Good afternoon George. How are you today?"

George answers, "I am fine. How are you?'

Bill responds, "I am fine." He sees Carl is already in the office. Bill says, "Hi, Carl. How are you?"

Carl answers, "I am fine, Bill. How are you? And how is Mattie?"

Bill answers, "I am fine. She is fine also."

Erin calls on the intercom. "Ed Woodworth and Charlie Wilson are here. Should I send them in?"

George responds, "Send them in."

Ed and Charlie come in and exchange pleasantries with George, Bill and Carl.

George continues, "You caught the one alleged rapist responsible for sixteen rapes."

Bill replies, "Yes. I have much news, but I am sure you have heard much of it already."

The mayor replies, "Congratulations on the success. Even though it is not the rapist from here it is good to get these Bastards off the street."

Bill replies, "Yes. But I have good news about the Nottingham Harbor case and the sixteen related cases. I also have good news about the three other suspects we have been trying to identify. None of this has been on the news for obvious reasons. As you probably heard I side stepped any questions about the case in Nottingham Harbor. The AG and I do not want to spook the guy if possible. So be vague about any questions. It is simply we do not want to chase these guys half way around the world. Just remember what it will cost to chase any one of these guys across the country. We are not quite ready to identify a specific suspect. Remember when we discussed the situation about catching this guy Richard Robinson. He was not the Nottingham Harbor suspect. I mentioned that catching anyone of these guys with the technique we are using would change the game. It has. We have received over 800 new names with locations and other related information in just the last week. The information relates to the other four groups of cases. Nottingham harbor is now our top priority. Mattie is processing the names. We are meeting tomorrow to discuss the information. However the amount of information is going to take a couple of weeks to sort out and organize. As you know Mattie teaches summer school this year and cannot abandon the kids and her teaching. We got information from all the other towns with the same suspect as Nottingham Harbor. We have also had calls from some of the towns about where to send more information. So I believe there will be more names coming over the next couple of weeks. We need to keep all this information confidential. If you pass on any of this information to the council members emphasize the confidentiality and the cost of not maintaining strict confidentiality if the information spooks the suspects."

The mayor says, "I understand the confidentiality as related to the cases. I do want to tell the council something interesting and good about the Nottingham Harbor group of cases."

Carl doesn't say anything he looks toward Bill for an answer.

Bill says, "Mattie, Linda, and Vivian believe we have a suspect, an alleged rapist, for the Nottingham Harbor group of cases. We are in the process of confirming various pieces of information. We are close to making an arrest. We are doting the 'I's and crossing 'T's. We want to be absolutely sure everything is absolutely legal."

George replies, "I will emphasize confidentiality, but I do need to tell the council we are making good progress. A couple of them asked how come you caught the rapist from the other town and not the Nottingham Harbor."

Bill replies, "Tell them the truth. We got lucky on the other case. The information simply identified him first. It did exactly what the AG and us believed would happen. It spurred on a lot of the local police to find and provide information on the other cases including the one here in Nottingham Harbor. We are putting a priority on the Nottingham Harbor cases, but from the amount of information we have received we may identify the suspect in the other three groups of cases simultaneously. This will not interfere with the Nottingham Harbor case, but will get us a lot of help from the state police and from each of the AG's. I think you realize this will be very good politically. Emphasize that the council members need to keep their respective mouths closed until the announcements of the capture of the suspects. Then you and they can brag about how everyone supported the effort. I obviously will not contradict whatever you guys say about the support. George, you and the politicians can handle the politics."

George answers, "Thank you. When are you meeting with Mattie?"

Bill answers, "Tomorrow, Please do not mention Mattie's name when discussing this. I am worried she could become a target of one of these guys because of her involvement. I may have Sandra my assistant move in with Mattie or Mattie move in with Sandra until this is over. You understand my concern."

George replies, "I understand. Having Sandra and your assistant staying together may be a good idea. If you think it is necessary then do it. Mattie is too nice and good to be hurt by any of this."

Bill says, "Thank you. I do love her. The AG is arranging to do this if necessary. Carl, do you or Ed have anything to add."

Ed adds, "Richard Robinson has been arraigned in Maine as well as in New Hampshire. I think he is going to plead out in Maine. Have you heard about New Hampshire?"

Bill responds, "Not as of this morning."

Carl asks, "You have many more names for Nottingham Harbor cases?"

Bill answers, "Yes. There are over 800 new names from all across the three states. We also got some DNA information and sketches. My assistant, Sandra, and Mattie are entering the data and will sort it soon. I am not sure how many names are related to each of the remaining four cases."

Carl says, "I actually found a few more names directly for Nottingham Harbor. There is a small Bread and Breakfast two exits to the East on I-95. I realized I had not checked before."

Bill responds, "More is better in this case. I will communicate with all of you as soon as I have an improved list from the ladies. Have a good day. Secrecy is the watch word."

Ed says, "I will be talking to all of you also. Have a good day."

Charlie says, "None of the rapes committed by the guy responsible for the Grindal cases were in Vermont. Also none of the rapes committed by the Nottingham Harbor rapist were committed in Vermont. However for the other three groups of cases there were rapes in Vermont. So I want these guys as much as you guys. I am waiting my turn."

Carl says, "Have a good day, guys."

Charlie says, "All have good day, also."

George says, "Good work Gentleman. Keep it up."

Bill leaves and as he passes Erin, he says, "Erin have good afternoon.'
Erin says, "You to Bill."
Carl, Charlie, and Ed say good afternoon also.
Carl returns to the police department.
Ed heads up to the East to his Barracks.
Charlie heads to his Barracks in Vermont.
Bill returns to Concord.
Thursday and Friday pass without much happening.

SATURDAY IN THE SECOND WEEK OF JUNE

Bill arrives at Mattie's house about ten in the morning. Mattie answers the door. She sees it is Bill and unlocks the dead bolt on the door. She says as she opens the door. "Come on in Bill. I have some coffee ready. I am going to get some Bacon and Toast ready. You like Jelly with your toast? Do you want an egg?"

Bill replies, "I can skip the egg. How are you this morning?"

Mattie continues, "I am fine. How are you?"

Bill answers her, "I am fine."

Mattie was sitting at the dining room table working on the computer before Bill arrived. Bill sits down at the dining room table as Mattie walks to the kitchen. She says, "Breakfast will be ready soon."

Bill answers, "Take your time. We have all day. I talked to George on Wednesday at his office. Carl, Charlie, and Ed were there also. We discussed the general progress and all the additional names that have and are coming in from different towns. Although the mayor is not my primary concern, he is politically connected and it is good to keep him happy."

Mattie continues as she sits some butter and jelly on the table, "I think we have 900 new names with detailed information attached. It is good in one way but it is slightly overwhelming."

Mattie continues fixing breakfast. Bill can hear the bacon frying. Mattie is making herself an omelet. She walks back in with the silverware. Bill says' "Can I help?"

Mattie answers, "Relax. I have it under control."

Several minutes pass. Several more trips to and from the kitchen and breakfast is ready. Mattie returns from the kitchen and walks around to the side of the table where Bill is seated. She bends down and kisses him. He returns the kiss. Mattie sits down on the end of the table. She says, "Let's say grace before breakfast. I would tell the kids it is a prayer to start the day." Bill joins his hands and joins her in a simple grace before they start to eat.

Mattie says as she begins to eat, "It is going to take all next week to catalogue the new names. I hope Linda, Jane and Vivian can wait that long. I think George is more anxious. Several of the police and mayors in the small towns are also anxious."

Bill replies, "They have to wait."

Mattie continues, "The news of the arrest had the effect we expected."

Bill answers, "It is interesting that suddenly all the other towns began to search for more names. It was a great motivation."

Mattie continues, "Is the toast and bacon OK."

Bill answers her, "Great."

They both sit there eating slowly and smiling at each other without saying anything. Bill gets up and makes a second cup of coffee. He says, "Mattie do you want another tea?"

Mattie answers, "Not now. I will get another a little later."

As they finish breakfast, Bill helps Mattie clear the table. Mattie says, "I have put a few of the names on the computer so far."

Bill replies, "Can you use help?"

Mattie answers, "Yes, I can use some help. Maybe Sandra can type the information into a file. I do have to teach summer school all week. I can give her a dummy file for her to enter the data. I can then copy the data into the primary spreadsheet."

Bill says, "Let me call the office and see if Sandra is there today. Are you ready to give her the data?"

Mattie answers, "Yes. She can make a dummy file and enter the data in the correct columns."

Bill calls the office. The phone ring several times. Sandra answers, New Hampshire State Police, Officer Davenport here. How can I help you, Bill?"

Bill speaks, "I am over at Mattie's house to look at all the data we have received. There are 800 to 900 new names with associated data. Can you help type the data into a spreadsheet file?"

Sandra answers, "I can type the data. I need to know Mattie wants the same format we have used for the other data."

Bill continues, "Let me put Mattie on the phone."

He hands the phone to Mattie. Mattie takes the phone and says, "Sandra, how are you today?"

Sandra answers, "I am fine Mattie. How are you?"

Mattie replies, "I am fine. You are familiar with the column headings. I think you have most of the E-mails. I have the letters with about 200 names. I will give them to you. Do you want us to come over to the office or would you like to come here?"

Sandra answers, "I will drive over now."

Mattie replies, "Yes, Do you know where I live?

Sandra answers, "I know where you live. I will be there in half an hour"

Mattie responds, "See you in half an hour. Drive carefully. Goodbye."

They both hang up.

Mattie turns to Bill, "Sandra is coming over."

Bill answers, "OK. Do you need help with the dishes?"

Mattie answers, "No, read until Sandra arrives."

In about 20 minutes, Mattie comes into the living room. She says, "I have finished the dishes. I am going to the dining room and prepare a file for Sandra."

Bill says, "OK."

Fifteen minutes pass and the doorbell rings. It is obviously Sandra. Bill goes to the door. He does check to be sure it is Sandra before he opens the door. It is just a habit from being a careful cop. He says, "Come in, Sandra."

Sandra replies, "Hi, Bill."

He says, "Mattie is in the dining room. Come with me. He shuts the door.

Sandra says, "OK. Lead the way."

Mattie has moved to the sun porch. Sandra walks in and says, "Hi, Mattie."

Bill says, "I will leave you two to discuss the data and the files."

Mattie says, "Hi, Sandra. Grab the chair."

Sandra sits down and Bill returns to the living room.

Mattie and Sandra work on the files and the data for about a half an hour. Finally the ladies return to the living room. Mattie gets Sandra a paper bag for the regular letters. Bill says, "Are you all organized?"

Mattie replies, "Yes, I believe we are organized."

Sandra says, "Yes, I can help with this. Bill you are OK with me doing this in the office?"

Bill answers, "I am fine with you doing it in the office. You may have to interrupt the typing from time to time to take care of a more pressing problem, but this is a priority otherwise. We want to solve the rape cases."

Bill continues, "I do want both of you to consider another idea. I am a little worried about Mattie's safety because of her involvement in the rape cases. I may have to ask you to move in with Mattie if there is some threat from one of the suspects. I know this is a surprise to both of you. We can discuss the possibility."

Sandra and Mattie are both surprised by Bill concern. Sandra says, "I can if it is Ok with Mattie. Do you really think a threat is likely?"

Mattie says, "Never considered the possibility of a serious threat. I am OK with Sandra staying here."

Bill replies, "Just take it under advisement for now."

Sandra says, "Goodbye, I will see you Monday, Bill. I will be talking to you, Mattie." She goes to the door and Mattie follows and says, "Have a good day, Sandra."

Bill and Mattie talk about the list of names for a little time. Finally they go to lunch in Concord. Bill stops by the office for a few minutes after lunch. He drives Mattie home. They make a date for dinner at about

7PM. The rest of the weekend goes by without any serious incidents for Bill to handle. The next week passes quickly. Sandra gets most of the names entered and the information checked. Mattie has to concentrate on her school class. Saturday morning is very nice when Mattie arrives at Bill's office. Bill and Sandra are already in the office. Mattie greets Sandra as she enters, "Hi, Sandra. Thank you for the lists you send me yesterday by E-mail."

Sandra replies, "You are welcome. I still have more names and information to enter. I will be finished next week. The list of new names has slowed down."

Mattie continues, "I did look at some of the information last night. Come on in. Join the discussion with Bill and I."

Sandra answers, "OK."

She walks into Bill's office.

Bill says, "Good morning."

Mattie and Sandra reply, "Good morning, Bill"

Bill asks, "How are the lists coming?"

Mattie replies, "Very good. Sandra has most of the information entered and I sorted some of it. I will wait to make any decisions until all the names are in the file. We will be slightly behind the name data entry because more names keep coming in every day. However most of the names are going to be in the list by next week."

Sandra confirms Mattie's answer, "I have about 80% entered and should finish by Wednesday."

Bill says, "That sounds good. I am not trying to pressure either of you, but I am curious about the results. George is probably anxious about the Nottingham Harbor results also."

Mattie continues, "We have names from every town associated with the Nottingham Harbor case. But I have not identified a suspect as of last night. I may be able to complete the sorting by tomorrow some time. We do have names from most of the other towns involved with the three other groups of cases. I will do a more careful sort when I get home and over the next few days. I do need to grade tests for my class and prepare for next week. Summer school moves very fast."

Bill says, "You have to do the necessary work for your school class. We have time."

Mattie replies, "I am doing the school work first."

Sandra interjects, "I will continue entering the names onto the lists"

Bill says, "I believe we just need to continue. I do not have much to do until we identify suspects."

The next week passes like normal. Mattie is able to devote three evenings to the data reduction. Sandra finishes entering the remaining names including a few that arrive on Tuesday. Bill and Barney concentrate on the normal business of the state police department.

Bill arrives on Saturday about 10 AM. Sandra is already at the office. As Bill enters he says, "Good morning Sandra."

Sandra replies, "Good morning serge. Is Mattie coming today?'

Bill answers, "Yes. She should be here any minute. She told me last night that she has some interesting news." He goes to his office.

A few minute pass and Mattie arrives. As she enters, she says, "Good morning Sandra. How are you today?"

Sandra answers, "I am fine. How are you?

Mattie answers as she enters Bill's office, "I am fine." She continues, "Hi, Bill."

Bill answers, "Hi Mattie. How are you today?"

Mattie answers, "I am fine, Bill. How are you?"

Bill continues, "I am OK. I am anxious to hear the news." He calls to Sandra, "Sandra, please join us."

Mattie replies, "I sorted most of the names. On Nottingham Harbor group of cases I got a match for twelve of the sixteen towns. For four towns about eighty miles northeast of here I did not get a name match. It is like a hole in the data. In the second group of cases I got a single name match in fourteen towns. In the third group of cases I got two names in fourteen towns. The two names are missing from the same three towns. The fourth group of cases I have three suspects. I have to get with Linda and have her check the physical characteristics of each of these suspects from their driver license information. The good news is we do have a suspect or suspects that match to most of the rape cases."

Bill asks, "Why do you think there is this hole as you called it in the Nottingham Harbor cases?"

Mattie replies, "It could be we need more names from those towns. It could also be the suspect lives in the vicinity of those towns and did not need to stay at a local residence?"

Bill asks, "The twelve towns where there is a match to one suspect, what is his name?"

Mattie replies, "His name is Jeff Willison. I have to talk to Linda on Monday or you can talk to her. She can pull his driver license information."

Bill thinks for a few seconds and then continues, "A couple of years ago there was an accident in Nottingham Harbor. Carl told me about it. The driver of the one car was a Jason Willison. He had been at the pub, but was not intoxicated enough to be charged with DUI. The accident was not his fault the other driver came through a stop sign. Jason Willison lived near the area you are describing. However the fellow Jason was in his early seventies but is could be a relative of Jeff Willison. Sandra, Carl should have records on the accident?"

Sandra replies, "He should. I will call Carl. Should I do it now?"

Bill answers her, "Let's finish the discussion, then you can check. Mattie's idea, that the suspect lives in the area, may be a good guess."

Mattie continues, "That sounds like a good match for the Nottingham Harbor case. For the second case I have the name Gary Kipling. The data indicate he probably lives in New Hampshire, but works here and other places in New England. Again Linda should be able to get driver license data."

Bill injects, "So we have more or less firm suspects in two groups of cases."

Mattie continues, "Yes. I am going to talk to Linda, Jane and Vivian on Monday or Tuesday and have them run the names I have on the other two cases through the DMV. If I can get the physical characteristics from the driver license information it may narrow the suspect list. One of the names from the other two groups of cases is a firm suspect."

Bill continues, "We should talk to Linda first. From this point forward we need to be sure that all of our actions are strictly legal. The suspects are alleged suspects and Linda needs to verify any moves we make. I will have a discussion with Linda on Monday morning to verify any subpoenas we need. We all know that it is critical to be strictly legal and maintain confidentiality. If the guy in the Nottingham Harbor case is living where we suspect, then the state police can pursue an arrest. My self and the locals will simply be observers. It is Ed Woodworth's territory."

Sandra says, "I will call Carl about the information on the accident."

Mattie says, "Here are the names for all four groups of cases. I wrote confidential across the top of the pages to remind us how to handle the information."

Bill says, "Good idea. I do want you and Sandra to isolate yourselves from the cases. We never know how one of these guys will react to being arrested or pursued before the arrest."

Mattie and Sandra nod in agreement. Sandra gets up and goes to the outer office."

Bill continues; "I will be over at about 7 o'clock. We should celebrate the progress."

Mattie answers; "See you at 7 o'clock. Have a good rest of the day."

As Mattie leaves, she says, "Sandra, have a good day. See you soon."

Sandra replies, "Same to you."

Mattie and Bill go to dinner at Seabrook to celebrate the progress. Mattie's math background is really helping the progress."

Bill arrives Monday morning about 9 AM. Sandra greets him, "Bill, Carl found the information on the accident. He FAXED me the report. I put the report on your desk."

Bill replies, "Thank you. I am going to be busy calling Linda today."

Bill takes the list of the names Mattie identified from his desk. He looks in the Rolodex for Linda's office phone number. He should know it from memory, but he forgets it. He dials the number. The phone rings four times and then goes to Voice mail. "You have reached Linda Smyth, Assistant District Attorney in the Attorney General's office of New Hampshire. I am in court this morning. Please leave a message. It may be late afternoon before I can respond."

Bill speaks, "Linda this Sergeant Bill Simpson. We have identified suspects in the rape cases. There are seven names for the four groups of cases. We only have one name for the Nottingham Harbor group. Need you to check driver license information in order to check the physical profile of the suspects. Starting now the suspects are alleged suspects and we need to tighten the legal pursuit of information. We may need various subpoenas. I will talk to you later. We are treating the names as confidential for now. Hope you are having a good day."

Bill cannot do any more until Linda returns his call. He calls to Sandra. What do you know about the town of Willsburg where the guy Willison lives or lived?"

Sandra responds, "I looked up information on the town. The sheriff for the county and the chief of police are both named Willison. If our suspect is related to the sheriff or chief, we may need to be more discrete with inquires."

Bill answers, "Yes, very discrete. Linda is not going to be in her office till late in the day."

Bill calls the local state police barracks. He knows the captain personally. Captain James Burns answers the phone. After a polite exchange Bill begins, "Jim we have identified a number of suspects in the four groups of rape cases. I am going to need your help to arrest them once we have warrants from the AG."

Jim replies, "Are the suspects from Maine or living here?"

Bill answers, "I am not sure at this time about all the suspects. However the suspect in the Nottingham Harbor cases appears to reside in Maine. It turns out the local law enforcement has the same last name as our suspect. I am talking to Linda Smyth later today about subpoenas and other information. When she believes we are ready I can use your help for an arrest."

Jim replies, "I will help or at least the local state police will help. Let me know when you and we are ready to move."

Bill continues, "Thank you. I will be in touch. I am just giving you a heads up at this time. Have a good day, Jim.

Jim replies, "Bill you have a good day. I will be awaiting your call. See you soon."

Bill answers, "Likewise."

They both hang up.

Bill spends the rest of the day awaiting Linda's call. He goes to lunch." The afternoon passes slowly. Bill doses around three o'clock for fifteen minutes. Nothing is happening. He goes over to the diner for a piece of pie and coffee. As he returns Sandra says, "No one has called Bill."

Bill replies as he walks into his office, "Thank you."

It is four fifteen when the phone rings. Bill answers, "Sergeant Bill Simpson. How can I help you?"

Linda Smyth says, "This is Linda Smyth. I got your message. Can you fill me in on the suspects? I was in court on a robbery case until the Judge got tired of the Lawyers and recessed the trial till tomorrow."

Bill continues, "We have identified seven suspects. That is Mattie has identified the suspects in the other four groups of cases. There is a firm suspect in the Nottingham Harbor case. His name is Jason Willison. We need to confirm his general physical characteristics from his driver's license information. Then we will need to determine if we can get a public DNA sample. Then we will need an arrest Warrant. Any subpoena will be your call. We also need to verify his residence to pursue an arrest. One problem is the town where we believe he is living has a sheriff and chief of police with the same last name. The Maine state police will help with the arrest when we are ready to move. Ed Woodworth and Jake Burns are both on the task force."

Linda replies; "I will get one of my assistants to prepare all the information over the next couple of days. Do you believe there is a more urgent effort needed?"

Bill answers; "I do not believe the suspect knows we are on to him. He could commit another rape, but we have no way of knowing one way or another."

Linda responds, "We should have information by the end of the week. I will have it FAXED to you."

Bill says, "Thank you. The FAX is safer than the internet."

Linda continues, "How about the other names?"

Bill answers, "There are six names for the other three groups of cases. One group has only one name, but we believe he resides in New Hampshire from some of the motel information. There are two names for the third group of cases and three names for the fourth. Mattie has made a data sheet for all this information. Sandra my deputy is ready to FAX the sheets to you. I just wanted you to be in the office before we FAX the data."

Bill says, "let me tell Sandra to send the data sheets." Bill calls to Sandra, "Sandra, please FAX the suspect data sheets to Linda now."

Sandra responds, "Ok."

Bill returns to the phone call, "Linda the FAX is on the way."

Linda replies, "Hold for a few minutes while I go across the hall and get the FAX."

Bill says, "OK. I will hold."

Linda comes back in about four minutes. She says, "I have the FAX. I will get my assistant to work these names also. I will have her send the information to Sandra. She can forward it to Mattie.

Bill answers her, "Good Plan. I will talk to you later in week. Mattie or Sandra will also be in contact. Good-bye for now."

Linda replies, "Good-bye, Bill. Have a good evening." They both hang up.

Linda calls her assistant Beverly, "Bev can you come in here, please."

Beverly replies, "OK. But I need a minute to save the data on my computer."

Linda says nothing and waits until Beverly comes into her office. "Bev, I need you to take this list and search driver license records for the men on the list. You may need to call Jane and Vivian in Maine and Vermont.

I need their pictures and physical characteristics from the driver license data. We do not need a subpoena to obtain this information. However, I need for you to keep the reason for obtaining this information and the information confidential. DMV does not have a need to know. No one else has a need to know, except Jane and Vivian, what you are doing. Just report what you find to me only. You understand the information involves potential suspects in serious crimes."

Beverly replies, "I understand, Linda."

Linda hands Beverly a copy of the FAX. She says, "Some of the information should be helpful in locating the correct suspect."

Beverly looks at the list and says, "I should have the information in a few days possibly tomorrow. Is that quick enough?"

Linda replies, "A few days to obtain accurate information will be more than satisfactory."

Beverly leaves and Linda continues with other work.

Bill calls Mattie after he hangs up with Linda. Her phone goes to voice mail. Bill says, "I just FAXED Linda your list of suspects. She says she will have her assistant search the driver license records for more information about each of the suspects. Talk to you later."

Bill walks to the outer office. He says to Sandra, "There is not much I can do until the information from Linda arrives. If she calls have her FAX the information. No internet use on information about the potential suspects."

Sandra replies, "Right serge. I understand. NO leaks."

Bill continues, "I am going to walk outside for a few minutes."

Sandra replies, "OK."

A few days pass. Things are about the same every day. Linda sends a FAX that has the physical characteristics for five of the seven suspects provided by Mattie. Bill reads the FAX. The data for the suspect in the Nottingham Harbor case matches the characteristics described by the victims.

Bill calls Linda, "Linda this Bill Simpson. The suspect for the rape in Nottingham Harbor has the physical characteristics of the rapist described by the victim here and by the victims in several of the other towns. I think we got this guy. I would say we can issue a warrant for his arrest.'

Linda says, "I will start the paperwork and go to a judge for a warrant. As soon as I have a warrant we can call the Maine state police and proceed with an arrest. I will also get a subpoena for a DNA test."

Bill replies, "Thank you. I will wait to hear from you before we take any action. Have a good day."

Linda responds, "You have a good day, Bill."

They both hang up.

Bill calls Jim at the state police. The phone rings several times and Jim answers. "Captain Jim Burns, Maine state police, Bill how can I help you?"

Bill replies, "I think we got one, Jim."

Jim replies, "Good. I like to catch the bad guys. What are the details?"

Bill continues, "The guy's name is Jeff Willison. He and his father live in Willsburg. I understand the sheriff and the chief of police of Willsburg both have the last name of Willison. We will need to be extremely careful in dealing with the arrest."

Jim interjects, "The Willison's are protective of their little town. A couple of our people have run into the situation. I remember an incident several years ago involving a bar fight in Willsburg. At least one of the family members was involved. I will check on the incident. We may get lucky. There may be a blood sample at the local clinic. Linda Smyth could get a subpoena to check the DNA."

Bill continues, "I never considered the possibility that there is a blood sample that could be used to check the DNA."

Jim replies, "Some blood samples are kept for records and some are not. It is worth a try."

Bill says, "In any case we need to plan our strategy for the arrest. We will need to tell the sheriff and the chief before we proceed to arrest Jeff Willison."

Jim says, "We have to assume they will follow the law even in the case of a relative."

Bill replies, "When we arrive in town to make the arrest will be soon enough."

Jim replies, "Yes. I will arrange to take a couple of other officers from headquarters with us. I will also get several officers from nearer barracks to help. The local chief of police may not want to participate because it does involve family members. He may or may not be helpful. I am sure they will support a peaceful arrest for the protection of their family member."

Bill says, "As soon as I know the paperwork is available I will call you. I wanted you to know where we are in the process. Have a good day. Jim. Is Jake Burns a relative of yours?"

Jim replies, "Yes, he is a cousin of mine. Why?"

Bill says, "Jake is on the task force so he will be in on the arrest. Ed Woodworth is also on the task force. They will be joining us for the arrest."

Jim responds, "OK. I will plan for them to help on the arrest."

Bill says, "You can call them and talk to them about the arrest. They both know who the suspect is."

Jim responds, "You have a good day, Bill."

They both hang up.

Bill calls Linda again. The phone rings several times. Linda recognizes Bill's number as she answers, "Bill so soon."

Bill replies, "Yes, Linda I have some interesting information."

Linda says, "What have you found?"

Bill continues, "There was a fight in a bar a couple of years ago in Willsburg involving at least one of the Willison's.

According to Captain Jim Burns the participants ended up in the clinic. There may have been blood tests. The clinic may have kept samples for their own protection. If your tech can find the samples and the related data using a subpoena, we may be able to run a DNA analysis prior to the arrest."

Linda says, "That is interesting. Do we know the particulars?"

Bill continues, "Captain Jim Burns has the particulars and can provide them to your tech."

Linda continues, "I will have Bev call Jim."

Bill continues, "Thank You. Have good day."

Linda immediately has Bev contact Jim to follow upon Bill's information. Bev contacts the clinic. The clinic does not have any blood samples from the incident. There is no way to determine the DNA. Linda contacts Bill and Jim with the information. She also explains that Jane had the Judge in Augusta issue an arrest Warrant and a subpoena for the DNA test. It will be up to Bill and Jim to exercise the Warrant and Subpoena. After Jim talks with Bill they decide on the next morning.

Bill, Ed, Jake, and Jim will all drive separate vehicles. Jim makes arrangement to have several other officers in the surrounding area to be standing by on the radio in case the guy runs. The plan is to show up at the Willison farm at 9:00 AM.

Jim, Bill, and Jake show up at the Willsburg Police station. They ask for the chief. He invites them into his office.

The chief Martin Willison greets the party, "Good Morning gentlemen, how can I help you?"

Jim speaks, "We are here to arrest a suspect in a series of rapes. Unfortunately, you are related to the suspect. You are personally not involved in the crimes. We thought you might not want to participate in the arrest. However as local law enforcement, we are inviting you along.'

Chief Martin says, "Who is the suspect?"

Jim continues, "Jeff Willison. The information we have is he lives on a farm with his father. Is this correct?"

The chief answers, "Yes. The farm is about 5 miles to the East."

Jim continues, "How are you related to him?"

The chief answers, "His Father is my cousin. So Jeff is a second cousin."

Jim continues, "This is a state police matter, but you can come along. Since he is a relative you may be able to talk him into surrendering without violence. This is Bill Simpson. He is the a state policeman from New Hampshire. He is here as a member of a three state task force to identify and arrest criminals. One of the rapes occurred in his hometown. Several occurred in New Hampshire. The other person is Jake Burns of the Maine

State Police." There should be another state police, Virginia Keller already watching the farm. Several other officers are aware we are making the arrest."

The Chief continues, "Should I come with you or use my own car?"

Jim replies, "Can you take a deputy with you? You can use your car."

The chief replies, "I will take Sam my senior deputy."

Jim continues, "Let's roll. No sirens."

The five people head out of the office for their respective vehicles. The chief follows Jim at a reasonable distance."

In about eight minutes they arrive at the farm. Jim stops next to Virginia's car. He rolls the window down next on the passenger side of the SUV. Virginia rolls her window down. He says, "Virginia any activity?"

Virginia replies, "Nothing."

Jim continues, "Stay here in case someone comes out. If that happens try to block the gate."

Virginia replies, "OK. Jim. Be careful."

Jim pulls up to the gate on the driveway.

Bill steps out of his SUV and walks to the gate.

As he passes Jim he says, "I will get the gate."

Jake replies, "That is OK.

There is only a loop of rope holding the gate closed. He removes it from the post and swings the gate open. He motions to Jim, Jake and the chief to enter. There is a post on the fence that Bill can use to hold the gate open. Jim pulls the car near the house and to the right. The chief takes the left side. Jake and Bill pull into the middle area.

Jason the father is inside and sees what is going on outside. He dials his son's cell. The phone rings and Jeff answers. Jason says, "Jeff I do not know why the police are in the yard, but you better not come home. Are you in trouble? What did you do?"

Jeff says, "Lay the phone on top of the dish cabinet so I can hear what is going on. I will hang up if they want me. Love you pop."

Jason answers as he put the phone on the dish cabinet where it cannot be seen directly. "Love you too. Do what you have to do."

Bill is standing by the car. Jake and Jim approach the door. The chief and his deputy stand near their car. Jim turns and looks back. He is checking where the other people are standing. He likes the spread. He holds up his right hand and makes an OK sign with his thumb and forefinger. Jake and Jim stand to either side of the doorway. Jim wraps on the door and says in a load voice, "STATE POLICE. OPEN THE DOOR."

There is NO answer from inside. Jim repeats the command, "STATE POLICE. OPEN THE DOOR. WE HAVE A WARRANT FOR THE ARREST OF JEFF WILLISON."

From inside a voice says, "One second."

Finally the door opens. The person is obviously the father, Jason. He says, "Can I help you?"

Jim asks, "Can we come in?"

Jason replies, "Why?"

Jim continues, "We have a warrant to arrest your son Jeff. Is he home?"

Jason replies, "No. He is out working in one of the fields. He knows this is not strictly true. Jeff is some miles to the East. You can step inside." Jason realizes Jeff can probably hear them on the phone.

Jim starts the conversation, "We have this warrant for his arrest. In fact we have two warrants. One is from Maine and one is from New Hampshire. He allegedly committed a number of rapes. There is enough evidence for a judge in each state to issue these arrest warrant."

Jason replies, "My son is not a rapist"

Jeff is miles away but can hear this on his cell. He knows it is time to run. He hangs up the cell phone. He knows there is a side road about two miles to the East that leads to the Canadian border. The road is closed at the border. However he should be able to still escape. He knows there is a toolbox in the trunk. There are fields along the border. Cutting the fence will get him into Canada. He drives out of the store parking lot at normal speed and drives toward the side road. Even though he is on the run he is smart enough to control his speed and watch how he drives. About fifty minute pass and he can see the border. He stops and observes the border.

Nothing is moving. He gets out of the car and finds a pair of dykes in the toolbox. He watches for a few more minutes. There is no obvious motion on either side of the border. He thinks there may be an electric signal in the bobbed wire of the fence. He strips a couple of pieces of wire that are long enough to bridge the gap in the wire. He cuts the top wire and rolls it back. He carefully hangs it on the one post. He repeats the process for the second wire. He drives across the border. He makes a loop in the end and uses a short piece of his wire to tie it off at the post. He figures that if either of the border patrol personnel flies over the area the fence will look like it is not cut. He drives up the road on the Canadian side at nominal speed. Five miles in from the border the dirt road meets the highway. He turns on to the highway and heads northeast away from the border.

He has some friends further out the Atlantic Providences toward the Gaspe Peninsula. Hopefully he can stay with them a few days to formulate an escape plan. Two hours have passed, since his father called.

Martin Willison and Jim have searched several outbuildings and the barn. Bill has walked around the house and barn outside. There are three cars on the property. Neither of these cars is registered to Jeff. Jake calls headquarters and asked them put out an APB on Jeff and his car. He reminds the person at headquarters to notify the Canadian authorities to be on the lookout for Jeff and the car. Tell the Canadian Mounties that Jeff Willison is a fugitive and can be arrested and detained if located. The border patrol and border guards are notified. Several hours have passed by the time everyone is looking for Jeff and the car. By this time Jeff is about seventy-five miles east of the border. He is getting hungry and is going to need gas. He looks in the glove compartment and finds the envelope with some Canadian money. He gets to a small town. There is general store and an old gas station. He parks near several old cars and walks the two hundred feet to the store. He goes in gets several cold sodas, two packaged sandwiches, some chips, and couple of Danishes. He pays for the food with Canadian money. He heads back to the car. He opens one of the sodas and the one sandwich. He starts the car and pulls up to the road. He does see any police cars. So he turns on to the road and continues east. Twelve miles down the road there is a large town. There is a gas station. He still has some Canadian money. He walks into the station and checks the Map rack. He opens the one map and decides it will do to get to his friend's place. He folds it back together. The map is three dollars. He still has twenty-five Canadian dollars. He gives the clerk two tens and says he wants to buy twenty dollars of gas. He says, "How much is the map?"

The clerk responds, "Three forty with tax."

Jeff hands the clerk four dollars. Jeff asks, "Is there a bank in town with an ATM machine?"

The clerk answers, "Yes, about two city blocks down this main street."

Jeff thanks him. He goes outside and pumps the gas. He then drives to the bank. His need for more cash overrules his thought about someone tracking his account. His ATM card works and he get the limit of $500 Canadian. He pulls around behind the bank building. He opens the map. He locates the town. He sees a side road that heads south for about fifty miles to a larger town. He decides to follow the road south. If someone does access his bank account he thinks that using the ATM here and then again fifty miles to the South will leave a false trail. He checks the road and leaves the bank lot. He gets to the side road after going about a city block. He starts down the road. He obeys the speed limit by just staying slightly above it. It takes two hours to get to the town where the road ends. He sees a pub and restaurant and pulls into the parking lot. The place is fairly crowded. He parks in the corner of the lot. He needs to rest. He dozes off for two hours. When he wakes he drives thru town and spots a bank. The ATM is under a canopy on the side of the building. He realizes he has already taken the cash limit for the day. So he pulls through and goes back to the pub. It is about ten-thirty in the evening. He needs to kill an hour or more. He opens the map. He studies the map. There is a road to the South a couple of miles to the West. He opens another soda.

He spots the side road and turns left into the road. The road is rough, but paved. It is about sixty miles of fairly rough and slow driving. He only passes two cars. He gets to the road that will take him to the town. He turns left and drives about four miles to the town. It is after one in the morning. He drives thru town and sees a bank. The ATM is again under a canopy on the side. He pulls in and inserts his card. The screen on the machine gives him the usual selection. He punches in Withdrawal and asks for $500 dollars again. The machine dispenses the money. The receipt shows he only has fifty-three dollars left in the account. He sees a bar down the Side Street and heads for the parking lot. There are enough cars in the lot to cover his being there. He eats the second sandwich and drinks a soda. The soda is warm. He reads the map. There is road about six miles to the East that heads more or less in a Northeast direction. He starts to go east and sees a gas station on a road headed south. He turns around and heads for the gas station. He uses his credit card and fills up. He realizes getting gas at this station will look like he is continuing south. He leaves the station and turns south just in case the attendant is watching. About a block south he sees a town street running to the West. He turns into the street. Two blocks down the street there is a street headed north. He turns into it. It takes him back to the main drag. He turns and heads east. A couple of miles down the road, he spots a car with the lights flashing. He slows and turns into a driveway. He turns off the lights and ducks down on the seat. The Canadian Mounties' car goes by the driveway. Jeff waits a minute and then backs out of the driveway. He continues east to the side road he located on the map. He turns left into the road. It is a rough road also, but probably not highly traveled. He comes to an intersection with a better road. There is an all-night gas station on the one corner. He pulls into the station and parks around the far side. He decides this place will be OK for a nap. He puts the seat back and tries to sleep. The sunrise wakes him up. He needs the rest room and could use something to drink and eat. He goes into the station. He goes to the restroom. He picks up several sodas and two sandwiches and a pie. He pays the clerk. He gets back to the car. He looks at the map. The side road continues northeast for another twenty or so miles. So far he has not been spotted by a Mountie. He looks at the map and realizes he can get to within about hundred mile of his friends place without using any main roads. He sees there are two roads that will get him to within a hundred miles of his friends place without going on a main road. He decides to continue that far. He continues. It takes three hours on these side roads. He stops short of the intersection and examines the map. The road he is on crosses the main road and meets a road coming from the southeast that goes directly into the town. He uses the route to stay off the main road. As he comes into town he spots a shopping mall. He pulls into the parking lot. His car will blend in with all the other cars in the parking lot. He can rest before continuing the trip. It has been a day and he has gotten away clean.

CHAPTER 16

BACK AT THE FARMHOUSE WHAT HAS HAPPENED SINCE YESTERDAY

Meanwhile back at the Willison farmhouse, Bill and Jake are discussing the situation. After about ten minutes it is obvious Jeff is not coming back and Jason is not going to provide better information. The search warrant covers all the buildings at the farm. Chief Willison and his deputy join Jim and the other state police to conduct a search of the barn. Bill walks a wide circle around all the buildings and observes several vehicles behind the barn and at another out building. He writes down the license number, the make, and model of each of two vehicles. The third vehicle has no license. As he walks back to the front of the house he calls Sandra on his cell.

After a few rings Sandra answers, "Hello serge. How can I help? Did you and Jake get the guy?"

Bill replies, "No. I am going to give you the description of three cars here on the property. Need you to trace the ownership of them thru the Department of Motor Vehicles (DMV). Need the information quickly. Tell them it is fugitive situation and we need an immediate response. Also need to know the license and make of any cars owned by Jeff Willison. Make sure they understand that the fugitive is wanted for a criminal felony. He is assumed to be armed and dangerous. He is fleeing possibly toward Canada. The state police and I need this information now. This is not a traffic stop."

Sandra replies, "I already have the DMV on the other line. I will call you back."

Bill continues, "I do not have my Laptop. Jake may have his. Get the information. Jake is a couple hundred feet away. Here is the license and model information." Bill reads the information to Sandra.

Sandra types the information on her computer. She asked Bill to hold a few seconds. She punches the bottom for the DMV line. She says, "Sue, are you still there?"

Sue replies, "Yes, Do you have the info."

Sandra responds, "Yes. I am getting the info over the phone from Sergeant Bill Simpson. I will forward it to you from my computer. The criminal is a felon and possibly armed. Sergeant Bill Simpson and several state police are in the field. I need you to hold. Give us a minute to get the information on the computer. OK?"

Bill is walking toward Jake.

He continues with Sandra, "Have DMV send the information to Jake Burn's computer."

Martin Willison walks up. We found two trucks in the barn. I am having DMV check the ownership. Martin is holding his computer. Bill says, "I have DMV on the phone from my office. I am having our inquiries expedited. I will tell them to expedite yours as well."

Sandra says on the phone, "I heard what you said. Do I have all your information? I have three cars. I will tell Sue to check on Chief Willison's inquiry. I will call you back. I can send it to Jake."

Bill says, "Good send it to Jake. As soon as you get the answers call me."

Sandra hangs up.

Bill turns to the chief and Jake and says, "Sandra has a contact at Maine DMV. She should have the car information quickly."

Jake nods OK.

Jim and Sam join the group. Virginia arrives in her vehicle. Sam says, "Here is the vehicle information for Jeff's car. I already put out an APB on the car and Jeff and notified the border patrol and the Canadian Mounties."

Bill says, "The chief and I are having the other cars we found checked for ownership. They probably belong to Jason."

Chief Willison adds, "The truck in the barn is definitely Jason's. I see him driving it regularly. Jeff is probably driving his own Chevrolet SUV. Sam you know his SUV. That is the one you flagged in the APB?"

Sam responds, "Yes, chief."

The chief asks, "Can you tell me little more detail about the crimes?"

Bill replies, "Maybe you heard about the arrest in Tennessee of an alleged rapist, who allegedly committed a number of rapes in Maine and a couple of alleged rapes in other states. Well we were tracking Jeff with the same mathematical techniques as we used for the guy Robinson. We have DNA evidence and other physical identification that matches Jeff Willison. Jeff is allegedly connected to between twelve and sixteen rapes. Obviously he is an alleged rapist until there is a trial. But there is enough information for a judge in Augusta to issue the subpoenas and search warrants. A judge in Concord issued warrants and subpoenas for the crimes in New Hampshire. The techniques we are using were developed by a mathematics teacher and are similar to techniques applied to other crimes. We have a team of State Police and ADA's from Vermont, New Hampshire, and Maine pursuing a number of alleged serial rapists.

The assistant district attorney in Augusta, Jane Cordova, has been reviewing and processing the information provided by the team on the rapes in Maine. The assistant district attorney in Concord, Linda Smyth, has been reviewing and processing the information provided by the team on the rapes in New Hampshire. The team has been gathering and sorting the information for over four months. Both ADA's have asked us not to spread the detailed information around, because all the information could be evidence in a trial. The consensus of the team and the ADA's is that Jeff is the alleged rapist.

Bill says' "I am going to contact Jane Cordova and get a subpoena for access to his bank account and credit cards."

Jim says, "Yeah, shut them down."

Bill emphatically says, "No."

Jim says, "Why?"

Bill continues, "When I was working on several cases with the Boston force we discovered a neat trick. Unless the fugitive was trying to access stolen money, we would monitor the account, but not denied access. We could get almost instant response on where the accounts were accessed. Consequently we knew where to look for the fugitive. It takes a good technician, but with legal access the information is very timely."

Jim replies, "That is neat."

Bill calls Jane and sets up the subpoenas. He asks her to have one of techs in the office to trace the accounts, but not interfere with Jeff's access."

THE NEXT MORNING

Bill, Ed, and Jake are having an early Breakfast at the local diner. Ed and Jake dismissed the need for the other officers.

At about 7:30 AM Jane calls Bill. She says, "I am sorry for the delay, but the judge was not at his office. My tech is on the problem now. The card was used twice over night. He is in Canada about a hundred and fifty miles east of the border. He turned South after midnight. There was no more activity this morning. I already told captain Weatherite, you will be contacting him momentarily. He has a copy of the fugitive Warrant. Here is his number.

Bill calls. After two rings the phone is answered. George Weatherite answers, "Canadian Mounted Police, Captain George Weatherite here."

Bill replies, "This is Sergeant Bill Simpson. Jane Cordova of the Attorney General Office of Maine contacted you?"

George replies, "Yes. Seem you Yanks have lost a fugitive up here. I guess you would appreciate if we caught him."

Bill replies, "Yes. He came across the border sometime yesterday. I suspect he crossed at some unguarded crossing. He used a credit card at FILLITUP GAS N GO and later at SMART GAS. It appears that he is headed south toward the coast. He is not a stupid criminal. So the turn south may have been intentional."

George replies, "We will look to the Northeast also."

Bill continues, "You read my mind. He could be armed, but we are not sure he is armed. He is probably driving side roads. But I have no idea where he is headed."

George replies, "We have eight Mounties in the area. I will get some extra Mounties headed toward the area and call in several off duty officers. We should saturate the both areas. Jane gave me his description and the description of his car. Our system is a little different than yours. The Mounties cover local and national law enforcement."

About an hour passes and George calls back, "We have the suspect under surveillance. That was a good call. He is headed northeast on a back road. I have an unmark car following him. Two other cars are closing in front of him. We should stop him momentarily. We had our attorney check the Subpoena and the Fugitive Warrant. He confirmed everything is in order. I do not know how he got over the border, but we have no record of his entry. Thus we have cause to arrest and detain him. I'll call you guys back as soon as we have him in custody."

Bill replies, "OK. Tell your guys to be careful."

George answers, "We will. Good bye."

They hang up.

The Mounties have the road blocked around a bend just past a stream bridge. Both sides of the road are deep ditches. A local car is left through the blockade. The car tracking the suspect's car reports they have passed the last crossroad about a half-mile from the bridge. Two police cars are parked diagonally across the road just past the bridge. A third car is parked parallel to the road just behind the other two. The chase car is slowly closing on the suspect. As Jeff rounds the curve before the bridge he spots the police cars blocking the road. Momentarily he contemplates running. Realizes he can't go to either side. He stops on the bridge. The chase car blocks his escape to the rear. Officer Jones approaches the car from the rear. He yells, "Turn the engine off. Keep your hands where we can see them. Use your left hand to open the door. Get out slowly with your hands in the air. You are under arrest for several offenses."

Jeff considers the situation. He is surrounded in a place with NO exit. Jeff yells, "I am coming out. I don't have a weapon." He does what the Mountie had told him. Immediately two other Mounties surround Jeff and hand cuff him.

The one Mountie says, "You are wanted as a fugitive in the US. And in Canada for not checking in when you crossed the border. There may be other charges. You will have a chance to present your side of the case before a Magistrate in the morning. You do have the right in Canada to remain silent until the hearing. As a US citizen the US Embassy will arrange for your legal council."

Jeff says nothing as the Mounties place him in the one police car. The one Mountie gets into Jeff's car. The keys are still in the ignition. The other police cars move to one side of the road. The Mountie moves Jeff's car to the side of the road. There are several local cars waiting to get by over the bridge. The Mounties talk for a couple of minutes. The one car with Jeff in handcuffs follows Jeff's car with the Mountie driving to a town about twenty miles away. There is a Magistrate at the town for tomorrow's hearing. The Sergeant calls George, "Sir, we have the suspect under arrest. We told him not to talk about his side of the arrest. The US Embassy will need to be notified to provide an attorney for a hearing tomorrow. The hearing is only to determine how long we can hold him. As you know, the Embassy in these cases usually contacts a local Canadian Attorney."

George says, "I will have the Police in the US to contact their State Department also. Everything went smoothly?"

The Sergeant replies, "No violence. He surrendered peacefully. I'll be talking to you."

They hang up.

George calls Jake and Bill on Jake's phone, "Jake here. This is George Weatherite. We have your guy under arrest. There will be a short hearing in the morning. I think we can hold him with respect to a violation of Canadian Law. He allegedly crossed the border illegally. We can handle the fugitive warrant separately. Call your State Department and have them contact the US Embassy in Ottawa to provide legal representation."

Jake replies, "I will call the attorney general's office in Maine and they will call the State department."

Simultaneously Jake and Bill say, "Thanks."

They hang up.

Jake calls Jane and explains the situation and asks her to contact the State Department. Jane follows through with the State Department. She reminds them this is a dangerous fugitive and we need to dot the "I's" and cross the "T's" on this operation. Bill calls Linda and asks her to do the same. Linda follows through immediately.

Ed Woodworth joins Jake and Bill to discuss yesterday and this morning. The Diner is crowded this morning Linda calls Bill, "Bill this is Linda Smyth. The Attorney General is prepared to take over the New Hampshire cases with the Canadian Government and the Mounties. They are holding him on a charge of illegal entry into Canada. He will be detained until he can be returned to the US. He cannot make bail or otherwise be released on the charge of illegal entry. Ed, Jake, and You may need to go to Canada and escort him home. The Mounties will accompany you to the border. This will probably be next week. You should plan two days for the trip. I will talk to you as soon as the extradition is arranged. You should hear from Jane with a similar request."

Bill replies, "Ed, Jake and I don't have anything to interfere with bringing the guy back."

Linda continues, "Good. Say hello to Mattie for me. I'll be talking to her also in a few days."

Bill continues, "OK, Good bye."

Ed's phone rings. It is obviously Jane on the phone. She says, "Ed this is Jane Cordova." She tells Ed the same thing Linda told Bill.

Ed replies, "Linda Symth called Bill just a couple of minutes ago. We are prepared to go to Canada and bring the suspect back to the US and to both states. Jake is going along to assist."

Jane continues, "Good. I and Linda will be talking to the three of you about the specific arrangements."

Ed replies, "OK. We will be talking to the both of you. We are just sitting down to breakfast after a long day and night."

Jane says, "Have a good breakfast and good day. Tell Jake and Bill congratulations on a job well done. Of course, congratulations to you, also."

Ed replies, "Thank you. See you in couple of days. We catch them when we can."

Jane giggles and says, "Have a good day. Drive carefully home."

They hang up.

Ed says to the guys, "that was obviously Jane. She told me the same thing Linda told Bill. Probably next week, we will go to Canada to bring the suspect back to the states. I am ready for breakfast."

The waitress takes their orders. They talk about the families and Jake and Ed ask Bill about Mattie. Finally they pay the bill and engage in a couple of minutes of small talk before starting for home. Tomorrow will be an easy day just paper work on the trip.

THE NEXT DAY

Bill enters the office at about 9 AM. Sandra greets him, "Ed, Jake and You caught the guy. Congratulations."

Bill answers, "Not Exactly. The Canadians caught him yesterday morning."

Sandra continues, "He got across the border."

Bill replies, "Yes. Not sure where he crossed. We tracked him from a couple of credit card uses. The Mounties stopped him about one hundred and ninety miles into Canada. He was driving a zigzag route to confuse us. It looked like he was headed south from the credit card use, but he was headed northeast. Canada is holding him for an illegal border crossing. By the way congratulation to you for your fast response and help. We needed your help also. Everybody worked together to bring a serious criminal to justice."

Sandra says, "All in a day's work."

Bill says, "Thanks anyway."

Sandra just says, "OK, Serge."

Bill continues, "Linda and Jane are arranging for his extradition. I am glad to be back. Actually they may not need a formal extradition. I think the Canadians are going to throw the guy out because he crossed the border illegally. We just need to be at the border when they send him back."

Sandra replies, "Glad to see you are back in one piece. Mattie is probably glad also."

Bill continues, "I have to call her. She is in class. I will tell her all about the little trip."

Sandra continues, "Have you told Carl or George Bernard, the Mayor?"

Bill continues, "I am going to call Carl now. I am going to let Carl tell the Mayor.

Bill calls Carl. The phone rings four times. Carl answers, "Chief Carl Kramer, Nottingham Harbor Police Department. How can I help you, Bill?

Bill responds, "I am going to help you with your buddy the mayor. We caught the Nottingham rapist. I should say alleged rapist. Actually the Canadian Mounties caught him about 200 miles east of the border. He apparently crossed the border illegally. The Canadians are holding him on an illegal entry charge. They can hold him indefinitely on the illegal entry charge. There is no bail. The US State department is negotiating his return the US. There is NO need for an extradition hearing, since he is illegally in Canada. They are going to simply throw him out into our arms at the border. You can come along and drive his vehicle back to Concord.

"You can have the pleasure of telling Mayor Bernard. However I need him to maintain silence for a few more days, maybe two weeks. We know who the third suspect is. We want to make it easier to catch him. Remember the suspects are legally alleged suspects until a trial. I will stop by Nottingham Harbor after we return from Canada. I can tell you and the Mayor all the gory details."

Carl responds, "I will be glad to go with you guys. I will be looking forward to hearing the entire story.

Bill continues, "I will call you Monday with the travel schedule. I am sure I will be coming by Nottingham Harbor on the way to the border. Ed and Jake will join us near their Barracks. Till then have a good day and weekend. Remind the Mayor about being silent for now.

Carl answers, "You have a good day and say hello to your lady, Mattie. And I will tell George silence for now."

MATTIE'S MESSAGE

It is later in the afternoon when Mattie calls. Bill picks up the phone and says, "Hi, how are you/"

Mattie replies, "I am fine. How did the trip go? You were gone longer than I or Sandra expected."

Bill continues, "Well I met Ed, Jake and several deputies. We connected with the Chief in Willsburg and his deputy. They were supportive. When we arrived at the farmhouse the father was there, but the son was not. The son somehow realized we were there and he took off. The Canadian Mounties caught him the next day. We were at the house till morning. I slept in the car and Ed and Jake slept in cell bunks at the Willsburg jail till morning. Any way I returned tired. So I took off yesterday. The suspect Jeff is being held in Canada for crossing the border illegally. Linda and Jane are working through the State Department to bring him back here. There is some possibility the Canadians will simply expel the guy at the border. They are cooperating we just need to coordinate the time and place. When he walks across the border we will arrest him. Linda and Jane are working the problem."

Mattie listens then comments, "So, that is two. There are three more to go."

Bill says, "Linda has located the third one living in New Hampshire. I can handle this one with my deputies. We can talk more on the weekend. I will call Saturday, but do you want to go to Seabrook to celebrate?"

Mattie says, "Yes, I will expect your call on Saturday."

They hang up.

Bill spends a quiet Friday. He reviews a couple of armed robbery cases, but has no obvious suspect. He writes a rough draft of the report on the chase and capture of Jeff Willison. He calls Mattie on Saturday about noon and they agree that he will pick her up at 6:30 PM. Bill arrives at Mattie's house at 6:25 PM. He wraps on the door. Mattie comes to the door and looks through the peephole to be sure it is Bill. She unlocks the door, opens it, and says, "Come in Bill."

Bill comes in. He kisses her on the cheek. She says, "I'll be ready in a few minutes. Have a seat."

Bill sits down on the sofa and says, "Take your time. The reservation is for 8."

Mattie walks back to her room and finishes applying a little makeup and jewelry. She combs her hair a little bit and returns to the living room. She fusses with her pocket book and then gets a coat from the foyer closet. Bill gets up and helps her with the coat. She looks around the room. She turns off a light. She says, "Ready."

Bill answers, "Yes."

They walk to car after Mattie locks the door. Bill opens the passenger side door and Mattie gets in. Bill slides into the driver's side. They fasten their seatbelts as Bill starts the car. Mattie looks at the four CD's in the door pocket and opens the Patsy Cline CD and places it in the player. Bill has turned the car and driven to the road. They talk a little and listen to the CD. When they arrive at the restaurant, Bill parks the car and opens the door for Mattie and they walk into the restaurant. The hostess seats them in the corner. Bill helps Mattie with her chair. They sit down and start looking at the menu.

Bill says, "How are the kids?"

Mattie replies, "They are good. How are yours?"

Bill responds, "They are good."

Mattie says, "I am glad we are catching these guys, but actually I would like to talk about more pleasant things."

Bill says, "We do need to congratulate ourselves for the success."

Mattie continues, "I agree, but crimes are so depressing."

Bill says, "You are going to be finished with summer school in two weeks. Am I correct?"

Mattie answers, "Yes."

Bill continues, "Let's plan on going to the beach one or two days. We could go to Conway for a day. It is a little far but we can make it if we leave early. Maybe go to Nottingham Harbor one day."

Mattie answers, "I would love to do those things"

Bill says, "We have two weeks to plan. We can talk more on next weekend. I will have some time off after we return from Canada."

Mattie asks, "Do you think this trip to Canada is dangerous?"

Bill says emphatically, "NO. The Canadians have him in custody. He won't be armed. It should be a piece of cake. It is going to be four of us."

Mattie continues, "OK. I will only worry a little."

Bill continues, "Probably the most dangerous part of the trip is driving to the border and back to Augusta."

Mattie replies, "You are coming back to Augusta not Concord?"

Bill responds, "Yes. He committed more crimes in Maine than in New Hampshire. We are going to give Maine first chance to prosecute. I won't need to be involved once he is arraigned in Maine.

Bill says, "Let's concentrate on the vacation days."

Mattie replies, "OK."

They discuss going to various places for vacation.

Bill changes the subject. He says, "My brother and Sister are talking about having a cookout at the farm for Labor Day. You are obviously invited. I was talking to Ed and Jake about Labor Day. I think I will invite them with their families to the farm. What do you think?"

Mattie replies, "I like the idea. I will come if you are inviting me."

Bill says, "You are invited. You are my lady."

Mattie replies, "I will come. You are my guy."

They sit quietly eating for several minutes and just smiling at each other.

The waiter breaks the silence, "How is everything? Can I get you anything?"

184

Bill says, "More ice tea, please. Mattie do you want another wine?"

Mattie replies, "Yes?"

The waiter leaves and returns in a few minutes with the ice tea and the wine.'

Bill says, "Thank you."

Bill is thinking 'Mattie is so nice.' Mattie is thinking the same thing about Bill. Their relationship is becoming more serious, but having been married to loving spouses they are not ready for the next steps.

They order some desert and coffee.

They finish and drive back to Mattie's place. They spend an hour sitting on the sofa and just holding each other. They finally kiss good night and Bill leaves. They are in love, but their first spouses are still on their minds. They need a little more time.

CHAPTER 17

NUMBER TWO AND THE TRIP TO CANADA

On Monday Bill arrives at the office around 9:30AM. He says, "Good morning Sandra."

Sandra responds, "Good morning, Serge. How was your weekend?"

Bill answers, "The weekend was great."

The phone rings just as Bill is sitting down with his coffee. He answers the phone and says, "This is Sergeant Bill Simpson, New Hampshire State Police. How can I help you?"

The Mayor says, "This is Mayor George Bernard. Congratulations on catching the Nottingham Harbor rapist. I should say alleged rapist. I will hold announcing the catch to the press until you catch the third guy. I understand your concern."

Bill says, "Thank you. There were a number of people responsible for the capture. I will be up to Nottingham Harbor next week and I will explain all the details. We are starting on the chase to catch the third rapist. As soon as we capture him then you can make a big announcement about capture of the rapist. Until we capture the third guy silence will be very helpful. I am also anxious to announce the successes. Please don't mention my lady Mattie in connection with the identification."

George continues, "I am on board with your concerns. You have my support, 100%."

Bill replies, "Thank you, George. I know all of this has various political overtones, but our first duty is to catch and prosecute the criminals and protect the people from the criminals."

George says, "I agree completely. I am a politician, but I have relatives and friends in addition to the general public that are and can become victims of these criminals. Keep up the good work, Bill. Be safe until we talk again. Definitely tell the other officers involved to be safe. Have a good day, Bill.'

Bill responds, "You have a good day, George."

They hang up.

As Bill hangs up Sandra says, "Linda called about ten minutes ago."

Bill replies, "Thanks. I will call her immediately."

Bill immediately picks up the phone and dials Linda's number."

The phone rings four times and Linda answers, "Linda Smyth assistant to the attorney general of New Hampshire. How can I help you?'

Bill replies, "Bill Simpson here. You called. What do you want?'

Linda continues, "I did recognize your phone number. I have the tentative schedule for the return of Jeff Willison to the US. I talked to Jane and she has the paperwork for Maine ready. I have the New Hampshire paper work ready. Who is going along?"

Bill responds, "Ed, Jake, Carl and myself."

Linda continues, "Ed and you will arrest Jeff Willison separately. Each of you should read him his rights and explain the full list of the charges will be provided when you arrive at Augusta. Jane and I will be in Augusta when you return to present a formal list of charges. We will have court appointed attorney in Augusta to represent him. As you know you should not question him during the trip to Augusta. You can allow him common human courtesies. Record the reading of his rights and the presentation of the charges. Carl is going along?"

Bill responds, "Carl is going along. He will drive Jeff's vehicle to Augusta. We are going to have to stop for gas and lunch. Ed, Jake, and myself have all transported prisoners before. The trip should be straight forwarded. We should be in Augusta by dinnertime on Thursday."

Linda responds, "Jane has scheduled an arraignment for Friday morning. Here is the schedule.

Linda continues, "The Canadians are planning to return Jeff to the border on Thursday Morning. The four of you should go up to the crossing at I-95 on Wednesday afternoon and stay overnight. Jake has a State Police

Van for these kinds of transfers. The both Attorney Generals have said we will cover your cost to stay there and your expenses. So unless something changes Wednesday is the schedule. Jane and I will have the Canadian contact names. Remember both Ed and you need to read this guy his rights at the border. And make sure you have Jake and Carl witness the reading of his rights as soon as he crosses the border. Make sure he is in the US at the time. Jake says he is taking a simple video camera. One of the custom officials should video the reading. Then serve the subpoenas. As I said we will appoint an attorney when you get Jeff to Augusta and get a sample of his DNA. I know you know how to do this, but I am just going over the procedure so we do not make a stupid mistake. He will be transferred to Concord for arraignment in New Hampshire sometime the following week."

Bill replies, "I know. Send me an E-mail at the office and send one to Ed, Jake and Carl with the procedures in writing. Make sure Jane does the same."

Linda replies, "In about hour as soon as I write it down."

Bill says, "Thank you. Have a good day. Talk to you later."

Linda says, "I will include instructions for applying for your expenses."

On Wednesday Ed, Jake, Carl and Bill travel to the Canadian Border. They introduce themselves to the American Border guard and to the Canadian Border guard. The Border Guard Officers explain who will be on duty in the morning. They go back to the small motel. The clerk tells them about a Diner in the next town. They go to dinner. Returning to the motel they sit in Bill's room and chit-chat till eight and watch a TV till ten while drinking some beer and eating some snacks.

Thursday finds Ed, Jake, Carl, and Bill waiting at the Custom Station on the US side of the border. The Mounties with Jeff Willison are due to arrive shortly. It is about 10 AM. Jake talks to the custom officers about the transfer. The one officer Bob gladly volunteers to photograph the transfer and reading of the rights. The Canadian Mounties arrive in three cars one is Jeff's car. Ed, Jake, Carl and Bill go to the border with Bob. The Mounties bring Jeff to the border crossing. They remove the cuffs and tell

Jeff to cross the border. They tell him he is being returned to the US for crossing the border illegally. Any charges the US has are not their concern. Several US custom officers and two Canadian officers are standing on the Canadian side. Since he has not been charged with the crimes committed in the US, there is no need to worry about any extradition problems. Jeff momentarily looks around and hesitates crossing the border and realizes there is really no place to run. The one Mountie says, "Sir you might as well return to the US. If you do not, the judge says you will be charged with illegal entry and spend many years in a Canadian Prison. Since the crimes in the US do not carry the death penalty, the Canadian government will never grant you political asylum. When you get out of jail in Canada you will be returned to the US."

Bill says, "You will be tried on return to the US with the crimes that you are charged with in the U.S. and spend more time in a US jail. You might as well surrender now and face the music."

Jeff looks around and says, "Ok. I surrender to you guys."

Jake says, "Please step over here and surrender in the US."

Jeff steps over the border. Jake motions to him to stand by a fence on the US side. The Canadian officers are watching the scene. The custom official from the US has been photographing the scene since the Canadians arrived. An officer on the Canadian side is likewise photographing the scene with a video camera. Jake starts with the arrest. He says, "Jeff Willison is your name? Please answer Yes or No?"

Jeff answers, "Yes."

Jake continues, "I am Jake Burns a State of Maine State policeman on a task force to find you and other serious criminals. You are charged with multiple crimes of raping women. The full lists of the crimes are shown on the warrants from Maine and New Hampshire. Policemen from the two states will now formally charge and read you your rights."

Ed Woodworth says, "I am Ed Woodworth a Maine State Policeman. Jeff Willison you are charged by the State of Maine with multiple counts of rape in the first degree. I am going to read you your rights." When Ed finishes he asks, "Do you understand these rights. Do you want to speak to attorney?"

Jeff answers, "I understand my rights. I do want an attorney?"

Ed responds, "You are going to be transported to Augusta Maine where a court appointed attorney will be provided. You are under arrest by the State of Maine."

Bill says, "I am Bill Simpson a New Hampshire State Policeman. Jeff Willison you are charged by the State of New Hampshire with multiple counts of rape in the first degree. I am going to read you your rights." When Bill finishes he asks, "Do you understand these rights. Do you want to speak to attorney?"

Jeff answers, "I understand my rights. I do want an attorney?"

Bill responds, "You are going to be transported to Augusta Maine where a court appointed attorney will be provided. You are under arrest by the State of New Hampshire. Once you are finished in Augusta with the arraignment on the charges in Maine, you will be transported to Concord New Hampshire to be arraigned on the New Hampshire charges."

Jake continues, "We are going to take you to Augusta, Maine. There you will be interviewed and an attorney will be provided before you are questioned or interviewed. On the drive we will be stopping for lunch and if you need to use the lavatory. Do you need the lavatory before we start? The chief of Police Carl Kramer of Nottingham Harbor is going to drive your car to Augusta. He is on temporarily assigned to the Attorney General of Maine. Do you need the lavatory?"

Jeff replies, "Yes I could pee."

Jake replies, "Bill will escort you into the restroom. One of the custom officials is going to be outside so there will be NO place to run. When you are finished, you will be handed cuffed for the trip."

Jeff says, "Ok."

Jeff goes with Bill and the custom officer to the restroom in the station. The custom officer checks the restroom and waits for one person to leave. He motion to Bill to escort Jeff into the restroom. He stands outside. One person approaches the door. He says, "I need you to wait. We have a prisoner using the room." If you are in a hurry, you can use the handicap room across the hall."

The fellow walks over to the handicap room."

In about two minutes Jeff and Bill come out. Bill says, "Jeff, please place your hands behind your back. I need to cuff you."

Jeff complies.

They head back outside to Jake's SUV. Bill places the suspect into the back seat on the passenger's side of the car. He takes a leg chain on the floor and places the cuff around Jeff's ankle"

Bill goes around the car and gets into the backseat on the driver's side.

Carl has pulled Jeff's car next to Jake's car. Jake tells Carl he does not need to absolutely follow them but they will be stopping for lunch around 12:30. He asks Carl, "Do you have my cell and Bill's phone number?"

Carl answers him, "Yes. I programmed all three of phone numbers into my cell earlier. I am going to follow you. I will try to keep you in site, but not follow you to close. I know how to get to Augusta. Do you all have my cell?"

Jake answers, "I have your number."

Ed says, "I have your cell, Carl."

Bill says, "Likewise."

Jake says as he gets into his car, "Bill will call you if we stop for gas or the lavatory and lunch. Ok. Let's Roll."

Carl gives Jake a thumb up. Jakes gives the border guys a thumbs up. One of the Canadians beeps the horn.

Ed, Jake, and Bill do not expect any problems for the trip except normal traffic.

About a half an hour into the drive Carl calls Bill. Bills phone rings. He answers, "Bill here."

Carl says, "I am sorry. I should have noticed and said something. I am going to need gas. There is less than a quarter of tank."

Bill says, "There is a rest area about ten miles ahead. Do you have enough gas to get that far.'

Carl replies, "Yes."

Bill says, "OK. We will stop there."

They hang up

Bill says to Jake, "that was obviously Carl. Jeff's car needs gas. You heard me tell him we will stop."

Jake responds, "OK. The Canadians drove that car almost 200 miles to the border. I forgot to ask Carl to check the gas before we left the border."

Bill says, "It is OK."

A few minutes pass. They are approaching a rest area with a gas station. Carl is behind them a few hundred feet. Jake signals to turn into the rest area. Carl follows. Jake stops short of the parking area. Carl pulls alongside. They roll down the respective windows. Carl says I am going to get gas and hit the head. I will wait on the other side of the pumps"

Jake says, "Go for it. We are going to park also."

Jake pulls the car to front of the lot but away from other cars. Jakes says, "I can use the head also."

Bill says, "Ed and you can go to the head and get more to drink. I will wait with the prisoner."

Carl drives the wrong way across the parking lot. As he stops next to the SUV a Maine State trooper pull alongside of the car. Carl steps out of the car. He is obviously armed and so is Bill. The trooper draws his gun. Carl says I am a cop. I have identification. Bill says the same thing. The trooper says use your left hand and show me your identification. Carl shows him his chief of police badge. Bill shows him his New Hampshire State police badge. The trooper says, "Neither of you have any jurisdiction in Maine."

Bill says, "Actually we do. The two Maine State Police inside and us are on a task force for the three states. The prisoner in the SUV is being escorted to Augusta and then to Concord for arraignment. The prisoner is a wanted Felon."

Jake walks up and says, "Is there a problem."

The state trooper recognizes Jake. He says, "Sergeant you are with these two guys."

Jake answers, "Yes. They are on a task force to capture serious criminals."

The trooper responds, "Well he went the wrong way at the front of the lot."

Jake says, "He is driving the suspect car. We need to coordinate this operation. I am sure he was careful, but it is important we stay together."

The trooper says, "OK. Be careful. You can understand my concern."

Jake says, "It is Ok. No harm no foul."

The trooper says, "Do you want an escort?"

Jake replies, "NO. We are trying not to attract attention. Thank you."

With that Ed walks up. The Trooper recognizes Ed. He says, "Hello, Sergeant. Are you with these guys?"

Ed motions for the trooper to come over away from the SUV. He says. "The prisoner is an alleged rapist we are bringing back from Canada. I need you to keep quiet about this. Talking about it even a little could jeopardize us catching several other felons. Do you understand? Secrecy is paramount. You will read about this operation in a few weeks."

The trooper answers, "I understand. I did not see anything. I just had a normal routine patrol."

Ed says, Thank you, have a good and safe day."

The trooper gets back in his car. He says, "You guys have a good day."

Ed says, "It is taken care of. Bill you need the facilities before we leave."

Bill says, "Yes." He turns to Jeff. He says, "Jeff do you need to use the Men's room."

Jeff answers, "NO. But I could use a bottle of water."

Bill says, "OK."

Bill goes into the building. Jake gets a second chain from the rear of the SUV. He loops it through the leg iron chain. He says, "Jeff, I am going to undo the cuffs. You can put your hands in front and I will cuff you so you can drink the water." Jake hands Carl his weapon. Ed draws his weapon. Carl stands back. Jake cuffs Jeff to the chain in front of his lap. He reconnects Jeff's seat belt. Ed climbs into the back seat. Bill returns and hands Jeff the water. Carl goes back to Jeff's car. Jake gets into the driver seat. Bill gets into Passenger seat. Bill then says, "Jeff, if you do anything violent or cause a problem we will be forced to place your hands behind you. We are being civil to let you drink the water. So please act accordingly."

Jeff replies, "I am thirsty. I recognize you guys are all armed."

Jakes gets back on the highway. Jeff actually dozes. Around Noon Bill calls Carl, "The next rest stop has several food shops. We are going to stop for lunch. Are you still behind us?"

Carl answers, "Yes. I can see you about five hundred feet in front of me. I will follow you into the rest area."

Bill replies, "OK."

They pull into the rest area. Bill and Jake ask Ed and Jeff what they want. Ed stays with Jeff and the car. Ed is out of the car and has his weapon. Carl joins them. Lunch goes without any problems. Jeff says he needs the restroom. Bill and Jake escort him to the restroom. Ed hangs back but walks along. Carl stays with the vehicles. Once they are back in the vehicles, Jake and Carl head out onto the highway.

In late afternoon they arrive at the Local Augusta Police Station and place Jeff in a holding cell. Jane and Linda arrive with a court appointed attorney. They have Jeff brought to an interview room with themselves and the attorney. Jane reads him his rights again. Jane asks him some questions and repeats the charges against him. Linda confirms that the reading of his rights applies to the crimes he committed in New Hampshire as well as those in Maine. Jane finally tells him and the attorney there is a similar hearing tomorrow to formally present the charges and set bail, etc. She tells the attorney he can set in the room and discuss the charges and hearing with his client. Linda tells them there will be another hearing in a few days in Concord New Hampshire when the proceedings are finished in Maine.

A half an hour passes and the attorney asks to leave and Jeff is returned to the holding cell until tomorrow. Jane tells the attorney that the hearing is tomorrow at eleven AM. She reminds him that as a court appointed attorney he must be there tomorrow. He can discuss with the judge after the hearing about continuing to represent the client or if he has any conflicts. Please be prepared tomorrow. The charges are serious and the judge will not be sympathetic to a poor representation. Tomorrow's hearing is only about the charges in Maine.

Jane says as the attorney leaves, "Have a good evening."

He thanks her.

Friday morning 10:45 AM finds Jane and the lawyer James Harwood in court. Linda is only an observer. A Sheriff's deputy brings the suspect in at about 10:55 AM. He joins James at the defendant table. The bailiff announces the judge, "Please stand the honorable Judge Petersmith presiding."

The judge says: "Please be seated."

The judge sorts a couple of papers on the desk. He addresses the Bailiff, "George, please explain the reason for this action this morning."

George answers, "Your Honor, we are here for a hearing and reading of the charges against the suspect Jeff Willison. You will or will not set bail after hearing the charges. The Assistant District Attorney is Jane Cordova and the lawyer for the defendant is James Harwood. He is appointed to serve the defendant for this hearing. I think you know the players except the defendant."

The judge calls on Jane "Jane are you prepared to present the charges?"

Jane answers, "Yes Your Honor."

The judge continues, "Mr. Harwood, are you prepared to represent the defendant in this hearing."

James answers, "Yes, Your Honor."

The judge says, "Mrs. Bush can you read the charges."

Jane continues, "Mr. Jeff Willison is charged with fifteen counts of rape by the State of Maine over the last four years. He is also charged with fleeing to Canada to avoid arrest and prosecution."

Jane hands the bailiff a sheet of paper with the charges listed. The bailiff gives the paper to the judge.

The judge looks the paper over and asked, "This is the same list that was given to Mr. Harwood and the defendant?"

Jane replies, "It is an exact copy of the list I personally provided the defendant and James last evening during an interview. Mr. Willison was read his rights at the border in the US after the Canadian Mounties expelled him from Canada for illegally crossing the border. He was not extradited for the crimes he committed in Maine. Mr. Harwood is aware of these facts."

The judge continues, "Mr. Harwood you heard what Jane said. Do you agree with what she said?"

James Harwood replies, "She has stated the facts accurately. I was told what she said last night at the interview."

The Judge continues, "Jeff Willison how do you plead?"

Jeff talks quietly for a minute to James. He said, "I plead not guilty."

The Judge continues, "These are serious felonies. Do you or your attorney have anything to say, before I set bail and a date for the trial?"

James stands, "Your Honor. There is nothing to say. I will be asking the AG to consider a plea bargain."

The Judge turns to Jane "Is there a possibility of a plea bargain, Jane."

Jane replies, "I have not had the time since yesterday to consult with the AG about the charges and a plea. I will talk to Mr. Harwood and the AG on Monday."

The Judge continues, "Considering the seriousness of the charges, Mr. Willison will be held without bail at least until a plea bargain is accepted or rejected. I will expect to hear from you, Jane, and Mr. Harwood before the end of next week. Mr. Willison, do you understand you should talk to your attorney about any plea the AG offers?"

Jeff nods yes.

The judge says, "Mr. Willison, please answer out loud."

Jeff answers, "I understand Your Honor. I will talk to my Attorney about a plea."

The judge says, "Thank You. I understand the suspect is wanted in New Hampshire also. Is this true Jane?"

Jane answers, "Yes your honor. State Police of both states arrested him at the Canadian Border. Linda Symth the ADA from New Hampshire set in on the meeting last evening with Mr. Harwood. Jeff is well aware that New Hampshire will indict him in a few days."

The judge says, "Linda has the state of New Hampshire made a formal request for extradition?"

Linda replies, "Your Honor. Jeff Willison was arrested and transported here by state police from both states. We have a request that he be held without bail and transported to New Hampshire for arraignment when the proceedings are finished in Maine. I would have thought your honor was aware of the request."

The judge says, "I am not. He turns to the bailiff."

The bailiff says, "Your Honor, I am not aware of said request. I will check."

The Judge bangs his Gavel on the Desk and says, "Mr. Willison you are to be held in the local jail until the request for your transport to New Hampshire can be confirm. This hearing is complete. I need to see you, Jane, in my chambers about another matter. It has nothing to do with this proceeding, but since you are here can we have a short discussion.

Jane replies, "Yes, we can Your Honor. I do need a personal moment."

The Judge is standing. "Take the moment you need, and then come to my chambers."

The judge leaves. James addresses Jane. He says, "I will call you about a meeting next week."

Jane replies, "Any day but Monday. The AG will not be back until Tuesday. I can contact him, but he is out of town on personal business."

James says, "OK. I will talk to my defendant and talk to you Tuesday."

The sheriff's deputy is standing by to escort Jeff back to Jail. James turns to Sheriff and says, "Can I speak to my client for a moment?"

The sheriff's deputy says, "Ok but just a moment." He steps away.

Jane has left for the ladies room.

James says, "You understand these are serious charges. First do not talk to anyone about the crimes or the charges. Particularly do not talk to a cellmate or other prisoners at meals. They could use the information to reduce their charges. Obviously do not talk to anyone that is an official.

Think about whether you want to plea bargain. You are facing most of the rest of your life in jail if convicted of all the charges. Don't do anything stupid. In all likelihood the AG will offer you a plea bargain. I have to go over the evidence against you. That I could not do since last night. I will talk to you on Monday and have our ducks in order for the meeting next week. If they want to do a DNA test refuse, but tell them you will talk to me about whether you can summit to the test. If they present you a subpoena for the test you can still refuse until you consulted with me. They understand that requirement. Do you understand what I have told you just now?"

Jeff replies, "Yes. No information to anyone. Thank you for representing me today."

James continues as he motions to the sheriff's Deputy, "I am finished. Thank You. Jeff I will see you Monday."

MEANWHILE BILL, ED, JAKE AND CARL
HAVE RETURNED TO HOME

Ed and Jake leave for their respective Barracks in upstate Maine. Carl heads back to Nottingham Harbor. Bill heads for Concord New Hampshire. The case against Jeff Willison is in the hands of the ADA's. Tomorrow and next week will bring another suspect and a new set of problems.

Carl meets with George Bernard, the mayor of Nottingham Harbor, the next morning. Carl reminds the mayor not to say anything to the press about the latest arrest. He tells George that they know the third suspect. They need a few days to make the arrest. George agrees to keep the information secret.

Mattie is glad to see Bill is home safe and sound. Sandra congratulates Bill on the arrest.

Mattie and Bill plan their mini vacation.

CHAPTER 18

THE THIRD SUSPECT IS GARY KIPLING

Ed, Jake, Carl and Bill completed the Transport of Jeff Willison from Canada and moved him to Augusta last Friday. Mattie and Bill have Dinner to celebrate their success. The alleged Nottingham Harbor Rapist is in jail in Augusta. Jane is preparing to prosecute Jeff Willison. Linda is preparing to bring him to Concord for prosecution in the New Hampshire cases. They are at Saturday evening dinner at the Restaurant in Seabrook.

Mattie says, "I am not enthused about spending much time during dinner talking about the rapist stuff. But I will tell you that Linda and I have identified the other two rapists. We believe we have the identity of all five rapists. Obviously the first two have been caught. Number three is living in New Hampshire. Number four is living somewhere in upstate Maine. Number five is living in New York or at least working in New York. Ed, Jake, Charlie, and you are going to have some more fun chasing these guys across New England."

Bill replies, "We will get together next week to discuss the details. I agree with you, this dinner is to discuss more pleasant things." Mattie and Bill continue their dinner. Bill takes her home after dinner. They spend some time at Mattie's quietly together.

Monday comes too soon. Linda calls and Bill answers, "Sergeant Bill Simpson, New Hampshire State Police. Sorry Linda recognized your number after I started my standard answer. How can I help you?"

Linda replies, "Hi, Bill. Are you and guys ready for another chase?"

Bill answers, "We can handle one more. What do we need to do?"

Linda answers, "The third suspect is Gary Kipling. He lives on a farm in New Hampshire. He has raped in all three states. Bill you are going to be the lead for this operation. Ed, Jake and Charlie Wilson should be along. If this guy runs he can easily get to Vermont or Maine. Vivian and Jane will have subpoenas and warrants for their states also. All of you are on the task force and can assist in either of the three states. He could also run to Canada. If he heads for the border I will notify the Canadian border police to detain him. Be careful the guy has used a gun to threaten the victims during the rapes. Remember all four of you should observe the reading of his rights and the serving of the subpoenas and warrants."

Bill replies, "I am going to call Ed, Jake, and Charlie now. Are you calling Vivian and Jane for their subpoenas and warrants?"

Linda answers, "Yes. You should have Ed, Jake, Charlie and yourself check the subpoenas and warrants. FAX copies of all the warrants to all four of us as soon as Vivian, Jane, or yourself have them. I am going to do the arrest on Thursday if everything is in order."

Bill responds, "We will check them and we will call you if there are any problems. There is a state policewoman in barracks near where he lives. Her name is Barbara Greene. I will call her. Can you FAX a copy of the search warrant for the property to Barbara?" She can check the property tomorrow for the address and any out buildings or vehicles on the property."

Linda responds, "Good idea. Do you know her phone number?"

Bill answers, "Yes. Let me give you her number. Wait till I call her."

Linda responds, "I don't yet have any of the paperwork."

Bill says, "OK. I will be talking to you. Have a good day."

Linda answers, "You have good day also."

They both hang up."

Bill calls Barbara Greene. The phone rings at the barracks. The desk sergeant Sam Apple answers, "Sergeant Sam Apple, New Hampshire State Police, how can I help you."

Bill responds, "This is Sergeant Bill Simpson. I wanted to talk to Officer Barbara Greene."

Sam replies, "Officer Greene is on second shift this week. Can I help you?"

Bill continues, "I need Barbara to check on the subpoenas and warrants related to the rapist we are going to arrest later in the week. I need her to verify the address and details about the property. Check the county records, etc. I do not want her to serve the paperwork. This guy is probably armed and dangerous. He is an alleged rapist. There is paperwork from Maine and Vermont as well as New Hampshire. The paperwork is going to be FAXED to her from three ADA's. We just need the paperwork verified. No foul up because of typos. She has done this before. The task force guys are going to make the arrest. She is not going to serve the paperwork or even approach the guy. Can you have her call me?"

Sam answers, "Yes, I will. I also will tell her to make this her top priority."

Bill continues, "Thank you. Have a good day. I will be talking to you and your captain on Wednesday. We will need several officers from your barracks. Tell the captain."

Sam replies, "You have a good day."

They hang up.

Bill calls Ed, Charlie, and Jake he tells them about the FAXES from Linda, Jane and Vivian. He explains that he is having Barbara check the information also. If there is anything even questionable please call the ADA and be sure the problem is clarified. This guy has shown a tendency to be violent toward his victims. We want to be sure we get this guy clean.

Bill calls Linda. The phone rings five times. Linda answers, "Hi, Bill. What's up?"

Bill responds, "I am waiting for Barbara Greene to call me back. She is on second shift. She should still be able to help check the data. I called Ed, Jake, and Charlie about the FAXES you are sending. I will have Bernie and Sandra check the paperwork you send me. Barbara should get back to Jane, Vivian, or you directly. By Wednesday evening or Thursday morning we should be ready to arrest the guy. I will be talking to you on Thursday."

Linda responds, "Good. Have a good couple of days until then."

Bill continues, "Same to you."

They hang up.

By Thursday morning everybody has read the paperwork three times. Barbara has verified the address and described the property to Linda, Jane, and Vivian. There are several houses on the property. There is a main farmhouse and several other buildings that appear to be bunkhouses or secondary residences. Bill is convinced they are ready to go. Linda has determined the guy is a worker on the farm. He travels throughout New England. Barbara observed he is home on Thursday morning. She has told Bill. The one question is he going to be home on Friday.

Bill calls Charlie, Ed, and Jake. He explains the team is going to meet at the motel near St. Johnsbury Vermont on Thursday evening for dinner. After breakfast they will head for the farm to execute the arrest warrant on Friday. He calls Barbara and asked her to join them for dinner and breakfast to help in the planning of the arrest. Everything is coming together nicely.

Around noon on Thursday Bernie, Sandra and Bill head for the motel in St. Johnsbury. He knows that Charlie, Ed, and Jake are heading to the motel also. Sam Apple from Barbara Greene's barracks joins them as extra help. Sam and Barbara do not need to be members of the task force since they will only be operating in New Hampshire. The members of the task force check in to their respective rooms. Sam and Barbara are local. They call Bill. He tells them to meet for dinner at 6:30 PM.

Bill arrives in the restaurant dining room at about 6:25 PM. The rest of the team arrives by 6:35 PM.

Matilda the waitress comes to their table. She says, "How can I help you ladies and gentlemen."

Bill answers, "Coffees all around, except the ladies want tea. Bring some ice water for everyone. Most of us like cream and sweetener. The ladies probably want some lemon for the tea. We will be ready to order in a few minutes."

Matilda says, "OK." She counts the number people. She continues, "I will be back shortly with the drinks."

Bill says, "Thank you."

Bill starts the serious conversation, "We need about an hour to get to the suspect's house and set up. There are multiple buildings on the property. So we will need to disburse across the property. Ed, Charlie, and myself will approach the main farmhouse. Barbara you need to position yourself where you can see the front entrance. After we move onto the property you can block the driveway at the road. Sandra I want you behind the main house. There are several outbuildings that look like bunkhouses. There is a barn. Bernie you take the barn. Jake you take the right end of the bunkhouse row. Sam you cover the left of the bunkhouse row. Be careful this guy is probably armed. After we check the main house Ed and I will come around to bunkhouse row."

Sandra says, "What time tomorrow?"

Bill says, "Let's have breakfast at seven. We should leave about eight. We should arrive at the farmhouse at about nine. Barbara told me there is a roadhouse about two miles South of the farm driveway. We will stop there. Then Barbara can move up to observe the farm. She will report back. We will then move to the farm and take up the positions. We can make sure there are NO additional questions at breakfast. Get a good night's sleep. Let's finish dinner. Make sure you wear your vests and your weapons and ammo are ready."

Matilda returns to the table to take their orders. After Matilda leaves with the orders Bill continues, "Sandra and I checked the paperwork from all three states. Charlie, I need you to check the paperwork from Vermont. I need Ed to check the paper work from Maine. Barbara, I need you to check the paperwork of all three states with regard to the description of the property and things like the addresses.

Barbara says, "I checked them yesterday, when Jane, Linda, and Vivian sent me copies."

Bill says, "I know you did. Just run through them again."

Everybody passes the paperwork around and reads it until Matilda returns with the food. The paperwork looks complete and accurate. The team is ready to go in the morning.

Bill says, "We want his guy. He has been violent to the victims on occasion in addition to raping them."

Matilda returns with food.

Matilda says, "You are all state police, but not from the same state."

Bill answers, "We are here on a mission. We obviously cannot discuss the details. It is does not involve the motel or the restaurant. We are just guests like any other guests."

They spend the rest of dinner engaged in chit-chat about their families and friends. Bill picks up the bill. They slowly leave for their rooms.

Bill calls Linda. The phone ring five times and Linda answers her cell. "Hi, Bill. What's up?"

Bill replies, "The courier caught up with us about an hour ago. I have the originals of the subpoenas and warrants from all three states. We just finished dinner and the discussion about the arrest tomorrow. I just wanted to check that there are no changes."

Linda continues, "Good. There are no mistakes or changes. Ok. Be careful. I will talk to you after the arrest."

Bill replies, "OK. Have a good evening."

They hang up.

Bill says, "I am going to read these one more time. Sandra, can you read them after I finish each document?"

Sandra replies, "OK."

The waitress comes over to the table. She says, "Can I help you?"

Sandra says, "Can you get me another tea, please?"

The waitress replies, "Certainly. Are you all with the police?"

Sandra answers, "Yes, but we cannot discuss why we are here."

The waitress says, "You are not in uniforms."

Sandra answers, "We were simply traveling today. The 'civvies' are more comfortable."

Bill says, "Can you bring me cup of coffee also?"

The waitress leaves to get the coffee. She returns in a couple of minutes with the tea and coffee.

Bill says, "Thank you. You can have someone clean the rest of the table."

Bill is reading the second subpoena. Sandra is reading the first subpoena. They add sugar, lemon, and cream to their drinks and keep reading. A young lady comes over and starts clearing the table.

Bill and Sandra finish in about fifteen minutes. As Sandra finishes, Bill says, "Have a good evening Sandra. I will see you in the morning."

Sandra responds, "See you in the morning."

They head to their respective rooms.

THE NEXT MORNING

It is 6:50 AM as Bernie arrives in the dining room area of the restaurant. Bill arrives at 7:05 AM. The rest of team members are there.

Matilda the waitress comes to the table and asks, "Are you ready to order?"

Bill answers, "I believe we are ready."

Matilda motions to Sandra and says, "Let's start with you."

Matilda takes all of the orders and says, "How many want coffees? How many want hot tea? Let me put the orders in and I will bring coffee and tea to the table."

Matilda comes back with regular and decaf coffee and then brings the hot tea. The cream, lemon, and sugar and several sweeteners are on the table. Matilda asks, "Anything else?"

Bill looks around the table and he says, "I think everyone is satisfied for now." Several people nod their approval.

Bill says, "Everybody is clear on their respective assignments at the farm. Barbara you have an unmarked car?"

Barbara responds, "Yes, I do Bill."

Matilda walks over and places two carriers of molasses and maple syrup and ketchup on the table. Bill nods thank you. She says, "About five more minutes for the food. The uniforms look good."

While eating, they chit chat about different topics. It is quarter to eight as they finish.

Bill says, "We should meet by the cars at a little before eight. I am going back to the room for a few minutes. Go to your rooms for any last minute needs. Make sure your weapons are OK. Does everyone have the vests on? Make sure you have them on. This guy is violent. See you all in a few minutes." He gets up and walks to his room. He pays the bill as he passes the cashier.

They all get in their cars and head out.

Bill and Ed go last in Bill's SUV.

Barbara arrives first at the Roadhouse Diner at about 9:04 AM. By 9:10 everyone else is at the lot. They park off to the side as a courtesy to the regular customers. Bill is out of his car and motion to everyone to join him. Barbara went inside right after she arrived. Bill sees her empty car and figures she is inside. A couple of the guys say they need the restroom. Bill tells them and anyone else to use the restrooms. We will wait. I want everyone to be comfortable. Barbara comes out. She walks over to Bill and says, "I am ready. Should I go now?"

Bill replies, "Yes go ahead. Observe from as far away as possible. Call me on my cell when you are in place."

Barbara leaves. It is about four minutes to the farm.

Barbara parks on a little rise in the road. She can see the farmhouse and the driveway entrance. She calls Bill.

Bill's phone rings three times, Bill answers, "Hi, Barbara. Are you in place?"

Barbara replies, "I can see the house and the entrance. Nothing is happening. No action."

Bill continues, "Ok we should be there in five minutes. Are you on our side of the entrance?"

Barbara answers, "Yes, I am." She hangs up.

Bill says to the other officers, "Barbara is in place. She is on our side of the entrance. Ed and I will be in the lead. We will open the gate. Then just roll in and take up your positions. Are there any questions?"

Nobody asks anything. Bill says, "Let's roll. Follow me." He and Ed jump into the SUV. The other officers do likewise and follow Bill. They spread out a little. Five minutes pass. Bill gets to the farm entrance. Ed gets out and unlatches the gate and hooks it open. He jumps back in and they proceed to the front of the farmhouse. Everyone else follows and takes up their respective positions. Charlie parks in front of the house. Ed and Bill are walking toward the front door. Bill looks around and sees Charlie. He jesters to Charlie the 'OK' sign. Sandra calls him on the walkie-talkie. I am in place Bill.

Bill acknowledges her message. He says to Ed, "You take the right side and I will take the left side of the door."

Bill raps hard on the door and yells, "**POLICE. OPEN THE DOOR. WE HAVE A WARRANT FOR THE ARREST OF GARY KIPLING. OPEN THE DOOR.**"

A small older man answers. Bill holds up the Subpoena and Search Warrant and says, "Sir, step outside. This is a search warrant to allow us to search this residence."

The man is slightly confused. He says, "Who are you looking for?"

Bill says, "We are looking for Gary Kipling."

The man says, "He left for White River about a half an hour ago."

Bill says, "Oh, Shit."

He says to Ed and calls to Charlie "We had better check the house thoroughly."

Bill says to the old man, "Who are you?"

The man answers, "I am Charles Brown. This is my farm. Gary Kipling is one of my hired hands. He lives in the bunkhouse around back. He lives in house "B". He shares the house with George Starling. Why do you want Gary?"

Bill says, "He is wanted for committing a number of felonies. We have this search warrant to search all the buildings on the property."

Charles says, "Well I cooperate with the police. But I do feel this is an invasion of my property."

Bill says, "We are not after you or anyone else living here. You said Gary went to White River Junction Vermont."

Charles says, "Yes. He is going there to get supplies. Some of the supplies are for the farm and some are for various workers. He should be back in a few hours."

Bill says, "I need you not to call him or contact him in anyway."

Charles says, "I will not, but there twenty people working here. I cannot guarantee someone else will call him."

Bill says, "OK. I have to search the other houses.

George has seen the police. He calls Gary. Gary answers his cell phone. "Hi George What's up? Do you need something from White River?"

George answers, "No. The police are all over the property. Not sure why. Do you have a legal problem? There must be eight or nine policemen?"

There is knock on door. Bill yells, "**THIS IS THE POLICE. WE HAVE A WARRANT FOR THE ARREST OF GARY KIPLING. OPEN THE DOOR.**"

Before George hangs up he says, "They are looking for you." He hangs up. He yells back. "I am coming to the door. I am Gary's roommate. He opens the door."

Bill says, "Please step outside. This is a search warrant for the property."

George says, "I am George Starling. I share the house with Gary. He went up to White River for supplies."

Bill says, "Do not contact Gary. We are going to arrest him."

George says nothing.

Bill turns to Ed. "We need to search this house completely."

Bill turns to the roommate, George. "Can you sit at the main house until we are finished."

George says, "Can I get the newspaper and my glasses on the table?"

Bill says, "Let me get them off the table."

He returns to the porch.

Bill says, "You can have the glasses, but I need to keep the paper."

George walks toward the main house.

Bill calls to Sandra. "Sandra, you should help Ed search this house."

Bill goes to the patrol car. He picks up the radio. He calls headquarters. He says on the radio, "The guy is headed to White River. Put out an APB and see who can cut him off in Lebanon on our side of the river."

Bill calls on the radio for everyone to gather behind the main house.

Charlie says, "The guy is going to White River Junction in Vermont."

Jake says, "How did he find out we were about to arrest him?"

Bill replies, "I think he is just going to get supplies. But if he gets into Vermont then we need to have the Vermont State Police arrest him. I do not think he knows we were going to arrest him. It is just bad luck on us."

Bill says to Charlie, "We need you to call Vermont with an All Points Bulletin (APB) to arrest the guy on site. You take the lead with Vermont and White River Junction Police. Contact Vivian to have her back up the APB."

Bill turns to Bernie, "Call Linda Smyth and issue an APB in New Hampshire. Call the Lebanon Police."

Bill says to Ed, "You take over here and get his living quarters searched. I want Barbara to remain on the gate. Get someone else to assist her. I am going to White River and follow him until he is caught. Charlie and Jake you are with Sandra and me. Keep this place secure."

Bill says, "Let's roll."

Bill stops at the gate and says to Barbara, "The guy is going to White River for supplies. We are going there also. I told Ed to send someone else to back you up on the gate. No one comes in; No one goes out, except our guys. Verify any medical emergency."

Barbara responds, "Got you serge."

They are on the road about ten minutes and Bill's phone rings. He hands it to Jake. Jake answers, "Jake Burns here. Bill is driving."

Bernie says, "This is Bernie. I contacted Linda and the Lebanon Police. Linda is having an APB issued for Gary Kipling in New Hampshire. Everybody should have it within ten minutes. When I called the Lebanon Police, they said an officer will be at the bridge over the Connecticut River to White River Junction."

Charlie says, "I just got off the phone with the police chief in White River. He said they will patrol the town looking for Gary's car."

Bill is on Interstate 91 headed south at 90 mph. He has the lights flashing, but no siren. They are still 30 minutes from White River Junction.

Charlie's phone rings. He answers it, "Charlie here. What's up Bart?"

Bart answers, "I believe we missed him. I think he is across the river. I saw a car meeting the description just going on the bridge. I have no jurisdiction in Vermont."

Charlie responds, "We have already notified the White River police and the Vermont State Police. White River has a small police force. We were told he was on a shopping trip. There are only a few stores where he would go in White River."

Gary knows the police are probably after him. He stops long enough to get gas. He thinks that he better head west. As he exits the gas station he sees a patrol car in the food store parking lot. He turns away from the patrol car and heads for the road out of town. Back roads are slower, but the main roads are patrolled more. There is the possibility that Vermont is not aware he is fleeing. He heads northwest toward the Crown Point Bridge. There is also a small cable ferry at Ticonderoga. If they know he is in White River, the police will think he is going to go west on Route 4. Three hours pass. He hasn't seen a patrol car on the back roads. After coming over Middlebury Gap he is on Vermont 25 approaching Vermont 17 at Crown Point. He does not see a patrol car sitting in a farm. The patrol car does see his car. The officer calls the car sitting near the bridge on Vermont 17. He also calls on his cell the New York troopers sitting on their side of the bridge. The car on route 25 closes behind him. The trooper on route 17 has the road blocked just east of the intersection. The New York troopers have blocked the bridge traffic from the west and one car is blocking the bridge just to the west of the state line. Gary realizes the car behind is closing fast. He speeds up hoping to get to the New York line. As he approaches the intersection he realizes route 17 is blocked to the east. He turns toward the bridge. He realizes the bridge is blocked. He turns into the small park next to the bridge the patrol car is now a few feet behind him. He tries to make a U-turn in parking lot. He is going way too fast and slides onto the grass between the Lake Shore and the parking lot. The car goes into the Lake. He scrambles out the passenger side window and starts to swim across the Lake. A New York trooper with a bullhorn yells if you make over here we will arrest you. Turn around and swim toward Vermont. It is closer. Gary considers his situation and decides to swim toward Vermont. The Vermont troopers are standing on the shore and fish him out of the water. They hand cuff him and wrap a blanket around his upper body. They read him his rights and explain to him he under arrest. They tell him he is being taken to Vergennes Vermont where they get him dry clothes before he is processed any further. Also he can request medical examination. They ask him if he understands these rights and this other information. He agrees he understands. They call Charlie and tell him Gary is in custody. Charlie suggests they meet in Rutland where

Gary can be detained temporarily at the local police station. Charlie, Jake, Bill, and Sandra drive across Route 4 to Rutland. They arrive before the troopers from Vergennes arrive. The local police are slightly surprised by their guests. They politely provide them with some coffee and a place to sit while the group waits for the troopers. Jennia is one of Vivian's assistants explains to the desk Sergeant that what every facilities they require while the prisoner is here are under the jurisdiction of the Vermont AG's office. This is not to usurp the local authority but to be sure the prisoner is held under the authority of the AG's office. There will be several state troopers who will help guard the prisoner and they will need to reside here until he is transferred to Montpelier or back to New Hampshire. Jennia says, "Sorry for the inconvenience."

The Sergeant replies, "That is OK. What did this person do?"

Jennia answers, "He allegedly raped a number of women in Maine, New Hampshire and Vermont. And he fled across New Hampshire and Vermont today. He is considered a felon, but legally he must be considered an alleged felon until tried in court. You know the game."

The Sergeant continues, "All too well."

A half an hour passes. The state police arrive with the suspect. The one officer, Bill Lincoln, comes in and sees Charlie and the desk Sergeant talking. He walks over and says, "We have the suspect in the car. Where do you want us to put him?"

The Sergeant calls the one other Rutland policemen, "Hey Smitty show Bill here the empty cell where they can put the suspect."

Smitty answers, "Right Serge. Come this way Bill." He walks Bill Lincoln through a door and down a short hall to the cellblock. "I understand this guy is a serious felon."

Bill Lincoln answers, "An alleged felon. He is wanted in Maine, New Hampshire, and Vermont. So he may be here a few days or we may take him to Montipelier for arraignment. He has been read his rights."

As Bill Lincoln and Smitty return to the lobby. Bill Simpson comes back in from the restroom. Bill Simpson walks over to the desk sergeant's desk. He says, "Charlie what has happened since I left for the restroom?"

Charlie responds, "The suspect is out in the car. Bill Lincoln here has arranged for the Rutland police to hold him until we can arrange for his transfer to Montipelier. He has been read his rights. Do you want to do it again and record the reading?"

Bill Lincoln says, "I am going to bring the prisoner in from the car."

Bill Simpson says, "Yes. We will record it here as soon as he is inside."

Sandra says, "I will get the video camera." She goes out to SUV.

Bill Lincoln goes to the car. John Louis is standing outside the police car. Gary is inside. John and Bill bring the prisoner inside the lobby.

Bill Lincoln says, "We read him his rights, but we did not ask him any questions. We just had him put on dry clothes in Vergennes. He went swimming in the lake when his car went into the lake. We have a towing company pulling the car out of the lake. We are taking it to Vergennes until we are told where it should be sent. The car will be under police control at all times."

Bill Lincoln and John Louis return to the lobby with Gary Kipling in handcuffs.

Bill Simpson says, "I am going to read him his rights while Sandra records the reading. I believe you read him his rights, but by recording the reading with witnesses erases any doubt about the procedure."

Bill Simpson then says to the suspect, "You are Gary Kipling? Please answer yes or no."

Gary answers, "Yes."

Bill continues, "You are charged with committing a number of rapes in Vermont, New Hampshire, and Maine. A detailed list of the crimes is attached to this warrant for your arrest. I am going to read you your rights. This is being recorded. These two officers are witnesses to the reading. Officer Charlie Wilson is from the Vermont State Police and Ed Woodworth is from the Maine State Police. I am Bill Simpson of the New Hampshire State Police." Bill reads Gary his rights. Bill asks, "Gary Kipling do you understand these rights?"

Gary answers, "Yes. I want an attorney present for any questioning."

Bill says, "Because you are wanted in all three states, the officers from all three states have witnessed the reading of your rights. There is a question I need to ask that is not about any crime you have allegedly committed or other actions. Do you need medical attention and/or do you need any medical treatment or take any medicine? Medical treatment will be provided if you require it."

Gary answers, "No."

Bill says, "If at any time during your incarceration you require medical treatment you only need to ask and it will be provided. You will be arraigned in the morning. The arraignment hearing is simply to determine if you can be held in jail before your trial. As soon as the judge appoints an attorney to represent you we will notify you and provide a copy of the charges to your attorney."

Gary says, "I do not have an attorney."

Bill responds, "An attorney will be appointed by the judge for tomorrow's hearing."

Bill continues, "I have here a subpoena for your DNA. I will wait till tomorrow to request your DNA. Your Lawyer can advise you about providing your DNA."

Bill motions to Sandra to stop the recording. Bill turns to the desk Sergeant and says, "Smitty can take Mr. Kipling to the cell. Remember he is to be single celled. The Vermont AG's office is in charge of Mr. Kipling's incarceration. Two Vermont State Police are going to be here in about fifteen minutes. The two State Police will be here until the arraignment tomorrow. If Mr. Kipling must be moved, the State Police must handle the move. This is a technicality not a reflection on your Force. You are going to have plenty of visitors tomorrow. Just verify their identities. Charlie Wilson is a Vermont State Policemen and is on the task force. He will be here in the morning and can take charge of the Kipling case."

Bill motions the desk Sergeant aside. He says, "This guy has allegedly raped 16 or more women. All three states want this guy. So we are making every effort to not foul up the arrest. Please pass on all of this Information to the next shift."

The desk Sergeant responds, "I understand. No mistakes."

Bill smiles and says, "Correct."

THE FOLLOWING MORNING

Vivian Bush arrives at 8:30 AM. She asks the desk sergeant to speak to Gary. The sergeant says, "Ms. Bush the prisoner requested an attorney after being read his rights. You are aware of the request."

Vivian answers, "Yes, I am. Thank you for reminding me."

The desk Sergeant calls officer Sam Horse, "Sam can you take the Lady to see Mr. Kipling. She is an ADA from Montipelier. It is OK for her to enter the cell, if she request entry. Stay in the cellblock."

Sam Says, "Come with me Madam."

As she passes the outer door to the cell Vivian says hello to the one State Trooper sitting near the door. He responds with a good morning.

Vivian follows Sam into the cellblock. She recognizes Gary as they approach his cell.

Sam says, "This is Mr. Kipling."

Vivian responds, "Thank you." She says to the second State trooper you need a break. Sam and I can handle the duty for a few minutes.

The trooper says thanks and says, "I was just about to ask Sam to spell me for a few minutes."

She addresses Gary, "I am Vivian Bush an ADA with the Vermont Attorney General's office. I will be the prosecuting attorney in court today. I am not your attorney. When you were first arrested you requested an attorney be present during any questioning. Do you still want an attorney?"

Gary replies, "Yes, I still want an attorney present."

Vivian continues, "Do you want a specific attorney or is a court appointed attorney acceptable to you during this initial arraignment hearing?"

Gary asks, "If I want a different attorney for other legal proceeding I can request a change. I do not have another attorney at this time."

Vivian continues, "The attorney that the judge is appointing is Robert Bowers. He is a local attorney with criminal law experience he will represent you in court today. I will present him with the list of crimes for which you are charged. You will have time to meet with your attorney before the court hearing. There is an interview room in the lobby of the station. It is secure and you can talk freely to your attorney. Robert Bowers will be here shortly. He will identify himself. About 11 AM the State Police will transport you and Robert to the courthouse down the street. Do you have any questions?"

Gary says, "None at this time."

Vivian continues, "I repeat. I am Vivian Bush, the ADA from Vermont. There will be two other ADA's in court; Jane Cordova from Maine, and Linda Smyth from New Hampshire. You are wanted in all three states. There will be additional hearings after today, but today's hearing only involves the crimes in Vermont. Ask your attorney any and all questions on your mind. There is a subpoena for your DNA. You need to ask your attorney about the subpoena for your DNA. You should ask your attorney about everything I have told you."

Gary says, "Thank you for the information."

Vivian responds, "It is my duty to inform you of your rights and the charges against you. You are welcome."

Vivian turns and leaves. Sam unlocks the cellblock door and motions to Vivian to go first. He follows.

Vivian walks to the Desk Sergeant's desk. Vivian addresses the desk sergeant, "An attorney Robert Bowers is going to represent Mr. Kipling in court today. I am meeting with the judge and Mr. Bowers to formally appoint him as Mr. Kipling's attorney. When Mr. Bowers arrives please provide him and Mr. Kipling with a private interview room. Their discussion must be considered as an attorney client privileged interview. Nobody else is to record or listen to the interview. Do you understand?"

The desk Sergeant replies, "I understand. I will see that the procedure is followed."

Vivian says, "Thank you. Have a good day."

The desk sergeant responds, "You have a good day. Get the guy."

Vivian has already turned toward the door. She gives the sergeant an OK with her right hand. She drives over to the court. As she enters, the courthouse guard says, "Ms. Vivian the judge is waiting for you in his chambers.'

Vivian replies, "Thank you." She stops at the ladies room and the proceeds to the judge's chambers."

Vivian raps on the door. A voice from inside says, "Come in." Vivian enters.

Judge Wilkenson is sitting at his desk. He says, "Good morning, Ms. Bush."

Vivian replies, "Good morning Your Honor."

The judge says, "This is Attorney Robert Bowers. We have been waiting for you."

Vivian responds, "I was over at the police station. I wanted to be sure they understood about the secrecy for the interview between the prisoner and Mr. Bowers. I also informed Mr. Kipling about today's proceedings and Mr. Bowers representation."

The judge turns to the court stenographer, "Are you ready, Linda? Ms. Vivian and Mr. Bowers are you ready to proceed?"

Linda answers, "I am ready your Honor."

Vivian responds, "I am ready judge."

Robert respond, "I am ready, your Honor."

Judge Wilkenson proceeds, "Robert Bowers, I asked you yesterday whether you could represent Mr. Kipling the defendant in this case. Do you have any conflicts with this representation?"

Robert responds, "I have two other cases before the court at present. However, they are not related to this case. Except for a scheduling conflict I can handle all three cases. Since you are the judge for the other two cases, any scheduling conflicts would apply to you as well as myself."

The judge says, "I will interpret your answer as a no conflict."

Robert says, "No conflicts, your honor."

The judge turns to Vivian and says, "Ms. Bush do you have any objections to Robert Bowers representing the defendant?"

Vivian answers, "None."

The judge continues, "I will ask the defendant at the start of the court proceeding if he has any problems with Robert Bowers as his attorney. Mr. Robert Bowers I appoint you to represent Mr. Gary Kipling for the arraignment hearing and all following legal actions against Mr. Kipling. Mr. Kipling can request your replacement at any time."

The judge says, "Ms. Vivian Bush, as the ADA from Vermont please give copies of the charges against Mr. Kipling to attorney Robert Bowers."

Vivian answers, "Robert Bowers as the attorney of record for Mr. Gary Kipling here is the documentation on all the charges from the State of Vermont. There is a simple list of the charges and detailed warrants for each charge. He is a fugitive from New Hampshire and is also wanted in Maine. I will ask the ADA's from New Hampshire and Maine to provide a list of those charges. There is a subpoena from Vermont for a DNA sample in the paperwork. This arraignment only covers the charges from Vermont."

Judge Wilkenson says, "This arraignment only covers the charges in Vermont. However the court is aware that Mr. Kipling is a fugitive from New Hampshire and Maine. Mr. Kipling will not be released until a ruling can be made on his return to the either of the other two states. I am going to review the paperwork again before the arraignment. I am going to schedule the arraignment for 11:15 AM today. Any questions before I close this proceeding."

Vivian and Robert simply each say OK.

The judge says, "This procedure is closed. Mr. Robert Bowers you are the attorney to represent Mr. Kipling. Court will convene at 11:15 AM. Thank you."

Vivian says, "Robert, do you know where the Police Station is here in Rutland."

Robert says, "Yes, I have been there a bunch of times."

Vivian says, "I told the desk sergeant you would need a secure interview room to confer with Mr. Kipling. The sergeant will ask you for identification. See you in court."

Robert replies, "Thank you. See you in court."

The judge interjects a comment; "Please have the desk sergeant call the bailiff if you are going to need more time with your client. I hope you will be ready by 11:15 AM. But it is important you do everything legally," Robert replies, "I don't think I will need more time, your Honor."

The judge says, "OK, I will see you and Vivian at 11:15 AM."

Robert and Vivian leave.

Jane and Linda are waiting at the front of the courthouse for Vivian. Vivian introduces Robert. Robert says, "Hate to run but I must go to the police station." He leaves.

Linda says, "Bill, Ed, and Jake are on the way."

Vivian says, "Charlie Wilson is at the Police Station. There is a Diner down the street. Why don't we go down there and wait?'

Linda says, "I will call the guys and tell them to meet us there."

Vivian says, "I will call Charlie."

They walk to the Diner. Charlie arrives at 10:10 AM. At about 10:15 AM Bill, Ed and Jake arrive.

Evelyn the waitress comes over and asked what each of them would like. They all order a little to eat and drink.

Vivian says is there anything we need to discuss.

Linda says, "Nothing. The judge has a fugitive warrant from New Hampshire and Maine. He should not release Gary after the hearing."

Vivian says, "He said that Gary would be held until each of you submit paperwork to move him."

They continue to talk about other things.

ROBERT BOWERS INTERVIEWS GARY
AND THE ARRAIGNMENT

Meantime at the police station, Robert Bowers addresses the desk sergeant, "Good morning sergeant. I am Robert Bowers. I am the attorney for Gary Kipling. Here is my identification. I will need to use your interview room. Please have the prisoner Gary Kipling brought to the interview room. Your interview room is secure?"

The desk sergeant responds, "The room is already. Vivian Bush prepared everything for you. The interview room is over there. I will have the prisoner brought in immediately. We have been waiting for you. Turn on the light and have a seat." He continues, "Officer Bart can you get the prisoner Gary Kipling and bring him to the interview room?"

Bart replies, "Right away, Sergeant." He goes to the cellblock and brings Gary back to the interview room.

Bart says, "Mr. Kipling, please have a seat." Bart releases one of the handcuffs and connects it to the security rail on the table. He continues, "Just tap on the door glass when you are ready to leave." Bart leaves and closes the door behind him.

Robert flips the lock on the door. He says, "I am Robert Bowers an attorney with criminal law experience. I was appointed by Judge Wilkenson to represent you in the hearing today. Although the judge just appointed me formally about fifteen minute ago, he had told me yesterday. The ADA, Vivian Bush, had the charges FAXED to me yesterday. So let us cover a couple of formal questions and procedures.

"I am going record this interview. Everything you tell me is covered by Attorney-Client privilege.

"Are you satisfied to have me as your attorney? Please answer yes or no."

Gary replies, "Yes, I am."

Robert continues, "You were read your rights and you requested an attorney."

Gary answers, "I was read my rights when they pulled me out of the lake, yesterday. The State Police Sergeant from Vermont read me the rights again and recorded the reading with witnesses from Maine and New Hampshire. All three states have brought charges against me."

Robert continues, "Ok that is acceptable. Were you interviewed or questioned."

Gary answers, "I was not questioned. The lady ADA did explain what the hearing was about today and that you were going to be appointed as my attorney."

Robert continues, "She did not question you."

Gary continues, "Only that I understood what she explained. She said they had a subpoena for a DNA sample, but I could talk to you first."

Robert continues, "They made no attempt to get a DNA sample."

Gary answers, "No. They asked me if I had any medical problems that required medicine."

Robert continues, "OK. Today the hearing is about whether you will be held in jail or released on bond. It is unlikely you will be released. The seriousness of the charges preludes any bail. If the judge asks how you would plead to the charge, plead not guilty. Look at me if you are asked any questions. I will give you an OK sign then answer. Do not admit any guilt. You can ask for my advice on any question. Be very polite to the judge and the prosecuting attorney. The arraignment does not determine your guilt or innocence. We will approach those problems later. The judge can hold you in a local jail or send you to prison. You want him to hold you in a local jail at this time. So be polite."

Gary says, "I understand."

Robert continues, "I will see you in court. I know it is hard to relax, but try. If you have any medical problem the state is required to take care of it immediately. After today's hearing I will come back and talk to you. I may suggest another attorney to help with your defense. I have no problem defending you, but after I study the charges in more detail I may recommend help. There will be a series of hearings related to the charges in New Hampshire and Maine. I will represent you at those hearings also. I can practice in New Hampshire and Maine. It will be a day or two before I have the information on those hearings. You can refuse to provide a DNA sample. The state will continue to pursue their need for a sample and the court will finally order the sample to be taken. If you agree I will insist that two samples be processed, one by the state and one by a lab of our choice. This eliminates the possibility of a mistake or any funny business. I will see you in court at 11:15."

Gary says, "OK. See you in court. Thank You."

Robert responds, "I am your attorney. I only answer to you. I am here to defend you, innocent or guilty. You are NOT guilty until found guilty in a court of law. Do NOT talk about the case to anyone except me. Other prisoners can use the information you tell them to testify against you as a trade for lowering their punishment."

Gary says, "I understand."

Robert raps on the window of the door. Bart opens the door. He says, "You are finished?"

Robert checks his recorder to see it is off. He answers Bart, "Yes."

Robert walks to the desk sergeant desk and says, "Mr. Kipling is due in court at 11:15. You have been contacted formally about delivering the prisoner to the courthouse?"

The desk sergeant responds, "Yes. He will be there on time. The judge doesn't blame the prisoners for being late. He blames us."

Robert says, "Have a good day Sergeant."

The desk sergeant says, "Same to you, sir."

Robert returns to the courthouse. It is 11:00. He uses the restroom and then goes to the courtroom. There is nobody in the room. He sits at the defendant table. He relaxes. At about 11:10 Vivian, Linda, and Jane come in. Vivian sees Robert and walks over to him. He stands. Vivian says, "Robert Bowers this is Jane Cordova the ADA from Maine on this case. They shake hands. This is Linda Smyth the ADA from New Hampshire on the case. They shake hands. Bill Simpson the one State Policeman and Linda have been leading the charge on a number of rape cases. I am sure you will be meeting them again when Gary is arraigned in the other two states.

Robert responds, "Thank you for the introduction."

Vivian goes to the prosecution table. Jane and Linda take seats in the gallery. The stenographer and the bailiff enter the courtroom. Bill, Ed, Charlie and Jake enter and take seats in the gallery. The bailiff gets up and goes to the judge's chambers. He comes back in a couple of minutes. The sheriff brings the prisoner in and removes the handcuffs. Gary takes a seat with his attorney.

The bailiff stands up and says, "Ladies and gentlemen, we are going to have a few minute delay. The judge has a personal phone call." He sits down.

About five minutes pass. The judge opens the door to his chambers. The bailiff stands and says, "Please stand. Court is in session, the honorable Judge Wilkenson presiding."

Judge Wilkenson says, "please be seated. Sorry for the short delay. The wife called. Even judges have bosses."

Everyone laughs.

The judge says to the bailiff, "What is the matter before the court today?" The judge knows but it is a formality to record the information.

The bailiff answers, "The matter before the court is the arraignment of Mr. Gary Kipling on various charges brought by the State of Vermont. This is a hearing to determine whether Mr. Kipling will be released on bail or held in jail until his trial."

The judge says, "Mr. Kipling please stand. Please read the list of charges."

The bailiff reads the charges.

The judge says, "Mr. Kipling are you represented by an attorney?"

Robert Bowers stands. He says, "I am Mr. Kipling's attorney. He has accepted me to represent him."

The judge says, "Attorney Bowers you have read the charges and have you had time to consider the case with respect to this hearing."

Robert answers, "I have."

The judge says, "Who is representing the state?"

Robert and Gary sit down. Vivian stands. She says, "I am Vivian Bush Vermont ADA. I will be the prosecuting attorney for this hearing."

The judge says, "Mr. Gary Kipling. You have read the charges. This is not a trial but a hearing about setting bail. However I have to ask how you would plead if this were a trial."

Gary stands. He answers after looking at Robert, "I plead NOT guilty."

The judge says, "You can be seated. Vivian, what does the state request with respect to bail or incarceration?"

Vivian answers, "The state requests incarceration. As you know all the charges are serious felonies. Mr. Kipling was trying to run when he was caught. He has no permanent resident here in state. He has only out of state relatives. He has allegedly committed similar crimes in two other states. He is a fugitive from those states."

The judge turns to Gary and his attorney, "Robert can you comment on bail verses incarceration."

Robert stands and addresses the judge, "We acknowledge that ADA Vivian has stated the facts correctly. We would request that Gary be held in local jails if you refuse bail."

The judge sits quietly for a few moments. He speaks, "Considering the seriousness of the charges and the lack of any local ties, I am going to incarcerate Mr. Kipling until his trial. I will permit him to be held in local jails rather than a state prison. Is there any other business?"

Vivian says, "There is the matter of a subpoena to request a DNA sample."

The judge says, "Robert are you requesting the subpoena be blocked?"

Robert says, "I have review the subpoena and cannot request that the taking of the sample be blocked. I do request two samples be processed. One sample is to be processed by the state and one sample by a lab specified by the defendant."

The judge says, "Then I order the samples be taken and be processed as you requested. The results can still be accepted or rejected at the time of trial."

The bailiff stands and says, "Please stand. Court is adjourned."

Judge Wilkenson stands. He says, "Vivian can you bring the ADA's from New Hampshire and Maine to my chambers. Thank You."

Vivian answers, "Yes sir. Can you give us a few minutes?"

The judge says, "Take a little time."

Five minutes pass.

Vivian brings Jane and Linda to the Judges chamber. She asks Bill, Ed, Charlie and Jake to wait outside.

Vivian knocks on the Judge's door. Judge Wilkenson says, "Come in Please."

Vivian enters and says, "Good day Judge."

Judge Wilkenson replies, "This is not a formal meeting. I just want to understand about all the crimes this man has committed."

Vivian says, "I would like to bring the State Policemen that were chasing him. One of them Sergeant Bill Simpson can explain the other crimes."

The Judge says, "Bring them in."

Vivian opens the door and says, "Guys come in." She introduces the other ADA's and the guys.

The judge says, "Mr. Simpson can you explain the charges in the other states."

Bill replies, "We are on a task force to identify and hunt down serial rapists. We have used some math and good old fashion police work to identify these criminals. We have captured two rapists that have allegedly committed about thirty-five rapes in the three states. Gary Kipling has been identified as the third rapist. Legally he is an alleged rapist, but we have enough evidence to have the arrest warrant and the subpoenas. There is a lady mathematician that is tracking the rapists for us."

The judge says, "How does the tracking work?"

Bill responds, "The lady matches the physical characteristics from a number of rapes. She matches the DNA from the rape kits. We check motels and rooming houses in the area around the area where each rape occurred and compare names. When we have eight to ten locations with the same name then we start concentrating on that person as a possible suspect. We use public information like driver licenses to be sure the physical characteristics match. If everything checks out and matches for the rapist then we close in on the guy who we have identified."

The judge says, "Very interesting. Linda and Jane you want this guy also."

Linda responds, "I don't want him. The state of New Hampshire wants him for five rapes in New Hampshire.'

Jane says, "The state of Maine wants him for four rapes in Maine. Linda and I are preparing papers to request extradition to each state. We definitely want to try him also. We want to be sure he stays in jail till he is old and gray or dies. He has been violent while committing the rapes."

The judge says, "Thank you for the information."

Vivian says, "Hope this helps you understand."

The judge says, "Thank You. Have a good day."

Vivian responds, "You are welcome your honor. You have a good day."

The others nod their approval of Vivian's comments.

They leave. Once outside the judge's chamber Vivian says, "Everybody ready for lunch."

Bill says, "I am."

Jake says, "The little diner down the street?"

Vivian responds, "That's Ok with me. Everyone OK with the diner?"

Nobody disapproves. So they head out of the courthouse and walk to the diner.

Bill says, "Charlie you need to move Gary's car to an impound facility."

Charlie replies, "It is already at an impound lot in Montipelier."

Bill calls Barbara. The phone ring five times. Barbara answers, "Hi Bill."

Bill responds, "Have forensic team finished at the bunk house?"

Barbara answers, "Yes completely. They found several weapons and several pieces of clothing. The lab is processing the evidence as we speak."

Bill says, "Good. Talk to you tomorrow."

CHAPTER 19

THE FOURTH SUSPECT CHARLES BILLINGS

Mattie has identified the last two suspects from the five groups of cases. Linda Smyth has reviewed her findings and agrees. The two suspects are Charlie Billings and Marshall Brickman. Charlie lives in upstate Maine. Marshall lives in New Hampshire. Mattie told Bill on the weekend.

Bill calls Linda on Monday, "Good Morning Linda. Hope you had a good weekend."

Linda replies, "I had a pretty good weekend. Did you and Mattie have good weekend?"

Bill replies, "We celebrated our success and Mayor Bernard's public praise. Mattie told me that you and she have identified the last two suspects and located number four."

Linda continues, "Yes. The fourth suspect is a survivalist type. He lives near Baxter State Park in Northern Maine. I talked to Jake a little while ago. I was going to call you. Someone interrupted me before I could call. Jake told me Ed Woodworth lives near the town of Sherman to the east of the park. Jake said that the two of you could stay there and plan the arrest. Please call Jake."

Bill replies, "Ok. I will call Jake. Are you processing an arrest warrant and subpoenas to search the property?"

Jane and Vivian are processing arrest warrants and subpoenas, also.

Linda continues, "They will be ready tomorrow morning."

Bill says, "Ok. We will pick them up and head for Sherman in the morning. Good bye for now."

Linda replies, "Good Bye."

Bill calls Jake, "Good Morning. How are you this fine Monday morning?"

Jake replies, "I am fine. How are you Bill?"

Bill replies, "I am fine. Linda told me you have a friend in Sherman where we can meet and plan the arrest."

Jake continues, "You know Ed Woodward and I attended and graduated from the police academy in the same class. We have been friends since then. I am going to call Ed and arrange for us to meet on Wednesday at his place. I am sure he will want in on the arrest. If we have the rest of the team along some of us will need a motel."

Bill says, "More the merrier."

Jake continues, "I am going to have one of the officers near Augusta drive the Maine warrants and subpoenas up to Concord. Charlie should pick up the Warrants and Subpoenas from Vermont. We should be able to head for Sherman around 11 AM. Ed's wife is a good cook, so we should have dinner at their house Tuesday evening. I am told that this suspect does not respect law enforcement. I am going to have several local officers and several state police participate in the arrest."

Jake continues, "Before you called I talked to a local officer and he knows this guy. He is a real survivalist and gun toting radical. I think we will want help. The guy knows the area better than most other people. We need to be prepared for a chase and a long day."

Bill continues, "I will bow to your judgment. I will see you in the morning about 11 AM."

Bill calls Ed. The phone rings five times. Ed answers, "Sergeant Ed Woodworth Maine State Police. How can I help you?"

Bill replies, "Hi, Ed. Bill Simpson here."

Ed says, "Hi, what's up."

Bill continues, "We have identified a fourth suspect. He lives near Baxter Park and is a survivalist. I have been told that he doesn't have much respect for authority."

Ed continues, "Why don't we meet at my barracks. It is on the way to Baxter. Is Charlie coming from Vermont?"

Bill continues, "Sandra and Bernie will be coming along also. Is there a motel we can use in the area?"

Ed thinks for a moment and says, "There is the Super motel in Sherman."

Bill continues, "I will make arrangements for Sandra, Bernie and myself. You will need to make arrangement for Jake. I'll talk to Charlie about his arrangements."

Ed says, "You and Jake should plan on staying at my house. We can plan the arrest at my house. Everyone else can join us at the house for dinner and in the morning for breakfast. Some people are definitely going to stay at the motel."

Bill says, "This is a very generous offer."

Ed says, "See you tomorrow around 11 AM. Tell the others to arrive here by the afternoon"

Bill responds, "11 AM. OK tomorrow."

They hang up.

Bill calls Charlie. The phone rings six times. Charlie answers, "Hi, Bill. What's up?"

Bill continues, "Mattie and Linda have identified two more suspects. They have located the fourth suspect Charlie Billings. He is a survivalist type. He lives near Baxter State Park in Northern Maine. According to a friend of Jake, he doesn't have much respect for authority. We are going to meet at Ed Woodworth's house about 11AM, tomorrow. I know it is short notice, but we want to get this guy. Linda, Jane, and Vivian knew whom Mattie had identified last week. They immediately prepared the paperwork.

"First, are you going to be able to make it tomorrow? There is a good motel in Sherman. Jake and you are invited to stay at Ed's house with me. If anyone else comes from Vermont they will need a room at the motel."

Charlie responds, "I will see you at about 11 AM at Ed's house."

Bill answers, "Sandra and Bernie are also coming. Bring your vest. See you tomorrow. Have a good day."

Charlie responds, "See you tomorrow."

They hang up."

THE NEXT MORNING

Bill leaves Concord at 6:30 AM in an unmarked SUV. Sandra and Bernie leave a few minutes later in a state police SUV. They drive to Sherman and Ed's house. Both of them stop for a little breakfast. Meanwhile Charlie leaves his barracks near White River and heads for Montpelier to pick up the paperwork from Vivian. Then he heads for Ed's house.

George Jefferson is coming from Augusta with the paperwork from Jane Cordova. He stops for coffee and a potty break. He continues to Ed's house. Ted Forester is coming from near the Canadian Border. Jim Bowers, Henry Davidson, and Jane McCullogh are from the barracks in Aroostook County. Allen Woodson and Barbara Linganore are from Penobscot County.. Will Van Sant from Piscataquis County is a Local Policeman. The Ranger Sergeant from Baxter Park, Howard Fireside is a Native American and like Jim Bowers can track anything through the forest. The last player is the Chief of the local volunteer fire department. They are all headed for Ed's house.

Ed stayed home today. He does make a run to the local grocery store in Sherman with a list from Melissa. She is going to prepare lunch for the crowd and later dinner. She needs donuts and Danishes for tomorrow morning. Ed gets everything on her list. He picks up some beer for the crowd after dinner. Ed returns home at about 10:15 AM. He helps Melissa but some of the food in the refrigerator and a cabinet.

Before coming to the planning session the local Aroostook County officer, Jim Bowers, drives up to the area where the suspect lives. He uses his own car so as to not appear to be the police. He has fished in this area and hunted in the fall. He refreshes his memory. There is a stream valley to the East of the suspect's cabin. There is a trail up the valley to a lake. He cannot directly see the cabin, but the land slopes up from the road and on both sides. He returns to Sherman and the meeting.

Bill, Sandra, and Bernie arrive at 10:45 AM. Ed greets them at the front door. Ed leaves the inner door open. By 11:15 the other players have arrived. Melissa has tea and coffee ready in the kitchen. Several people need the rest room.

Melissa has prepared lunch. She says, "Before you get serious about the arrest tomorrow have some lunch. Relax a little and then Bill and Ed can go forward with the serious stuff.

Bill says, "Let us enjoy lunch, but I do want to introduce you to each other. Tomorrow we are going to be working together. Just try to learn everyone's name. When you pass the lunch stuff you need to address each other by first names. It will help."

Ed says, "After lunch we are going out in the back yard for a little rehearsal."

Bill says, "I want each of us tell all of us a little bit about your background. It will help us to remember who is who."

As lunch progresses each person tells everyone a little bit about his or her respective background. At about 1:00 PM. lunch is finished.

Bill says, "It is time to get serious about why we are all here. My lady friend and the ADA's from New Hampshire, Maine, and Vermont have identified a suspect as serial rapist. They agree the person they identified, Charlie Billings, is the alleged rapist. We are here today to plan how we are going to arrest him. He is a survivalist and does not recognize our authority. Ed Woodworth and I have brought all of you here because this guy will probably try to run or may simply start a fight. I want to surround the house, which is more like a log cabin. Then we will call him out.

Ed continues the conversation, "Ladies and Gentlemen, as Bill said we are here to arrest the fourth suspect in a number of rape cases. I am sure you have heard on the news about Bill Simpson, Jake, and me capturing three rapists in the last few weeks. This suspect is number four and there is a fifth. The suspect has been identified as a survivalist and a loner living in a cabin between here and Baxter Park. His name is Charlie Billings. I think several of you casually know of this guy. The situation tomorrow could turn violent. So we are going in prepared. When I and several of you finish the briefing I would like you all to sit here and make sure you know each other and each other's names."

Ed says, "Jim Bowers is from Aroostook County and he is going to describe the cabin and the lay of the land around the cabin."

Jim begins, "The cabin sits on a knoll above the surrounding land. It has a front and back door and windows on all four sides. The walls are eight-inch diameter logs. Our weapons will not penetrate the walls. The cabin is 600 feet north of the road up a slightly curved driveway. To the east is a stream valley. To the west is a smaller valley. There is the shore of a lake probably a thousand feet to the north. There is a clearing in front of the house. The area is heavily wooded. When I was up on the property about 2 years ago, there were clearings around the cabin. The guy does go to a local firing range and the owner of the range told me he is an excellent shot and owns a variety of weapons and probably has lots of ammo."

Ed continues, "Jake Burns and Bill Simpson will be my seconds in command." I am going to separate you into two person teams and position you on the sides and rear of the cabin. Jake, Bill and I will approach from the front and attempt to serve the arrest warrant. As Jim says the guy does not recognize our authority. I am expecting the worst. The radio frequency is common to most of us, but I brought several extra radios so we can all be on the same frequency. Chief I need you to have an EMS unit positioned to the east of the property at the stream valley just in case. Linda Smyth the New Hampshire ADA and Jane Cordova the Maine ADA both want us to take the guy alive if possible, but not at the expense of one of us."

Melissa walks in and interrupts the discussion says, "Please excuse me. Please take some coffee and take a donut or Danish. Ed doesn't need all the donuts. I will have coffee and donuts tomorrow when you gather here.

Ed continues, "My kids have a play house in the back yard. They are grown and do not use it, but we are going to simulate the operation. The house faces in a different direction than the cabin, but we are going to change the directions of the house. Let's put your coffees down and I will lead the way to the yard. Each team should take one of these lights and everyone should have their flashlights. You need the flashlights for tomorrow, but not now.

They all go out to the yard and gather around the house. Jake says, "Let's come over here in front of the house but like we are on the road. Howard you take Allen and Barbara and walk up the road to my left. Turn in toward the cabin, but walk parallel to the driveway and then turn toward the cabin. Now Jim is going to lead Henry, Jane, and Will up the stream valley to my right. Will can stay in the valley while Jim leads Jane and Henry up closer to the cabin. Jim will come back down and join Will and they will continue down the valley and come up behind the cabin. Chief you will have your EMS team on the road at the stream valley over here to my right. You can sit the light on the ground. Remember this guy could fire at the lights."

Henry asks, "Are the lights on as we approach?"

Ed answers, "NO, use your flashlight for the approach. Minimum light during the approach. The Lights are used once we have the suspect's attention to indicate there are teams surrounding the cabin. Be careful he could fire at the lights. We are going to approach the cabin before dawn. Let's go back in the house and discuss any questions."

They return to the living room. They move around a little and sit down as the teams. Ed says, "We are going to meet here at 3:30 AM. That should give us time to drive to the site and be in place before dawn. I am basically finished with the set up for tomorrow."

The other people talk to each other on the team. The fire chief does ask Ed about the roll of the EMS team. Ed explains it is simply a precaution in case someone is wounded. Your guys will be far enough away to be out of the line fire. The chief tells Ed he will come with the team. He tells Jake and Ed he is going to use several of the guys and one of the ladies with combat medical experience. Ed agrees that is good idea.

Melissa walks in again and says, "You are invited to dinner at about 5:30 tonight."

They finish the serious discussions about the arrest at 2:00.

Bill says to Sandra, "Do you have all the paperwork?"

Sandra answers, "Yes I do."

Bill continues, "Get with Jim for a few minutes to verify the buildings on the property and the address."

Bill calls to Jim, "Jim, can you sit with Sandra and check the information in the search warrants about the property. Check the number of buildings and the address. Make sure the road name and stuff like the name are correct. You know the property. If you need to look again, please use the unmarked car."

Jim replies, "OK. We can sit here and go through the paperwork."

Bill says, "I am going with Ed when we finish. Sandra you know how to contact Linda, Jane or Vivian?"

Sandra says, "Yes, I do. They all told me that they would be standing by for corrections."

Jim and Sandra check all the paperwork. After the planning session most of the people head for the motel to check in. The locals head to their jobs for the remainder of the afternoon. Bill, Jake, and Charlie go with Ed to his barracks.

Bill, Jake, Charlie and Ed arrive back at Ed's house around 5 PM.

Melissa comes in from the kitchen and says; "I saw the story on the news. You are sort of a local celebrity."

Bill replies, "I am not sure I am much of a celebrity."

Melissa continues, "I have started dinner. Are the other people coming?"
Ed answers her, "Yes at about 5:30."

Melissa continues, "Make your selves comfortable while I cook. I hope you like baked ham. I made some meatballs and pasta if some you don't like the ham."

Bill replies, "I am looking forward to a home cooked meal."

The national news comes on. "The national news commentator is talking about the arrest in Maine of the serial rapists and the part Bill, Ed, Jake and Charlie played in the apprehension of the suspects."

Bill says, "If all goes well tomorrow, I wonder what the news is going to be?"

Ed says, "Instead of the Lone Ranger and Tonto, Maybe we should be called the sheriff's Posse."

Melissa walks in and says, "Maybe you guys are celebrities, but how about the women behind the posse."

Ed says, "You know that you are my celebrity."

Melissa replies, "I know. Bill, who is your celebrity? Jake and Charlie you are both married, so I can guess who your celebrities are?"

Ed says, "Bill has a lady friend, Mattie. Bill told me Mattie is a good cook. She is also the Mathematician who has been helping us with the data. We don't tell most people who Mattie is to protect her, but you can know."

Bill says, "Mattie has become my celebrity."

The doorbell rings. Ed says, "I'll get it."

Henry Davidson and Jane McCullogh from Aroostook County are at the door.

Ed says, "Come in."

He waits for Sandra and Bernie to come up to the porch. He says, "Come in."

Ed says, "Bill take over the door duty. I am going to get the wine and help Melissa with the table."

There is a wrap on the door. Bill gets up. It is Allen Woodson and Barbara Linganore from Penobscot County. Jim Bowers is coming up the walk to the porch. Bill says, "Come in dinner is almost ready."

A few minutes pass and the doorbell rings. Bill goes to the door. It is Will Van Sant from Piscataquis County. Howard Fireside is coming across the yard. The fire chief is just getting out of his SUV. Bill waits for Howard and the Chief before he closes the door.

Ed comes into the living room and says, "Dinner is served. Take any seat around the table." Ed is sitting at the one end nearest the kitchen. Melissa is sitting next to Ed. She is close to the kitchen. Ed says, "We always say grace before dinner and thank God for the good day. You are welcome to join us or not."

They spend dinner chit chatting about their kids and friends. Bill tells them about Mattie.

Bill explains that they should be here tomorrow at about 3 AM. Several local county officers will be joining them. One of the locals is going to scout the property. Sandra and Bernie excuse themselves and head for the motel. The other officers head for home or the motel. At about 10PM Bill, Ed, and Jake get their clothes from the SUV and prepare to shower before bed."

Melissa puts a few snacks on the table and tells them Ed and her have a midnight snack most evenings. Bill, Jake and Charlie join their host. Ed tells them he has invited the local officers to the house at 3 AM tomorrow. They watch the news on the TV. The Commentator again tells the story about the capture of the rapists.

Bill says, "Melissa and Ed we thank you for the hospitality.

Melissa answers, "I am glad you all are getting some of these criminals off the street."

MORNING COMES EARLY

Melissa gets up with Ed. She goes down to the kitchen and puts coffee on. Ed, Jake, and Bill get up and shave and prepare for the day. Ed gets ready also. Melissa has return to their bedroom and gets dressed. She puts some donuts and Danish on the table. She also puts some bread, jelly, butter, and places the toaster on the table for the other officers. It is about

3:15 AM when the first officers arrive. They begin to talk about the day. By 3:35 AM everyone is there and the EMS team has their vehicle outside. Our neighbors are going to call Melissa today to find out who needed the EMS vehicle. Ed says if anyone needs the facilities there is one in the basement and one at the end of the hallway and one at the top of the stairs. We are going to leave in ten minutes. It is about 20 minutes to the area of the suspect's house on the road. No flashing lights and no sirens. When we get to the stream east of the driveway we will deploy. Ranger Fireside brought his own unmarked SUV so he can drive the team for the west side up the road unnoticed. I am going to lead, but we do not want to look like a convoy. I will stop at the stream valley and the EMS vehicle can park there. Jim and his two teams will deploy up the valley. When each of you call-in that you are in place. I will call every team and tell you we are going up to the front of the cabin. You will hear me ask the guy to surrender. Then we will be playing it by ear. The EMS team is out of their vehicle and sitting on the back tailgate area. Ed repeats they should stay in place unless he or Jake or Bill calls for them. Bernie is with Sandra blocking the driveway.

Several minutes pass and the team at the back of the cabin call-in. They are the last of three teams to call in. Ed calls on the radio that the front team is moving to the cabin. Jake drives his SUV and Bill rides with him. Ed brings his own SUV to the driveway and then joins Jake and Bill. As they reach the front of the cabin there is just a sliver of Sun light on the horizon.

Ed takes the bullhorn from the SUV. Bill and Ed go up to the porch and approach the door. On a signal from Ed, Bill pounds on the door and yells "**POLICE. POLICE OPEN THE DOOR. WE HAVE A WARRANT FOR YOUR ARREST. COME OUT WITH YOUR HANDS UP. THE CABIN IS SURROUNDED.**" He is standing to the right side against the wall. Ed is standing to the Left side.

Jake using the second bullhorn announces the same thing, "**POLICE. POLICE OPEN THE DOOR. WE HAVE A WARRANT FOR YOUR ARREST. COME OUT WITH YOUR HANDS UP. THE CABIN IS SURROUNDED.**"

Nothing happens for about one minute. Then several shots come from the front window of the cabin. Bill quickly moves to the right and around several trees and finally takes cover behind an old tractor. Ed moves to the left and takes cover behind an old car. It is still too dark for the suspect to see Bill, Ed or Jake moving through the shadows by the trees. Bernie leaves Sandra at the driveway and moves up the driveway behind a number of trees.

Ed calls the three teams, "turn on your big light and get away from it as quickly as possible."

They do.

Ed calls on the Bullhorn again. "**MR. BILLINGS, COME OUT WITH YOUR HANDS UP. WE HAVE YOU SURROUNDED. WE HAVE A WARRANT FOR YOUR ARREST. LET'S END THIS PEACEFULLY.**"

From inside the cabin the suspect calls, "**I DO NOT RECOGNIZE YOUR AUTHORITY. YOU PIGS GET OFF MY PROPERTY, NOW.**" He fires another round at the SUV. It puts a hole in the passenger's side door.

Jake says on the radio, "We may have to huff and puff and blow the house down. It is a quote from children's book the three little pigs story. There are a few giggles on the radio. Charlie Billings goes around the cabin and looks out the windows and sees the lights on both sides and the rear of the cabin.

Ed calls on the bullhorn, "**YOU DO NOT HAVE TO RECOGNIZE OUR AUTHORITY. WE HAVE THE CABIN SURROUNDED. IF YOU COME OUT PEACEFULLY, YOU CAN ARGUE WITH THE JUDGE ABOUT HIS AUTHORITY. WE HAVE ORDERS TO BRING YOU IN ALIVE.**"

Nothing happens for two minutes. Charlie returns to the front window. He yells out again, "**I DO NOT RECOGNIZE YOUR AUTHORITY. YOU PIGS GET OFF MY PROPERTY, NOW.**" He fires another two rounds at the SUV. They put two holes in the passenger's side door.

The guys duck behind cover.

Jim and Will use the little distraction at the front of the cabin to move to the back wall. Jim is kneeling between the door and a woodpile. Will is at the corner with the east sidewall. Ed calls the teams to kill the lights. Jim calls Ed, "Will and I are against the back wall. I got the receiver volume turned down. Will is checking the windows. Maybe you can make some noise and cause a distraction at the front." Will ducks along the back window close to the west wall.

Ed calls to Charlie again. Suddenly Charlie fires several rounds at the SUV. One hit the window frame and ricocheted thru the driver side window and strikes Jake in the shoulder. Bill yells, "Jake is hit."

Jake yells, "It is my shoulder."

Ed fires several rounds at the front window. Will does get a good look into the one room from the west side window. He ducks and waits for the shooting to stop. The west side team does not fire. Will comes back behind the back wall. Bill ducks over behind the SUV. He says" Let me see your shoulder."

He pulls Jakes shirt off. He looks and says, "Looks like the bullet is still in your shoulder. He wipes the blood off the shoulder." Bill picks up the radio, "This is Bill. Jake has been hit in the shoulder. He is not bleeding badly. Chief can you hear me?"

The fire chief answers, "Yes. What do you want us to do?"

Howard instinctively drops back from the west and heads for the road. He calls Bill, "This is Howard. I am headed to the road and my SUV. The west team is holding otherwise."

Bill calls back, "What is your plan?"

Howard calls back, "I will get the SUV to the driveway, if you need to evacuate Jake."

Bill calls the chief, "Move the EMS team to the driveway at the road."

Jake says, "It is not that bad."

Ed yells to Bill, "Can you reach the microphone for the main transceiver in the SUV. Call for back up."

Bill pushes the button on the mike. He says, "This is Bill Simpson with Jake and Ed. We have taken fire several times from the suspect. Jake is hit in the shoulder. We need backup just in case."

The sergeant at the one barracks takes the call, "This sergeant Jones. I am reading you load and clear. What do you need?"

Bill continues, "We need several local or state police to block the road from the east. The Baxter State Park Rangers should close the exit from the park and send someone to block the road to the west or our site."

The sergeant has three thing started almost simultaneously. One of the officers calls the Park. One calls Penobscot County. The sergeant puts out a general call for several state police to move as quickly as possible to the site. Within three minutes the exit from Baxter is closed. There are six officers moving toward the site. Howard has reached his SUV. He calls Bill, "This is Howard. I am at my SUV. I am driving to the driveway."

Bill yells over to Ed, "Howard is almost at the driveway. Help is on the way. Do you want to take command?"

Bill says in reply, "No, you got it for now."

Barbara calls Bill, "I have moved toward the front of the cabin. I am still to the west side, but I have a clear shot at the front window, if you need covering fire."

Howard calls Bill, "I am at the driveway. I am ready to come up and get Jake. Can you help Jake into the car and he can lie on the seat till I get back to the road?"

Bill replies, "Hold one second."

He calls the other teams, "When the action starts, Barbara fire at the left window. Ed is going to fire at the right front window. The east and west side teams fire at the windows. If the suspect does not fire we won't."

Bill takes the bullhorn, "**CHARLIE IF YOU DO NOT FIRE WHILE WE EVACUATE OUR WOUNDED OFFICER WE WON'T FIRE.**"

Bill calls, "Howard proceed. We are ready. Everybody hold your fire unless the suspect fires."

Howard swings his SUV behind Jakes for cover. Bill starts to help Jake into the back seat. Suddenly the suspect fires several round at Jake's SUV. The teams instinctively return fire. Jake is in and Bill slams the door. Howard takes off.

In ten seconds the SUV is below the edge of the hill.

Bill goes on the radio, "Everyone OK."

Howard reaches the EMS team. They help Jake onto the Gurney and begin to evaluate his wound.

The firing stops as Howard disappears down the driveway.

The team in the rear calls Ed, "We have got a look at the inside. There are two rooms. The bedroom is on your right and a living area on your left. The rear door opens into the living area. The rear door does not have an obvious lock. I am going to the west side and try to see the door latch. Can you create a little distraction out front? Tell the west side team to not fire while I try to get a look."

Ed says on the radio, "You guys on the west side did you hear the no fire request."

The west side team replies, "Holding fire."

Ed can see Will has worked his way along the west sidewall. The sun is still to the east. Ed calls in the Bullhorn, "**CHARLIE HAVE YOU HAD A ENOUGH OF THIS FOOLISHNESS. COME OUT WITH YOUR**

HANDS UP. WE CAN ALL GET SOME BREAKFAST. THERE IS REALLY NO PLACE TO GO." Ed can see Charlie looking out the left front window.

Charlie is holding the rifle and pointing it up and out the window. He does not fire.

Ed says, "**I KNOW YOU DO NOT RECOGNIZE OUR AUTHORITY. YOU MUST RECOGNIZE WE OUT NUMBER YOU. THERE ARE TEN OF US AND MORE ON THE WAY.**"

Will calls Ed on the radio, "I got a good look. The door is bolted with a heavier bolt, but it will fail when we hit the door. There is a 2 by 12 about ten feet long back here we are going to use it as a battering ram. The door should break open."

Ed replies, "tell me when you are ready. I'll create a distraction."

Howard calls Ed, "Jake is OK. The EMS team is going to transport in a few minutes. There is a backup EMS team on the way about half way from Sherman to here. Where do you want me?"

Ed replies, "Howard hold where you are. The rear team is about to execute a break in."

Ed asks Will on the radio, "Are you two ready? I will have the other teams each fire three rounds slowly as a distraction."

Will comes back, "We are ready."

Ed says on the count of three, everybody should fire. Remember fire at the wall not the windows. He counts, "1.2.3"

All of the teams fire. Will and Jim run against the door with the 2 by 12. The door swings open. They drop the 2 by 12 in the doorway to hold the door open. Will steps against the left doorframe of the open door. Jim jumps over to the window. Will calls; "Charlie drop the rifle. We have you covered. It's over."

Jim yells through the broken window glass, "Charlie, got you covered here. Put your hands up"

Will yells again; "Charlie, we don't want to kill you. Be smart and drop the rifle."

Charlie looks over his shoulder and sees they have the drop on him. Furthermore they are well shielded by the cabin walls. He says, "I am putting the rifle on the floor." He slowly turns around.

Will steps into the room and says, "Put your hands up and don't move."

Jim comes around to the door and enters the room. He goes around to right and behind Charlie and pulls his hands down and places cuffs on his wrists." Jim pats him down for other weapons. Jim goes to the front door and opens it a little. He yells, "Ed and Bill it is over. You guys can come in." He opens the door more so Bill and Ed can see him.

Bill and Ed enter the room. Will is still holding a gun pointed at Charlie. Will says; "Ed, you and Bill need to take this guy."

Ed pats Charlie down again just to be sure he has no weapon. Bill calls Howard, "Howard can you bring the SUV up."

Howard replies, "Coming right up."

Ed leads Charlie outside. Bernie has come up to the front yard.

Bill calls the desk Sergeant at the State Police Barracks, "Serge we have the guy in custody. You can cancel the help. We do need a forensic team to search the premises. We have a search warrant. Have you heard from Jake?"

The sergeant replies over the radio, "I just called off the help. I will send a forensic team. It will take the about three hours to get there. Jake is at the clinic. He is stable. They are going to transport him to Bangor."

Ed comes out to Howard's SUV. Bill says to Charlie, "Can you hold the video camera while I read Mr. Billings his rights. Howard and Ed you witness the reading."

Bill reads Charlie Billings his rights. He asks Charlie, "Do you understand these rights?"

Charlie replies, "I do not recognize your authority."

Bill says, "That is fine. Do you understand what I said to you about your rights? Yes or No?"

Charlie says, "OK, I understood what you said. I do not agree with it. I do want a lawyer."

Bill says, "You are being taken to Augusta Maine. When we arrive a lawyer will be made available to you. This is the arrest warrant with the charges against you. Your firing on us and hitting our officer will cause you to be charged with more offenses."

Bill turns and says, "Can you two Penobscot County officers get your car and return up here? I need the scene and property secured until a forensic team arrives. You guys are the closest to your office. I cannot order you to stay, but I think you understand why I asked you."

The one officer, Allen Woodson says, "Barbara and I can cover the situation. We can wait till the forensic team arrives."

Bill continues, "Once the team arrives and has few minutes to settle in you guys can leave. They are armed and usually work alone. You might ask them if they are going to need more than the rest of the day. I will have a state police officer or two officers secure the premises at the end of the day."

Ed chimes in, "I have a second officer coming up at 4:30PM to secure the premises. I made reservations for two rooms at the motel just east of Sherman for the forensic team. The team is two guys and a woman. If they finish late they can stay till tomorrow before returning to Bangor. If they need more time they will be here tomorrow."

Bill addresses the other officers, "You can leave now. Don't forget to send copies of your reports and expenses to Linda Smyth in Concord or Jane Cordova in Augusta or Vivian Bush in Montpelier. Fill out the shooting reports to satisfy the requirement for use of your weapons. The investigation of all of this should be a formality, since we were fired upon first. Jake is being taken to Bangor. Call the hospital and send cards to the hospital."

And again thank you for your help. It is Jane's job to prosecute the alleged suspect for the crimes in Maine. It is Linda's job to prosecute the alleged suspect for the crimes in New Hampshire. Obviously none of us should disgust the case with anyone outside the AG's office or our respective commands. Again Thanks. I think we can say the alleged suspect is a bad guy as far as we know. Drive home carefully."

The various officers acknowledge Bill and Ed with a farewell salute or handshake.

Bill says, "Sandra and Bernie can stay for a little while Allen and Barbara go to Sherman and get brunch and a drink. You are going to be here for three to four hours. You might as well enjoy the nice morning wait."

They respond, "We will make the trip as quick as possible. Do you guys want anything?"

Bill says, "Ed and I are going to Augusta in Ed's vehicle. Sandra can you or Bernie bring my SUV back to Concord? Ed and I will stop with the suspect on the way to Augusta. Jake's vehicle must remain until the forensic team finishes and then someone from the state police garage in Bangor will pick it up. It must be processed for the bullet hits."

Bill and Ed move the alleged suspect into Ed's SUV and secure leg irons. They leave for Augusta. Jane Cordova is waiting with a court appointed attorney when Ed and Bill arrive. Jane immediately assumes command. She invites the court appointed attorney with the alleged suspect. She provides the attorney with the arrest warrants from all three states and a list of the new charges from the shooting.

Meanwhile up at the cabin after an hour the Penobscot County officers return. Sandra and Bernie leave for Concord. Three hours pass and the forensic team arrives. At about 4:30 PM an officer from Ed's barracks arrives to cover the night shift. Ted Forrester arrives at about 5:00 PM to help overnight. The forensic team returns at about 8:15 AM to finish the job.

Ed and Bill leave Augusta in the morning for Bangor to visit Jake. Sandra and Bernie in separate vehicles arrive in Bangor to visit Jake and pick up Bill. Jake is OK except for his shoulder. He is going to need several operations. The doctors have talked to him about going to an orthopedic hospital in Baltimore Maryland to repair his shoulder.. Bill calls Mattie and tells her about the capture. Mattie heard on the radio and TV about Jake getting shot. Bill had called her to say he was OK. It was not until He returned to Concord that she hears the entire story. After spending an hour at the hospital Ed, Bill, Sandra, and Bernie head for home. Charlie calls from home to ask Jake how he is doing. During the afternoon several of the other people call Jake to inquire as to how he is doing.

Bill and Mattie make plans to have dinner on Saturday. Even though they know whom the fifth alleged suspect is. They are willing to wait till Monday before starting the next pursuit.

CHAPTER 20

THE FIFTH SUSPECT
IS MARSHALL BRICKMAN

A few days have passed since the team captured suspect four. Jake is recovering in Bangor. Bill Simpson will be leading the capture of suspect five. At least two of the rapes were committed in Maine. Ed Woodworth wants this guy. Linda and Mattie have identified and agreed on the identity of the fifth suspect. Mr. Marshall Brickman lives Northeast of St. Johnsbury about twenty-five miles from the Canadian Border. Bill and Ed wonder if he another runner.

Linda calls Bill, "Mattie and I have identified the fifth suspect as a Marshall Brickman. He is a truck driver for a company Snickleman Trucking with several terminals around New England. It appears he works primarily out of the terminal in St. Johnsbury Vermont. Mr. Marshall Brickman lives Northeast of St. Johnsbury about twenty-five miles from the Canadian Border. I will E-mail you and Ed the exact address."

Bill replies, "Bernie and I will put together a plan for making the arrest. Have you issued subpoenas and search warrants for his property? Has Jane issued a warrant for the crimes he committed in Maine?"

Linda continues, "No. I just went to the judge this morning. I should have all the paperwork in order by tomorrow. He is a truck driver and may be out of town. His house is near the Vermont border and not too far from Maine. I talked with Jane and she told me the same thing. Her paper work will be ready tomorrow."

Bill responds, "I Am going to talk to the team about meeting in St Johnsbury, Vermont."

Linda answers, "Good idea. I will get the paperwork to you tomorrow. Till then have a good day. Be careful. I do not want another shooting like Jake."

Bill says, "Neither do I. But catching these guys is always a little dangerous and it is our job. I will call Ed and Charlie in a little while and begin making a plan to arrest Mr. Brickman. You have a good day."

They hang up.

Bill calls Ed. The phone rings five times. Ed answers, "Sergeant Ed Woodworth how are you, Bill? Halfway thru his answer he recognizes Bill's phone number. What's up?"

Bill says, "I am fine Ed. How are you? We have another suspect. The ladies identified a Marshall Brickman as the fifth suspect. He lives in New Hampshire. He works for Snickleman Trucking. Linda is issuing subpoenas and warrants for a Marshall Brickman the fifth suspect. She told me Jane is issuing subpoenas and warrants for Maine. He has committed rapes in both states. I am going to call Charlie also. We are going to need a plan."

Ed replies, "At the moment. I am running a Radar site on I-95. I can be ready tomorrow."

Bill continues, "Call me when you are finished. As I said we need a plan for the arrest."

Ed replies, "I will call you in about an hour. I will have broken off this operation by then."

Bill says, "OK. Catch those speeders. Have a good day, Ed."

Ed replies, "Only caught a few. You have a good day."

Bill responds, "I flying my desk today. Talk to you later."

They hang up.

Bill talks to Sandra for a few minutes and then calls Charlie. The cell phone rings several times. Charlie answers, "Sergeant Charlie Wilson. How can I help you?" He know this is not a regular call few people have his cell.

Bill responds, "It is Bill Simpson. How are you?"

Charlie answers, "I am fine. How are you? How can I help you?"

Bill answers, "I am fine. To answer your other question, I need you to help with the arrest of the fifth suspect. The guy is a truck driver and works for a trucking company in St. Johnsbury. He lives in upstate New Hampshire. We believe he has only committed rapes in New Hampshire and Maine. With Jake unavailable we really need you, Charlie. Linda and Jane are getting the paperwork in order. We are going to meet Wednesday in St. Johnsbury about 12 Noon to plan the arrest. Bernie and Sandra are coming with me. Can you make it?"

Charlie responds, "Yes, it will get me out of sitting for five hour at a Radar trap on I-91."

Bill says, "See you on Wednesday?

Charlie responds, "See you Wednesday."

They hang up.

It is about noon when Ed calls. Bill answers, "Sergeant Bill Simpson here."

Ed answers, "It is Ed Woodward. I can have several other state police available to help back up the arrest. What are your ideas on handling the arrest?"

Bill replies, "My primary idea is to wait until the guy is home. I think it would be difficult to chase the guy around all three states. If he is not home he will be in a few days. So let's make it easy on ourselves. Also I do not want the possibility of chasing a tractor-trailer up I-91 or another road. Other people could get hurt. What do you think?"

Ed continues, "I basically agree. We should be able to obtain Marshall's schedule from the trucking company. Linda should be able to issue a subpoena to his boss and include a gag order on discussing the information about the schedule with anyone but the owner's lawyer. We will need to talk to the owner of the trucking company in person. I am sure he will cooperate and keep the inquiries quiet."

Bill continues, "I will call Linda and get a subpoena for the inquiries."

Ed replies, "Good. I think we should have four of us at the house and couple more officers to monitor the route. We should use our cell phones for communications."

Bill continues, "As soon as I have the subpoenas we can meet in St. Johnsbury and make the inquiries about his schedule. Then we can drive up to his residence and scout the area. I will call you back after I talk to Linda and plan our little trip."

Ed replies, "That's good for me until then goodbye."

Bill comes back, "Goodbye."

They hang up.

Bill calls Linda at the AG's office. The phone rings five times and Linda answers, "Attorney General's Office, Linda Smyth here."

Bill replies, "Bill Simpson, here."

Linda continues, "What do you need Bill?"

Bill replies, "We need some kind of subpoena to obtain Marshall Brickman schedule from the trucking company without revealing to him we know the schedule."

Linda replies, "I can ask the judge to include a gag order on the subpoena, but you will need to explain this to whoever provides the information. Responsible management usually does not need such an order, but it does make it official. I should have it by early morning. Is that soon enough?"

Bill replies, "Morning is good enough. I'll talk to you tomorrow. You will FAX me a copy. I will need the original before Wednesday morning."

Linda replies, "I have court after lunch. The same judge should be able issue the subpoena. The FAXED copy is good enough as long as I have the original and can provide it to an attorney. You probably won't need that much formality. Just asks for the name of the company attorney and I will forward him or her a copy and mail an original, if they request it. I do have to go now. I can't be late for court. Leave Sandra all the information. My assistant will call her. Talk to you tomorrow. I've got to run."

Bill responds, "Go. Talk to you tomorrow."

They both hang up.

Bill calls Ed. Ed's phone rings three times and he answers, "Sergeant Ed Woodward."

Bill replies, "Ed, it is Bill. I have info on the subpoenas."

Ed responds, "Shoot."

Bill replies, "The bullets don't come through the phone, which is good thing. Linda is going to FAX me copies in the morning."

Ed says, "Funny. So do you want to meet me in St. Johnsbury at lunchtime tomorrow?"

Bill replies, "Sounds good. Meet near the trucking company? Then we can drive up to Brickman's house and scout the site. We can also scout the trucking company area just in case we make the arrest at the company site."

Ed says, "That sounds good. Call me in the morning to confirm. I am going to bring two other officers along to scout the sites. Do you have the subpoenas and warrant for the arrest?'

Bill replies, "No. I have asked Linda for those also. She is in court for the afternoon. I'll have my deputy, Sandra, call her assistant and make sure she is sending copies of those also."

Ed replies, "Call me in the morning. Talk to you then."

Bill continues, "I will. Till tomorrow have a good day."

They both hang up.

Sandra comes in and says, "I talked to Linda's assistant and we are on the same wavelength. You should have the subpoenas in the morning."

Bill replies, "Thanks. Need you to call her about the arrest warrant and the search subpoenas and be sure we have copies of those also."

Sandra replies, "I have a package delivered by a courier before lunch. It should be originals of those. Let me get it for you. I was waiting for you to get free from the other calls."

Bill responds, "OK."

Sandra goes and gets the package and returns to Bill's office. She hand the package to Bill.

He takes a letter opener from the desk drawer and opens the envelope. It contains the arrest warrant and the search subpoenas. He says, "Thanks Sandra. This is necessary paperwork. As soon as I get copies of the other subpoenas tomorrow we will be ready to go to St Johnsbury."

About five-thirty PM, Linda calls. Bill and Sandra have left already. She leaves a message, "I am sending the originals of the subpoena to obtain the schedule and to obtain Marshall's work records. I think you should hold the second subpoena until the arrest is made. There is also a subpoena to obtain a DNA sample after the arrest. Please read them all and be sure they are in order. No mistakes. Have fun and be careful. I have not talked to Jake. I understand he is home to recover before they start repairing his shoulder. Have Ed or you talked to Jake?"

Linda also calls Sandra's phone and leaves a message for her to remind Bill to carefully check the subpoenas for errors before presenting them to the recipients.

Sandra gets in at 9:30 AM. She listens to her messages. The first is Linda's message. Then Bill left a message he is going to be in at 10:00 AM. At 9:45 a courier arrives with another package from Linda. Sandra opens it. It contains two subpoenas for the trucking company. Sandra reads them carefully. She checks the spelling of the suspects name, the trucking company name and address. She checks to see that the requested information agrees with what Bill and Mattie have told her about the arrest. She makes a couple of notes about the information they are requesting.

Bill comes in at about 10 AM. Sandra says as he enters, "We just got two more subpoenas. I took the liberty of reading them. Linda left a message that you or we should check them for errors. The names and addresses are correct from the previous information we found. You should check to see the information they are requesting is accurate and related to the case. I am going to read the other subpoenas from yesterday."

Bill says, "OK. You read the ones from yesterday and I will read these new ones. First I am going to call Ed and tell him we have the subpoenas and I will meet him at about noon tomorrow in St Johnsbury."

Bill calls Ed. The phone rings three times and Ed answers, "Hi Bill how are things?"

Bill answers, "Fine. I receive original copies of the subpoena from Linda yesterday and this morning. My deputy, Sandra, and I are checking them to be sure there are no errors and we agree with information. I should be in St Johnsbury tomorrow by noon. We are meeting at the trucking company?"

Ed replies, "Ok. I will see you there. Do you want me to look the paperwork over? We could get some lunch while I look them over."

Bill says, "Sounds good. See you on the street across from the trucking company."

Ed responds, "See you at noon. I am coming in a plain car not a cruiser."

Bill continues, "I am coming in my own SUV not a State Police Vehicle."

Ed responds, "See you soon."

Bill continues, "See you at noon."

They both hang up.

Sandra comes in and says, "I finished these. There are no obvious errors."

Bill replies, "Thanks. I am almost finished these."

They both sit quietly until Bill finishes reading his batch of paperwork. He puts the paperwork into the envelopes."

He says, "I am ready to go tomorrow. I need to call Charlie again."

Bill calls Charlie, Charlie recognizes Bill number before he answers, "Hi, Bill. Have you got more information?"

Bill responds, "Yes. All the subpoenas and warrants will be ready by tomorrow. The plans are for Ed, Sandra, Bernie, you and myself to meet in St. Johnsbury near the trucking company. We will meet at a diner or café. I will have to call you when we get to town. I am planning to stay for several days. However, take care of your own reservations and come as civilians until we assess the situation. Bring your uniforms and vests for the actual arrest. See you about noon in St. Johnsbury."

Charlie responds, "See you about noon. Have a good rest of the day."

Bill says, "Same to you. Goodbye."

They hang up.

Sandra, Bernie, and Bill finish the day. Bill says, "I'll see you two in the morning. Have a good evening."

Sandra and Bernie both say, "Same to you, serge."

WEDNESDAY MORNING

Bill arrives at 7:30 AM. Sandra and Bernie arrive a few minutes later. Bill says, "I am taking my own car. One of you needs to take the State police SUV and one of you needs to take an unmarked car also. Make sure the siren and the lights work before we leave. Check the weapons and make sure you have your vests. I am doing the same. We need the paperwork. We should be ready to leave in a few minutes. Get a coffee for the trip. I know both are you are familiar with the procedures. I am just thinking out loud."

Sandra says, "I will be with you in a minute. I need the ladies room."

Bernie says, "Sandra, you can drive the SUV."

Bill says, "See you in the vehicles in five minutes." He checks his pockets and his weapon and his badge.

Bernie pulls up alongside of Bill. He hits the siren bottom and flashes the lights and says, "Weapons, extra ammo, vest and changes of clothes. I am ready.

Sandra pulls up on the other side of Bill. She says, "Weapons, extra ammo, changes of clothes, and vest. I am ready for anything, serge."

Bill says, "Weapons, extra ammo, vest, and changes of clothes. I am also ready. We will stop in about an hour for some breakfast. Let's roll." Bill pulls out first. Bernie waves Sandra to go ahead. He follows.

Bill likes to play Diana Krall jazz CD's or Patsy Cline country CD's while he drives.

About seventy miles from the barracks there is a small diner. Bill pulls into the parking lot. Sandra and Bernie follow. As they get out of the cars Bill says, "Let's get a quick breakfast."

Sandra and Bernie agree. It takes about forty-five minutes for breakfast. Then they are on their way again to St. Johnsbury.

It is noon as they come down the street in front of the trucking company. Bill sees a car with the driver sitting in it. As he gets closer, he realizes it is Ed. He pulls along the side of the car. He waves some one behind to come around. It is a side street. Ed rolls down the driver side window. Bill opens the passenger side window as he pulled up. Ed says, "There is a diner about three blocks down the street."

Bill replies, "Ok. Lunch sounds good. I will follow you. Have you seen Charlie?"

Ed says, "No. I will call him and tell him to meet us at the Diner." He pulls the car into the street. Bill, Sandra and Bernie follow. At the Diner they all turn in and park. They get out. Ed is talking to Charlie. Ed says, "Charlie is a few miles away. I told him to come to the Diner.

Bill gets to the door first and opens it. The others walk in and look for a table. There is a table for six in the far corner.

The waitress, Amanda, comes over with water glasses. She says, "Do you all want coffee?"

Sandra says, "I would like hot tea."

Amanda responds, "OK. I will be back with coffee and your tea in a couple of minutes."

Bill says, "Thank you. We have one more person coming."

Bill says, "Let us wait a few minutes until Charlie arrives. Then I can explain where we are with respect to the arrest."

They begin talking about what has happened since the arrest of Charlie Billings. Ed visited Jake and Sandra talked to him. They tell everybody Jake is doing OK.

Charlie arrives as Amanda comes back to the table with the coffees and Sandra's tea. Everyone says "Hi" to Charlie.

Amanda asks Charlie. "Would you like coffee also?"

Charlie answers her, "Yes."

Charlie sits down. He says, "What's the game plan."

Amanda returns and says, "Here is your coffee sir. And here is more cream. I will come back in a few minutes to take your orders. The menus are behind the salt and pepper shakers."

Charlie says, "I stopped in front of the trucking company. The sign says "Snickleman Transportation not Snickleman Trucking. Do you think this is a problem?"

Bill answers, "Not sure. I better check with Linda."

Bill picks up his cell. He calls Linda. The phone rings five times. Linda answers, "Linda Symth. How can I help you? Oh, it is you, Bill. Do you have a problem?"

Bill responds, "Charlie observed that the sign on the building at the trucking company reads Snickleman Transportation. The subpoenas read Snickleman Trucking."

Linda answers, "We checked that out. Snickleman Transportation is the parent company of Snickleman Trucking. Marshall Brickman works for the Trucking Company. The subpoenas are correct."

Bill says. "OK. I will tell Charlie and the others. We are all in St. Johnsbury at a diner having lunch. Everything is progressing. We are ready to plan the arrest."

Linda responds, "Sound good. Talk to you later. Be careful."

They hang up.

Bill starts the conversation, "First let me tell you what Linda explained about the name. Snickleman Transportation is the parent company of Snickleman Trucking. Marshall Brickman works for the trucking company. The subpoenas are correct. So here are the Subpoenas and Warrants." Bill hands Ed the two envelopes. He says, "The top envelope is the ones we need today. I want all of you to look them over."

The waitress walks up. Amanda says, "What can I get you fellas and the lady?"

Bill says, "Thank you, Amanda. Everyone let's order and then we can continue the discussion."

Amanda goes around the table and takes their orders. Sandra goes first and Bill is last. When they finish Ed opens the clasp on the envelope. He takes out the documents. He passes them around the table. Everybody should read all the documents. The first one is the subpoena requesting the employment records. The last one is the subpoena for the DNA test. Everyone is sitting quietly reading and passing the documents from one person to the next.

Amanda returns with a few of the drinks.

Ten minutes pass. Everyone has finished the documents. Ed says, "Has anyone found any mistakes."

Everybody responds, "No."

Bill says, "That's good. Several people checked them after Linda and Jane generated them. So I think we are good to go. When we finish lunch we can go to the trucking company and present the subpoenas. Linda did not think they would have any problem supplying the schedule information. She said we should remind them not to discuss the information with anyone."

Ed says, "I think that idea is good. It should not cause any problem with a responsible company."

Amanda returns with the food. She says, "Let me refresh those drinks."

Bill replies, "Thank you." The others nod their concurrence.

While they finish lunch they chit-chat about their families and friends. They talk about how Jake is doing.

Ed says, "I don't want to get too personal, but I gather you and Mattie are closer than coworkers"

Bill replies, "We date. It has not got more serious for now. We both were married and our spouses have passed away. We both have kids by the first marriages. Right now we are good friends. Because of Mattie's involvement in the math we are using to track these guys, I try not to mention her name with the program for her protection. She is very good with the math."

Ed replies again, "Hope you did not mind me asking."

Bill replies, "No, you can know, but I just don't want it to be public knowledge for now. Linda knows and my deputies know about Mattie's involvement. As far as our personal involvement the people around town know we date. There is nothing to be embarrassed about. Effectively we are both single and date."

They have finished lunch. Amanda come over and says, "any desert guys?'

Bill says, "None for me. You can bring the check as far as I am concerned."

Ed responds, "None for me."

Sandra and Bernie each say none for me. Charlie says, "I am going to grab a candy bar as I leave."

Amanda goes to counter and gets the check and returns and says, "Have a good day. You pay at the register."

Ed says, "Let me get it. I can put it on an expense account." He puts a tip on the table.

They leave and get in their respective vehicles. They drive back to the Snickleman Trucking Company.

Bill and Charlie park in the visitor parking spaces. They go in. The receptionist asks, "Can I help you?"

Bill replies, "I am Bill Simpson with the New Hampshire State Police and working for the New Hampshire Attorney General. This Sergeant Charlie Wilson of the Vermont State Police and he is also working with the AG's office. We need to speak with your owner, Neil Wilson."

Susie presses the bottom on the intercom and says, "There are two state policemen here."

Neil replies, "Please send them in."

Susie gets up and opens the door. She says, "Please go in." She shuts the door after Bill and Charlie enter.

Bill speaks, "I am Sergeant Bill Simpson of the New Hampshire State Police and I am working for the New Hampshire Attorney General. This Sergeant Charlie Wilson of the Vermont State Police and he is also working with the AG's office."

Neil says, "How can I help you?"

Bill continues, "We are not here about the trucking company or you. We are here about one of your employees. I am going to ask you to check that the intercom is off. We need the strictest confidence about this matter."

Neil looks at the intercom box and says, "It is off."

Bill continues, "We have a subpoena for the information. It is not that we believed you would not cooperate, but we need to be sure all the 'i's' are dotted and the 't's' crossed. This subpoena also imposes a gag order on the information you provide. In simple terms you are not to discuss the information provided or contact the alleged suspect about this conversation. Again this is not about you specifically or the company. It is about us needing to keep the information confidential. You can get your lawyer to review the subpoena."

Neil says, "I understand. So what information do you need?"

Bill continues, "We need to know the schedule of Marshall Brickman. When is he going to be back? I gather he is normally on the road."

Neil replies, "I will have to call my scheduler to the meeting. He is my Brother-in-law Joe Wilson. He is also one of the other two owners of the company. He makes the trucks move. My brother is the other partner and he runs the repair and service Garage. Joe will not have any problem keeping the inquiries a secret. He keeps the schedules confidential, we all worry about an outsider finding out about an expensive shipment and hijacking it. Let me get Susie to page him."

Neil switches the intercom on and says, "Susie can you page Joe and ask him to come here. We need some info he has."

Susie replies, "Sure Boss."

Susie pages Joe; "Joe Wilson the boss needs you in his office ASAP. In this case ASAP does not mean never."

Neil comments, "Did you hear that? Susie is young."

Bill said, 'I heard that from my deputy one day. I was slow responding and she said that over the radio."

Charlie says, "Never heard that before. When you think about that it does make strange sense."

Susie's phone rings it is Joe. "I need a minute."

Susie replies, "Neil has two police officers and he wants you to join them. Did you lose a truck?"

Joe responds, "I will be there in a couple of minutes. Stop joking around."

Neil says over the intercom, "This is an order. Do not speculate on the reason why our visitors are here. Do not discuss anything about this with any other employee. It is very serious you follow this order. Do you understand? No joking about it also."

Susie replies, "Sorry Boss. I will shut up about the visitors."

Joe shows up in the outer office. Susie says to him, "Neil said come right in. Better wrap on the door."

Joe wraps on the door. He opens it and enters. He closes the door behind himself. He says, "What's up?"

Neil says, "We are under strict gag order about what is discussed in this meeting. I do need to ask you officers. If I can tell my brother the third partner that this does not directly involve the company."

Bill replies, "Is he on site?"

Neil says, "I think I need to ask him to the meeting also. Is that OK?"

Bill responds, "Yes. He may be helpful."

Neil asks Susie to page his brother, Bill."

Susie does it without comment.

Neil says, "Do you want some coffee or tea while we wait?"

Charlie says, "I could use a coffee with cream and sugar."

Bill says, "I will take the same."

Joe says, "I will have the same."

Neil calls Susie again. "Susie can you bring us four coffees, three with cream and sugar and one for me with only sugar."

Susie replies, "OK boss."

A couple of minutes pass. Susie wraps on the door. She enters carrying a little tray with the four coffees on it. She sits it on Neil desk. Neil says, "Thank you Susie. That is all we need. Please shut the door as you leave. When Bill gets here send him right in. Tell him to grab his own coffee."

Bill says, "We should wait for your brother so we can explain this once."

Neil replies, "That's OK by me."

A few minutes pass. The four guys sip on their coffees. There is a wrap on the door. Bill, Neil's brother opens the door and enters."

Neil says, "Have a seat bro."

Neil checks the intercom. It is off. He says, "We are clear to speak."

Bill starts, "I partially explained our problem to Neil already. He said Joe could provide better help. He thought Bill, you should be in the meeting also. We gave Neil a subpoena to cover the information we need. The subpoena has a gag order about discussing the information we need and anything discussed in this meeting or on the phone and so forth about the matter related to the subpoena. Essentially we need you to not tip off the suspect named in the subpoena. The trucking company has done nothing wrong with respect to the subpoena. You certainly can discuss all of this with your attorney. Having said this I can essentially ask you for the information covered by the subpoena." Bill pauses. He continues, "Any questions so far?"

The brothers nod their heads, NO.

Bill says for the record can you each say you have no questions. They each do.

Bill continues, "The subpoena asks you to provide us with the schedule for Marshall Brickman until we can take him into custody. Essentially a verbal schedule would be excellent. We need Joe to update us by phone with any changes."

Charlie interjects, "I am going to give you my cell and ask you to call me with any changes to the schedule. But remember do not tip Mr. Brickman off."

Joe says, "No problem."

Charlie continues, "We believe he is out of town. Is this true?"

Joe continues, "Yes, he should be picking up a load in Georgia. He will be here in three days. Depending on how late in the day he arrives, he may go home or go to the refrigerated warehouse. I won't know that info till the last day."

Bill says, "We do not want to pull him over in the truck. I do not want him to run with the truck. We will let him come here or home or the warehouse and then execute an arrest warrant." We do have a subpoena to search the tractor-trailer, but the trailer is a formality. We will search the tractor, but the search should not take more than a day. We will probably want to be there when you open the trailer the first time. We cannot think of any reason the trailer or its cargo is a problem."

Neil replies, "Ok. Can you tell us why Marshall is wanted?"

Charlie responds, "Not details at this time. He has allegedly committed a number of felonies. Once we make an arrest you will learn more."

Neil says, "Now I remember where I have heard your name, Bill Simpson. You have tracked down several serial rapists."

Bill looks and replies, "Yes I have been in the news for the arrests. Please do not speculate about this case. Remember the court has imposed a gag order on everyone here. Just be good citizens and provide us with the necessary information. Some suspects that seem mild mannered and almost passive become violent when faced with arrest. We want to keep the violence away from your facilities also."

Neil says, "I am going to give you truck and trailer licenses. There is an electronic sensor on the cab that registers the weigh station and other information. You can track the truck as it passes weigh stations. I am sure you can get the information almost real time. The information should simplify your tracking efforts."

Joe says, "Give me a few minutes to printout a schedule. I will do it myself under the circumstances. Let me go to my office. I have a printer connected directly to my computer so no one will see the information." Joe gets up and leaves.

Neil says, "We are good for now. When you need more information, you will contact us."

Bill says, "Certainly. And thanks for the cooperation. The AG and us believe we did not need the subpoena to get your cooperation. The subpoena is for the lawyers, primarily the defense attorneys. It also protects you from any question about providing the AG the information."

Neil says, "I understand."

A few minute pass and Joe returns and says, "Here is Marshall's schedule for the trip he is on to and from Georgia. You recognize the times are tentative on a trip this far. Each driver has some flexibility with respect to stopping along the way. For instance, the schedule shows him leaving Georgia early today. He just left me a message that he left after lunch. The company down there did not finish loading the trailer until this morning. He should be here in three day, but it will be late in the evening. He will go home with the truck and plan to come in the morning to unload. You do have his home address? I wrote it down on here just in case you didn't have it."

Bill replies, "We have it. Thank you for this information. Thank you for the cooperation."

Neil says, "You are welcome. We will not talk about this to anyone."

Joe and Bill both nod in agreement.

Neil continues, "Have a safe trip till we see you in a couple of days."

Charlie says, "You guys keep rolling safely."

Charlie and Bill get up to leave Neil, Joe, and Bill extend their hands and shake Charlie and Bill's hands."

Charlie and Bill leave.

Once outside Charlie says, "Let's go see Marshall's property."

Bill replies, "OK. I will follow you."

Charlie replies, "Good. Let's go."

Charlie motions to Ed, Bernie, and Sandra to follow. They cross back into New Hampshire. At a small town about six or so miles from Marshall's house Charlie pulls into the parking area between the gas station and the general store. Everybody follows. Bill and Charlie get out immediately. The others follow. Sandra says, "I think I could use the restroom."

Bill says, "Go ahead."

Bernie follows and Charlie goes into the general store to get a coffee. Ed says, "I think I should follow Bernie." He does.

After a few minutes everyone is back standing in front of Bill's SUV. Bill says, "Everybody listen and tell me if the following game plan sounds good. Charlie, you and Bernie use your SUV. It is unmarked. Drive up and go pass the house and continue up the road a couple miles. Turn around and come back past the house and stop on the side of the road out of sight of the house. Sandra you go in a few minutes and drive up past the house and stop out of sight past the house. Ed and I will wait a few more minutes and drive up to the house and park in the driveway and approach the front door. There should not be any one home. If we get no answer, then we will walk around the house and look over the back yard. Since we have subpoenas to search the property going around the exterior of the property is no violation of searching the property. Because we cannot deliver the subpoenas to anyone does not violate search and seizure. We can leave and return to the road. I will call Sandra and tell her to return here. Charlie you and Bernie should see us come down the road. We will meet here."

Charlie says, "Are you ready, Bernie?"

Bernie responds, "Yes. Bill I am leaving the State Police SUV here. Let me make sure it is locked."

Bill says, "I will tell the gas station attendant we will be back in about half an hour."

Bernie says, "OK, Bill."

Charlie and Bernie take off. About ten minutes and they pass Marshall's house. They check the number and note the driveway. It is just a normal small two-story house. Bernie notes that beside the front door there is one on the West side of the house. They continue up the road for what Charlie judges is two miles. They turn around and head back. They pass the house and stop out of sight around a small bend in the road. A few minutes pass and Sandra drives by. She continues pass the house without acknowledging them. She stops out of sight. She calls Bill. Bill answers, "Bill, I am in place and Charlie is in place also."

Bill responds, "Ed and I are on the way."

About seven minutes pass and Bill's SUV passes Charlie on the side of the road. Charlie picks up the cell and calls Sandra. Sandra answers. Charlie says, "Sandra this is Charlie. Bill and Ed just passed me on the way to the house."

Sandra responds, "Thanks."

Bill and Ed turn up the driveway. They park about fifty feet from the front door. Bill says, "I will go up to the door. You hang back to the left."

Ed says, "OK with me."

Bill wraps hard on the door. He says, "I am looking for Marshall Brickman. Marshall are you home." Bill knows Marshall is not going to be home, but he wants to know that no one else is home. There is no answer. Bill repeats his call for Marshall.

Ed says, "Looks like we are alone."

Bill comes from the door. Bill replies, "Looks like you are correct. Let's just walk around the property and decide how we will position ourselves for the arrest." They both walk around the house and observe the windows and doors. They return to the front of the house. It is hard to see inside because of the curtains and shades. They walk back to the driveway. Bill continues the conversation, "We will need Charlie to cover the back. Marshall's personal car is parked out back. There are enough trees and bushes to the left of the back yard to prevent him from driving that direction. The driveway goes around the right side. We should block that side with a car. The tire tracks and crushed foliage indicates he parks the truck to the left front of the house, but maybe ten to twelve feet from the wall."

Ed says, "I agree. I hope this arrest goes better than the last one."

Bill says, "This guy does not have the reputation as with Billings."

Bill and Ed get back in the SUV and head down the road. As they pass Charlie and Bernie Ed motions to them to follow. He picks up the cell and calls Sandra to tell her they are returning to the gas station. About ten minutes pass and everyone is back at the gas station. Bernie gets out of the car and heads for the gas station rest room. Bill says, "I think we are ready for Friday evening. There is a Diner about ten miles south and over about five miles to the east. Marshall should not come past the Diner on the way to his house. I will send you the directions. We should be prepared to meet there after lunch on Friday. If I get a better estimate from the owner of the trucking company I will call Charlie and Ed. They can pass the information on to their people."

Charlie says, "I will have two more officers along I-91 to help. I will put someone near the trucking company office to observe. The refrigerated warehouse is in Maine. So Ed can you cover it. Maybe you can post an officer on the road between the office and the warehouse."

Bill says, "I will have two officers along the route from St. Johnsbury to here. I will have someone here in plain clothes to signal us as Marshall goes by or stops here. We will leave him get home and settle in for the evening before approaching the house.

We can go for now until Marshall is back from the trip to Georgia."

Charlie says, "One last thing. The several officers that patrol I-91 will be keeping a look out for the truck in two days. Their orders will be "report but do not interdict. Bill and I will talk to Linda and Jane and tell them not to post the warrants. If any officer checks the computer the warrants won't show. I will also flag the records for any officer to report the location of the truck, but do not interdict or stop Marshall and/or the truck for traffic violations."

Bill replies, "That should work."

Ed says, "I will tell everyone helping in Maine to follow the same instructions."

Bill replies, "I will talk to you in two days. Remember if at all possible we want to avoid a chase on the highway with a ten wheeler. Drive safely home."

Everyone says, "You do the same Bill."

They go to their respective vehicles and head home.

When Charlie gets to his barracks, he calls Linda. The phone rings five times and Linda answers, "Attorney General's Office, Linda Smyth, ADA. How can I help you?"

Charlie replies, "It is Charlie Wilson. We visited the trucking company and Marshall's home." We all checked the subpoenas and warrants.

Linda replies, "You and Bill?"

Charlie replies, "Bill, Ed, Sandra, Bernie, and me visited both sites and checked everything. Bill should verify these comments."

Charlie continues, "We served the Subpoena and explained the gag order. We met with the three owners, two brothers and a Brother-in-law. They provided the schedule information and explained Marshall Brickman would be back from Georgia in about three days. They understood the subpoena was a necessary formality to cover the situation legally. They will contact us if Marshall calls in on his way back. We explained they should just treat this as any other trip. We explained that we will need more information on his employment, but not until we detain him. We explained that we would prefer that Marshall was home or at the trucking company so that he was not tempted to run in the truck."

Charlie continued, "After we left the trucking company we headed up to Marshall's house and checked out the house and property. If we make the arrest at the house, we will have a good idea of the property and what we need to block during the arrest."

Linda replies, "That is good. What else do you need?"

Charlie continues, "Oh, I do need you to not post the warrant or any information that would flag his driver's license record. We want the police to leave him return to New Hampshire and home. Both Bill and I think he has no idea we are after him. He should simply return home like every trip."

Linda replies, "Ok. I have not post anything on Marshall. I will hold until you arrest him."

Charlie continues, "Have a good day and the next two days till I talk to you again."

Linda continues, "You have a good day. I will be expecting your call after the arrest."

They both hang up.

An hour passes and Bill calls, "The phone ring three times and Linda answers, "Attorney General's Office, Linda Smyth, ADA. How can I help you?"

Bill replies, "It is Bill Simpson. Did Charlie Wilson call you?"

Linda replies, "Yes. He told me things went well at the trucking company and with your checking out Marshall's house and property."

Bill continues, "Yes. It did. We are ready if the arrest occurs at the house and not the trucking company property. I will talk to you in a couple of days. Till then have a good couple of days."

Linda continues, "You do the same and say hello to Mattie."

Bill replies, "OK."

They hang up.

The next day when Bill arrives at the office Sandra says, "Captain James wants to see you today. He actually said if possible. After the last few months and the publicity about the arrests you and others have impressed Captain James."

Bill comments, "What gives you an idea like that?"

Bill goes into Captain James' office. Bill says as he enters, "Captain you wished to see me."

Captain James answers, "Bill you and your team are going receive an award for outstand work in reducing crime. Actually it is three awards. There is one award from each of the states. It will be presented at the Governor's Ball for July 4th. They want to honor Mattie for excellent work in identifying these criminals. I know you want her to remain anonymous. We will work something out to maintain her anonymity."

Bill says, "Thank You. We are going after the fifth suspect on Friday."

Captain James says, "Be careful, Friday."

Bill says, "See you later Captain."

Captain James, "One more question. How is Jake Burns?"

Bill answers, "Jake is generally Ok. However he will need two or more operations on his shoulder. He may need a prosthesis device put in his shoulder. I talked to Jake two days ago. He is home and obviously driving his wife crazy. She told him that she better not get her hands on the guy that shot Jake, but otherwise he is Ok. The other good news is that the fifth suspect is not as violent as number four."

Captain James responds, "Well, that is good news."

Bill replies, "Getting shot is not anybody's idea of having fun."

Captain James says. "See you next week. Be careful Friday."

Bill responds, "See you then."

Bill leaves.

Bill return to his office. There I nothing much to do until lunch. It is Thursday afternoon.

It is four o'clock when Ed calls. Sandra is out of the office when the phone rings. Bill answers it. He says, "Sergeant Bill Simpson, how can I help you?"

Ed replies, "It is Ed. I have some news on the suspect. Neil Wilson called. He said, "Marshall had called in. He is stopping in New Jersey just outside New York. He should be up here late tomorrow. I guess we better plan on going to the trucking company and Marshall's home tomorrow late."

Bill answers, "Ok. I will plan on coming up to St. Johnsbury around three in the afternoon. We could meet at the Diner where we had lunch."

Ed continues, "See you then. I will have three other officers to help. Around four or five tomorrow this afternoon he should be crossing into Vermont. I will have a couple of officers near the border of Vermont on I-91 looking for the truck. There is a weigh station a few miles beyond the border and he will either stop or pass through the electronic sensors. Linda gave me a subpoena yesterday for intercepting the information. We should have a very good estimate of when he will arrive in St. Johnsbury and at his home. I have arranged for one of the women officers to be at the gas station and the little convenience store near the corner of his road. She will be in plain street clothes. She will call me on her cell when he turns up his road. This is provided he does not stop in St Johnsbury. I will have a couple of officers patrolling I-91 near the exit for his house. Their orders are not to directly pursue or stop the truck."

Bill replies, "This sounds like a good plan. I will be in St. Johnsbury around three to be sure we are well ahead of his arrival at either place. Let's meet at the diner where we had lunch?"

Charlie continues, "Yes. The people I asked to track him along I-91 are senior officers. I met with them yesterday so they understood the game plan. They won't blow the operation. They understand the need for caution."

Bill replies, See you tomorrow."

Charlie and Bill both hang up the cell phones.

About 11:30 on Friday Bill, Sandra and Bernie leave for St. Johnsbury. They arrive at the Diner at about 2:40. Charlie is already there. His SUV is parked outside. Bill enters and sees Charlie at the table in the corner. He walks up and says, "Hi, Charlie. How are you, today?"

Charlie answers, "I'm fine. Marshall has not arrived at the Weigh Station."

The waitress, Amanda, comes over. "How can I help you guys?"

Charlie says, "I would like a coffee with cream and sugar also a piece of your apple pie."

Bill says, "Same on the coffee and a dish of vanilla ice cream."

Sandra says, "Hot Tea, but no pie."

Bernie says, "I will take the coffee and a dish of ice cream."

Ed walks in and comes over to the table. Amanda says, "Are joining these other officers."

Ed replies, "Yes. Coffee and the vanilla ice cream."

Amanda says, "I will bring you a pitcher of cream and sugar is on the table. Ok, were you guys here the other day?"

Charlie answers, "Yes, but we need to keep it quiet, police business you understand."

Amanda leaves to get the food.

Bill says, "I guess we just sit here killing time and wounding eternity."

Charlie replies, "How is Mattie?"

Bill answers, "She is fine. How is your family?"

Charlie answers, "They are fine, also. If you don't mind, I am going to get a paper to read while we wait."

Bill says, "I have a book in the car. I am going to go out and get it."

Bernie says, "Can I steal part of your paper Charlie?"

Charlie says, "Take the sports section. I am going to read the news."

Bernie says, "Thank You."

Sandra says, "I am knitting a sweater for my niece. I have it in the SUV. I am going to get the knitting."

Ed says I have a couple of magazines in the SUV."

Ed and Bill both get up. Ed says to Amanda, "We are just getting something to read while we wait. Be back in a minute."

Amanda brings the food to the table before Ed and Bill return.

As they come back in Amanda says to Ed, "If you need anything else just wave."

Ed answers, "Ok."

They sit down and fix the coffee and start eating and reading.

Sandra goes out and comes back in with her knitting."

Two hours pass and still no phone call. More coffee and a trip to the restroom is the only thing happening. A number of other customers have come and gone. As dinnertime approaches the traffic picks up. They all chit chat and exchange a few words of wisdom.

It is fifteen past five when Charlie's cell rings. George Sherwood the officer at the Weigh Station is on the line. Charlie answers, "Sergeant Charlie Wilson, State Police here."

George replies, "George Sherwood on this end. Your suspect just passed the weigh station sensor. He is doing about 65 mph headed north on I-91 as you suspected. I am going to proceed north after a few minutes pass. No need to close in on him at this time. Basically he is legal. I will keep in touch."

Charlie replies, "George, thank you. Drive carefully."

George says, "Always. Talk to you soon."

Bill says, "I obviously overheard the conversation. Marshall is in Vermont."

Charlie replies, "So the chase begins."

Bill comments, "The chase is slow at the moment."

Charlie says, "I have several other officers watching the route. Their orders are to observe, report, but do not intercept. It is will be dark by the time he arrives here. I think he will go home."

Bill comments, "Well that will be good. We can apprehend him without a lot of people around."

Charlie says, "Think I will have some more coffee and hit the head to empty out the last two cups."

Bill says, "Are you all getting Hungry, I am?"

Charlie says, "When I come back. I think we should order."

Bill says, "Ok."

Charlie gets up and walks to the restroom. Ed follows.

On his way back Ed motions to Armanda, "Come over in a few minutes, we will be ready to order dinner. Can you please bring the dinner menu?"

Armanda replies, "Sure, It will take a minute to finish these other orders."

Ed comments, "We are not in a big hurry."

Ed continues to the table and comments, "You probably heard me. I ask Armanda to bring a menu."

Ed asks, "Not to be too nosy, is Mattie a good cook?"

Bill answers, "Yes. We do go out a lot. Both sets of kids are out of the nest. The two sets of kids seem to get along when we do something together. My kids like Mattie and her kids seem to like me. My wife died of Cancer several years ago and her husband died in combat in the Army. So we are both free to marry, but right now our relationship is good friends."

Ed says, "I was not trying to pry."

Bill replies, "No. It is Ok, you ask. You are obviously married. How long?"

Ed replies, "Twenty-one years. We met in the last year of high school. I went directly to the State Police Academy from High School. I was a state police trainee until I was twenty-one. We got married after I became a full officer. We started having kids quickly."

Amanda comes over and says, "What can I get you guys and the lady?"

Bill says, "What do you recommend."

Amanda replies, "The Special is two Pork chops, potatoes, and a vegetable. If you want the fish is Talafia. It is very good tonight with the same vegetables.

Bill replies, "I will take the chops."

Ed says, "Same for me."

Sandra says, "I will take the Talafia.

Charlie says as he walks up to the table. "I will take the chops."

Bernie says, "Chops for me."

Amanda says, "Ok. Coffees?"

Sandra says, "I would like hot tea."

Bill says, "How about a soda."

Ed says, "Soda for me, also."

Bernie says, "Coffee for me."

Charlie says, "Coffee for me also."

Amanda says, "Four Pork Dinners and a Talafia Dinner. Two sodas, a hot tea, and two coffees. What vegetables and potatoes?"

Bill says, "What choices?"

Amanda replies, "Baked Potato, Mashed with or without gravy or French Fries?"

Bill answers, "I will take Mashed with gravy."

Ed says, "Same for me."

Sandra says, "Baked with sour cream."

Bernie says, "Baked with sour cream.

Charlie says, "French fries."

Amanda says, "I will bring you some butter and rolls. The fish comes with tartar sauce and lemon."

Amanda says, "Ok. For vegetables we have Green Beans, Applesauce, Lima Beans, Homemade Slaw, Stewed Tomatoes, Creamed Corn, and Baked Beans. You can have a small salad instead of the vegetable choice."

Bill says, "I will take the Homemade Slaw and can I pay for Applesauce also."

Amanda answers, "Yes. It is $1.25 extra."

Bill continues, "Ok. I will take the applesauce also."

Ed says, "I will take the Creamed Corn and give me the applesauce also."

Charlie says, "I will take Homemade Slaw."

Bernie says, "The same for me."

Sandra says, "Green Beans, please."

Amanda says, "Let me do a quick review." She reads each person's order back.

Bill continues, "Got the order fine."

Amanda says, "The Pork Chops take about ten minutes. Is that Ok? Are you guys waiting for someone?"

Bill answers, "The ten minutes are Ok. I cannot explain any details, but we are waiting for several phone calls. Hope you don't mind us sitting here. It is better than sitting in our respective SUV's"

Amanda replies, "No you are fine. Law enforcement officers are always welcome. I was just curious."

Bill continues, "We are probably going to be here for a few hours. None of us are from St Johnsbury."

Amanda continues, "Let me put the order in and bring you the drinks." She leaves and goes to the kitchen window."

Ed says, "Looks like you are making progress on the book."

Bill replies, "It's a murder mystery."

Ed says, "I get enough stuff like that on the job."

Bill replies, "Normally I do also. Mattie bought it for me. It has some DNA twists. She thought the twists were interesting."

Ed says, "I think I will see if there is an evening paper outside."

Bernie says, "I think I will see if there is another paper."

Charlie says, "What other papers are out there?"

Ed says, "I will let you know." Bernie and Ed walk outside.

Sandra is making progress on the sweater.

Bill continues reading. He says, "How is the sweater doing?"

Sandra answers, "The sleeves are complete. The front is coming along." She holds the front up. It has a moose on the front. She says, "My niece requested the moose."

Bill says, "It looks like a moose."

Sandra says, "I have a pattern for the moose."

Ed comes back in with the evening paper from Boston. Bernie has the evening paper from Bangor. They bring in several free papers from St. Johnsbury, White River Junction, and North Conway. They lay them on the table. Charlie picks one up from North Conway. They all sit quietly reading. Amanda returns with the drinks and she says, "About ten minutes on the dinners."

Bill replies, "Ok."

The guys keep on reading and Sandra knitting. Amanda returns to the counter to serve some other customers.

About ten minutes pass and Amanda returns with several dinners. She has to make multiple trips.

As they are finishing dinner Charlie's cell phone rings. He answers, "Charlie here."

Josh says, "This is Officer Josh Bradley. I am at the rest area just ten miles South of White River Your boy stopped here to use the restroom. He got something from the vending machine. He went back to the truck and is resting. He is less than two hours from the first St Johnsbury Exit."

Charlie says, "Good. Call me when he leaves. Have you seen George Sherwood?"

Josh says, "He just pulled into the rest area. Let me call him."

Charlie says, "Call me back after you two have talked."

Josh says, "OK."

Charlie replies, "Thank you. Have a good evening. Talk to you after the arrest."

Josh responds, "You guys have a good evening. Be careful during the arrest."

They hang up.

Charlie turns to Bill and says, "That was Josh Bradley. He is at the rest area about thirty miles south of White River. Our guy is resting there. He is less than two hours from St. Johnsbury. He is probably going to be late enough to go directly home. Let me call a couple of other officers."

Bill says, "Let me make a few calls also."

Bill looks in a little notepad that he uses to keep useful information. He dials a number. The phone rings five times and Jane answers, "Jane Ridgely here, how can I help you?"

Bill replies, "Sergeant Bill Simpson. Game is on. The suspect Marshall Brickman is thirty miles South of White River resting in his truck. We are estimating he will be here in less than two hours. I need you to get going. We have several people tracking the truck. I will keep you informed."

Jane comments, "OK. I am ready. I will leave here in about five minutes."

Bill continues, "That's fine. You are going to be in plain clothes. Wear your vest. Make sure you have your badge and gun. We need to be prepared for the worst. The suspect is a felon."

Jane answers, "I planned to wear a vest. I'll not show my badge or gun until I leave the gas station. I may need to show my badge to the attended, because he may wonder why I am hanging around for so long."

Bill says, "That's fine. You know how to handle a stake out."

Jane replies, "Keep me up to date. See you there."

Bill responds, "See you there. Be safe. Several of us are going to the Small Diner South and five miles East of the road the gas station is on. We will wait there until you see Marshall pass the gas station."

Bill and Jane hang up.

Bill says to the others, "that was Jane Ridgely she will be covering the gas station."

Meantime Jane gets her vest on under an oversized blouse. She returns to the dining room buttoning the blouse.

Jane's husband Charlie says, "Is the vest going to be necessary?"

Jane answers, "Better to be safe. The guy is allegedly a serial rapist."

Charlie replies, "Please be safe."

Jane answers, "I am only the lookout for the operation. It is going to be midnight before I return. Love you."

She bends over and kisses Charlie. He says, "Love you, too."

Jane leaves. When she gets in the car she checks the clip in her 9-millimeter and clears the chamber for the drive. She leaves for the gas station stakeout.

Back at the Diner Charlie has called Henry Clay the Officer patrolling I-91 just South of the St Johnsbury Exit. Charlie says, "Henry, the suspect is about an hour and a half from your location. Need to have you determine if he turns into St. Johnsbury or keeps going north."

Henry replies, "I am going to the crossover just after the first exit to St Johnsbury. Setting in the crossover I can see if he turns off the Exit. He will think I am running a Radar trap. If he doesn't turn I will wait till he is well past the exit and then head up the highway. I can see if he turns on the second exit from about a half of a mile behind him. I will call you when I determine which way he is headed. He could cross the river on the East side of St. Johnsbury and head for his house."

Charlie says, "We are aware of that scenario. Bill and I have that scenario covered. Let us know what he does at the two exits. I am not criticizing you about what you said, but I believe we are ready."

Henry responds, "Just making sure we are all on the same page."

Charlie says, "That is fine. Call me when you confirm his direction. Do not interdict the truck for any reason."

Henry says, "Standing by."

Bill motions to Amanda. He says, "Can you bring us the check?"

When Amanda brings the check he says, "Sandra can you charge this please. I will get you reimbursed."

Sandra takes the check and goes to the counter. Bill says, "Anybody need the facilities? We got a few minutes to finish your drinks and deserts."

In about four minutes everyone returns to the table. Amanda walks over to the table. She brings four coffees and a tea to go. She says, "Compliments of the house. Put the cream and sugar you want in them."

Bill says, "Thank You."

He turns to the team. He says, "Bernie head up I-91. He could exit the interstate and go directly toward his house. Find a place to observe the Exit. I will call you if he heads your way."

Bernie says, "OK."

Bill says, "If he does come off the road at that Exit, just wait a few minutes and then head for the small Diner. We will meet there. Barry Coolidge is headed toward the small Diner from the East. Jane Ridgely is at the gas station at the intersection a few miles from his house. ED, Sandra, and Charlie will stay here with me until we are sure he is heading for his house.

Bernie leaves. He heads to the Interstate and goes north to the exit where Marshall would exit for home. The Interstate is on the west side of the Connecticut River. Only some of the exits serve a bridge to New Hampshire. The trucking office is in St. Johnsbury, which is in Vermont on the west side of the river. Marshall's house is in New Hampshire and is on the east side of the river.

Bill, Ed, Charlie and Sandra settle in at the Diner and wait for more phone calls. Amanda comes over. You are not leaving.

Bill answers, "Not yet. Thanks for the coffees. We will drink them here. At present I think we will be leaving in about an hour and an half."

A half an hour passes. Charlie's phone rings. Charlie answers, "Charlie Wilson here."

Josh responds, "Charlie, Josh here. Our guy is on the move. He is pulling out on to I-91. I will wait a few minutes and follow him. George left for the south exit to White River Junction about ten minutes ago. He said he would call in when our boy passed that exit."

Charlie says, "Thanks Josh. Keep Tracking."

Charlie turns to the others and says, "That was Josh. Our boy is on the road again. He may be a rapist, but he is a careful trucker. George Sherwood is at White River waiting."

Bill responds, "Good."

Ten minutes pass. George calls Josh. Josh answers, "George, what is he doing?"

George responds, "Our boy has left I-91 at White River. He is going in town. I don't want to follow too close. You had better get north of town. Let me call Charlie."

Josh says, "Ok."

George calls Charlie. Charlie answers, "Charlie here. What is happening?"

George replies, "Our boy turned off I-91 at White River. He is headed into town. Josh is headed north of town. I can't follow too close."

Charlie says, "Stay on the line."

Charlie turns to Bill and Ed. He says, "Our guy has turned off I-91 at White River. He is in town. George is tracking him."

George says on the phone, "He has turned into a shopping center. Let me move so I can see the truck."

George sees Marshall get out of the truck and go into the grocery store. He continues on the phone, "He has gone into the grocery store. I am going to move so it will be harder for him to spot me."

Charlie responds, "Ok. He probably just needs food at home. Hang loose."

George hangs up.

Josh calls George. George answers his cell, "George here."

Josh says, "I am at the north exit. I am sitting in the gas station to the west of the exit. What is happening?"

George says, "Our boy has gone into the grocery store. All we can do is wait."

Josh replies and hangs up, "OK."

Fifteen minutes pass. Marshall comes out of the grocery store with a cart. He puts the groceries in the passenger side of the truck.

George calls Josh. Josh answers his cell. Josh says, "Josh here. What's up, George."

George replies, "Our boy just came out and put groceries in the truck. He is putting the cart in the cart rack. He should be in the truck in a couple of minutes. Stay on the line."

Josh says, "Once we know which way he is headed. I will call Charlie and tell him what is going on."

George says, "The truck is started. He is turning for the exit." There is a pause. George continues, "He has turned toward the I-91 ramps. I am waiting a little."

Josh says, "OK."

George says, "I have turned around, but I am waiting to follow. He just turned on the street with the I-91 ramps. I am closing the distance. I can see the ramps. He is turning north. You have the action now."

Josh says, "I am ready. Talk to you later."

They both hang up.

Meantime at the Diner nothing is happening either.

Bill says, "The waiting always kills me. I am ready for action. We are men of action, but the wait and watching is so necessary."

Ed answers, "I guess we are all the same. Waiting is not my favorite part of the job. It is necessary."

Sandra interjects, "That is why I brought my knitting."

Charlie says, "I am the same way."

Josh calls Charlie. Charlie's cell rings. He answers, "Charlie here."

Josh says, "George told me. He is back on the road and headed north. He apparently needed groceries. He should pass my location any minute."

Charlie replies, "OK. We are ready."

Josh says, "Anytime now."

A few minutes pass.

Josh says, "I see several trucks. I have binoculars. Just wait. A couple more trucks are just coming in view. None of them are our boy. Hang loose guys."

Charlie says, "We are hanging."

Charlie turns to Bill, Sandra, and Ed and says, "Josh is waiting for him to pass the north exit at White River."

Josh continues, "I think the truck coming now is our boy. This is our boy. He is cruising right pass the exit ramps. He is headed for St. Johnsbury. You guys have fun. I will follow him in a few minutes."

Charlie replies, "We are ready. See you soon."

Charlie says, "You guys heard part of the conversation. Our guy has passed White River and is headed for St. Johnsbury. Better call Henry and Bernie. We have got about thirty minutes till the he gets here."

Charlie calls Henry. Henry answers, "Hi, what's up? Where is our guy?"

Charlie says, "Our guy has just passed White River. He is headed here. Maybe thirty minutes. Be ready."

Henry replies, "I am ready. I will call as soon as I spot him."

Charlie continues, "OK."

They hang up.

Charlie calls Bernie. Bernie answers, "Hi, what's up? Where is our guy?"

Charlie says, "Our guy has just passed White River. He is headed here. Maybe thirty minutes. Be ready."

Bernie replies, "I am ready. I will call as soon as I spot him."

Charlie continues, "OK."

They hang up.

Charlie turns to Bill and says, "Everybody is ready."

Bill says, "He will probably get off of I-91. The question will be whether he stops at the trucking company office and yard or continues through town and across the river to New Hampshire. Sandra, can you find a place to hide nearer to the office? Don't try to stop him. Just observe and call us if he stops or continues to the bridge."

Sandra responds, "Let me go now and find a parking spot. There are a couple of side streets near the office."

Sandra picks up her stuff and goes to her SUV. She drives over to the office. She circles the several different blocks. She parks her SUV on a side street. She walks to the corner and sees the entrance to the yard. She calls Bill. Bill answers, "Yes."

Sandra says, "I parked on a side street. I am on foot. I can see the yard entrance. I can hide here behind a fence when he arrives. He should not see me. I put on my regular coat not the State Police Jacket."

Bill replies, "Good. Be careful."

Sandra says, 'As soon as I spot the truck I will call you. Be ready."

Bill says, "When he comes up the Interstate, I will alert you. Ed will be ready to back you up."

Sandra says, "Thank You. I am a qualified State Police Woman."

Bill says, "We all use back up."

Sandra responds, "I want back up. But I am a Police woman."

Bill says, "I know. That is why I sent you. As a woman you will be less obvious as a spotter. Just be careful."

Sandra responds, "Got you covered serge."

They hang up.

Twenty-five minutes pass.

Henry calls Charlie. Charlie answers, "Hi Henry."

Henry says, "Hi. Our guy just passed me and is leaving I-91 for St. Johnsbury. Tell Bernie."

Charlie responds, "Good, Come to the Diner in ten minutes. Use the back streets."

They hang up.

Bill has called Bernie. Bernie answers, "Yes."

Bill says. "Bernie this is Bill. Our guy has turned into St. Johnsbury. Come to the Diner by the back way."

Bernie responds, "OK."

They hang up.

Bill turns to Charlie. "Can you cover the bridge?"

Charlie gets up and replies, "I will get the bridge."

Charlie heads for the bridge to New Hampshire and finds a place to observe it.

Sandra calls Bill. Bill answers, "Yes."

Sandra says, "I see the truck. He is three blocks away. I am in my own jacket and hat. I look like a local citizen walking up the street. I am prepared. There is couple walking to a restaurant. So I should not be obvious. Here he comes. He is stopping in the street across from the yard. He is out of the truck. He has crossed to the yard gate. He is checking the gate. It is locked. He has crossed back to the truck. The truck is moving again towards the east. He is going to the river."

Bill says, "OK, Sandra. Come back to the diner. Charlie has the bridge covered."

Sandra responds, "I am coming back."

Bill calls Ed. Ed answers, "Yes."

Bill says, "You can come back to the Diner."

Charlie calls Bill. Bill answers, "Yes."

Charlie says, "Our guy crossed the river into New Hampshire. I could see he turned north toward his house."

Bill says, "Come back here. We will all head for the small diner."

A few minutes pass.

Sandra arrives at the Diner. Henry, Bernie, and Ed arrive next. Finally Charlie arrives.

Bill says, "Everybody wants a coffee or tea."

Bill calls to Amanda. He says, "Amanda can you get everyone a coffee to go. Sandra wants tea." He says to everyone, "Better make a rest stop before we head for the small diner near his house."

While Amanda gets the drinks, Bill and several of the people go to the restroom."

Amanda brings the drinks and everyone fixes the cream and sugar.

They return and sort of gather around the table. Bill says, "Let's head to the Small Diner."

Bill says to Amanda, "how much are the drinks?'

Amanda says, "Compliments of the house. Just get the criminal."

Charlie, Ed, and Bill thank Amanda for the hospitality. Amanda says, "Be careful out there."

Bill says, "Lets head them up and move on out. This is like a cattle drive in the old west. Only we are herding one steer."

Sandra interjects, "Yeah, but steers were all males."

Bill laughingly says, "Very funny. You are one of the cowgirls. Will let you come along."

Sandra responds, "I thought you meant we were the cattle."

Bill says, "No. Marshall is the steer."

They head for the small diner.

Bill calls Jane Ridgely. The phone rings four times and Jane answers, "Jane Ridgely here."

Bill says, "Hi, Jane. This is Bill. Marshall is on his way toward you."

Jane replies, "I am ready. I will call you as soon as he passes here."

Bill says, "I will be awaiting your call. Meantime we are headed for the small diner south of your location."

Thirty minutes pass. Jane almost freaks. She calls Bill from in her car.

Bill answers and Jane says, "The guy has stopped here and is ordering some food. When he leaves I will call you."

Bill says, "We are meeting at the small diner. We will wait until you call."

A few minutes pass and they arrive at the parking lot of the diner.

Bill motions to everybody to go inside.

Barry Coolidge is sitting at the corner table at the end of diner. Bill walks to the table and joins Barry. Ed, Charlie, and Bernie come in and join Barry and Bill. Sandra stops at the restroom. Henry fusses around in his SUV and then comes in. He stops at the rest room also. He comes over to the table.

Charlie says, "This Henry Clay. He is on the task force now. Josh is not. Josh is still patrolling I-91."

Bill says, "Charlie, have Josh go up to the end of I-91 near the Canadian Border. If Marshall runs north he can help us stop him at the border."

Charlie replies, "I will call him now." Charlie calls Josh and explains to him what Bill has suggested. Josh starts north and calls back to his barracks and tell the captain what he is doing."

Everything is getting in place for the arrest.

Bill says, "When we get to his house, we need to position ourselves around the house. Ed and Bernie can you cover the rear of the house.

Sandra and Barry you cover the left side. There is a door on that side, but you should have the cover of the tractor-trailer. Henry and Jane can cover the right side. We observed there are some trees and a woodpile for cover. Charlie and I will approach the front door. Relax until Jane calls."

A few minutes pass. Charlie's phone rings, He answers, "Hi, Charlie here."

Josh says, "Josh on this end. I am at the super 8 deli about five miles from the border. Call me if you need me."

Charlie responds, "OK. Stand by. I will call you when we are about to make the arrest."

Josh replies, "Standing by. I will be awaiting your call."

They hang up.

Bill's phone rings. He answers, "Hi. This is Bill."

Jane says, "Bill, Our boy is leaving the gas station. He is turning toward his house. I am going to wait ten minutes and follow. If he spots me, he should think I am on a normal patrol. I will just cruise by his house and continue up the road. You all should be able to move up to the gas station now."

Bill responds, "Be careful. We are moving to the gas station."

Bill turns to the others, "That was Jane. Our guy has headed to the house."

Charlie's phone rings. Charlie answers, "It is me, Josh. Someone is sticking up the Super 8 Deli. I can't ignore the robbery. There are civilians inside. Get me back up."

Charlie calls the barracks. The desk sergeant answers the phone. Charlie says, "This is Charlie Wilson. Josh Bradley is at the Super 8 Deli about five miles south of the border. The place is being robbed. Get backup and call the border patrol and the Mounties. These may be the guys that have pulled a couple of other robberies. We are going to break off the arrest and cut these guys off."

Charlie turns to the others who are listening. He says, "Josh is trying to stop a robbery near the border. We need to help."

Bill says, "You and Henry have jurisdiction in Vermont go. We will back you up on this side of the state line." They run to their vehicles and speed out of the lot with light and sirens on. Near Marshall's house they turn off the lights and sirens. They turn them on about a mile pass the house.

Bill says, "Bernie you head for the last road near the border. This is classified as a hot pursuit. You can stop the vehicle without a warrant." Bernie runs to the SUV. He speeds out of the gas station with the siren and light on."

Bill says, "Ed, you have no jurisdiction in New Hampshire, but you can report if the car is spotted headed south on I-91 as citizens."

Ed replies, "Got yeah."

Bill says, "Sandra, you are with me. We will cover the state line crossing. I will call Jane."

Bill calls Jane. Jane answers, "Hi Bill. What's up?"

Bill responds, "We have a little interruption to the arrest. Josh Bradley is trying to stop a robbery in Vermont. He cannot ignore the situation. There are civilians involved. After you pass the suspects house proceed to the state line and be prepared to block the road. As soon as we have better information I will tell you."

Meanwhile at the super 8 deli, Josh has crossed the road and approached the right side of the store. He peeks around the corner. There is a car running in the lot, but nobody is in the car. Josh ducks down and move along the window. Inside shelving blocks the robbers view. The one robber has a gun on the clerk. The other robber has a gun on the civilians. If it is the same robbers they have shot a clerk and a civilian. He checks his pistol and his back up piece in his ankle hostler. The clerk is scooping the money out of the cash register. The robber says, "Hurry up."

Josh swings the door open and says, "Police, drop the gun."

The clerk drops behind the counter and the robber turns toward Josh. He fires twice. The first bullet hit Josh in the chest. It stings, but Josh has his heavy-duty vest on because of the chase. The second bullet hits Josh in the right shoulder. Josh is left-handed and fires once at the robber. The bullet hits the robber high on the right side under the shoulder. The robber drops the gun on the counter. The gun discharges and the bullet shatters the hot dog case.

The clerk has a gun under the case and fires once at the robber. The bullet strikes the robber in the side. It is only a flesh wound. The second robber grabs a woman customer and using her as a shield starts toward the door. Josh backs farther behind the counter. He ignores the first robber trying to leave. The first robber is hit and is bleeding. The second robber is his problem. Josh backs around behind the counter. He says to the robber, "Let the woman go. If you leave her go I will let you go. If you shoot her, I will have to shoot you."

The robber gets to the front door. His friend is already in the car. He says to the woman pull the door open. She does as she is told. She opens the door enough for him to escape. The door is still blocking her. He shoves her into the counter and runs out and around the back of the car. By the time Josh is around the woman. The robber is in the car and has started out of the lot.

Josh identifies the car as a 2003 or 2004 Chevy Impala with New Your Plates. The first three letters are PWV. He grabs his radio. He calls the desk. The desk sergeant answers, "Is that you, Josh."

Josh forgets for a moment he is shot. He shouts into the radio, "Serge there are two robbers. They are white, they are in their thirties, one has brown hair and one has blonde. The brown haired one has green eyes and the blonde has blue eyes. The car is a 2003 or 2004 Chevy Impala, dark blue or black. It has a broken right taillight. New York plate that start with PWV. I hit the one robber in the right shoulder and the clerk hit him in the left side. The other robber is driving and not hit. I am hit in the right shoulder. I am not bleeding seriously. The one civilian woman was shoved into the counter and has cuts and bruises. There is other damage. We will need a forensics team."

The desk sergeant says, "EMS is on the way. They should be there in less than five minutes. I will get back to you in a minute."

The desk Sergeant put out an APB on the robbers, "There are two robbers. They are white, they are in there thirties, one has brown hair and one has blonde. The brown haired one has green eyes and the blonde has blue eyes. The car is a 2003 or 2004 Chevy Impala, dark blue or black. It has a broken right taillight. New York plate that starts with PWV. Josh hit the one robber in the right shoulder and the clerk hit him in the left side. The other robber is driving and not hit. Josh is hit in the right shoulder. He says he not bleeding seriously. The one civilian woman was shoved into the counter and has cuts and bruises. There is other damage to the store. We will need a forensics team. Charlie, how close are you and Henry?"

Charlie responds, "Just crossing into Vermont. We are about six minutes from the scene. We have people headed north and south and east at the New Hampshire border. Notify New York and the Canadians."

The desk sergeant responds, "The APB has gone to the Canadians, the Border patrol and New York State Police. I think we got them cornered. Be careful. They don't have much to lose. New York State wants them also."

Bill calls Charlie. Charlie answers, "Hello, Bill. I got to cover this. These are my guys and Josh has been shot. EMS is almost here. Josh is hit but is not bleeding much. The bullet went through his shoulder."

Bill comes back, "Chasing Marshall is on hold. I have people on the way to every Bridge into New Hampshire for about forty miles. Let's get these guys."

Charlie replies, "I have Henry chasing them south. I got Mildred Redmond coming north just below St. Johnsbury. New York wants these guys also. They are blocking the roads into New York State. The St. Johnsbury Police are blocking streets in the city. Hold the border, Bill."

Henry calls on the radio. "I think I have them in site on I-91. They are above St. Johnsbury headed south. I turned my lights and siren off. They are driving near the speed limit. There is an exit coming up. I am still a quarter mile behind them. They are turning off on the exit. I can see which way they are turning on the exit. They turned west. I am going to close up some. Can the other people hear me?"

Charlie says, "The Vermont Officers can. New York and New Hampshire officers cannot. I got Bill Simpson of New Hampshire and I am repeating the info to him real time. Serge Barry is communicating with New York. Keep Transmitting, we are all on board. This is a rolling road. I am losing them momentarily as they go over the hills. I am three miles west of I-91. I am continuing west. I have gone another two miles. I lost them. There is no crossroads. Where did they go? I am turning around. I am going to cruise back slowly. I am checking driveways. I just passed a driveway with a Chevy Impala. It is not a light colored car but it is too dark to determine an exact color. I am continuing for a little farther east. I need some back up."

Charlie responds, "I am coming south. Sam Wilson just arrived here. He can cover the investigation here until the forensic people arrive."

Henry asks, "Should I cruise back past the house?"

Charlie says, "No. I would recommend you hold where you are. Mildred, are you on line."

Mildred answers, "I am."

Charlie continues, "The St. Johnsbury police can cover St. Johnsbury. You can come north on I-91 and join Henry and I. We will wait here for you.'

John Davidson calls on the radio, "This John Davidson, I am about six mile south of St. Johnsbury. I am doing 85. I should catch up with Mildred at your exit."

Charlie says, "Be careful. But keep coming John. When Mildred and John arrive we are going to take these guys. Serge, keep several other officers headed this way. But we cannot wait any longer. Henry can cruise up the road and try and determine the address of the house. I am going to get Vivian on the phone and get a search warrant and subpoenas."

Serge replies, "There are only two additional officer close enough to do any good. I am going to ask St. Johnsbury to send a couple of officers. I am going to have them secure the grocery store scene. They can do this under the circumstances."

Charlie responds, "Thank You, serge."

Charlie calls Vivian Bush. The phone rings six times. Vivian answers, "Vivian Bush here."

Charlie says, "Vivian this is Charlie Wilson. We are in hot pursuit of two suspects that robbed a grocery convenience store. Josh interrupted the robbery and has been shot. His wound is not too serious. Josh shot one of the robbers. We chased them down I-91 and to their house on Smuggler's road. They do not know we know where they live. We got the New Hampshire and New York borders blocked. Henry is going to get the exact address. Can you get a search warrant and an arrest warrant? We probably don't need them since this is a hot pursuit situation, but let's do it anyway if possible. We know the car they used is a 2003 to 2005 Chevy Impala. The tags are New York and first three letters are PWV. The one guy is wounded. I think he is going to need medical help."

Vivian says, "OK. Get me the address. My tech is probably in bed, and so are the judges I would use. I will call you back in ten minutes."

Vivian calls Judge Pefferkorn. He answers, "Judge Pefferkorn, here. Who is this?"

Vivian says, "ADA Vivian Bush. I need several warrants like immediately, Your Honor."

Judge Pefferkorn responds, "You sound urgent."

Vivian says, "State Trooper, Josh Bradley interrupted a robbery in progress. Josh was shot but it does appear not to be too serious. He has partially identified the car. The other officers are getting me the exact address. Charlie Wilson would like us to cover the arrest and search with warrants. Is this possible?"

Judge Pefferkorn responds, "Damn straight. Tell me how to get copies to you?"

Vivian says, "My tech is going to get the car info and one of the officers on site will get me the address. The closest Barracks is north of St. Johnsbury. We can FAX them there. The original can be sent to the defendant's lawyers tomorrow."

Judge Pefferkorn responds, "Let me get to my computer. I have a standard form for the arrest and search warrants. I will call you in a few minutes to get the correct address and so forth."

Vivian replies, "Good."

They hang up.

Vivian calls Charlie. When Charlie's cell answers, she says "Charlie this Vivian. Get the exact address. I have Judge Pefferkorn working on a warrant. My tech is working on the car."

Charlie says, "Henry is on the way up the road to get an exact address."

Vivian says, "Call me when you have the info."

Charlie replies, "OK."

A few minutes pass. Henry calls Charlie. Charlie answers on the radio, "Henry, do you have the information?"

Henry says, "The address is 12142. There are two mailboxes on the same support. The even numbered houses are on the side of the road that corresponds to their house. The name on the mailbox is J. Parsons. I am stopped past the driveway. I cannot see the rear of the car to confirm the license number."

Charlie says, "Hold what you have got."

Henry responds, "OK. Let me call Vivian. I am going to park. I am going to walk back across a neighbor's property and try and see the license number. I have a small flashlight. I will call you on your cell if I get more information."

Charlie says, "Be careful. These guys are violent. We already have one officer shot."

Henry responds, "I am always careful, but we need more info."

Henry breaks off the radio conversation.

Charlie calls Vivian. Vivian answers, "What do have for me?"

Charlie says, "The address is 12142 Smuggler Road. The name on the mailbox is J. Parsons. Henry is trying to get close enough to get the entire license."

Vivian says, "Let me get my tech to check this additional info."

Meantime Henry has got to a tree line and hedgerow on the neighbor's property. He can see the car, but not the license. Henry watches the house for three minutes. There is no movement visible from his position. He moves toward the car. Suddenly the porch light comes on. Henry ducks back into the hedgerow and lays down. Somebody comes out to the car. It's a woman. She gets into the car. She turns the car lights on. Henry can see the license plate. The number is PWV734. He cannot move or call Charlie. She searches for a couple of things in the car. She shuts off the lights and finally returns to the house. Henry finally walks back across the neighbor's lawn to the road. As he walks up the road as he calls Charlie. Charlie answers, "Charlie here."

Henry says, "I got the full number. It is PWV734. There is also a woman at the house. She came out to the car for something."

Charlie says, "OK, return to your car. We should be coming up there in twenty minutes."

Henry replies, "I am walking back to the car and will wait to hear from you guys."

They hang up.

Charlie calls Vivian, "Vivian says, "Hi, Charlie. Got more info?"

Charlie says, "Henry got close enough to verify the car is a Chevy Impala and the full license plate number is PWV734. He also saw a woman come out of the house."

Vivian says, "The judge is going to issue a search warrant for the house. He will issue two arrest warrants for the John Doe suspects. You will be covered. J. Parsons is the owner of the house and property. The house is rented to someone else. In a couple of minutes you should have the warrants. I woke the judge up. So I will hear about this tomorrow. When Judge Pefferkorn heard that an officer was shot he told me the warrants were no problem. My tech is ready.

Charlie says, "As soon as I get the warrants and my other officers are here, we are going to execute the warrants and the arrest."

Vivian responds, "Good. Be careful."

Charlie says, "We will."

Mildred and John arrive at the gas station. Charlie gets out of his car. Mildred and John get out of their cars. They casually greet each other. Charlie says, "I am waiting for several FAXES. Relax until the FAXES arrive."

Mildred says, "I am going inside to the restroom. I will be back in a minute."

John says, "I am going inside and get a coffee."

Charlie says, "Go. I need to stay by the car until the FAXES arrive."

Ten minutes pass. Mildred and John have come back outside. The three officers chitchat while waiting for the FAXES. Charlie's cell rings, "Charlie here."

Henry says, "What's happening?"

Charlie replies, "I am waiting for the warrants from Vivian. Mildred and John are here with me at the gas station. I'll call you when we are ready. The FAX machine just started. Hang on." Charlie pauses. He looks in the SUV and checks the FAX. It is the warrants. He continues, "Charlie the warrant are arriving. As soon as I check them we will be ready to come up to your location."

Henry responds, "I am waiting about two hundred feet past the driveway. See you soon."

Charlie says, "I want to read the search warrant before we proceed. Let me lay the cell down. Stay on the line."

Charlie takes the warrants off the FAX machine. He checks the search warrant for the proper address. He picks up the cell and says, "Henry the address on the Warrant is 12142 Smugglers Road. You are sure that this is the correct address."

Henry answers, "The address of the neighbor's house is 12144 on the same side of the road. The house is on the even side addresses. The mailboxes in front of the property are 12142 and 12143. The logic is the house is 12142."

Charlie says, "OK. Here we come. See you in ten minutes."

Charlie hangs up.

Charlie says, "Let's go. We will meet Henry and figure a plan of action. No sirens or Lights. Spread out and drive up Smugglers Road and pass Henry. Turn around and stop off the road where Henry is parked."

Mildred, John and Charlie get into the respective vehicles and head up Smugglers Road.

Ten minutes pass and the three officers join Henry. They get out of their cars.

Charlie calls 911. When the operator answers, "What is the nature of your emergency?"

Charlie answers, "This is Sergeant Charlie Wilson of the New Hampshire State Police." I need an EMS team and an ambulance on Smugglers Road near the house at 12142. We are about to make an arrest and one of the suspects is wounded. I want to be ready to transport the wounded suspect. Connect me to the fire house."

The operator responds, "Let me call the fire house. Hold on."

She calls the firehouse. The only person there is the driver of the fire truck. She says" I have a State Police Sergeant Charlie Wilson on the line. I am going to have him call you directly. He needs your help."

The truck driver says, 'OK.'

The operator tells Charlie the firehouse's number.

He calls. The truck driver answers, "Fred Johnson. How can I help you?'

Charlie responds, "We are about to exercise a number of arrest warrants at 12142 Smugglers Road. Do you know where it is?'

Fred says, "I know the road. We will find the exact address."

Charlie says, "One of the suspects was shot by a State Policeman during a robbery attempt. As far as we know he is still alive. After we arrest him, he will need EMS help. Do you understand?"

Fred responds, "The EMS team works out of the local clinic. I am the only one here at the firehouse. This is a volunteer operation. I will call everyone to come to the address."

Charlie says, "That is fine, but tell them to stop at about 12000 and wait till I call. Do not use sirens or lights on Smugglers Road. Stop on the side of the road east of the actual address and wait."

Fred says, "I will tell the guys your instructions. Our chief lives in the 12600 block of Smugglers Road. Where are you guys?"

Charlie says, "We are on the side of the road in front of 12144."

Fred says, "Let me call the chief and have him join you. He can help to direct our other guys."

Charlie responds, "There are four of us on the side of the road."

Fred says, "Let me call him on his cell. And see how long it will take him to get there."

A couple of minutes pass. Fred comes back on the cell. Frank will be there in about five minutes."

Charlie says, "Good."

Fred says, "The others are less than ten minutes. Frank will give them instructions. Let me give you Frank's cell."

Charlie says, "OK. I can write it down."

Charlie says, "Thanks for now, Fred."

A couple of minutes pass. Frank pulls up in the chief's car."

Frank gets out of the car. Charlie says before Frank can ask, "I am Sergeant Charlie Wilson. This is Henry, Mildred, and John. We are about serve several warrants and to arrest two suspects wanted for shooting of officer Josh Bradley about an hour ago. They are in the house at 12142. As soon as you are in place block the road and wait for your team. We are going to block the road here."

Henry jumps into his cruiser and backs up the road and parks across the both lanes and turns the lights on. He is beyond the little hill where the suspects cannot see his car. Henry jogs back to where Charlie is standing.

The chief calls Charlie and says, "I have the lanes block to the east."

Charlie says, "Henry you cover the back door. Mildred and myself will cover the front door. John you go to this side of the house and be ready to help Henry or us. Henry did you see the right side of the house? Is there a door on the right side?"

Henry replies, "I observed the house from the road and there was no obvious door on the right wall."

Charlie continues, "We can use our radios for communications. Henry, you and John go across the neighbor property and get near the house. These guys have not been afraid to use their weapons. When you two are in place, I will drive to the driveway and stop. Mildred you follow me and block the driveway. Then get in my car. My running lights are fixed with a switch so I can go completely dark. I am going to call the local fire station and have them send a EMS and ambulance. We know the one guy is wounded."

Henry and John head across the neighbor's property. The porch light comes on. John heads up the walk. The man comes to the front door. John holds up his badge. John says, "I am with the State Police. Please go back inside and turn off the lights. Stay away from the windows on the east side of the house. I will explain after we are finished. Is there a basement?"

The man answers, "Yes. Why?"

John says, "Take the family down the basement quickly. There may be shooting. We are in hot pursuit of at least two suspects. Lock your doors."

The man slams the door and follows John's instruction. By the time John gets to the hedge row the house is dark. Henry says, "What did you tell him?"

John answers in a low voice, "I told him to lock up and take the family down the basement."

Mildred follows Charlie up the road. Charlie turns into the driveway. Mildred blocks the driveway. She jumps out of her SUV and jumps into Charlie's. They drive up to the front door. Mildred goes to the right and Charlie to the left. Charlie has brought his bullhorn. He whispers into the radio, "Ready Henry?"

Henry whispers back, "Ready as I will ever be. Go for it."

Charlie bellows on the horn, "**THIS IS THE STATE POLICE. OPEN THE DOOR. WE HAVE A SEARCH WARRANT AND ARREST WARRANTS. OPEN THE DOOR.**"

A woman's voice from inside says, "Just a minute." Charlie hears some commotion inside. The lock clicks. Mildred has her gun at the ready. The door opens slowly.

Charlie says, "Please open the door all the way, madam."

Charlie holds up his badge. He says, "I am with the state police. Please step outside."

The woman does slowly. Mildred waits until she is clear of the door. Mildred pulls the woman to the right side of the doorway. Mildred immediately cuffs her.

The woman says, "I am under arrest."

Mildred frisks her and says, "Just stand by the wall please."

Charlie looks inside and does not see anyone else. He says, "John, come around here."

John moves around to the front. Charlie looks into the living room. There is no one in the room. John enters and quickly ducks behind a large chair. John and Charlie hear what sounds like a door opening toward the back of the house. Henry is frozen against the back wall. He is holding a broom upside down. The one suspect starts out the back door. Henry sticks the broom between his legs. The suspect trips, falls, and yells. Henry is on top of him. Henry yells to the Charlie and John, "I got one of them. Before the guy can recover from the fall, Henry cuffs him. He frisks the guy on the ground and pulls him to his feet. You are under arrest. Charlie pokes his head out the door and says, "You got him?"

Henry answers, "Yea. Where is the second one?"

They hear john says, "Put your hands where I can see them slowly. The guy is lying on the bed. He can hardly move.

Charlie joins John. John holds his weapon on the guy while Charlie frisks the guy as best he can."

Charlie calls the chief. He says, "Chief, bring the EMS team. This guy is not in the best of shape. He is alive."

A couple of minutes pass, Charlie hears the chief at the front door. Charlie says, "Back here chief."

The chief enters with one other fireman. Charlie says, "I still need to frisks him completely. But he looks pretty bad off."

John is still covering the guy. The chief take a stethoscope from a bag and listens to the guy's heartbeat. He says, "Serge takes a pair of those gloves and search his legs and buttocks for a weapon."

Charlie does.

The chief says to the other fireman, "Let us turn him on his left side. Serge, search behind his back.' The chief looks at the guy's back.

He says, "Let's turn him on his right side." They do. Charlie searches behind the guy's back again. No weapons. Several other EMS guys enter. Two firemen bring in a gurney. They put an intravenous feed in his arm. A lady member of the team comes in with a radio system to monitor the guy's vitals. They have cut most of his clothes off. Let's get him on the gurney. Several of the EMS and firemen lift him onto the gurney.

Charlie says, "Procedure requires me to cuff him to the gurney."

The chief says, "OK. Just cuff him to the one rail on each side. Whoever rides along will have a key to the cuffs. He is weak and obviously has no weapons."

Susan the lady on the EMS team has secured a number of sensors to the guy's skin. She starts the monitors.

The chief says, "I was told he shot one of your guys, but as you know our job is not to judge a patient."

Charlie says, "My job is to be sure a patient does not do anything to your team or my officers."

The chief says, "You can relax. We are going to be here several more minutes."

Susan is obviously a nurse. She calls the clinic. And she calls the hospital in St. Johnsbury.

Charlie calls the other officers on the side. The woman and the second suspect are seated on the sofa. John is watching them. Henry is watching the wounded suspect. They gather around Charlie. He says, "We need to decide who goes where."

Charlie says, "There are three St. Johnsbury officers on their way here. I can deputize them to act as temporary State Police. We are going to lock the suspects up in St. Johnsbury for tonight. I was going to have one officer go with Mildred and the woman. I will have one go with Henry and the second suspect. John you can ride in the Ambulance. The third officer can guard the house until the forensics team arrives. Vivian will meet you guys in St. Johnsbury. I have to leave and join Bill Simpson and the team chasing the rapist. Vivian should be coming to St. Johnsbury."

Charlie calls Vivian. She answers, "Hi. Charlie. What is up?"

Charlie answers, "We have the two suspects in custody and a woman staying at the house. Three officers from St. Johnsbury are on their way to help. We need a forensics team to go over the house. John is going with the wounded suspect. I am going to read the other suspect his rights. You will need to read the wounded suspect his rights. He is not fully conscious. John is coming with him in the ambulance. You are going to have fun, but so are we. I have to get back to the arrest of Marshall Brickman the rapist."

Vivian responds, "I am leaving here in a few minutes. I should get to St. Johnsbury about the same time the suspects get there. How is Josh?"

Charlie says, "We been a little too busy, but I need to call the hospital. He is in the same hospital where the suspect is going."

The chief interrupts, "Charlie we are ready to transport."

Charlie says, "John are you ready to go?"

John responds, "Yes, I locked my car by the side of the house. I am ready."

The chief says. "John, I am sorry but the only seat is what we call the jump seat."

John heads for the ambulance.

Susan the nurse says, "Chief, I locked my car next to John's car. I assume the ambulance will be coming back here so we can get our cars."

The chief says, "Well we will get you guys back here. Just go."

The nurse goes to the ambulance. She checks the equipment is already. John gets in. The one EMS tech gets in the back. He says to John, "I am Bob."

John says, "I am John."

The driver and one other EMS get in the front. The driver says, "I am Fred. Are we ready to roll?"

Bob answers, "Ready back here."

The one fireman George with his own vehicle follows the ambulance. George's SUV has lights and Siren if he needs it.

They turn on the lights, but the siren is unnecessary at midnight on the roads up here.

The two male officers and a woman officer from St. Johnsbury arrive as the ambulance is leaving.

Charlie meets them. He says, "I am Charlie Wilson. The lady officer is Mildred Redmond and our other officer is Henry Clay."

The woman officer introduces herself and the two guys. She says, "I am Helen Green. This is George Williams and Fred Clinton."

Charlie says, "I am going send you, Helen with Mildred to take the woman to St. Johnsbury. Technically she is in protective custody."

Charlie turns to the woman and says, "I am sending you to St. Johnsbury for two reasons. The first reason is the ADA from Vermont will want to interview you. She will be at St. Johnsbury when you arrive. Her name is Vivian Bush. The second reason is I cannot leave you here until the forensic team finishes examining the house. Somebody will bring you back here if Vivian determines you are NOT wanted in this crime or others. Do you understand?"

She answers, "Yes."

Charlie tells Henry, "Please bring the guy over here."

Henry brings the guy over.

Charlie says, "I am going to read you your rights." He says to the guy, "You are charged with committing a robbery earlier this evening." He says to the woman, "You are not under arrest at this time, however you are a material witness." He reads them their rights. He asks each of them if each of them understand their rights."

They both answer yes.

Charlie says, "Mildred and Helen please take the lady in Mildred's SUV and go to St. Johnsbury. You must at least put handcuffs on her. This is protocol for transporting someone. Henry and George can you take the suspect in Henry's SUV to St. Johnsbury? You must handcuff the suspect and attach the leg irons once he is in the vehicle. Again it is protocol. Take them to the main police station in St. Johnsbury. You will lock up the suspect until Vivian can interview him. Don't leave Vivian alone during the interrogation."

The officers respond, "We got the job, Charlie."

Charlie says, "They have been read their rights. Do not ask them anything about the case. However you can take care of their human needs during the transport. Enjoy the trip."

Charlie continues, "You can leave. I need Fred to stay until the forensic team arrives."

Fred responds, "No, problem Charlie. I am going to lock the doors after you leave and just guard the house until the team gets here."

Charlie says, "The leader of the team is Marvin Hess. He should have two other techs along. Once they arrive you should be able to leave. They will take charge. The main thing is don't leave the premises. You can go to the car, but do not drive off the property. It is the chain of evidence requirement. I know you are familiar with the laws, but I am just making sure we are all working on the same rules."

Fred says, "I got you covered."

Charlie says, "Until this robbery and shooting happened, a task force that I am part of, was over in New Hampshire chasing a rapist. Long night. I am going. You have a good night."

Fred says, "Same to you Charlie."

Charlie leaves the house and gets into his SUV.

Charlie calls Bill. Bill answers, "Charlie is the chase all over?"

Charlie replies, "Yes. Are we going to arrest Marshall tonight?"

Bill says, "I was thinking that we should return to the small Diner and rest until maybe 4 AM. Then we can execute the arrest plan."

Charlie says, "That sounds good. We will all be rested. Sleeping in the car is not the most restful sleep, but it is better than nothing."

Bill continues, "I figure Marshall is going to get up tomorrow and drive to the trucking company office or the refrigerated warehouse. If we make the arrest around five o'clock at the house it should be easier."

Charlie says, "See you there in a little while."

Bill responds, "See you there."

After Bill hangs up his cell, he calls the other members of the team and explains to each of them to return to the small diner and get some rest. He calls the desk sergeant at headquarters and explains to him about what has happened and what their game plan is for the rest of the night. He asks the sergeant to call him at 3:30 AM so he can proceed with the plan. He asks the sergeant to round up a forensic team and send them to join the arrest team at about 5:30 AM. Bill drives to the Diner.

Bill drives about 30 minutes to the Diner. When he gets to the Diner he goes inside. He uses the restroom. When he comes out he approaches the waitress at the counter. Bill says, "As you can see from my uniform I am a New Hampshire State Policeman. Six other policemen are going to come here in the next half an hour. We are going to park over in the back corner of the lot unless someone objects. This has nothing to do with the Diner. We just need to wait until about 3:30 AM. The officer coming out of the ladies room is one of the policewomen."

The waitress responds, "There is no problem with parking over there until morning. I heard on the radio there was a robbery in Vermont at a store. An officer was shot. Do you know him?"

Bill responds, "Yes. He is a friend."

The waitress continues, "Is he OK."

Bill responds, "He will be OK. The wound is not very serious. He shot the one robbery. We caught the robbers about an hour ago at their house in Vermont."

The waitress responds, "Good for you."

Bill continues, "Thank You." He turns to Sandra and says, "Sandra, there is nothing to do until about 3:30 AM. So relax in the car."

Sandra responds, "Have a good night."

Bill says, "At least it is not a stake out where we need to stay awake all night. The desk sergeant is going to wake me at about 3:30. Good night."

Bill and Sandra go to their vehicles.

The other people arrive and go in the Diner. They come back and sleep in their cars.

Bills cell rings. He looks at his watch. It is 3:31 AM. He answers, "Bill Simpson here."

The desk Sergeant says, "Bill, it is 3:30. It is time to rise and shine."

Bill replies, "Thanks. I am going to rise. I am not sure about the shining part."

They hang up.

Bill gets up and steps out of the SUV. He stretches and yawns. He reaches into the car and turns the key. He honks the horn twice. He waits a minute and honks the horn again. He can see Sandra and the other guys are moving around. He walks to the Diner. Several of the others get out of their cars and walk to the Diner. The waitress Matilda greets them. "How are you all today? Was motel Beaufort comfy last night?"

Bill answers, "I think we are fine, but I need a coffee and the rest room.

Matilda answers, "The coffee will be ready when you come out."

Sandra and Ed come in while Bill is still in the rest room. Matilda asks, "What would you like?"

Charlie, Barry, and Bernie come in. Matilda asks, "What would you like?"

Jane went directly to the ladies room. When she comes out she joins the others at the table. Matilda takes all of their breakfast orders. In a few minutes Matilda brings them coffee and tea.

Bill starts the conversation. He says, "I am going to organize the arrest while we eat."

Everyone nods their heads in agreement.

Bill continues, "Jane, you should lead the way since you have been up the road twice. When you get near the driveway just pull on the side. Wait until we are together and then proceed to the driveway. The rest of us will drive up onto the property. Ed you should go first and Bernie and Sandra should follow you into the driveway. Ed you should go around the right side and cover the rear door. Sandra go left and Bernie go right. Position yourselves to intercept him. Charlie and I will approach the front door and call him out. Barry, you back up Charlie and me. Use the hand held radios. We can all hear everyone. Jane, after we are all up in the driveway, you block the driveway near the road. It should be morning twilight as we approach the property. Do not use sirens or lights. We should have the element of surprise on our side.

"Let's finish breakfast, use the restrooms, I will pay the bill. We should be ready to go by 4:30. I know some of you probably took off your vest to sleep. Before we leave the parking lot put the vests back on. Check your weapons. Does everyone have their back up piece? Everybody has a couple of extra clips or a extra two loaded cylinders. Are there any questions?"

They all respond, "We are ready, Bill."

Bill says, "I have one other item. A forensics team should be here between 5 and 6 AM to search the house and truck. We should be able to turn the operation over to their expert hands. I think we can transport the suspect to Lebanon and have someone pick him up there and take him to Concord. Linda can interview him in Concord. We will read him his rights, but not interview him on the way to Concord."

They finish breakfast and chit-chat a little. At about 4:20 they head for the restrooms and their vehicles. Bill pays Matilda. Matilda says, "Good Luck and be Safe."

Bill replies, "Thank you for the hospitality."

By 4:30 they are all in their vehicles. Bill flashes his high beams and waves Jane in front. They leave the Diner parking lot. There is little traffic on the route. They stop behind Jane's SUV a hundred feet from the driveway. Bill gets out. He walks up the line to Jane's SUV. Bill says, "Ready."

Jane answers, "I am ready serge."

He walks back the line. Everybody says in turn, "I am ready serge."

Bill flashes his high beam lights and then turns the regular headlight off."

Jane stops just short of the driveway. Everyone else drive around Jane and up the driveway. Barry waits for the others and follows Bill up the driveway. Everyone is on the radio.

Ed says, "I am in the back of the house."

Bill looks around to confirm everyone is in position. They are all out of the vehicles and using the vehicles as shields. Bill and Charlie are walking toward the house. They are about twenty feet apart. Charlie is on the right of the door against the wall. Bill is on the porch to the left of the door. Charlie reaches over and pounds on the door. Bill is on the bullhorn and says, "**MARSHALL BRICKMAN, THIS IS THE POLICE. OPEN THE DOOR SLOWLY WE NEED TO TALK TO YOU.**"

Charlie rings the bell and wraps again. Bill waits. Bill calls on the horn again, "**MARSHALL BRICKMAN THIS IS THE POLICE. WE NEED TO TALK TO YOU NOW. OPEN THE DOOR. THE HOUSE IS SURROUNDED. OPEN THE DOOR.**"

Bill and Charlie see a couple of lights come on. They can hear someone stirring around.

Marshall responds, "I need to pull on my pants. I am coming don't shoot."

Bill says in a normal voice, "Please open the door. Keep your hands where we can see them."

Marshall looks through the peep hole and see it is really the police.

The door slowly opens. Marshall steps in front of the storm door. Bill and Charlie can see his hands. There are no obvious weapons.

Bill says in calm voice, "Please step outside Marshall."

Marshall steps outside. Charlie instinctively steps behind him.

Bill asks, "You are Marshall Brickman?"

Marshall answers, "Yes. What is this all about?"

Bill says, "I have here a warrant for your arrest on a number of charges. Please place your hands behind your back."

Charlie secures the handcuffs.

Marshall asks, "What am I being arrested for?"

Bill answers, "You are being arrested by the State of New Hampshire for number of rapes. We also have a search warrant for your house and grounds and the truck you drive."

Marshall says, "I guess it is no use for me to say I am not guilty."

Bill says, "I am going to read you your rights. The district attorney will discuss guilt or innocence with you."

Bill takes out a little card and carefully reads Marshall his rights. Charlie and Barry witness the reading. Bill says, "Do you understand these rights?"

Marshall says, "Yes. I do want an attorney."

Bill says, "OK. We are transporting you to Concord New Hampshire. The ADA, Linda Smyth, will have an attorney appointed for you. Until then we will not be questioning you. During the transport you can request anything you require for normal human needs. Please take a seat in the back of the SUV. Barry sees that he is made comfortable. The leg irons are protocol for transport."

Barry walks Marshall to his SUV. Charlie follows until Marshall is secured in the back seat.

Bill says, "Bernie can you accompany Barry and Marshall to Lebanon?" Bernie says, "Sure."

Barry says, "I am the most rested. I can bring Bernie back here before going home."

Bill says, "Bernie I am ordering you to get a room. There is a motel over near the small Diner. Get a room and come down tomorrow."

Bernie says, "OK. Just charge it and I will cover the paper work."

Bill says, "Jane do you feel you are fresh enough to drive home."

Jane says, "I will stop at the Diner and get a coffee."

Bill turns to Sandra, "Go get a room at the motel. That is an order. I do not want anyone having an accident on the way home."

Charlie says, "I am going to drive to Vermont and then get a room. It has been a long night."

Bill says, "I am going to wait for the forensic team. Then I am going to get a room at the motel. We have done two good night's work in one night. So we all deserve rest. No accidents on the way home. Drive carefully. See you all tomorrow."

Charlie says, "Thanks for all the help. I agree with Bill two good night's work in one night. See you all soon."

Ed, Charlie, Bernie, Sandra, Jane, and Barry leave. Bill waits for the forensics team.

CHAPTER 21

NOTTINGHAM HARBOR PARTY

Mattie's techniques have identified them successfully. The task force lead by Bill Simpson has caught five serial rapists. It all started because of the rape in Nottingham Harbor. The directors of the golf club have decided to honor the team from the task force with a party. The principle players and the wives or husbands are invited. Carl Kramer and Mayor Bernard are also invited. The manager of the club sends out invitations after talking to Bill. The manager contacts Bill and tells him to talk to each member of the team. The party is free to the team members and their significant others. Four weeks pass between the invitations and the party.

At about 7 PM the team members begin to arrive. By 7:15 they are all at the party. There are a lot of regular members at the club for dinner. Bill and Mattie are seated at the center of the table. The table is arranged in a "U" shape. The waiter and waitress serve the guest with various drinks. After they serve a round of appetizers the manager, Melvin Wilson, takes the stage adjacent to the table.

Melvin speaks, "About two years ago a young woman was raped here in Nottingham Harbor. The rape occurred near the golf course. The crime made many people uneasy about being out in town after dark. There were other rapes here in Maine and in New Hampshire and in Vermont. Sergeant Bill Simpson of the New Hampshire State Police with the help of the Attorney Generals of the three states put together a task force to identify and arrest the criminals. Mattie Greene a friend of Bill's used her math background to sort through thousands of pieces of data to identify the rapists. State Policemen and Assistant District Attorneys from Vermont, New Hampshire and Maine worked to arrest and prosecute the criminals. Their efforts solved about eighty cases. So we here at the club are honoring the team members with their dedication and duty to the people of our three states."

The audience stands and applauds Melvin stops.

Melvin continues, "A special thanks must go to Jake Burns here at this end of the table. Jake suffered a shoulder wound during a gun battle with the fourth suspect. He has received an accommodation for his efforts. I am going to ask Bill Simpson to say a few words about the team. Bill."

Melvin hands Bill the mike. Bill says, "I want to introduce the members of the team. Please hold any applause until I finish the introductions." He begins with Jake and ends with Mattie. You all should know that like Chief Kramer, there are many chiefs of police across the three states that made invaluable contributions to the data Mattie compiled.

Bill continues, "I have one more thing to do."

Bill walks over to Mattie and says, "Without this lady's efforts I am not sure we could have accomplished the task of identifying the suspects. I now have a surprise. I met Mattie at church one Sunday at a Bazaar. I ask Mattie out. It was the first time either one of us dated since Mattie's husband died in combat and my wife died of cancer. We both have children from our first marriages." Mattie is smiling and slightly embarrassed by the attention. Bill kneels down by her chair. He takes a small box from his pocket. He opens the box and holds it up in front of Mattie. He says, "Mattie Greene will you marry me."

Mattie starts to cry. She answers Bill, "Yes. I will marry you Bill Simpson."

Bill places the ring on Mattie's finger. Bill stands up. Mattie stands. They kiss. The audience applauds. Bill hands the mike back to Melvin and they sit down. The team members congratulate Bill and Mattie. The women all want to see the ring.

Melvin says, "I guess there is going to be another party."

Bill says, "Let's eat. I am hungry."

The band arrives at 9 PM. Melvin comes to the stage. He says, "I am going to ask Bill and Mattie to take the dance floor. I understand one of their favorite songs is 'Moonlight in Vermont' so the band is ready."

The band starts playing "Moonlight in Vermont". Bill and Mattie start dancing. The other team members slowly join them on the dance floor. When the band finishes the song, the bandleader says, "Congratulation Bill and Mattie." The band begins playing other songs. Other couples from the club start dancing. After another song finishes Bill and Mattie sit down and finish their desserts. Around midnight the team members begin to leave. They thank Melvin for the party and the kind words.

TWO MONTHS PASS QUICKLY

A couple of Mattie's friends from school help her prepare for the wedding. The wedding will be held at the church where Bill and Mattie first met at the bazaar. Bill's brother, John, is going to be the best man. Mattie's Father is in his late eighties. He suggests that her brother, Ted, give her away at the wedding. Mattie picks out a beautiful blue evening gown as her wedding dress. Bill with John's help buys a tuxedo. Linda Smyth has the county clerk prepare a special blue license for Mattie and Bill. On the night before the wedding there is dinner for all of their relatives.

The wedding is 2 PM. on Saturday. The reception is in the church hall. After introducing Bill and Mattie to their friends at the beginning of the Dinner, Ted walks over to this lady friend and kneels down. He says, "Barbara will you marry me." Barbara responds, "Yes." It is a complete surprise to everybody. There is a round of applause from the people at the reception. Bill and Mattie congratulate Ted and Barbara. The reception goes on until 7 PM. Bill and Mattie go to the Bahamas for a Honeymoon. When they return to New Hampshire they move into Bill's house. John and Ted help them move some of Mattie's belonging to Bill's house.

THE END

Printed in the United States
By Bookmasters